Jasmine Johnson was bo   ᵇᵘᵗ lived in Britain since
she was a teenager. She ha   ι Media
& Communication Studies   ımpton.

C000261155

As well as writing racy no   t stories
and tantalising poetry, w   style of
her own. Her debut nove⎯ ⎯⎯⎯ ⎯⎯ ⎯   ⎯y The X
Press) won her The New Nation's Writer of the Year Award, 2001,
and is still kicking up a storm everywhere. She also writes plays
and children's stories.

Her creative talent was first recognised by her teachers some years
ago in a classroom in Jamaica. Jasmine draws her inspiration from
life, and in her *tell-it-like-it-is* style, she homes in on the subject
she enjoys exploring most: *relationships*. She boldly goes where
other writers fear to tread, leaving her readers wanting more.

Look out for two appetising tasters: two of her short stories this
autumn. *ONE SWEET, SWEET MOMENT IN TIME,* published by
Writers Without Border (Birmingham, West Midlands), in a
collection of poems and short stories entitled *The Shakespeare
Memorial Room,* and *RED SHOES AND SEVERED TRUST,*
published by Avocado Press, Coventry.

Due to a high volume of readers' requests, Jasmine is currently
working on the sequel to MR SOON COME, with a view to
adapting it to the stage. She is also collating an anthology of her
poems and short stories for future publication.

Jasmine would like to take this opportunity to thank all her readers
who have *'spread the word'* and made her debut novel Mr Soon
Come so successful. She sincerely hopes you enjoy *THE DEVIL I
KNOW.*

Published & Distributed by
Xaymaca Books
PO Box 10886
Birmingham
B5 7YX
West Midlands, Great Britain
Tel/Fax 0121 440 2459
E-mail: xaymaca@book1.freeserve.co.uk

A CIP catalogue reference for this book is available from the British Library.

Printed and bound in Great Britain by Biddles Limited

ISBN 0-9544175-0-X

THE DEVIL I KNOW

JASMINE JOHNSON

For Marcia
'Enjoy!'
Love Jasmine x x
30/5/05

XAYMACA BOOKS

Author's ACKNOWLEDGEMENTS

Respect and thanks to...

My proof-readers...

Natasha Harding, *'Big up!'* and **Karin Reitner**, *'Danke Schoen!'*

My mum whose kindness has no limit and **my dad** who must have invented the art of laughter. *'Thank you both for everything'.*

My supportive brothers **Errol** and **Neil** whose drive, determination and ambition left me with no room to even consider *'giving up'.* 'Thanks for your valued support, bros. May you both enjoy the fruits of your labour *'to the max'.'*

My brother **Kevin.**

My sisters **Jacqui** and **Yvonne**. *'Thank you both for your love, support and encouragement. Love those sisterly chats. Strong blood'.*

My nieces and nephew **Shari**, **Khamilla** and **Jerome**. *'Love you'.*

My brother-in-law **Barry** and cousin-in-law **Byron**. *'Thank you both'.*

Bev & Lanny *(The Xaymaca Experience). 'Thank you'.*

My cousin and dearest friend **Janet Harrison**. *'Little lady, big heart... The wind beneath my wings'.* 'Thank you for being there'.

Sue Brown. *'Wishing you blessings in abundance'.*

Ikenna, Althea, Ron, Wesley, Jerome, Richard, Allison, Everton, Yvette, Mark, Paulette, Andrew, Jeannette, Patrick, Francis, Phillip, Leonie. Auntie Dorcas, Uncle Sony, Auntie Joyce, Uncle Prosper, Auntie Daphne, Uncle Labon, Uncle Lenny. *'Love you all'.*

All my family of **Kings** in Jamaica. *Big up!*

Ann & Ashley Crooks, Tom & Marie, Ruth & Eddie, Tony, Pansy: *'Neighbours from heaven'.*

Michael Forbes, *'Thank you for your valued time and unbelievable patience'.*

The Sting FM, PCRL and **New Style** crew. *'Respect'.*

*

But most important of all!! Thanks to my fifteen-year-old son, **Andre**. Thank you, son for those laughs in your *clowning-around* moments, and also for your patience and understanding.

Nuff respect. Follow your dreams, Son. May they all come true.

PROLOGUE

Come Ethiopians come, I've got a message for you
Come Ethiopians come, I've got a message for you
Zion gates are open wide, Zion gates are open wide
Zion gates are open wide, Come Ethiopians come...

When Lijah was not cooling out in the quiet *(for the want of a better word)* corner of a rammed-out session, sweet reggae music playing with his brain cells, Sting FM would be his saviour. Tonight it was Father Jarvis. Larger than life, the King of Revives was digging deep into his vintage selection, sounding out big people with nuff all-time-greats. How was he to know that he was healing a troubled brother with his musical expertise and his wicked selection?

'Elijah Zephaniah Benjamin'... Lijah sat emerged in a mound of bubbles, dosing up on Sting FM's cultural radio waves. The dread repeated his own name over and over again, wondering who would have chosen it. His mother Nettie? Or his old man Lothan? He had never asked. So biblical, the whole thing. He didn't even know why it mattered, but figured it would more than likely be his mother. And now she was on his mind again.

Lijah was twenty-five years old when his mother died and still, after so many years, he hadn't gotten over it. Nettie was much too young to die. *'No age at all'*, was always Lijah's thought. And each time he would think about her, the dread would have a job stopping himself from crying. And no, he isn't a big girl's blouse. Just a regular human being with a heart that pains from time to time. And talking about it Nettie would be ten times worse. Gloria had told him that that was exactly what he should do. Cry. *'Who said men aren't suppose to cry?'* she would ask hypothetically, as they would engage in a heat of passion, his tears washing her ebony body and the voice of John Holt washing over them like sprinkles of tropical rain. And like a mother comforting an upset child, she would play meaningfully with his locks – a comforting gesture he had always adored.

Only Gloria knew that anger and an upset state-of-mind triggered Lijah's urge to *fuck*. They had talked about it on several occasions, and would not put it in any finer terms. *Making love* just wouldn't do, for it was most certainly not that. It was like punching a punch bag. Letting off steam. Getting rid of pent-up frustration. Lijah's anger would lay dormant for a while, and like the bubbling centre of a volcano, it threatened mighty eruptions from time to time. And so spates of anger and frustration would erupt, so Gloria would cool him. And she would wait again for the next one. And in her waiting she would battle with the suspicion that there was something deeper than his mother's demise troubling him. But he had not talked about anything else, so she didn't ask. But these eruptions were real problematic, so entangling in heavy heats of passion was just a temporary safety net. These problems needed to be rooted out. *Permanently*. Or like cancer, they could become seriously malignant.

Lijah knew that the only person that held all the answers to his mother's short-lived life was his old man. *Lothan Zechariah Benjamin*. He knew also that before his spirit could settle, several uneasy questions had to be asked. He felt, however late, he owed it to his dear mother. The frequent visits to her grave, placing her favourite flowers and talking diligently to the spot where she was laid to rest, was never gonna be enough.

'No wonder they call this t'ing a think-tank to raas', Lijah thought, periodically topping up with hot water as soon as his bath would cool down. His heavy knee-length locks hung majestically like a lion's mane over the edge of the bath, resting on the spotless bathroom tiles. The house was quiet. Peaceful. He was relaxed. Yet in the stillness of things, he missed her like breath: *Gloria*, his queen. So even freedom has its price.

For the first few months, he had enjoyed the freedom from Gloria's obsessive fixing, fussing, and hoovering. As opposed to *his* nuisance: *a horny reaction to anger and frustration,* those were *hers*. A habit she had picked up from her mother Hortence Fontaine.

Gloria understood and loved him to the bone. It was unnatural for them to be apart. He and Gloria went far beyond sex. They figured they had a bond that no other woman or man could ever sever. No other love. No great sex. No amount of money.

Lijah cast his eyes around his immediate space and reminded himself that it wasn't *their* house. It wasn't the house he and Gloria once shared from way back when. It was Bernadette's house. But that's another story.

Earlier that morning, he ended a week of nights at the wretched tyre-making plant and was more than grateful for the break. *'Fuck'*, he was thinking aloud. *'I can't even see myself doing this for the next five years, let alone until I'm sixty five to rahtid. Jah know'*. He thought of his old man, who gave his life to the railways and was so thankful for a measly handshake in the shape of a gold watch, he couldn't find the words to express his gratitude'. Now, he chuckled to himself, knowing full well he wouldn't stay anywhere long enough to earn a tin can, let alone a golden handshake.

"Oi! Sugar!" A strong Jamaican accent, followed by the loud tooting of a car horn, amidst a clatter of engine, pulled him from his thoughts and reassured him it was Saturday night. It was Jaro, a dread whose voice had never failed to take Lijah back to the *front-line*. And to his youth too. Good times and bad. The good times were *good*, but the bad times? He'd rather not recall.

"Whaap'n, Sugar?! Yuh ready feh mek a move?!" Yes. A blast from the past. The past of the real *'dread'* days, when most new recruits leaned full-heartedly and faithfully into the teachings of His Majesty, Haile Selassie. The Lion of Judah was the strongest motif, hanging from windscreens in Ford Capris. When the word *Rastafari* rolled off tongues like ice off hot pavements. When young black heads were crowned with knitted red-gold-and-green stripes. They were the days when locks sprouted from every young brotha's head like wild fire. When brothas lived together in tribes. A union all authorities tried to disperse. When their women seek the most flamboyant head and body African wraps and pleased their *'Emperors'*, *'Heads'* or *'Commanding Generals'*, to the fullest. When sistas would change their names with pride, to *Naptali, Makeda* and such delightful names all descendants of Africa should be proud of. Names, that strongly affiliated them with Ethiopia and distant them from Babylon *and its* mentality. Each one was learning a new concept of *'self'*, and the *'each one teach one'* tactic was catching on. Fast.

They were important times, when the twelve tribes of Israel each had a place of their own and respect was shown. But on the contrary too, it was when black parents whose reluctance to *understand* stood firm, as they relentlessly opposed the very possibility of their daughters *'taking up'* with a rastaman. And with opposition from descendants of Africa, what scope was left for white employers to understand? They too discriminated through FEAR. *False Evidence Appearing Real.* Fear of the unknown. They had no evidence of what they should fear, but they feared it anyhow. It was the *unknown* they didn't want to *know*. The Ethiopian affiliation thing was the farthest from their agenda of understanding, yet it was homing in on them like (in the words of a misguided English man) *'stink bombs in an enclosed space'.* Their *FEAR,* at times was manifested in the form of cynicism: Rastamen's hats for instance, were demised to simple *'tea-cosies'* by little old ladies.

Enoch Powel's *'Black Star Liner'* promise gave hope. Hope to Rastas and hope to white employers. The former hoping to escape to the Promised Land, and the latter hoping to *help* gladly, with the *'opening of the gates'.*

"Me soon come bredrin!" Sugar held his head out of an upstairs window and bellowed back to Jaro.

" 'Urry up Sugar! Runnings an' t'ing!" Jaro urged.

Like clockwork, around that time on a Saturday night, Jaro would come calling for his idrin Sugar, who to Lijah's surprise lived only two doors away from his newly acquired abode. Bunti was always at the front of Jaro's ride. Sugar was a new acquaintance. He did not go back as far as Lijah and the other dreads.

Jaro, Papa Dread, Reds, Bunti and Lijah went back a long way. To times he had tried to elude from his head. And to good times. Times when *'front-line'* was *'front-line'*. When dreads used to burn calli-weed together and reason on a righteous level. Papa Dread would reason with them, making no apologies for Black Spirituality, Repatriation and African Liberation. And the good old Ital herbs. But even then it was joked that bredrin had something against doorbells and knockers. The *Voice* must be heard.

Apart from the fact that Gloria had sent Lijah packing, the memories of his mother and the memory of the most devilish time in his life, were the only ones he believed could ever make him cry. But on the subject of his mother, when he wondered if his old man had treasured his gold watch more than he did her, he wanted an answer.

The radio wasn't too high, but the old guy next door made it known in no uncertain terms, that he had no taste for, and will not be acquiring one for reggae music. It seemed as if reggae music to him was like the voice of a Jew to Hitler. And there he was, sandwiched between Lijah and Sugar, who dished out the wickedest baseline, like sweet pumpkin soup.

"Don't you know about the noise pollution law?!" the old man shouted, as he banged his walking stick against their adjoining wall. Bang! Bang! Bang!

Lijah hated that. *Banging.* It was as if someone was holding his brain and squeezing: its cells squirting through their fingers like minced meat. Banging to him signified torture. It triggered horrible, torturous memories of his mother Nettie. And now her song came to meet him like a punch. That hearty song she would sing, as she would lie there in that captive bed. Before she had lost her speech that was. Oh how she would sing. And sing. And sing. Wearing the verse, thin. Yes, it came to him now like a taunt:

I see the stars, I hear the rolling thunder
Thy power throughout the universe displayed

It rode over Sting FM. Over the old man's banging. And into his very soul. It was a wicked memory. Evil. And still, unexplained.

Then sing my soul, My Saviour God to Thee

How great Thou art, How great Thou art
Now he needed Gloria. The only real solace to his suffering.

He eased out of the bath, dripping all over the bathroom tiles, then the soft red carpet, to gain access to the remote. He lowered the sound on Sting FM, a sacrilege notion, if ever there was one, then walked slowly back to his bath. And still his mother's voice didn't leave his head...

Then sing my soul, My Saviour God to Thee
How great Thou art, How great thou art

A temporary distraction from his pain, Sugar's voice rescued him. "Yes I! Weh yaah seh?" Then the revving of an engine spelling an exodus. An exodus to some place in the second city. A city, that not unlike New York, never really sleeps.

Apart from wondering about the way the old man had treated his mother, Lijah often wondered how it would have been if he himself had granted her wish. Her one expectation of him. Although a grown man, he felt guilty. To add to his pain, he found another reason why he too could have let her down. He remembered it well; the glint in her eyes when his teacher had told Nettie: *'your son could be anything he chooses to be, Mrs. Benjamin. He could be a brain surgeon if he wants to.'* His mother had smiled and looked an expectant look into his eyes. And he had returned a promising one into hers. And he meant it. But he was only sixteen years old with influential friends. The *wrong* influential friends, who saw grammar school as *'a w'ite bwoy t'ing'*. That would be dissing his street cred. And as for university! No one around him even gave it a thought. They all saw that as a *'brain-washing'* t'ing. And that would be cutting no cultural dash.

Lijah was brainy all right, but at times for the benefit of his friends, he would purposefully play it down. Disguise his true intellect. It was true; he could be whatever he wanted to be, like his teacher had said. But what he could have done with then, at sixteen, was a positive black role model. A mentor. Someone with a different influential attitude from the inexperienced piers who themselves needed guidance. Someone to teach him how to take the important things from life. Or from *Babylon*, as he would often put it. Education for one. But he hadn't met Papa Dread until way after he had left school. Papa Dread would have drummed home The Emperor's belief, that education is the basis of greatness: the power pride and prosperity of a nation.

And that wasn't all. By the time he met Papa Dread, Lijah had seen a part of life no young black male had any business seeing or experiencing.

Yes, as a youth he did time. That good old Borstal shit. *Borstal*, but he would refer to it, no less than *'Prison'*. Led by pressure, Lijah had dared to enter an off-licence with a metal piece: the likes of which he had only seen on TV. Nervously, he held the devilish piece of metal to the off-licensee's head and demanded the contents of his till. "Gi...Gi...Gimme yuh money," he rattled, nervously. But he was clearly not cut out for that and could not pull the trigger, so he was rumbled by the owner's son who sneaked up and overpowered him from behind.

When the police swung their wagon in front of the shop, young Lijah pissed himself. Literally. His older and smarter accomplice who was sat waiting in a shiny, black Ford Capri was long gone, leaving only the scent of his sorry ass and Lijah behind. Busted. The sucker had pulled the young, green and vulnerable youth into a world way above his head and left him to take the wrap.

And Lijah had done just that. *'Taken the wrap'*. Kept his mouth shut. Tight. He didn't know who he feared more: the law or his accomplice, who had told him, *'I don't tek kindly to grass. If yuh get ketch, don' call me name... or yuh is dead meat'*. As *Evil* himself spoke, he ran his palm over his gun. That was the first time Lijah had felt the warmth of his own piss trickling down his legs. He was in too deep to back out. Fear had convinced him of that. He didn't do the *blood in* thing, but he felt that the *blood out* was as sure he had woken in a cold sweat, on that infamous morning.

There were times when the eyes of this brotha would meet his, and Lijah would see only begging. The nonverbal *'begging for forgiveness'* only an evil sinner could ask so deeply for. But there were other times when this *'begging'* would take on a ruthless difference.

Lijah could never forget. And he probably would have forgiven this brotha, but due to what he went through behind bars, his troubled mind would not allow him to. Now he feared for Kunta, his own son. Hoped to Jah he would not pass through any of Her Majesty's doors of captivity. But more so, he hoped Kunta would not cross the path of this brotha, who had placed a metal shooter in his youthful hand years ago. A brotha who had hid behind the name of Jah for the longest time, moving skilfully with the times, among respected brothas. With the chains of guilt hanging heavily around his neck. Guilt that could well turn to disaster.

Lijah's physical sentence was shortened for good behaviour, but mentally, he would serve it for the rest of his life. But not so much the time spent in prison itself. No. It ran much deeper. Hypothetically and literally. An incident he had only told Papa Dread about. Not his mother. Not his closest idrin Festus. Not Gloria. No, not even Gloria. As far as they all knew, he did time. Paid his dues to society and returned home to *forget.* But he knew more. He knew too, that there are some things that black men just can't or won't tell. No sir. They would rather die. Rather it ate away at their brain cells like a malicious virus, sent to a computer's memory.

It's a sad thing, but numerous ex-inmates from black communities everywhere are doing time for life: all clinging to that half that can never be told. To them, it's the *greatest taboo.* It's a Blackman t'ing. It's called pride.

Gloria was Lijah's rock, but even she would be spared the details of this one.

'Know what they know', Papa Dread would have told him. *'Be a cog in the machinery of British industry. Ease into the 'know' of its economy. Take from it today, what you can manipulate tomorrow. Take, take, take like they did from us in Africa. But hold steadfast to 'who' you are. Share it with your sons and daughters'.* And that would have been the key to a host of 21st century doors. Doors, that once inside, would reinforce themselves against the painful cries of struggle, struggle and more struggle. Struggles that have long gone left the *'issue'* stand and have become *'life'.*

Papa Dread had an old head. Always did. So old a head, that it was in his early twenties that he acquired the title *'Papa'.* He was born to *shield,* and would take it to considerable limits – especially if the demise of young black youths were in the equation. Even when the consequences may be detrimental to his own welfare. If his theoretical voice could not be heard, he would pull up his sleeves and do the practical. And if the youth were extra sentimental to him, there would be no telling what this old rastaman might do.

'Where are the influential black people in high places in Britain? Or Birmingham for that matter?' Lijah asked himself as he topped up his bath with hot water. *'I could have been one of them',* he answered his own question. *'But that's just it: could have been'.* He couldn't even be sure *'who'* he was now. Not even a semi-dread. Just a black brotha with a fine head of locks with no meaning other than its existence. Locks that sistas had got used to, and curious white women craved to touch, like chastised babies reaching out to the forbidden.

Though not with pride, he had already secretly claimed a *'Fallen Rasta'* status. A status Gloria had long gone accepted. Not unlike a backslider from a Christian church. For the doctrine and philosophy of it all had left him, or he them. For good, it seemed.

Dread Locks cyaan live inna tenement yard
Dread Locks cyaan live inna tenement yard

11

Too much sussu-sussu-sussu, Too much watchy-watchy-watchy...
Father Jarvis licked out the rootsy rhythm and Lijah nodded his head to
the sweet reggae beat. It reached his very soul. The King of Revives
pulled up the rhythm and took it from the top. The short pause allowed
the faint sound of a car engine easing onto the drive. Its light shone
through the bathroom window, as if making a statement.

As always, Bernadette had arrived home *unexpectedly*. Beautiful, free-
spirited and mysterious, this sista gave off an empowered aura you would
think twice about challenging. In her own rights, it seemed she was
streets apart from Gloria. Lijah rarely asked questions, and when he did,
he got little or no answers. The dread had no reins on Bernadette. In fact,
her attitude said, *'Don't even try'*.

She was his landlady. Lover. Therapist. Sexual healer. Call it what you
like. All he knew, she was unlike any other women he had ever met.

He opened his eyes and alerted his mind to the sound of rattling keys.
Then he cleared the bubbles away from his manhood and peered
purposefully at the masterpiece Jah had blessed him with.

"You haven't drowned have you, Lijah?!" The approaching sound of
Bernadette's voice gave him a lift, in more ways than one.

"Come fin' out nuh!" he shouted back, doing some serious under-
water fumbling, loving the fact that he was at the front of the queue on
that great *dick-dishing* day. *'Who seh Jah isn't black?'* He amused
himself with his corny thought.

"Move over then," Bernadette commanded, her seductive voice
brushed his soul. She was now in the bathroom, standing over him like a
mistress. She pulled her T-shirt over her head, revealing her firm, black
breasts. She had taken her jeans off on the landing, and now her firm,
unwrapped ass was in his face. With a difference to the way he was
missing Gloria, he had been missing Bernadette. He hated her London
trips but couldn't do jack. Beggars couldn't be choosers. Gloria had
rejected him, and Lucy wasn't really his thing. Yes, Lucy. Juicy Lucy. A
whole new kettle of blonde fish. But Bernadette was certainly a *night
nurse* who could most definitely quench his thirst any time.

Father Jarvis must have known...

Night Nurse... Only you alone can quench dis yah thirs'
Lijah mimed the words silently, in anticipation, as he stared dreamy-
eyed at Bernadette's beautiful body. It was just what he needed – the
wickedest therapy yet. Tonight his emotions were ruffled. Mixed up. He
was under the weather, big time. And like a volcano, he had to erupt.

Bernadette eased her sexy body into the hot bath, teasing his manhood
with her red, nimble toes. Massaging his scalp and playing with his

dread-locks, she took control. She always did. Hooking his moist tongue with hers, she kissed him passionately. Now she wasted no time. Easing herself gently onto his ready yardstick, yoga playing a part in her erotic art, she quenched her own thirst.

Although not as much as Gloria, seemingly, this sexy beast had come to have almost an in-tune understanding of Lijah. She had always been a friend of his family, and seemed to know what was troubling him. She had come to know too, that his mother's plight had affected him much more than his sister Faye and his brother Roy.

"How are you, Lijah?" It was almost as if talking in the middle of love-making added something to her pleasure. Only Lijah was the opposite. *'Let a hungry man eat. Talk can come later'*, could almost be the interpretation of his hesitancy.

"A'right. But yuh know I don' like talkin' when I make love."

Making love in unusual trysts turned Lijah on to a point of uncontrollable passion. Kitchen tables, on the stairs, in a pile of washed laundry in the spare room. Anywhere away from the traditional bedroom. But most of all, in the bath or under the warm torrents of a shower. The first time he had tried it with Gloria, she had said it was his rebellious inner-self being manifested. He had chuckled at her psychological analysis.

Now, conversation could wait. Bernadette understood. She held still, the whole length of Lijah inside her. Appreciating the warm bath water around him, and the well-needed bath mat that gave purchase to his ass, he grasped the cheeks of her ass and readied himself, almost saying grace for the acceptance of *'what he was about to receive'*.

"Don't move a muscle," she whispered seductively, as she tightened the muscles of her woman around his hard dick, like a boa constrictor holding its prey, easing, gripping, easing, gripping as she pleased. She moved no other part of her body. The pleasure was new to him and she had many more in store. Oh yes. Pulled them out like tricks from a magician's hat. Lijah wanted to die a sweet death as she moved up and down his shaft in a cow-milking fashion, blowing his mind beyond explanation. Amazed at the way she gripped him, her vagina muscles tight around his shaft, he opened his eyes and looked puzzled and questioningly at her. It was pleasure to die for, and he could have sworn he had done that. Oh yes. *Died and gone right off to heaven.*

And all the time his seductress commanded, *'Don't move a muscle Lijah... Just ... stay... firm...yes... like the spear of an African hunter."*

And him, floating on ecstasy, whispered, *"You are one raas claat phenomenal woman, Bernadette... t'raas... "*

CHAPTER * ONE

Gloria stood in the pouring rain, soaking up its torrents, as the sweet melody of John Holt seeped into her head. Unshaken by the torrential downpour, she let the heavy drops beat against her face, cascading hurriedly down its plumb-like surface, quenching the closed corners of her mouth and eyes. Like a ritual, she held her hands up to the heavens, as if giving thanks to Jah for the downpour. Several sistas hurried by, running for shelter, worrying more about their hair getting wet, their perms going funny and the ruination of their weaves, more than anything else.

Gloria had not noticed a passer-by: a distinguished looking white woman taking a long, hard, quizzical look at her, mumbling to herself. *'Mmm God'*, the sceptical middle-aged woman had said, *'Suppose she'll be hugging a tree next'*.

Despite the downpour, the day was hot, and humid. This was not the norm for Gloria. Not in an open park anyway. She had always found the rain therapeutic, but standing in her own garden was the most public she would get. Today, she herself and the question of what insanity really was, crossed her surprised mind.

'Black women don't do dem t'ings unless dem mad', a sista said to her friend, as they hurried up the ramp towards the MAC, not realising that her voice was thrown much further than she had expected.

Minutes later, when Gloria sheltered, crouching behind the wheels of her Corsa, shivering and staring into space, the reality of her actions hit her. In her staring, she saw not what was physically in front of her, but what could have been. *Future-wise.*

Of late, she had not let herself think too much about it, for when she did, she needed torrents like the ones earlier, to wash away her tears. Tears that came when she remembered her shattered dream. Her dream to become one of the first newscasters on British TV. A dream that she felt sure could have become a reality. For she had believed in herself, and all the teachers from Chapleton Girls School in Leeds, who expressed their belief in her ability to excel. Reach for the skies. Be one of the best.

Teachers would tell her parents (who themselves were equipped with only the basics in education), how promising their daughter was. And the Scottish headmaster, who held Mrs Fontaine around her shoulders when he said, *'The only person who could prevent Gloria's ambitions materialising, is the girl herself. The girl could be a brain-surgeon if she wants to'*.

'Are you sure your teacher wasn't Mrs Bridgwater?' Lijah had asked

her the first time Gloria told him about her teacher's high expectations of her. *'Or perhaps all teachers seh dem t'ings to all parents. Dat is de same t'ing my teachers dem used to seh. Still, if we both have such wonderful brains, imagine what our children will be like'*, he had joked.

Gloria did not regret having her daughters Ikesha and Khamilla and her son Kunta. In fact she could not imagine life without them. But she never ceased wondering what the whole package would be like: Lijah, her children and her dream career. But she knew there is a different ending to every road, and somehow, for her, what she wished for didn't happen.

As she started her engine in an attempt to leave the serenity of the chosen spot at Cannon Hill Park behind her, Gloria glanced over at the pages of written A4 sheets, on which she had recently started to exercise her passion. Writing had always been her passion, and it was always at the low ebbs in her life that this passion would burn, like a lustful desire. She reflected on the short stories and meaningful poetry she had written and discarded. The ideas for plays she had let fall by the wayside, gather dust on forgotten shelves, only to sit in audiences watching other people *'getting on with it'*.

Now, she let John Holt beat upon her heart with her favourite song. The song that clung to the dimness of the room that night: the night she lost her virginity to Lijah, over twenty years ago.

Take the ribbon from your hair, Shake it loose and let it fall
Lay it soft against my skin, Like the shadows on the wall
Come and lay down by my side, Till the early morning light
All I'm taking is your time, Help me make it through the night...

...she sang along with John Holt, drying tears from her eyes and wishing she could stop them flowing. Now she wondered how much, or even if, Lijah had appreciated taking it. Her virginity.

She flicked out the John Holt tape and eased in another old Faithful. It almost pained her. Teddy Pendergrass played mercilessly with her heart-string. Why was she doing it to herself?

Looking back over the years
I guess I've shedded some tears...
I tell myself time and time again...

And she had known, without a doubt, that the recent beckoning of her tears had everything to do with the most recent happenings in her life. Happenings that made her feel inadequate. Lacking something. Not enough for her man.

When Gloria lived in Leeds under her parents' roof, with the dream of becoming a sparkling newscaster, everything was gonna be fine. She left

school with six A' levels and a promise to be general dog's body in a
BBC studio in London. In those days, that wasn't looked down on.
Working your way up on a youth training scheme was something. It
wasn't sneezed at or daunting.

Three months before she was to leave for London, Gloria spent a
weekend in Birmingham with her friend Kizzy. On that Saturday night
the girls met their heart-throbs. Two Birmingham Supas, Lijah and
Festus.

The club was Rialto, a then kicking night-spot, with nuff level vibes,
and music to keep any raver rocking all night. It was the days when
names like Matumbi, Quaka City, Mafia Tone and Coxon were
household ones. Young and love-sick, Gloria soon lost her ambitious
desires and could see nothing, or hear no other, but Lijah.

Likewise, Kizzy fell for Festus in the same way.

Not long after their meeting, Gloria fell pregnant with Ikesha and her
trip to London had disintegrated into wishful thinking. And when the
pressures that came with teenage pregnancy, a mother's disappointment,
and a father's anger became too much, the only solution for her was to
shack up (her mother's term) with Lijah in his self-contained bed-sit in
Handsworth. This bed-sit was a far cry from her parents' four-bedroom
house in Leeds. Even that was a battle in itself for Gloria, since Lijah
shared a house with a few other dreads. He must have been the first to
break tradition and moved his woman in. In those days, it wasn't the
done thing. Gloria soon got used to the regular chanting of doctrines,
chanting down Babylon and the lifting up the name of Haile Selassie.

A visit from Gloria's parents one unexpected evening was an ordeal
for all. Mr Fontaine, in his Kingly character, was trying hard to shine his
sacred torch on a situation that didn't please him. Head of a church in
Leeds, he had come to repossess what he thought was rightfully *his*. His
precious daughter.

The whole situation was *trying*. Lijah, *trying* to cope with being seen
as a lesser being. Gloria, *trying* to be piggy-in-the-middle, having to take
sides between her man and her parents. And to cream it all, Mrs
Hortence Fontaine, regurgitating her words of protest like a scratched
record, *'Pack yuh t'ings an' come home!' Wid yuh Rasta stupidness!
Look at de state a yuh head! An' to t'ink of dat lovely head a hair yuh
did have. Comb yuh hair! Wha' kin 'a nat-up nat-up t'ing dat? Dis falla-
fashion t'ing will bring yuh into open shame! Yuh is disgracing yuh
family! I can hardly look de bredrin dem in de face! I cyaan tek de sussu-
sussu any more!'* But then, she could not have known that all the
brethren that threw words like hailing rock-stones would soon have to

listen to bigger ones crashing fiercely against their own windows. The Rasta culture was coming like a force. And one to be reckoned with too. Emperors would need Empresses, like the sun needs the sky. So daughters had better shape up!

But that wasn't all. Gloria wondered if her mother had a short memory. She wondered if she had forgotten that no one was perfect. Not even her Reverend husband. For he, way back when, had sinned. Fornicated. And Gloria had not forgotten either the image of this woman's face, or the sound of her name. This woman (one of many) that her Reverend Father had copulated with. She could never forget her name, as her mother had thrown it in anger too many times in her father's face. And she had seen her face for the first time across a busy Soho Road. Hortence had come on a weekend visit to see Gloria and her grandchildren and had pointed this woman out, almost in shock. "Oh Lord," she had said, "There is that Zelda. She was one of your father's 'kip' women. She must be living in Birmingham now. What a small world. I wondered why I haven't seen her in Leeds. It looks like everybody runs to London or Birmingham. Everyone runs to the big cities. Perhaps they think they can hide their dirty deeds better. More people, more shadows to hide behind."

"*One of*, Mum? *One of?*" Gloria had asked, "So how many women did he have. I thought my dad was holier than Thou."

"Gloria, nobody knows the trouble I bear wid yuh faada. The secrets. The hush-hush. Some of the things I closed my ears to."

"And you never said a word when I was growing up. And to think, he nearly crucified Lijah for just being a rastaman? And you were backing him to the fullest, Mum. What was all that about?"

"Gloria, you wouldn't understan'."

"What's there to understand, Mum? My Reverend father slept around and you accepted it, yet my man wore locks and if you could have burnt him at the stakes, you would."

Hortence saw the truth in her daughter's argument. She half grimaced, half smiled, sighed, then embarked the tip of a huge iceberg. Yes, the mere tip. Of course, there were better places to discuss 'The lustful life of Reverend Fontaine', than a crowded Soho Road in Handsworth, so Hortence simply filled Gloria in on a few of her father's activities, ending her conversation, "You are only child for the marriage, Gloria, but don't be surprised if there aren't several half brothers and sisters scattered around in Leeds. When I met yuh faada, he was a sweet-bwoy. Womanisa. He found the Lord, but he still needed willpowa to ovacome the temptation of de flesh. We prayed night an' day. We fast an' pray 'bout it. But dis t'ing was really strong."

Gloria noticed her mother's uncomfortable state as the Zelda got close to them. She didn't seem to recognise Hortence. Gloria took a good look at her face. So good a look, her image became an imprint on her mind. And after that, she would see her from time to time. And each time, as she watched the swish-swashing of her frock-tail, Gloria would imagine this Zelda in a compromising position with her Reverend father: a hard image to conjure up. But the uncanny thing was that Zelda would never have the slightest clue as to who Gloria was. She was only a little girl back then, and besides, Leeds is a long way from Birmingham.

And now, as her father played the perfect respectable dad, Gloria wondered if he knew that she knew that he had messed up on his wedding vows. And under the title *Reverend* too!

So here they were in the *House of the Dreads*, high-pitched chants dashed in-between Hortence's words, battling with them. Contrasting. Floating from the living-room like shadows formed in a midday sun. Strong. Prominent. Standing their ground: *'Jah! Rasta Fari! Haile Selassie! King of Kings an' Lord of Lords! Conquering Lion of the tribe of Judah! Jah! Rasta Fari!'*...

It was the dreads' weekly meeting, and nothing would stop them. A young Papa Dread, Jaro, Reds and Bunti were carrying the *red-gold-and-green* banner with pride.

Kizzy sat waiting in Festus' room. She had already been through it all with Mama Maya, her adopted mother: a Jamaican woman who had an abundance of love to give, and no chance of producing a child of her own. Mama Maya, in her *'mother-hen protectiveness'*, thought Kizzy deserved better than someone who wanted her to *'throw the comb away'*. Besides she had already been through one battle on the hair front with the staff in the home where Kizzy came from. Staff who did not know how to deal with the slightest hint of African hair, so they had given up and left it to grow wild.

So room for compromises and understanding was filled with nothing but Mama Maya's memories of how she got Kizzy and her adopted sister, Fiona, from that God-forsaken children's home, and reared them into fine young ladies. And to her reckoning, *'fine'* did not go with *'uncombed hair'*. Nor did it go with any other doctrines but that of Christianity: of which bible Festus and Lijah had told them was misinterpreted and given to Africans a *'disguised ulterior motive. More disguised than the way Europeans 'taken' the gold. The artefacts. The people'*.

But Mama Maya and the Fontaine's were settled in their acceptance of what they thought was right, so that day, Lijah's attempt to persuade them would be like trying to fill a basket with water, so he didn't attempt to.

And Lijah's low-pitched voice, ignoring the wishes of Mr and Mrs Fontaine and daring to drop a bigger pebble in the already angry ripples, *'I man is a peaceful rastaman. I jus' want you to leave me an' my queen to live as one. Jah! Rasta Fari!'*

Gloria was their one and only child. Lijah's claim to her had cut them like a knife: *'My queen '*. Hortence left in tears, and Reverend Fontaine, disappointed and defeated. They spent years remembering her in their prayers. With permanent lumps in their throats, they were totally convinced their daughter needed deliverance from the man she loved. They had no time to look at his heart. He was simply judged by his locks.

One of the hardest facts for a mother to swallow was the fact that the child she pushed painfully from her womb was not hers to keep. Unlike an item of material gain.

But in all this, Gloria needed time to think for herself. Lijah himself had a lot to learn, and, in his own way of expressing love, clouded Gloria's dreams, made her his queen, clad her in red, gold and green and controlled most of her life. He was the Emperor. And although it was there, lying dormant like a simmering volcano, the Empress' own strength had no chance to shine for her own *'self'*. She was blinded by love, clouding the path to her once craved desire to be a newscaster. It conquers all: this love thing.

In this bed-sit, Lijah and Gloria did everything together. Ate, slept, cooked, argued, changed nappies, made love and farted. She wasn't weakened, but stunted. Like a brand new tyre that had a fatal encounter with a nail.

She cooked him ital food, made him nuff Sexy, Irish moss and Guinness punch. She was there for his every beck and call. Back in the days, the Fontaines had thought that some Rastamen had got the teachings slightly wrong. They ran t'ings. Lijah ran things from his teachings, and when they found out that when their daughter would menstruate, she would (in the nicest possible way) be subtly banished from his bed, for she was daubed *'unclean'*, they flipped. But that was the real deal and Gloria was simply in love with a dread.

Kizzy had once scolded her sister Fiona for saying, *'You could almost see the brown on your nose, Gloria. You think the sun shines out of Lijah's ass'*. Not to her face however.

And later they made another baby, Kunta.

Just after the birth of Kunta, the council saw it fit to re-house them.

They had built up enough points to warrant space to breathe. And before that, as parents do, Mr and Mrs Fontaine saw it fit to forgive, *for the sake of their grandchildren.* They had practised what they preached and forgave, inviting Lijah into their home, trying to hide their fear of *'what the brethren and sistren would say'.* And Lijah had joked as they travelled up in his gleaming Ford Capri, that strange Sunday afternoon, singing at the top of his voice: *'Guess who is coming to dinna! Natty Dread Locks!'* but his joke did nothing for Gloria's nerves. She had known that locks behind their 'Christian' doors would be like a *'ragga'* behind *'Royal'* doors.

Putting fun and joke aside, life was hard. But as Lijah reached another stage of maturity, he played his part like a man, supporting his woman's needs. Money was tight to mention, but he worked hard to provide the best he could. Whatever else he carried for his father, he carried his words of advice securely in his subconscious. It was hard for him to do otherwise. The words were said with mighty conviction:

'Kids dat are brought up on dirty money will be soiled for life. Son, mek sure yuh put food on yuh table by the sweat of yuh brow', his father used to tell him, even before he had sperm. *'And neva mek no woman min' yuh. A man dat stretch out 'im han' an' tek money from a woman is no man at all'.*

Lothan, Lijah's dad would always say the latter with such depth, Lijah would wonder if he was chastising himself. And he would wonder too, which woman in his old man's day would have money to give a man anyway. Certainly not his mother, God rest her soul. She died at no age: fifty years old. And from what he was convinced, her death was from a broken heart. And though it didn't matter: not a penny to her name.

By the time Ikesha was three and Kunta two, Lijah had worked every hour God sent and came up with a healthy deposit for a place of their own. They decided to leave some of their unwanted past behind. Like acquaintances who, when the righteousness of the rastaman flew out the window, it left them with only their locks. Bredrin who lived on the edge and only for the present day. Bredrin who lived in the fast lane, where bandulu dealings, badness and dirty money were the keys to their lives. Bredrin who were beginning to make stereotypical views of *the black man* a reality. Ones who did not just throw their combs away, but also, the *'true aim and philosophy of a true rastaman'.*

At first, Lijah and Gloria's decision to buy a house was criticised, questioned, kicked up against the wall by people who were simply intimidated by the house-buying game. Sadly for some, the sense and sensibility of it all was not weighed up against the dead money they themselves were paying to keep landlords laughing weekly, all the way to the bank.

Lijah and Gloria didn't leave the hood through snobbery, or cowardice, like some speculators claimed, but trouble was brewing, and the writing was on the wall. Besides, like his mother Nettie used to say, *'A coward man keeps sound bone'.* Coward was farthest from his persona, but from his reckoning, *'Natty Dread didn't fancy going on another one of Her Majesty's holiday'.*

From where they were standing, the writing on the wall was foretelling a frightful future. It was Gloria's old head, adamant stance, the twinkle in their children's eyes and the need to prove to the Fontaines that all was not lost, that helped Lijah's determination not to bring his children up in the hood.

Although, at that time, Papa Dread (everybody's mentor) saw things differently. *'It nuh matta w'ere yuh bring yuh pickney dem up Rasta. If dem gwine bad, dem gwine bad',* the older and well-respected dread who shared the house with them, had told Lijah when he told him of his plans to *ease out. 'Give de yout' dem de teachings of His Majesty. Leggo all devil's philosophy, an' yuh yout' dem will be a'right man'.*

Lijah only wished he could believe it was that easy.

They bought their first three-bedroom house in upper Edgbaston, which soon showed the sense in their nonsense.

Gloria had been proud of Lijah and her children, and to a certain extent, she was contented with her Psychology degree, a *'mature student'* acquisition. She had not felt the same about doing a media degree, as she detected a thick layer of *'ageism grease'* on the first ladder of media, which would make it much harder to climb. But it goes without saying that every time Moira Stewart, Trevor McDonald or any black news reporter graced her television screen, a deep *something* would fill her.

The Perry Barr roadblock couldn't have come at a worse time for Lijah. He hated being late back with Khamilla but this time he had no choice. The armed response team had randomly chosen him for a stop-and-search. He was used to it, but ever since Lucy had donated that red Roadster Sports, his chances of getting stopped rocketed ten-fold.

Lijah sang just to keep his head from exploding...

> All ova me, Babylon dem all ova me
> All ova me, Babylon dem all ova me...

"Would you mind stepping out of your vehicle, sir?" one of the six boys in blue that gathered around him asked.

"What's the problem, officer?"

"Just a routine check, sir. Can I ask where you're coming from?"

"And what's that got to do with routine?"

"The quicker you co-operate sir, the quicker you can be on your way."

"One Stop shopping centre. I just took my daughter shopping. I hope that's not a crime, officer?"

"D'you possess any form of drugs, sir?"

"Yes officer. Me have a one-spliff."

"And where is that, sir?"

Lijah couldn't help but to recall a track from yesteryears...

> *Oh oh oh DC... don't yuh touch my calli*
>
> *Oh oh oh DC... don't you touch my ishence*

He reached into a breast pocket, produced a pitiful spliff and handed it to the officer, who opened a small bag for him to drop it into.

"Wha' d'you guys do with all these pittances of spliff you confiscate daily officer? Throw them in the bin?"

"I'm afraid you're going to have to accompany two of our officers, down to the station, sir," the officer emphasised, pretending he didn't hear Lijah's sarcastic question.

"What for? A one-spliff? Why don't you guys spend your time catching real criminals?" Lijah should have held his tongue, but he couldn't. "What yuh gonna do when they change the law, officer? And I don't think it's gonna be long before the government see sense and do dat."

"Change the law? What d'you mean, sir?"

"What yuh gonna do when they change the law and *down-grade* the *high-grade*?"

"*High-grade*, sir? You've lost me."

"Neva mind officer. But I think you're just gonna have to buy your own, then."

"Excuse me?"

"Like I said, officer, neva mind."

Not long after, Khamilla stared as her dad stood spread-eagled across the bonnet of a police car, experiencing nuff touch-up-touch-up, an' feel-up-feel-up. "What's my daddy done?" she asked in a frightened voice, turning to see another two searching the side of her seat and underneath Lijah's seat.

"Hello, Sweetheart. What's your name then?" the female police officer tried the friendly-friendly.

Khamilla ignored the officer's question and stared even harder at her dad being frisked like a common criminal. "Is my daddy going to jail? What's he done?" Confused, she started to cry.

"Would you like a sweet?" the female officer exposed a fist full of sweets. Khamilla's tears fell on them, flowed over a wrapper or two and came to rest in the folds of the officer's palm. "Don't cry. It's ok."

"But you're gonna take my daddy to jail."

The officer twisted round from her crouched position, as if to observe what the sad little girl was seeing.

"No. We'll do nothing of the sort, Sweetheart. We're just doing our jobs. We're just looking for bad people. But because we can't really tell who the real bad people are, we have to stop a few people every now and then."

"Why?"

"Just to see if they're carrying things that might hurt good people like you and your dad."

"But my dad don't have anything that will hurt anyone."

"I'm sure he hasn't. So, are you going to tell me your name?"

"Khamilla."

"Khamilla, your dad is just coming with us down to the station. Would you like to come with me in my car?"

"To the station? Why?"

"Your daddy just needs to talk to us some more."

"Khamilla! Yuh a'right?" Lijah shouted across to his daughter.

"Yes." Khamilla sniffled. "I'm coming with you to the station. In the police car."

"There," the officer handed Khamilla a sweet. She took it, then stared again at her daddy as he entered the police car.

"I'm ok, Khamilla. Daddy's ok." Lijah assured her. Then he looked up and caught the eyes of the driver in a slow-moving silver BM. Yes. Those same eyes. The ones that would take him again, to a time and place he'd rather not be. The burly, blonde man looked purposefully at him; it sent shivers down his spine. But now a new thought. He drove a silver BM. And though there are thousands of silver BMs out there, Lijah sarcastically challenged the officers in the car in which he was sitting. "That silver BM would probably give you better dividends, officers. Wasn't the get-away car in that bank robbery the other day a silver BM? And wasn't the driver said to be a burly, blonde bloke? So you let him cruise by and stopped an innocent dread with nothing but a one-spliff and a frightened daughter?"

The officers ignored him. He expected nonetheless.

Lijah didn't know how to explain to Gloria how he came to be carted off to the beast man's yard, he and their dear daughter, without sounding as if he was making excuses. But he needn't worry too much, since, in a funny kinda way, it was a weird adventure for Khamilla: one she couldn't wait to tell. But as far as far as Lijah was concerned, the caution he got for holding a stick of weed was well over-done.

CHAPTER * TWO

When Gloria walked into her house, Ikesha, Kunta and his girlfriend Shari had made themselves comfortable in the living-room. Her children had their own places, but still kept their keys to her house, so it wasn't unusual to return home to find her house fully inhabited by them and their friends, conversations going any-which-way. The family was close like that and Gloria would not have it any other way. Besides, however much he'd like to think he was a man, she was Kunta's rock. He depended on her more than he himself realised. If he didn't turn up for his rice an' peas on a Sunday, she would worry and dial his number.

Kunta had put a brave front on the separation between her and Lijah. Too brave a front in fact. Gloria likened it to 'not crying at a funeral', and she dreaded the result.

"Hi kids!" Gloria shouted before shutting the front door.

"Yo! Mum!" Kunta shouted back.

"Hi, Mum!" Shari and Ikesha said, their voices synchronised.

They all waited for her entry into the sitting-room, but it was somewhat delayed. Ikesha gave her time, then she discarded her book, got up and headed for the kitchen. She had detected something not quite right in the grain of her mother's voice. Besides, Gloria's hesitancy to enter the sitting-room confirmed that all was most certainly, not well.

"Mum?" she said, looking questioningly at her mother.

"Yuh a'right, Sweetheart?" Gloria asked, trying to turn the concern away from herself and onto her daughter. She averted her eyes from the kettle and tried to force a normal conversation, turning away again, just as quick.

"Have you been crying, Mum?" Ikesha asked softly, rising above her mother's act.

Gloria turned and answered with her eyes.

Ikesha hugged her. "What's the matter, Mum?" As if she didn't know.

"Shhh...Ikesha don't mek a fuss," she said. "Yuh know me 'ave me moments."

She was hoping her tears would have subsided back at Cannon Hill Park, but they hadn't. Perhaps the torrential rain wasn't enough. Or perhaps, today she was hurting too much. She dabbed her face with a tissue, widened her eyes and headed for the sitting-room to greet her son and girlfriend face-to-face.

Kunta sat diagonally across the settee, resting the cheeks of his ass on its edge, the base of his spine against a cushion, his long legs stretching for what seemed like miles across the room like a blown-down obstruction after a storm. It didn't seem that long since he was struggling to climb into the very same settee, upholstered three times by his mother's expert hands.

Shari sat on his lap, her far-gone maternal belly pointing south, she herself looking no more advanced than a baby. In less than two weeks, they were 'expecting the topsy-turvy responsibility' of teenage parents. With Kunta only nineteen and Shari just turned eighteen, nappies could have waited.

"Yuh not pregnant by any chance are you girl?" Gloria joked, realising the size of her bump.

"Think so," the over-pretty, bright-eyed young girl replied, smiling. She was a dead ringer for Alicia Keyes, and though pregnant, it was hard to imagine her losing her virginity. Innocence clung tightly to her face like a baby to its mother's breast.

"Bags packed?" Gloria asked in her usual caring tone.

"Yeah. Everything's ready ain'it, Kunta?"

"Yeah. Propa."

"Kunta, you know you're not to leave her for a minute now, don't you?" Gloria half chastised, then proceeded to leave the room. It was obvious that a new thought had occupied her mind.

"Yeah, Mum, I know," Kunta's voice trailed after her.

"He'd better not," Ikesha stared a playful threat at her brother, then she settled herself into the side-chair in which she was previously sitting. She put her head back in her book and a pair of headphones in her ears.

Soon, the noise of the hoover broke the silence and Gloria's humming emphasised her mood. A mood only Ikesha and Kunta could pick up on. Hoovering and humming spelt gloom. Gloria hummed... *'And I still... haven't found... what I'm looking for... '*

Then a pause in the dirt-monster allowed the sound of the doorbell. Gloria opened the door and Lijah walked in holding Khamilla's hand. He had lost that sure-footedness he had when he lived there.

"A'right G?" These days Lijah's tone was always low. Careful. Like a peasant talking to a King. Walking on eggshells had nothing on this. What with Gloria's cutting silence, the aftermath of shame and a forever-existing guilt, it was almost as if he was commanded to tread carefully.

"Me a'right." She barely managed the words. "How come you took so long? You should have been here two hours ago."

"Cha. Some stop-an-search business. An' guess who happen to be a random motorist?"

Khamilla, their sweet five-year-old had already rushed towards her mother. Gloria was kissing and hugging her tight. Lijah proceeded to the sitting-room and beheld the rest of his family. "Kunta, whaap'n?" He touched fists with his son; a replica of himself, apart from his locks and the good few inches in height Kunta had given him. He stroked Shari's bump and kissed the side of her face. "Bwoy, me still not sure 'bout dis gran'dad t'ing yuh know."

"Well, if all goes well, you've got no choice, Dad," Shari presumed the in-law status.

"Ikesha! How's me book-worm baby?" He diverted his attention to his older daughter, kissing the side of her face as he poke. Ikesha was the replica of Gloria as a teenager.

She lifted her head from her book, removed her headphones and kissed her dad. "Yuh a'right, Dad?"

Lately, where Lijah was concerned, Ikesha evaded the subject of her parents' situation. It bothered her, but although she had always been there for her mum, and although she wished they would sort out their differences, she figured they were old enough (*although seemingly not wise enough*) to sort their lives out. She was seriously trying to sort her own out. Putting it on the right track. Starting as she meant to go on.

"Surviving, Sweetheart. It's all about surviving. Yuh done know." Lijah was clearly making a point. He turned purposefully and looked at Gloria who was now standing in the doorway. '*My queen* ', his eyes said, but the words had better stay where she would tell him they belonged: *up his ass*. But whatever happened, he knew she would always be *his queen*. Despite her thought, she understood his silent way of communicating and gave him a sharp look.

"You?" he looked again at Ikesha.

"Safe, dad. Even safer when I finish my media degree. I'll be twenty-one then. Then dad... I'm going backpacking. For a year."

"You're what?!...Backpacking?!... Where?... Why?... Yuh mad?!"

"Dad, I'm young. I'm gonna enjoy life while I can. A group of us are going. It'll be fun. Don't wanna spend all me life hanging around Birmingham you know. I wanna see a bit of the world before I settle down an' have babies an' all that. And I hope I get my news reading job before that too." The girl was too pretty for words, and her high hopes and assertiveness emphasised it even more. The matter-of-fact way she spoke about trailing across alien parts of the world made her beauty even more of a mystery. She had beauty, brains and now, a sense of adventure no one saw coming.

At first, it was Kunta who would have been expected to express desires to spread his wings and fly far away from the family nest. From a child, Ikesha possessed an old head, but not an adventurous spirit. She would cling only to her room, her books and a tatty old worry-blanket that would be constantly stuck up her nose, as she sucked on her tongue. The combination gave her comfort. But it seemed that one day she woke up. Maybe one day in between the tight bookshelves in her university's library.

Kunta looked at his sister in amazement. "So what's wrong with Birmingham? Nah man, Ikesha. Yuh cyaan do dat man. Is only w'ite students do dem backpacking t'ings deh. Dem t'ings is dangerous man. Don't yuh 'ear all dem weird t'ings happening to back-packers? Listen to de news Ikesha, man. You could get kidnapped. Killed. All sort a t'ing can happen."

It was fright for his sister's safety that made Kunta make negative comparison. In all their squabbling, deep down they were best friends. Cared more for each other than they openly let on.

"Kunta, don't be so narrow-minded. Bad t'ings happen everywhere. If they're meant to happen to you, backpacking or not, they will. Look what's happening on the streets of Birmingham. People our age gettin' shoot up lef' right an' centre. I'm more likely to get shot standing at a bus stop than on a backpacking trip. Anyway, where's the dare in you Kunta? I wanna do t'ings before I'm old. Before dem nappies, sleepless nights an' all dat rubbish." She felt the need to repeat herself, "That's not all to life, you know."

Shari looked at her, and Ikesha felt a little guilty for preaching in front of the young mother-to-be. She didn't mean to worry or even demean her. Just giving her views on the real deal.

Kunta jumped to the rescue. "Don't talk like dat in front of her Ikesha man. It won't be dat bad. I'll be there for her."

"What d'you mean it won't be that bad, Kunta? For one, I don't see any tits on you. Are *you* gonna help with the breast-feeding?"

Shari went a shade paler, smiling nervously, as if breast-feeding was news to her.

"Nah, man, we've got one a dem express t'ings to express de milk in advance. You don't need to frighten her, sis'." Kunta hugged Shari at the same time, as if trying to make it better.

"Yeah, an' make sure you're not just there for the first few weeks, Kunta. *Always*. Like Mum said Dad was when we were born."

Lijah glanced at Gloria, seeking an acknowledgement for his recent commendation. A small brownie point that was hardly worth the mention, considering his present standing with her.

"Why yuh stressing me, Ikesha man?" Kunta knitted his brows. "Jus' because yuh at university, yuh coming wid yuh righteous lecture. Yuh always 'ave yuh head in dem dyam books. An' all yuh ever listen to is dat classical rubbish. Cha." The truth hurts and the young man was on the defence. The reaction was natural. Now his attack was fright for himself. It's true that he had not really thought seriously about the business of fatherhood, and his sister had suddenly hit it right home to him. Two years ago when he met Shari at a hip-hop and garage rave, making babies wasn't a conscious decision, but, not for the want of the knowledge of safe sex, the overwhelming passion of youth took the wheels. Now, though reluctantly, raving with their hip-hop, rap and garage buddies must stay on the back burner for a while. In their youth, they had plunged upon themselves the responsibility of their own youth. It wouldn't be long before a gurgling bundle of joy (or pain) would come crawling into their lives.

"Classical rubbish, Kunta? Why do you call it rubbish?"

Kunta looked quizzically at his sister. "Well, what's wrong wid hip-hop and garage?" He reflected on his position as *DJ Romeo* for a recent pirate radio show he and a few friends had put together over a year ago, catering for their own crew and beyond.

"Nothing. Nothing at all, bro'. But Kunta, what's wrong with having my head in my books? *You* need to read more. Open your mind. Life is not all about rap, hip-hop, garage and trousers fighting for purchase 'round your ass, you know. Nelson Mandela, Martin Luther, Malcolm X, Denzel Washington and Jessie Jackson read books. These are people who should be you role models."

Lijah listened to his daughter's strong reasoning, his eyes constantly fixed on the side of Gloria's face and his mind on the first day they met, back in 1982. He remembered the fiery, determined young woman that stood out from the crown in a corner of Rialto's. How he fell in love, not just with her beauty and innocence, but her strength, ambition and sense of pride. And how he had gradually watched her change, as love conquered all. And how he had plucked up the courage to tell her that he had done time, and breathed a sigh of relief when she didn't treat him as a leper, but as a youth that had stumbled on his way to manhood.

Gloria could feel his eyes on her. Almost as she could, that same night at Rialto's. And almost telepathically, together they shared a silent sense of pride towards their daughter, wishing, in their silent ways, that her dreams would materialise.

Little Khamilla was ignoring the whole adult thing. She stared curiously at Shari's bump, bubbling with excitement at the fact that inside was her little niece or nephew: big sister Ikesha had explained it all to her. Being more advanced than a regular five-year-old, she understood perfectly.

Ikesha continued, "And I listen to classical music when I study, Kunta. It helps to relax the mind. Focus. In fact, you know I listen to all kinds of music. Reggae, Calypso, Jazz, Blues, R&B... and yes, Hip-hop and Garage. But each to their own and I can't say they're my favourite." As she spoke, she got up, walked over to her brother and stuck her headphones in his ears. She wanted to prove a point. What blurted out was not what Kunta expected. *A classic*, but not from his surmising, *classical*. Instead, Sizzler's *'Black Woman An' Child'* filled his ears. Further along the tape, if he cared to wait, Garnet Silk would entertain him. The two artists were among Ikesha's favourites.

Kunta smiled and nodded his head to the crucial lyric, postponing his immediate problem for a little while.

Then Ikesha rounded off her point by shoving her book under his nose. Nelson Mandela's *'Long Walk To Freedom'*. Yes. Old head. Grandma Fontaine had told her that since she was a mere six years old. Now, her friends were of a slight difference from Kunta and Shari's, who would probably view her not as boring, but different.

Shari eased forward slightly to allow enough space for the book.

Lijah looked on, still with pride. He was bemused as to the extent of his daughter's force. He knew where she got her determination from, but felt sure his little girl would not be held back. She would know no boundary. Born with sight of the final frontier in her view, and would reach for it.

Gloria walked back to the kitchen. She had already forced back her own sadness and smiled at the mini feud between her children, battling out their differences. She remembered how not so long ago, all they argued about were toys, who had taken what from whose room, who had worn whose named T-shirt without asking, and whose turn it was to wash-up.

"Have you ever spent time to read any of these books, Kunta?" Ikesha stressed her point by pointing to the mahogany bookshelf, calling out titles in a condescending yet playful, high-pitched tone, as if her brother couldn't read them for himself.

"Neva min' dat, sis. When was the las' time yuh tek een a session?"

Ikesha raised an eyebrow at him.

"Yeah," he stressed, "a real session. Dem play Sizzla inna dancehall, yunnuh. Yuh wanna get out more, Sis'. Get out an' dance...Ah tell me 'bout book." He kissed his teeth and looked to Shari for support, but by now, she was somewhere else. In the land of thoughts. Something Ikesha had said got her juggling things in her head.

Ikesha was somewhere else too. Transported to the last time she took in a session. It was the Hurricane nightclub. More or less, she was dragged there by Sista Scorcha, a distant cousin but close friend of the family. Sista Scorcha was the hottest mover on Birmingham's dance-floors. In order to keep ahead of her title and to hold on to that infamous trophy, she followed every known sound system around, like chicken do, mother hens. She wore snippets of cloths for skirts, and skimpy tops that fought to control her tits. Yes. The sista was well-endowed too: an added requisition.

'*Come out tonight, Ikesha*', she had said. '*Leave de books dem feh one night*'.

Ikesha was strong, but Scorcha had more persuasive power than a double-glazing salesman. And somehow she had persuaded her to do some hardcore socialising. It opened her eyes to dancehall moves she had never seen before. Sista Scorcha for one showed her moves she wouldn't have thought possible. She moved her body like a rag-doll. Yasso, desso, indeh, outdeh, rock-an-go-dong, rock-an-come-up. A real man-tease. But that was one of the requisitions for holding the title.

But that was not the chin-dropper for Ikesha. It was when a bona-fide Jamaican, Scorcha had not known, came up behind the flexible dancehall queen, placed his groin against her ass, stretched his blinging hands in the air and moved rudely against her ass. Ikesha had a job controlling her reaction. Scorcha, however, took it like a pinch of salt. Legs spread widely, back bent, ass reaching out to meet his groin, she gave as good, busying her ass against his dick like a blender against cake-mix. '*Then what if she had known him?*' Ikesha had asked herself.

And two records later, when his bredrin had asked Ikesha, '*Gimme a dance nuh pretty girl?*' she had refused politely, knowing full well she could not even begin to entertain the thought, let alone *do* those moves. '*So wha'?*' he had challenged, yard style. '*Is why yuh come out? Feh dance? Or feh stan' up inna de place like yuh nice? Yuh nuh dance wid man? Yuh is a lesbian?*'

Ikesha had cowered, and it was Scorcha herself, who saved her with her lip, from this guy, who was about to take the dance anyway, consent or not.

So yes, Ikesha remembered it well.

"Well," Ikesha addressed her brother, "*you* shouldn't be taking in no session for a while anyway, Kunta. The only *club* you should be seeing is the one your woman's in."

That was a bite, if ever there was one.

"Easy Ikesha, easy," Lijah begged. "How yuh a cou'se up yuh bradda suh? Gee."

"Don't worry, dad. My time wi' come," Kunta promised.

Lijah eased into the kitchen to join Gloria, leaving the kids to their cultural battle. Khamilla followed, twisting her ponytails and holding onto her father's leg and wishing with her big brown eyes. "Don't go Daddy, I don't want you to go."

Lijah looked down at his little angel, his free-flowing locks sweeping the top of her head like roped door tassels.

"Khamilla, don' start dat man. Yuh know daddy have to go."

"When are you coming to take me again?" she asked, staring up at him, bubbles of tears waiting to burst out.

Gloria was not comfortable with Khamilla's behaviour of late. Her psychology degree had highlighted more to her on the human behaviour front than she had bargained for, or ever dreamed possible. She hoped their splitting up wouldn't affect Khamilla too much, but the five-year-old was already showing signs of missing the permanent presence of her father. She had started to wet the bed again. Khamilla's antennas were more receptive than they all thought. Gloria didn't need to ask. She knew it was down to their splitting up. She knew she could have done the *'for the sake of the children'* thing and let Lijah stay, but she found it hard. Having him in her bed, touching her after he had touched another woman, was like allowing her greatest phobia to crawl all over her naked body. *'Something'*, she had told Kizzy, *'men just don't understand'*.

Lijah himself had been on the end of Gloria's analysing theory, and didn't need to ask how deep she would go with this one. And if push came to shove, he knew he would be blamed for the majority of Khamilla's unstable disposition. It wouldn't have been half Gloria's fault for chucking him out, but mostly his, for messing with a mysterious white woman and screwing the baby-sitter. And of course, the *Bernadette* thing would be added ammunition. The final bullet in her gun.

Lijah had already ran his usual spiel about '*Black women taking on the European way of dealing with t'ings. Breaking up the traditional African family. Grasping independence like a staff. Building strength from their one-parent-family situation and leaving their men with nothing to do but to be stereotyped'*. He chose to ignore the real reasons why women are taking control of their lives, and masked it with a blanket of praise for

African women, who he claimed, *'stay with their men, through thick or thin'*.

Lijah had gotten so used to being blamed, it had soon become no big deal. Though subtly, Gloria had used her psychological analysis and told him he was partly to blame for his mother's demise (*a very sore point, opening his wound of guilt even more*). He had already taken some of the blame and was trying to live with it, but (*although she did not intend it to be*) her emphasis on the subject was, at times, painful for him. She told him, *'You should have confronted your dad when your mum was hurting, Lijah. She needed you. Faye and Roy had already left, but you left when she needed you most'*.

To a certain extent she was right, but his mind was not strong enough to cope with the reality that surrounded him then. He shielded himself with his new-found religion, Rastafarianism. Escaped and hid in the arms of The Kings of Kings and Lords of Lords. Haile Selassie.

Gloria didn't blame his choice of escapism, but what he had escaped from, leaving it to go bad, like a lost mango.

Besides, Lijah figured he wasn't the eldest son. Roy should have been there to confront their father. Tackle him with his broad chest, adorned with The Queen's medals. Fight for his mother's rights. Used his Royal Air Force stature, and protected her. Instead, he served the Monarchy, which now sees him only as a number, if it sees him at all.

And even on his return to England, Birmingham wasn't good enough for him. Not just because he had moved 'up', but also because he had moved 'away'. Away from the past. In a way, Roy must have felt that in his own way, he had chastised his old man. At the funeral, the most crucial time when families should unite, he did not speak to his dad, even when he tried. A 'silent treatment' that cuts.

And besides, Lijah had never felt comfortable with his father ever since he returned from Her Majesty's service. If it weren't for his mother, Lijah would have returned to the streets. He had dented his father's pride and now he would stick out like a patch of darn on old dungarees.

Lijah resented his father's silent, chastising stares, almost as much as his father resented his very being. At times, Lothan would sit in his car if Lijah was in the house. Other times he would walk sideways like a crab, as if trying to avoid the passing breeze of his own son. *'How could you?'* his body language would say, *'how could a son of mine spen' time in prison?'* And of all the things his old man would do, or say, nothing could be worse than his cutting despite.

It was only in later years that things changed. Lothan swallowed his pride and spoke to his son like a man, giving him more fatherly advice, adding to the ones he had already given him, a boy.

But everyone had laid blame. Found new escapism. Tried to heal themselves by leaning on the post of everybody else's faults.

Gloria stressed, "You were the one who saw, heard. You told me yourself you used to watch the sheepish expression on your dad's face. Heard the guilty shuffling of Dora's feet."

And Lijah would recall the pretentious black nurse (who claimed to be Nettie's best friend), whenever he would enter the house unexpectedly. He would catch her shifty glances. See the hurried *'shit-get-dressed-quick'* action in his old man's body language, as he would guard the living-room door to give her chance to make herself descent.

And he had seen too, the bed that held his mother captive: slave to its discomfort, with nothing to offer but its frustrating familiarity, laughable wishes and those infamous bed sores. Yes. Bed sores and an everlasting soaker-upper for her tears.

And Lijah had puzzled too over many other things. Like his sister Faye's and his brother Roy's reluctance to return to Birmingham after the funeral. Even for a visit. Everyone runs from life, he reckoned. Frightened to face up to their fears, as if they were seven-headed giants, and their swords of confrontation having no effect. Lijah had always said that if they had all *'come together'* and talked, rather than 'go apart' and suffer in silence, things might have been much different.

He had puzzled too over his Uncle Stan. *Stanley Augustus Benjamin.* Uncle Stan was Lothan's younger brother. A quietly spoken man with a mysterious air about him. Uncle Stan didn't speak much, but women loved him - black and white. But he didn't have much time for black women. Almost as if somewhere in his past, a black woman had hurt him. Cut him to the core. So now, he sported only white women.

'What's happened between you and Uncle Stan, Dad?' Lijah had asked, sometime after his mother's funeral.

'Me an' yuh uncle, Stanley jus' don' see eye to eye, Lijah. Jus' mek sure seh yuh try to live good wid Roy', Lothan had answered, obviously trying to be as evasive as possible.

But of all the strangeness surrounding his family, (next to the demise of his mother) Lijah found this one rather strange. Besides, it seemed sacrilege that they didn't get on, as Uncle Stan was the spitting image of Lothan. No joke. Looks wise, they were two peas in a pod. Uncle Stan was about five years younger than Lothan, and had come to England about a year after Lijah was born. The memory Lijah had of his uncle, had never faded. He could remember, as a child, Uncle Stan coming to the house with a different woman every time: none of them black. And sometimes he would come alone and sit cool and quietly, looking like an American soul singer. To Lijah's reckoning, Uncle Stan would speak only when an argument had strength, or a comment was of substance. It was almost as if he didn't want to waste his breath on futile chit-chat. But Lothan didn't see it that way. Lijah could remember his old man saying, *'Stanley too dyam sneakin'. Him gwaan like 'im quiet, but 'im can be sneakin' at times. Ginnal.'* And in spite of Lothan's surmising of his brother, no steps were taken to stop him coming to the house. Still, it didn't change Lijah's view of Uncle Stan. He respected him to the bones. At least, back then. Or even until he had grown into a man and questioned the meaning of *'respect'*.

Now, on the streets of Birmingham, he would see Uncle Stan only now and then. Like Faye and Roy, he too seemed to have taken the option of *'keep yuh distance'*. And whenever Lijah would see him: mostly as they drove in opposite directions, Uncle Stan sporting a gold tooth, gold chain and a pony-tail that suited him down to the ground. A pony tail that would look ridiculous on most other black man his age – all Uncle Stan would say was, *'Yuh a'right, Lijah? An' how is Faye when yuh 'ear from her?'* It was almost as if there were no Lothan. No Roy. Or even Gloria and his grand nieces and nephews. Just Faye.

Lijah knew that Faye was always Uncle Stan's favourite, and it was good to know that an old uncle cared so much about his niece, but his question was becoming irritable. Like the annoying grate of a scratched record. Unlike the question he himself would like to ask Uncle Stan: *'What really happened between yuh an' me old man? You're brothers, yet yuh don't speak'.* But time will always be longer than rope. Lijah figured that one day he might pluck up the courage, to ask.

But Lijah could never tell Uncle Stan how Faye was, since he just didn't hear from her. She was lost; it seemed, in the depth of France, forever. And Lijah would wish for the *'coming together'* of his family. To see them all around a big table. Eating together. Talking. Like close black families do, on Sunday afternoons. But as he saw it, it was never gonna happen. His family was given to him, and him, to them. Family is one thing one cannot choose.

"Soon babes. Soon," Lijah addressed his crying daughter, dragging himself back from days gone by, and wishful thinking. He had acknowledged the fact that Khamilla was missing his permanency, badly. "I'll be coming back soon." Lijah picked Khamilla up as he spoke, then rested his eyes questioningly on Gloria, a begging question filling them. Ever since their break up, they spoke with a difference. In silence. Body language. Any other means away from verbal communication. More so, Gloria spoke through music. She always did. In good and bad times. She would let her music ride him. An appropriate song would tell Lijah what she was thinking or even feeling. And when her stereo wasn't on, she would sing or hum. And it would reach the pit of his soul. Ride every strand of his locks. Seep through his silk socks, kicking his black ass - like nuisance road-chippings against prestige bodywork.

But Lijah had his way too. Through his eyes. His silent presence. The agitated shaking of his right leg. The rising of his manhood, triggered by anger and frustration, pushing hard against the inside of his thighs like a frustrated snake. Anger and frustration made him horny. Gloria had always known. They understood each other to the max. They knew too that, most of all, people hurt the ones they love most.

Their love was one of such depth; their parting could almost be likened to separating Siamese twins. It was only Gloria who had been there for him, when not even his ital brew could take away the painful memories of his mother's suffering. A pain not even his idrins could detect. Not even Festus who he was the closest to.

"How are you, G? *Really.*" Lijah leant against the work surface of the new kitchen they had both paid for not so long ago. The need to sit down was quashed by the blanket of animosity that generated from Gloria. She hated him. But it was the aftermath of a too-deep love that had crossed that infamous thin line. Turned over on its back like a troubled tortoise.

"I'm fine. How much time yuh gonna ask me dat?" She tried to strengthen her voice. As she spoke, like therapy, she skilfully rolled individual pieces of dough into round and oblong shapes, dropping them one by one into the rich, bubbling soup. As the well kneaded cornmeal dumplings fell with grace onto the tops of neatly diced yellow yams she had recently dropped in, she was taken back to Leeds, when her mother first taught her to make red peas soup, gongo soup, stew peas an' rice, rice an' peas - the works. In those days, there would be a mound of salt beef, pig's hock, pig's tail – whatever it took to make her mother's pot tantalising: the aroma from her kitchen on a Saturday sending out an invitation to all who passed by.

In those days too, the way to a man's heart was through his belly. Whatever else he would love outa street, he would always come home to his good food. Hortence would swear by that, and in a way, it sent a signal to Gloria, compelling her to be a chef in her kitchen.

She had already learnt to be a lady in her living-room, but being a devilish whore in the bedroom took backstage. She thought she knew her man. And although she wanted to know him more and to share what she knew, she was cagey with his pride. She loved him and enjoyed making love to him, for a while, missionary (*though orgasmic*) was as good as it got.

Back then *(yes, back then, since today, his locks serves the purpose of that of a favourite jumper);* Lijah was a *true* rastaman who didn't touch *Pork*. So pig's hock, and pig's tail, were out. That too was unclean. An insult to his sacredness. So though tasty in its own right, Gloria's red peas soup had never tasted like her mother's. The main ingredients were missing.

"How's work?" he tried again, wishing he could *back weh wid de small talk*, and hug her. It wasn't easy. They had come too far to be this way. From the inexperienced yet satisfying taking of her virginity, to the sharing of a single bed. She knew no other. And if variety is really the spice of life, she knew nothing of it.

"Fine. How's Bernadette? Yuh *landlady-come-lover?*" Gloria jabbed, tight-lipped and purposeful, her resentment cutting through his soul and her corn-meal dumplings taking the physical force of her anger.

The taunt pierced Lijah's heart. "So we goin' down dat road again G? Is you chuck me out yuh know. Whatever situation I'm in, is you sen' me to it." Lijah eased his daughter onto the floor, catching a deep look and a hateful cut-eye from his queen.

"Listen G," he stated with curt directness. "Me mekin' a move. As always, I man don' like de vibes. I'd love to stay an' have some a dat peas soup, but de vibes nah seh not'n G. Jah know, I don't like dis fussin' an' fightin' t'ing. Yuh done know. Whatever me doin' outa street, is yuh me love, but me nah get nuh lovin' from you G. I am a man. Jah know, me have needs. A jus' so."

"And I suppose as well as Bernadette, yuh still fucking Faithlyn. An' dat w'ite gyal as well." Gloria was hurt and wanted to hurt back. Besides, admitting his needs didn't help. It was basically saying, '*Yes, I'm having sex*', *a man need to have sex*'. She had known, but had rather he didn't confirm it.

Lijah looked hard at her, his brows knitted questioningly. Her language perplexed him. It wasn't her style to use foul language and it confirmed how much she was still bitter.

"Yuh wouldn't like me soup anyway Lijah," her 'cutting' tactic still in use. "Pork inna it." She totally ignored his latter statement about fussin' an' fightin'. "Oh... sorry... I was forgetting... of course yuh eat *pork* now."

Lijah knew exactly what she meant. A black woman scorned can be the most spiteful. He thought of Lucy the blonde, the start of his downfall. The woman who dangled her cash, gave him access to her gash and gave Gloria the reason to suspect him of foul-play on the night-shift.

Lijah chose not to answer and returned to the living-room with a lump in his throat and Khamilla in tow. He kissed Ikesha, Shari and Khamilla, touched fists with Kunta and left, dying from Gloria's unwillingness to give, and the sound of Khamilla's pleading voice, saying, "Daddy! Daddy! Come back!"

But now, the force of Gloria's need to hug him was one to be reckoned with. It had swung like a pendulum that had earlier got stuck on the opposite side. But she wouldn't hug him, so she fought it and let him walk, staring at his disappearing figure, his long dread-locks swinging proud down his back. She remembered the days they barely touched the nape of his neck. The days she washed, dried, twisted and pampered them. Well after all, she was his Empress. His queen.

She soothed Khamilla by giving her a piece of dough to roll. She glanced again at Lijah as he climbed into his MRS Roadster Sports, still doubting his ability to afford the sweet ride. When she had asked, his explanation was curt. Hurried. She didn't push it.

She knew he would come back to stay tomorrow if she asked him to, but like she wouldn't hug, or be civilised to him, she wouldn't. Too proud to ask. But like her father Reverend Fontaine had told her years ago: *'Pride cometh before a fall'*. He had known full well what he was talking about, but practicing what he preached, was another thing.

'Would Lijah talk about his mother to another woman?' Gloria asked herself as she tilted the lid slightly on the bubbling pot of peas soup. As far as she knew, he had only ever confided in her. She had always soothed him unconditionally. Comforted him in his difficult moments. Moments his idrins wouldn't have dreamt, existed. Like most men from the 'dread' days, it was almost as if it was a must that Lijah masked himself with hardness. A far cry from the real Lijah only she knew.

Gloria wondered too, how he would cope this year, on the anniversary of his mother's death. Like previous years, the memory of the day, would take another little bit of him.

"A'right, Mum?" Ikesha joined her mother in the kitchen again, pulling her from her thoughts. Her little sister was now sitting comfortably on her left hip.

"Yeah. Me a'right."

But Ikesha knew otherwise. She had felt the pain in her father's goodbye. And now, almost touching the hurt from her mother's aura, mixed with the aroma from a bubbling pot, the air in the kitchen was stiff.

CHAPTER * THREE

It was Saturday afternoon and the Soho Road was buzzing with a buoyant, cultural air. In one infamous area, everyone willingly spread their seemingly happy-go-lucky mood around. Reggae music boomed out of four separate black men's rides, threatening to make the sound clash between Vibes Injection, Mighty Crown, Will Power and David Rodigan a farce. The loud jabbing sounds of black women's laughter danced like waves, ducking and diving the regular sounds of police sirens.

A wicked aroma of freshly baked West Indian bread, bun, gizzardas, cut-cakes, grater-cakes, cheese, and salt-fish patties oozed out onto the street like whiffs from Mama Liza's kitchen. The queue for the 'Yard-style' delights span for some distance, stretching itself way 'round the bend and up onto Thornhill Road. A purposely placed police wagon stood its ground, its presence said, 'Too many blacks in one place. There might be trouble',

Now the impatient, yet steadfast queuers watched him scavenging in a bin on Soho Road. Montie. The black, drunken tramp. His over-grown dirty-white hair, untouched by a comb for what seemed like forever, made him look scary.

"Laad have mercy!" a loud talking woman said when her eyes beheld him. "W'at a sin inna Inglan' eeh sah? I hate to si black people inna dat situation."

Kizzy looked on in despair from her position in the queue, wondering why it should feel so strange. So unacceptable for a black man to be in that state, in a land where he had come to better himself. It had never bothered her too much seeing a white man in that position. After all, it is England. The white man's land. And where better for his downfall, than his own land. But a black man? It just didn't feel right. But that was all she could do. *Wonder.* It wasn't her problem. It was somebody else's. Or perhaps nobody's problem at all. Not even Montie's. For him, it wouldn't be a problem, but a life situation.

Festus picked up the old man's image in his rare-view mirror, as he sat waiting for Kizzy. As he watched, sorrow filled his eyes and anger darkened his face. His forehead became wrinkled. His eyes narrowed. He opened his door and made his way towards the old unkempt, shameful looking man, who was now rummaging in a convenient bin. "Leave de bin! Here," he lowered his voice now. "Tek dis. Get yuhself some food. Yuh sleep in yuh flat last night?" Festus spoke to the pitiful-looking man as if he (the man) was a child. Pangs of anger jabbed his belly and he tried hard to control himself. It was almost as if he knew that this man once had grace, and had now fallen from it, face down into open shame of no return.

The queuers puzzled at the dread's concern.

"Whaap'n, Festus?!" a brotha shouted, "yuh turn Good Samaritan now?"

He kissed his teeth and ignored the cynicism.

Festus knew his woman was watching. She always did. Watched and wondered how come he could be so sympathetic to a vagrant, yet had no mercy when he would beat her ass.

Some of the people in the slow-moving queue found the man pitiful, and saw Festus as a Good Samaritan. Some found him disgusting and saw Festus as weird for caring. The *'I'm alright Jack'* attitude would have been more acceptable. Some found pleasure in watching this gutter situation. A sort of enjoyment from perverse voyeurism they themselves would not have even known they possessed. None; neither the pitying nor the disgusted would have offered help. In their silent judgement, they saw no further than the situation in front of them. A loser. A good-for-nothing tramp, who could not have possibly emerged from a woman's womb.

The old man stretched his hands forward, gripping the note that the dread was handing him. "T'ank yuh, Son. God wi' bless yuh." It was what the old man would say most of the time when Festus would show him mercy. Festus would sometimes pick him up in his car, take him to his flat (cold and musty from un-inhabitation) and see that he had a bath, a change of clothes and a hot drink. But at times there was no chance of that. Most of the time it would be impossible. Of late, Montie had been almost always out of his mind with drink, drinking away it seems, his pain. A weary wanderer on the streets of Handsworth. They called him The Handsworth Tramp. Sometimes when his senses would return from their leave, and when familiar stares from black, questioning eyes would put him on trial, he would shout from his dribbling, toothless mouth, *'Tom drunk, but Tom nuh fool!'*

Festus was deep in thoughts when Kizzy pulled on the handle of his car door. The scent of the old man was pushed away by the aroma of fresh bread, bun and a thick slice of Jamaican cheese: their son Fari's favourite. Festus reached out to help her with the bag, but Kizzy winced, pulling it away. "No Festus. What if yuh hand touch dat man? Me sorry feh, him but him look so nasty. Yuh don't know what yuh might ketch. Mek sure yuh wash yuh han' before yuh touch Fari."

"How yuh so fuckin' snobby 'oman?! De man is a human being, yunnuh! He is somebody's son, Kizzy. He was born from a woman's belly t'raas."

Kizzy stopped in her tracks, perplexed at his defence for the tramp. "I
didn't say he wasn't human, Festus, but he was just searching in the bin.
Can you imagine de germs?" Kizzy settled herself in her seat, securing
her seatbelt at the same time, stretching the process like a well-needed
anchor. She hated when Festus got into a mood. Whatever his problem
was, it would be hers later. You see, he would bust licks up-side her head
in a wave of anger. But she would forgive. Yes she would. That once-
too-many forgiveness, in her search for reasons why, and coming up with
the same answer all the time: *'He's the devil I know'*.

But today, she couldn't help but think, *'Even a tramp took precedence
over me... even a fucking tramp'*.

A force of gravity threatened to suck her permanently into the back of
her seat, as Festus stepped on the gas, leaving the vicinity of Soho Road
behind.

CHAPTER * FOUR

Lately, more than ever, Lijah spend nuff time meditating. Thinking of
everything. Hurting his queen was one thing, but the fear of her using
their daughter Khamilla against him became an obsession. Before things
had calmed down to the stage where they could talk, let alone negotiate
about him seeing Khamilla on an arrangement basis, he had visited the
house on separate occasions and felt the wicked force of her spite. It's a
serious thing. It should be said, 'Hell *really* hath no fury like a *black*
woman scorned!'

Gloria would pick Khamilla up and wrap both her arms around her, as
if forbidding her to look at her father. And Lijah had detected that the
word *'Daddy'* from Khamilla's lips was almost like a swear word to
Gloria's ears and knew she wished him harm. It was ripping him apart.
He loved Gloria, and hated the situation as it was. More than anything,
he hated picking up and dropping off their daughter like some borrowed
tool.

He had previously told Gloria how sorry he was for hurting her, but
wanted also to explain how he really felt. How it really happened. To
make her understand that sexual temptation - like the baby-sitter thing,
was more compelling than that of hunger for food. Besides, Faithlyn had
pushed fresh pussy under his nose. And he was hungry.

As far as he knew, Gloria was always faithful to him, and would give
him all the reasons why men are dogs. So like that infamous night when
she asked, *"Are you screwing the baby-sitter?"* He remained silent.

He had wanted Gloria back from the day she chucked him out. He pleaded, literally, but to no avail. He could feel her hurt and wanted to love her, turn the clock back. But the wall she had built around her was so solid; he had given up trying for a while.

One Sunday afternoon, just like the one he had gathered up some of his belongings from the drive, he sat on his own doorstep with a full heart and a buzzing head, listening to ecstatic moans seeping from his letterbox. That day, he developed a psychological contempt for red SAABS. It was parked in front of his house like an *apostrophe S,* showing ownership of his drive. *Feh real.*

Lijah knew that whatever Gloria was doing, it was through spite. Getting her own back. Something told him she wasn't enjoying it, but suddenly it hit home to him how she must have really felt, actually seeing him giving the baby-sitter what she had claimed to be rightfully hers. He supposed she wanted him to feel what she felt. That *'two wrongs'* trying to make *'one right'* thing. He did it in their house, so why shouldn't she.

It was then that Lijah realised the seriousness of the situation. Shit. There was another man walking through his door, climbing his stairs and seemingly, rocking his woman's world.

Khamilla was young and vulnerable and he quickly developed a serious phobia: a phobia of his daughter calling another man daddy! Besides, he needed desperately to know *who* drives a red SAAB. *'Seem like a dodgy character',* he would say. *'Why would anyone want to black out their window? Dis bredrin mus' have somet'ing to hide to raas'.*

And he had wondered too, where Gloria's ecstatic moans were coming from. The bed they once shared? The thought alone jabbed his heart. Men had killed for less. He needed to talk to her. *Seriously.* But just then, sucking salt was what he had to do.

That same evening after a long walk to clear his head, Lijah returned to his rented accommodation to find Bernadette sat on the living-room floor, cross-legged, in a black leotard, responding to a relaxation video. Even now, recalling his first intimate encounter with her would arouse him.

"You're early, Lijah," she had said without turning 'round.

"Yeah, I suppose I'm earlier than normal." He used the opportunity to view her emphasised figure through her sexy leotard. Diana Ross sprang to mind.

Bernadette's living-room was red. A hot, intense red and she made no excuses for that. He remembered the first time she showed him 'round.

She had described herself as a passionate, sexual and sensual being. Explained something about the importance of having all her senses engaged. Speaking with a poetic tongue, she had said, "Among other colours, red is welcoming to my eyes. The voices of John Holt, Dennis Brown, Beres Hammond, Frankie Paul and Garnet Silk are music to my ears. The feel of silk, satin, the torrents of a warm shower, and the easy touches of fingertips against my body do wonders for my sense of touch. The aroma of musk, lavender, jasmine, burning tar and my mother's cooking soothes my sense of smell. And I love the taste of ice-cold shandy, chocolate of any sort, seedless grapes and mangoes. Yeah. That's me," she purred.

Lijah had concluded that only Bernadette could make the simplest of things sound so dynamic. Sensual.

"Why are you so tense?" She asked.

He wondered how she could know, without touching him, or even turning to look at him.

"Am I?" He eased his locks to one side and sat on the spacious settee.

"I can feel it from here, Lijah. Here. Sit down." She patted the spot beside her.

Lijah was puzzled and hesitated.

She looked up at him and firmly said, "C'mon Lijah. I don't bite."

He adhered to her request.

Still, he felt awkward. Presumptuous. Presumptuous for presuming that Bernadette was instigating what he thought she was.

"See. That wasn't so bad, was it?" she said, patronisingly.

Lijah smiled nervously. He became coy, almost shy. A feeling he didn't relish much. This is the woman he spent his youth wishing he could be lucky with. And now when the wishing had stopped and respect stepped in, here he was confronted with a situation he was finding difficult to deal with – simply sitting by her on her living-room floor!

Bernadette eased herself up onto her knees and shimmied gracefully behind him. He wanted to ask her what she was doing. And why? Why him?

"Relax, Lijah." Now she was kneading the front of his shoulders and the side of his neck with her strong fingers. "Oh such knots. It's not good for you, you know. All this tension. Bad for your health." Lijah had forgotten that she had ran her own massage parlour somewhere in Birmingham after returning from France. Already he was beginning to relax. "Did Gloria ever do this for you?"

He didn't want to be reminded of Gloria just then. For all he knew, (*although the thought of it cut like a knife*) she might have been in a compromising position with a SAAB driver. "No," he mumbled back.

Now, she eased her fingers lightly over his lips, eyes, nose and chin. A host of new sensations took over his body. He wanted to hold her, but felt he had to wait for her permission. Besides he wasn't sure whether he was being simply massaged, or blatantly seduced.

Suddenly he felt her warm lips between his right shoulder blade and the side of his neck. Her palms had found their way under his T-shirt and were working their way all over his chest and down past his navel.

"Hey...Bernadette...What's this? *Really*," he asked, trembling with arousal and still not sure if he should make a move.

"You're tense. A little touching and caressing won't hurt. Do you the world a good."

She removed his T-shirt, running her tongue down the length of his spine, all over his back, caressing his nipples. The silence in which she performed her pleasure turned him on even more.

The reason for this treatment was above him, but he wasn't gonna complain. He simply relaxed into her grip like putty.

A short while after, she reached down towards his waist and proceeded to unbutton his jeans. He did not protest. Now, apprehension was not even a slight thought, but he still could not help wondering, '*Why me?* And, '*Didn't Bernadette have a man?*'

Her smell was erotic. Different. She always had a foreign edge about her. The idea of her being his sister's friend, his brother's first girlfriend and Jacques' ex-wife, flew out of his head fast, taking his inhibitions with it. Besides, Bernadette no longer spoke of any of them. And now her attention was going to be the healing he needed to deal with the Gloria situation. But at the time, he did not know how much.

She put her face into his neck and it felt safe. Right. Reassuring. Reaching for a lavender-scented cushion, she placed it on the floor behind him. Gently, she eased him into its comforts, manipulating the roots of his locks with such expertise, he wondered if she had had a dread in her life before. Some women have an uneasy way of dealing with dreads.

Now, for the first time, he saw her eyes like he had never seen them before. They spoke to him in a non-verbal way he had never experienced before.

"Don't move," she whispered now, kissing his lips gently. Then she left the room, but only for a few seconds. Returning with a bottle of lavender oil, she knelt over him with mastery. He adored the attention and the sexual silence was erotically golden.

Lijah's whole body ached with an unexplainable wanting for Bernadette.

By now, he had expected it, so when she attempted to remove his jeans he was not surprised. Periodically, she penetrated his eyes through the dimness of the room, with a language of pure passion.

He was proud of his erection and was delighted when she stroked it firmly. "Oh... my... God!" she sighed when she first discovered the size of his blessing.

Bernadette commanded him to lay face down. She placed a cushion under his neck, one under his ankles and one in the small of his back. She undressed and sat astride his buttocks. It felt sensational. Using gentle, erotic pressure, she worked upwards from his buttocks, her thumb pushing inward along his spine.

"Oh, Bernadette. Dis is wicked. Jah know," he mumbled. "But why me?"

The seductress said nothing, but worked all the way up his spine and out to his shoulders, bringing her hands slowly down his sensitive sides and down to his buttocks again. This she repeated several times until he was almost floating.

Now Lijah felt the time was right, so he turned 'round and began to stroke her firm breasts. She approved silently and he marvelled at the firmness of her bottom, the softness of her neck and the ease of her loins.

He had to be in heaven. Erotic massage. Never in his whole life had anyone made him feel so good, by just touching him. Not even his queen, Gloria.

"D'you know how to use this thing, Lijah?" Bernadette perplexed, fumbling his manhood like a prized gear-stick. "Can you handle it?" she added, almost as if she was referring to him driving an exclusive motor.

He smiled and said '*Tes' me nuh?*' Something most brothers would say, whether or not they were sure of their chances of passing that test.

Now the smell of lavender came with a newness to his senses. It wasn't from the cushion under his neck, but from the lotion, which Bernadette was now rubbing into his shaft, her fingers emulating a cluster of firm, erotic vibrators.

He wanted to speak but something in the air commanded him not to.

"Have you had many lovers, Lijah?" Bernadette broke the silence again. Somehow, it seemed she owned the right to. It was her show. "Would be a waste if you hadn't. With a tool like this? Well..." Now she talked directly at his weapon. Her tone was low. Erotic. Sensual.

He attempted to answer but for the first time, her warm lips gripped his, her tongue probing deep into his mouth, manipulating his taste buds with her sweet lavender kisses. Then she eased up. Just when he was floating at the highest level.

"Well? Have you?" she almost demanded.

"A few," he replied.

"So you know a lot about love-making then?"

"I suppose so."

"Somehow I suppose you've just *fucked* a lot of women, Lijah. There's a difference between that and making love to them." Her tactile attention continued, as she patronised him.

"Where is the relevance in this, Bernadette?"

"You don't think it matters to me whether you are a plain fucker or a great lover? Jacques... Mmm," she moaned, almost sorrowful," he was a great lover. But French men usually are."

Lijah felt as if he was being compared – one of the worse things a woman could ever do to a man. Unless of course she was telling him *he* was the best.

"Life isn't all about being physical in bed, is it? There are much more important things." He put up a defence.

"Like what? Marriage? Two point five kids? Mortgage? Making sure your pension's up-to-date?" There was sarcasm in her voice and Lijah tried to read her. At the same time he checked and found that after all, he didn't have all of the things Bernadette just reeled off. He wasn't married. He had no pension. Yes, he had a mortgage and he really wasn't sure what *point five* kids were supposed to be. He had three. "Do you have a problem with those requirements?" he asked, although he felt it was the wrong time for them to get deeper into that kinda conversation. He'd rather be getting on with the matter at hand. Satisfying his burning desire.

"I've tried that shit before, Lijah. Yes. But life's got a way of kicking you in the face when you least expect it. Now? I live life. Life doesn't live me. I was married: where's that got me? Careless, I know, but I have no pension. My house is paid for, so I have no worries there. And as for the two point five kids? I can't have them. I don't suppose Jacques would have married me if he knew. Still," she paused, kissed him, then said, "he's got someone who can now. She can give all the kids he'll ever want."

"Is that why you and Jacques split up?" Lijah pried again, hoping Bernadette would elaborate more on the break-up, "he's left you for someone else?"

Bernadette ignored Lijah's question and said, "You know, there was a time when I suspected Jacques of being bisexual. He was spending so much time with his best friend, Pierre, doubts were creeping into my head. But I was wrong, Lijah. So wrong. It wasn't Pierre at all." She stood up and stretched, doing some yoga stance. And now, the strongest urge yet, came over Lijah. He trembled, weak in the presence of beauty. He stood up, held his chest against her back, cupped her firm breast in his palms and felt his whole body melt with desire. His breathing became uncontrollable. His wantings lavish. His manhood, protesting strongly against restriction, throbbed avidly against the firm cheeks of her ass. "*Jeeesas Chris'*," he sighted, almost weeping, as he tried to contain the pleasure that overwhelmed him. As he whispered '*sweet somethings'* into the back of Bernadette's neck, sealing them with warm moist kisses, he wanted her like the sweet forbidden.

Why hadn't Gloria ever aroused him *so*? Not that she didn't arouse him at all, but never *so*. And now he was beginning to think about the notion that, *the way to get over one woman, is to get a woman like Bernadette, under him'*.

Bernadette pulled away and took his right arm. "Come Lijah," she whispered seductively, leading him towards the stairs. He loved her authoritarian action. The light was dim, and as he walked behind her, something told him his sex life was about to be revolutionised. *Feh real*. They were both hot and Lijah opened his mind to receive the experience of his life.

Bernadette led him to a room of divine decadence. A king-sized bed was cosily placed in a far corner. Light softly dimmed. Soft embroidered, gold-trimmed pillows were neatly placed; too perfect to be disturbed.

'*Raas claat!*' was his first thought, imagining himself in a place more fantastic than Birmingham. It was almost like a dream. And he felt safe. Safe and horny.

"I hope you're not a narrow-minded black man, Lijah. Or, I dare say, our time together won't be much fun." Again she eased her left hand firmly over his manhood.

'*Damn tactile this woman'*, he thought. '*To rahtid*'.

"Does the thought of bondage frighten you, Lijah?" she continued matter-of-factly, freaking him out. But he didn't show it.

"Bondage?" he asked. "Sounds like some slavery t'ing." But he wasn't entirely naïve. "Er... well... I suppose it depends on de kinda bondage yuh mean."

She laughed, dimmed the light even further and pushed him firmly but playfully, into her classily dressed bed, his body, he felt, not worthy of its touch. '*Bwoy, dis is like a dream to rahtid'*, he mumbled.

Lavender filled his senses again. He craved this woman's offering and waited with baited breath.

Bernadette pulled out a drawer and produced two long strips of material, advancing towards him with silent reassurance in her eyes. The word *kinky* crossed his mind.

"Trust me," she whispered, crossing his legs and tying them firmly at the ankles. He laid back and let it all happen. Shit! If his idrin Festus could see him now. Only a few days ago they dissed things like this. Said only kinky judges and the briefcase brigade would do dem t'ings.

She proceeded to his wrists, firmly securing them to separate bedposts, showering him with spates of kisses in between. Like giving an impatient child little treats before dinner. He surrendered to her every move.

Now, she touched a button on the headboard above his head and a low wave of classical music seeped into the silence. At first he was bemused. You see, hard-core reggae music was his thing. The only classical music he would hear was what would seep out of Ikesha's room when she studied.

Now she teased him with self-satisfaction, attending purposefully to herself. Selfish though it seemed, it heightened his wanting.

"Bernadette," he sighed. And the man in him quizzed, asking all kinds of questions. For one, *'What kind of woman had Bernadette become? A mistress? Seductress? Or simply, like she said, a sexual, sensual being who was simply, living life?'*

Now she eased forward, brushing her lips teasingly all over his vulnerable body, letting up as soon as he began to appreciate the sensation of her warm, moist mouth. Then she stood back, watching his sweet torment, stroking herself teasingly.

Lijah was unable to move, and the memory of her lips all over him blew his mind. He was bursting with excitement.

Now she came towards him again, still teasing, this time, pressing carefully with one finger on his scrotum, as she held his manhood firmly, administering rapid hand movements. Her tongue, her fingertips and her woman worked over the most sensitive parts of his body, not allowing him to instigate any touching at all. Still... he couldn't even if he wanted to. The brotha was in some serious bondage. *Feh real.*

Again, she abandoned him, but lay beside him, totally avoiding tactility. Instead, she concentrated on herself. Stroked her breasts, now enjoying it like never before, she moaned in ecstasy. Lijah was jealous. He couldn't stand it any longer. Forty years old, and this was the most mind-blowing, frustrating, sensual moment he had ever experienced.

"Untie me, Bernadette. Me cyaan tek dis nuh longer. I need to enter you now!"

"Easy." She loved the control and it showed. She kissed him sensually, using her expert tactility almost mockingly, bringing him to a climax that could kill. And maybe he was killed. Died that infamous *'little death'*.

"You see, it's not all about penetration, is it, Lijah? When will you guys ever learn?"

Now, she untied him quickly, stroking him again in her erotic silence.

He held her tight, kissed her hand and cried like a baby, his eyes telling her, that never before had he felt such deep passion.

He was exposed to feelings, sensuality and seductiveness he had never known possible.

"Hush," Bernadette commanded in a whisper. Still in control, her sweet voice seeped, like silk, into his soul. "Hush... hush... hush." She played with his locks, stroked his face, and eased her soft fingers over his lips and into her mouth. She stroked the surface of his black skin and tasted his salty tears.

This mysterious woman had unleashed the baby-like side to Lijah. Exposed him too, to his feminine side. Sides he didn't know existed. Sides most brothas would rather not get in touch with. Bernadette beckoned a language from his inner soul, connected him to a kind of intellect he had had hidden deep within. She had given him a taste for passion that would stay on the taste-buds of his mind, forever.

Now he knew that reading about certain things in magazines, or even watching tacky blue movies were nothing but theories, but to find a woman who was willing to give him the pleasure of realisation, was the ultimate *'other'*. Lijah had found her. But still, Gloria laid heavy on his mind.

The Monday morning after that enjoyable Sunday night, found Lijah in Bernadette's bed, his long, flowing locks wrapped around her slender, firm, ebony body. It was a different kinda loving. Sweet, yet unattached. A different feeling from being with his queen. He was awoken by a kiss to the nape of his neck and the warmth of her body covering the length of his back. She smiled at his hard, readiness and the extent to how much he was obviously aching for her. To his reckoning, the feeling was mutual, so now, for Lijah, the real fireworks would begin. Bernadette rolled onto her back, her erotic, non-verbal command loud enough to wake an impotent man. Lijah didn't hesitate, and took her like a newly-freed prisoner, hungry for the letting-out of a host of pent-up frustration. Easing himself into her for the first time, his patience got the better of him. Almost forgetting his own strength, he rocked her world to a point of no return.

It was good. So good, that sleep had taken them, like the effect of hypnosis, to a calm quiet place. Lijah woke an hour later to an arm across his chest, warm breath against his right ears and that familiar voice saying, "I'll make you breakfast." Bernadette kissed him and he watched her rise from their love-nest.

"Morning," he said, reflecting on their previous entanglement.

"Feeling ok?" she asked, pulling on a beautiful, black, silk kimono over a likewise body. And beautiful, black and silky was an understatement. Bernadette's body would have the owners of lap dancing clubs singing for their supper. They would do anything to recruit her for her assets. She drew the bedroom curtains, and even that had an erotic art about it.

Now, the light of the new morning enabled Lijah to see fully, the contents of her bedroom. He glanced thoughtfully around it, thinking himself somewhat lucky. He had known brothas who got the push from their women, and ended up with their heads in their hands, or like wandering sheep. Or even mental. But here he was, in an almost *'Caviar'* situation, although, he didn't know if given the chance, he would give up his *'ackee-and-salt-fish'* situation for it. It was at that point, he found himself thinking about Gloria again. He wanted to hold her for old time's sake and wondered if she was missing him. But now she proportioned the blame. They were both at fault. He had messed up and pushed her into the arms of a SAAB driver. And she had rejected him and pushed him into the arms of not just another woman, but a serious *'love nurse'*. *Feh real.*

Lijah must have drifted too deep into his thoughts of Gloria, for Bernadette's voice almost startled him. She had re-entered the room with some different kind of *'morning delights'* on a tray, saying, *'Of course we're gonna have fun. Lots of it. Just as long as you understand that I'm a free spirit. So don't get hooked on me."* She was almost over-confident. *"I'm all the friend you're gonna need, Lijah. Trust me."* She bit seductively into a slice of toast, managing to make even that a turn-on.

Lijah stared questioningly at her, then helped himself to toast, marmalade, boiled egg, coffee and croissant. He would have preferred ackee-and-salt-fish, but one cannot have it all.

Gloria stayed on his mind.

"So... d'you wanna talk about her?"

"Who?"

"Who else? Gloria of course."

He wondered if she was reading his mind.

She continued, "Or even this thing with this Lucy chick? Or that silly baby-sitter shit?" She chuckled and sipped coffee from a gold-edged china teacup. "Anything. I'm all ears. I'll be your lover, friend, agony aunt... whatever you like, Lijah..." She paused, looked into his eyes and stated with a passion, "But I just *won't* be your *wife*. Wives: common-law or lawfully wedded get the worse end of the stick. They might think not, but they do. They walk down the aisle in a flowing white gown, potpourried confetti showering down on them, yet as soon as they fold away that wedding gown, they begin that long skivvy through life. The husband's attention finds its way onto another woman. She gets the flowers, the wine and the *always-perfect* man. Everything."

"Sounds like you're speaking from experience, Bernadette." Lijah was reminded of Jacques again. That fine looking French brotha she married and lived in France with for years. "You can't say every marriage is like that, can yuh?"

"Show me a marriage Lijah, where the man would say no to the delights that laid at the meeting of another woman's thighs, and I'll prove to you that Hitler wasn't racist."

"So why is this infidelity t'ing always aimed at men?" Lijah defended. "An' why yuh t'ink every man mek pussy tu'n dem fool?"

"Well... Lijah...didn't you?" That was a wicked upper-cut. Straight to his abdomen. He was almost winded by her sarcasm. "Men are already fools Lijah, but pussy will always help them to be bigger ones."

He threw his toast aside. Appetite left with his pride. "Why did you and Jacques break up anyway?" he asked with purpose. "I thought you were made for each other. Like Faye and her guy. You both seemed to have found perfect partners. Was a third party involved? You seem bitter."

Bernadette glared at him, but still she ignored his question and asked, "Heard from Faye lately?"

"No. Not for a long time. I just hope she's ok. France isn't that far, but it can be, when your sister is there and un-contactable. She moved, but her new address is a mystery. I know there was a lot a things going on in her head. With Mum's death, and all that was going on with the old man, but..."

"Faye is a survivor, Lijah. Your sister is like her niece, Ikesha. Strong. Sensible. A go-getter too. Gets whatever she wants, Faye."

"Don't you two keep in touch? You were best friends," he asked.

"Don't *you* two?" she answered his question with a question. "You're her brother."

Before Lijah could address what he saw as undiluted sarcasm, the phone rang and Bernadette picked it up. After a few *'yeahs, mmms,* and *oks* and *I'll call you later'*, she clicked off. But she seemed to have forgotten where they had left off and said, "So? Who d'you wanna talk about? Gloria? Lucy? Or that naughty little baby-sitter, Faithlyn?"

The strange air about Bernadette intrigued Lijah immensely. Again, he stared questioningly at her and despite her mystery, he couldn't help but draw to her beauty. Gone are the days when women over forty looked their age. Today they carry their age well, but Bernadette most certainly takes the biscuit. Forty-five and looking more like twenty-five. She had certainly reached her peak. Peak in experience, peak in maturity and with all inhibitions out the window.

"You most probably won't meet another woman like me, Lijah. Being away from England for a while changed me. Besides, I find continental black men more fun. Unlike the English ones, *Ahhhrrr.*" She covered her mouth and did a fake yawn.

"Are we really that boring? *Ahhhrrr.*"

"Tell me about it."

"Don't you mean we are not as *kinky* as continental men?"

"Call it what you like. Still boring. *Ahhhrrr'*.

Lijah laughed. "Is there any pleasing you women?"

"Lijah, you stay the way you are. If you're happy the way you are, then don't change. It's just that I have an open mind about everything now. I've come to accept that none of us owns each other. It's just a thing society has conditioned us to think. Still, I don't try to change or condition anyone's mind to the way I think. I just do my thing." She kissed his lips and stroked his ass.

There was a pause and she added, matter-of-factly. "We could even talk about your mother. Is it not her best friend that your dad married? From the tone of your voice the other day, I knew that was troubling you most."

Lijah nearly choked on his toast, but styled it out. He couldn't even remember telling Bernadette about his mother, but he must admit he had had a few measures of fire-water after Gloria had given him his marching orders. He had only ever consciously told Gloria about the sore subject around his mother, and was now wondering *how much* he had told Bernadette. Now he felt exposed.

"Don't look so worried, Lijah. We've all got at least one painful subject in our heads, skeleton in our closet. Whatever. Trust me. I'm a friend. I was your sister's best friend, remember? But it was even hard for her to talk about it, even though she was in France for most of it. I

didn't push her. So I won't push you. I know you only talked about it
that time because you were hurting from the break-up between you and
Gloria. What is it with men? Do you all think God made your hearts
harder than us women?"

Lijah thought hard and meaningfully about the term *Phenomenal
Woman*. He had only just tangled with Bernadette, yet he had truly
convinced himself that she was just that. *A Phenomenal Woman*. It
wasn't just her sexiness that turned him on. It was her aura. Her mystery.
Her very being. The way she made things looked simple. The difference
with which she seemed to approach life.

She pressed the button at the head of her bed again, but this time she
had him shaken, stirred and mixed in deep emotions. Gloria's song
seeped into his head, taking him back to that first day. The day he took
her virginity.

Take the ribbon from your hair...
Did Bernadette know this was his and Gloria's song?
Shake it loose and let it fall...
He looked into her sexy eyes and asked the question.
Lay it soft against my skin...
But she replied only with the expression of her own desires.
Like the shadows on the wall...
Discarding a tray of unwanted breakfast, she proceeded to heal him
again, with her sexual touches.
Come and lay down by my side...
Again she kissed his lips, tasted his tears. Aroused his desires.
Till the early morning light...
"Are you ok?" she whispered.
"Yes. But let's not talk right now." And Dennis Brown helped him
along…
All I'm taking is your time...
So help me make it through the night.
Lijah was almost stifling with hurt. Worse when he remembered his
and Gloria's promises to each other. And that she had helped him
through many crucial nights. But at that crucial, hurting moment, Gloria
wasn't there. So he pulled Bernadette closer, entered the gates of her
heaven. Poured his hallelujah into her glory, seeing her as a fine
substitute. '*A man's sexual need must be fulfilled*', he told himself. And
that it was. *Feh real*. Well and truly fulfilled.

It was late Monday evening. Lijah sat in his Roadster Sport in a secluded
spot at the far end of Cannon Hill Park, reflecting on last night, this

morning, Gloria. And Bernadette.

The thought of Bernadette was trying hard to dominate. He remembered being just ten years old when he met her. She was just fifteen. Back then she didn't even look at him. She had that teenage crush on his older brother Roy, who was sixteen at the time. All the girls liked Roy. He did everything that was perfect. Good. Outstanding. Including fulfilling his mother's expectation of him. His picture – him clad in a proud Air Force uniform, permanently graced their fireplace, with their mother constantly dusting it down like a precious piece of china. Protecting it. Like Roy protected his Queen and Country.

Roy was the model son, but in his own way, he was selfish. Not mean, but selfish. If it was possible, he'd buy you the world, but don't expect to share his. As a child, his selfishness was unlike other children's. If Roy had a toy that gave him pleasure, he'd rather save his pocket money to get you your own, rather than letting you play with his.

Once Lijah watched jealously through the keyhole into the bedroom they shared, as Roy and Bernadette had their first kiss, wishing it were him. And later, although Lijah hadn't literally witnessed it, he knew that childish kisses had most certainly led to teenage sex and more.

But years went by and Bernadette grew. Grew out of Roy, childish kisses, teenage sex and out of Birmingham. She met and married Jacques, a French brother, who took her away to France. Roy joined the Air Force and headed off to Germany. And later, Lijah found trouble: bad influences, which led to the sacrilege walls of a prison cell. An experience he locked deep within his soul. Rastafarianism. And his queen, Gloria.

Bernadette had kept in contact with Faye, who, after several visits to Bordeaux, fell in love with the city too, and later with a French brother.

After a while, for whatever reason, Bernadette and Jacques broke up, leaving a void in Bernadette's life. Five years ago, age forty, she came back to England. She and Lijah bumped into each other on several occasions. They chatted briefly about life, the old lady, the old man and very briefly about Jacques: Bernadette seemed to find the subject painful, so she more or less dismissed it, rather than talked about it.

By that time, Roy too had ended his time in the Air Force and later, after training, secured himself a job in the Police Force somewhere in London, where he worked himself up to a well-paid post. Good old Roy, the police force loved him and from what Lijah had heard from the grapevine, he married a blonde, had three kids and the house, cars and the holidays to go with. But like Faye, Roy might as well be in France and un-contactable.

By then, Lijah was thirty-five years old with a family - Gloria, Ikesha, Kunta and a newborn Khamilla. The boyish crush he had on Bernadette had long gone out the window, with *grown-man's-lust* struggling hard, to stay dormant.

Bernadette sported a sexy French accent. She would wear her hair loose and free around her face, its thick strands sitting careless and sexy on her shoulders, complementing her slender neck, defined shoulders, perfect velvet skin, and perfect white teeth. And almost as if she was born with it, a light, sexy, musk aroma oozed always, from her aura. Gloria would have killed him if she knew *how much* her man lusted after this beauty. When Gloria was not around, as Bernadette would speak: oblivious it seemed, to Lijah's sexual existence, he would admire her deeply, trying hard to ensure that his sexual desires remain undetected.

But Bernadette treated him like a brother. He had put it down to the one she never had. The thought of her never looking at him *'that way'* was a fixture in his head. And not daring to make any kind of suggestion to her, he left it at the *'respect'* stage. He respected her, more so because of the way she remained kinda *'loyal'* to Jacques, even though they had broken up. As if she was hoping for reconciliation.

Previously, the thought of sharing a roof with Bernadette would have been more like a dream. So when she suggested he rested in her spare room after Gloria chucked him out, he took her up on the offer, still holding up that torch of respect. So the thought of them becoming lovers was even farthest from his mind. Now, here he was, dick throbbing at the very thought of her. She had become a sex therapist who soothes his pains away. And he had several. Ones he could talk about and that infamous one in particular, that he'd rather not.

And though not on the same keel as the old lady and his deep-rooted one, Gloria, who used to be his remedy, had become a new spouting root of pain. And when his pains would get too much, Bernadette would cover him. Put her tender arms all over him and cover him. And sometimes, she'd put him to some kind of test. Physical test. She would totally forget tenderness and make him work. As if it was a part of the healing process.

Almost lost in thoughts he opened his eyes only when a couple in a slow moving car admired his wheels. A sweet donation from Lucy. But he had no energy left to think about Lucy now. Lucy needed a host of new brain cells. He started his engine and headed for the city.

CHAPTER * FIVE

At first the abuse was verbal. Mental nastiness. Cutting words and wild accusations that had no more strength than a fart in a storm. Then came the physical, escalating slowly but surely to a serious point of no return. That first push. The condescending pokes at her chest with his brutal index finger. To the wilful squeezing of her neck.

Then came the guilt, when it was cleverly smoothed over with roses, dinners, gifts and nuff dance-hall niceness. Emotional blackmail to be blunt. And Kizzy would assist in the smoothing over too. Yes. Not forgetting the clever smoothing on of make-up over her Nubian face, (*an action that had previously been so forbidden for Empresses*). Make-up to hide tell-tale bruises.

And then came a time when the smoothing-over had subsided and excuses took over: '*I fell in the bath*'. '*Bumped my forehead on the cupboard door*'. '*Accidentally scratched myself*'. Excuses that were short-lived to the *not-so-stupid*, like Fiona, Gloria and Lijah.

The first slap had started on a coach trip to London. It was meant to be pure niceness. Gregory Isaacs had just flown in and the whole of Birmingham it seemed was doing an exodus to take in the exclusive show. The whole of Birmingham too, had seen the slap reaching Kizzy's face. And likewise, they had seen the determination of Fiona, Kizzy's adopted sister, to flatten Festus. And Fiona had never been one for making threats. No. She promises and delivers. *Feh real.*

Papa Dread had made it his business too, to pull Festus up about it. In his books, it was a weak man who beats his woman. He detested women beaters, like he did *enemies in his camp, dealers of shit* and *gun-slingers*.

And no doubt Lijah had his say. '*Yuh cyaan do dem t'ings man. Yuh cyaan jus' embarrass yuh 'oman suh. Moreover not in-front a people. Festus dat is fuckries blood. Yuh nuffi deal wid dem t'ings*'.

The slap was triggered by a simple smile. A smile Kizzy had dared to return innocently to a handsome dread in the opposite aisle of the packed coach. Festus had called it flirting. Insecurity had engulfed him. The green-eyed monster had grabbed his throat and was choking him. He couldn't control himself.

For a while it looked as if it was going to be a one-off. Or that Festus had taken Fiona's threat seriously. Or even looked closely at Papa Dread's and Lijah's reasoning. But a year later and thereafter, the memory of that first slap surfaced every time they argued, bringing with it added extras: the landing of a clenched fist against her head. An active right foot in the small of her back. And the wilful wrenching of her sacred locks from their roots.

'If a man hits you once, he'll hit you again, and again, and again', Fiona had told her from the first time on that coach, and now, years later, she didn't need to say, *'I told you so'*. Today she had accompanied Kizzy to the dentist to replace a missing front tooth, punched out with brute force. The women had sat in the dentist's waiting room talking about the most recent ordeal.

"What if I was having an affair?" Kizzy asked hypothetically.

"What d'you think?" Fiona asked. "You'd be dead."

"I don't know if I should stay with him, Fi'. I'm seriously thinking about it."

"It's only just now that you've started to think about it, Kizzy? And anyway, what's there to think about? You can't stay with a man who raises his hands to you!" Fiona tried now to lower her tone in the quiet waiting room when she noticed the attention she was attracting. "Listen Kizzy, you know my views on the physical abuse thing. I'm talking from experience. You can't forget Winston. He got off the first time he hit me, but *he* hit the kitchen floor the second. Mama Maya had taught us too well for us to end up as beating sticks for men. What d'you think she would say if she knew Festus beats you?"

"Fiona, I don't even want to think about it. I think before she kills Festus, she'd kill me for taking it."

"That day when I took that Dutch-pot to Winston, I didn't even think of the consequences," Fiona continued. "All I knew was, I wanted him dead. Until you've been physically abused yourself, you cannot begin to understand how it feels." A renewed anger heightened her voice, attracting bemused glances again from patients who previously had their eyes in old, recycled magazines, out the window and on their own feet.

It was no joke. The man could have been dead, but Kizzy chuckled as she remembered Winston, aka *Bush Tea*. More so, the call from Fiona one Friday night saying, "*I think I've killed the bastard!*"

Winston was an apprentice dread who had not learnt the golden rule: *'A rastaman is a peaceful man'*. Another brother who had defaced the *upstanding* philosophy of the *'true'* rastaman. Not unlike a corrupt church leader or a bent cop. He needed to visit Jamaica. Live up in the hills for a while. See how rastamen run t'ings.

"Hey, have you heard anything of him lately?" Kizzy enquired.

"Hell, no. The last I heard he moved to London. Doing some mobile food thing. Y'know, carnival an' stuff. In fact, lately when I go to any carnival at all, my heart skips a beat every time I see a black man selling dumplin', fry fish an' dat. Not that I'm afraid or not'n. I'd bus' his head again if he ever tries that shit. But you know how it is when you see an ex? Especially one that used to beat your ass."

Kizzy couldn't relate to the former. She didn't have an ex. Like Lijah was for Gloria, Festus was her first and only man. But she could identify well with the latter part of Fiona's statement. She had had her ass beaten more often than a run-away slave. *Feh real.*

"Especially if he's got a Dutch-pot scar over his forehead, hey Fi?" She couldn't help being flippant, forgetting for a moment, her missing tooth.

"Yuh damn right," Fiona agreed.

"Kizzy Sewell?" The voice of the dental assistant entered the room. "Would you like to come with me?"

"Sure," said Kizzy, following the white-coated lady into the dentist's room.

Fiona picked up an over-read magazine from the untidy pile on the table in front of her. A picture of Naomi Campbell graced the front cover. She dully flicked its pages and came to rest on an article about a model who could no longer work the cat-walk because of scars obtained from being physically abused by a jealous lover. Fiona smiled cynically, sympathising at the same time. The scar-faced model looked a pitiful sight, though still beautiful. *'Men'*, grunted Fiona to herself. *'When will they learn that their powers lie not in their might, but in their ability to rise above the massa's tactic?'* She kissed her teeth, then read the article to the end, shaking her head periodically.

Kizzy eased her right index finger over the extra-dark birthmark, just above her left collar-bone. It was an unconscious ritual she often performed: like one would bite a nail, or suck the tip of his/her tongue. Or sniff a comfort blanket. The intriguing mark stood out like a sore thumb against her caramel skin. The replica of the map of Jamaica, it would be the topic of conversation everywhere she would go. Mama Maya would say jokingly, *'Your mother must have been thinking about Jamaica when she was pregnant'*. West Indians have an explanation for everything and Kizzy had soon become familiar with a few.

Now, she gathered her locks, taking care to secure every strand. Then she wrapped them with her most recent head-wrap, with colours so vibrant, you might have thought it was weaved by a native African. Now, letting it fall gracefully down her back, she admired herself in the mirror.

'There's a natural mystic flowing through the air' ... .

She sang to the tape in the background, Bob Marley's voice seeping into her bones. He was one of her favourite singers. Affiliation must never be ruled out.

Her cotton robe, also of great vibrancy, was already artfully wrapped around her petite body. Her earrings were woodcarvings of the map of Africa, and as always, her face as warm as the sun. Short of silver coins and amber and coloured glass beads, the sista could give a Songhai bride a run for her culture. She was the picture of a true Empress. The night was destined to be fun. It was a revival night at The Scratchers Yard and the one Father Jarvis was about to pull another healthy crowd. Did it every time. Kizzy and Gloria hardly ever missed any of his sessions. Besides, Kizzy almost always needed them. His selection was like vintage wine and the DJ's cheerful voice was guaranteed to make any troubled soul perk up. *Feh real.*

As she stared at her image, Kizzy recalled the chat-up line Festus had used to woo her. *'Whaap'n, me Nubian Princess? Yuh look irie tonight. Me cyan hol' dis dance?'* Though he had not known how much, it was a great honour to her to be called *'Nubian'*. The strong cultural air about it gave her a sense of *something*. Something to hold onto. Prior, although she hanged with black girls (*mostly of Jamaican background*), picking up patois with an authenticity Festus was surprised at, Kizzy had never been sure of *'who'* she really was. She knew she was adopted. And that her maternal mother was white. But all she knew of her father was two words on her birth certificate, *'father unknown'*.

But of course it wasn't hard to figure out that this *'unknown'* father was of a hue complexion. But unlike other mixed race people (like the ones who went to her school), Kizzy knew neither one of her parents, and although she loved Maya, it was hard to explain how odd it felt, especially when she considered the possibility of her blood parents being *'out there'* somewhere.

Ever since she became old enough to be *'aware'*, the notion of being different from Fiona gnawed at her, and the urge to ask questions came earlier than Mama Maya had expected.

Unlike Fiona, Kizzy was not too much of a hue appearance. Her caramel skin, her not-so-African nose, her far-from-nappy hair that took forever to form dread-locks, well after Festus had introduced her to Rastafarianism, had long gone convinced her that she was not full black.

Though both girls were beautiful in their own rights, Fiona's skin was like olive. She was always the stronger of the two - strikingly pretty, but as a teenager, she was a real tomboy, ignoring this prettiness everyone fussed so much about.

On that crucial explaining day, just before Mama Maya explained to the girls how they came to be so different, she told them how they came to be adopted. But now, Kizzy had become hungry for more answers.

Answers to questions like, *'Why didn't Mama Maya have a husband?'...* And Aunt Patricia... *'Who was she, really? Since she wasn't their 'real' auntie.'*

Aunt Patricia was a jet-black woman who Fiona had told Kizzy, *'must have been from a generation of Africans who had managed to have escaped the massa's rape'.* About a shade or two up from Fiona's, her skin was like that of a star apple – black, shiny and unblemished. Over-tall, yet she was never seen without high heels. Said they made her feel elegant. She was pretty, sturdy, with high cheekbones and child-bearing hips: hips that as far as they knew, bore not one single child. She had a deep belly laugh and breasts that could comfort any child. And she could eat too. Much more than any man who would dare to challenge her. But she wasn't fat. Just sturdy. Her hair was a flow of black, shiny mane, which fascinated the girls whenever she would let it down. And that was a rare occasion, since it was almost always tied up in a bun. And when one day Kizzy asked her how she managed to have such a nice head of hair, she replied, *'Me comb it an' pray'.*

Even though she was young, Aunt Patricia had a striking patch of grey that streaked in a straight line, from the ridge of her forehead to her crown. It gave her character. Like her tallness, her unique belly laugh and comforting breasts. And beautiful hair.

When Kizzy and Fiona were small, like lullabies, it was the comforting melodies of Aunt Patricia's deep chuckles in the dead of her visiting nights, followed by Mama Maya's stern whispers that would lull them both to sleep. Her accent was slightly different too. A bit more up-market than Mama Maya's. At times, the girls would stretch their little ears to listen, as Aunt Patricia would recall memories of Jamaica, ending sentences in clichés like, *'you could take the boy out the country, but you couldn't take the country out the boy. Real country bumpkin he was'.*

And one morning, when Kizzy had innocently asked what a country bumpkin was, both girls had detected an urgency in Mama Maya's voice: a *fear-like* urgency, coupled with Mama Maya's gentle yet firm push at the back of her head, as she would usher her off to another place in the house, as she'd ask, *'Why yuh listening to big people's conversation child?'* And Fiona had watched that pensive look on her face: a look that asked, *'Lord have mercy. What else must the child have heard?'* And she had never forgotten that look that Aunt Patricia had given her. A look that asked the same question, but with more depth, *'What else must you have heard?'*

Apart from being a *more-than-once-a-year Santa,* Aunt Patricia stayed a mystery. All the girls knew was that Aunt Patricia came from Luton.

She would visit at certain times of the year, bringing an abundance of sweets, gifts, clothes and hugs. She had a comforting smell of kuss-kuss, bay rum, lavender and moth-balls, all mixed in one. And she protected Mama Maya like a mother hen would a lost chick. Not unlike Mama Maya would protect them.

And like Aunt Patricia and the reason Mama Maya hadn't married, the whole truth about their real parents remained a mystery. A subject Kizzy and Fiona had discussed several times. Mostly at nights, as they listened to Mama Maya fill her hot water bottle (*the only warmth she had*) and climbed the stairs alone, peeping 'round their bedroom door, as if to make sure they had not left her. Especially those long '*miss-you*' nights when Auntie Patricia didn't come to chat to, laugh with and protect her.

The girls knew that Mama Maya had lost a love. Someone she had cared for dearly. They knew though, that she did not lose him through death, but they weren't quite sure how, since whenever Aunt Patricia would mention it, Mama Maya would stop her abruptly at a crucial point. It was obvious that the subject pained her. And since the girls were brought up not to pry in big people's business, Kizzy knew that until she was a '*big person*' herself, she would not ask.

'*I adopted you as I can't have children myself*', Mama Maya told the girls that day in her explaining. '*I have a lot of love to give. It would be a sin to waste it*'. She didn't explain how she found out that she couldn't have kids, but her eyes would soon light up when she would speak of the day she found them: in that pitiful home, where un-mothered, unloved children waited for a chance to be *chosen*. To be *loved*. Where black kids wandered around with un-creamed faces, ash-dry feet and that infamous un-combed hair: on which she would stress so much – '*De staff need to be educated on how to treat black people's hair*'.

It was 1997 (six years ago), when Mama Maya returned to Jamaica - in her own words, '*to die*'. And Kizzy had told her, '*Mama, you have lots of life left in you. Much more than Aunt Patricia*'. Aunt Patricia had returned to Jamaica herself, less than a year prior.

The year previous to Mama Maya's return, Kizzy and Fiona had spent three weeks in the house she had built in Kingston. It was divine. Kizzy loved Jamaica and had always said that if Festus would come, she would live there.

Prior to 1997, Mama Maya had made her will. And when she had satisfied herself with the fact that all was well with her two daughters, she showered them with hugs, kisses, tears and more motherly advice, then boarded an Air Jamaica jet back home. But not before threatening Festus with a promise of serious reprisals, as old as she had been.

'*Festus,* she had said, '*hurt a single lock on Kizzy's head and you'll have me to deal wid'*. But Mama Maya didn't know she was already too late. Much was kept from her. She had not known that the abuse had long gone set in like a contemptuous familiarity. Her too-late threat had come as a result of her smelling a recent rat. But nothing was confirmed, since Kizzy denied it when she had asked her. She had detected though, that Festus had a temper. From day one, she had told Kizzy that his eyes spelt an inexplicable rage.

Fiona could have enlightened her, but she didn't. She figured it was nobody's business but Kizzy's. And she should be the one to tell it. Like she wouldn't tell Kizzy Mama Maya's business. Unless of course, for some crucial reason, she had to.

But Mama Maya knew she needn't worry about Fiona. Winston might have had his one lick, but there was no way this sista would let another man hurt her without putting up a fight. Unless he held a gun to her head of course. After the episode with Winston, her karate classes were like weekly rituals. Fiona possessed the secret of '*drive*', determination and that good old '*I don't give a damn*'. Mess with her at your own mercy.

It was at the airport that Mama Maya faced her fears and gave Kizzy her blessing on searching for her blood mother. She knew it would be hard since all she had was a name. Nothing else. No address. Just the slightest tip of an iceberg. An iceberg Kizzy had thrown to the back of her mind, until of late, when the desire to find out the real truth about herself surfaced again, plaguing her like a nasty secret, shaking from the inside of its closet.

Fiona was different. She had no wish to know her true parent. No more than she needed to be told that Kizzy was no more *blacker* than she was, because she wore dread-locks. Nor she, any *blacker* than Kizzy, because of the darker shade of her skin.

As Kizzy paid the final attention to herself in the mirror in the living-room, Bob Marley's *Redemption Song* kicked in, almost in union with Festus' lazy, breathy stretching and yawning. He showed some life. He had been dozing for the past hour on the living-room couch, having not had his full quota of sleep since the night shift. He had broken it mid-stream to do some crucial runnings outa street. Besides, of late, the *tyre-making, spirit-breaking, blood-sucking* plant (in their words) was doing his and Lijah's heads in. The subject was high on their topics of conversation.

"Bwoy... Princess, yuh looking irie," a sleepy voice assured Kizzy. Festus had caught sight of his woman in her majestic apparel. Tonight he was in a sweet mood. A flip-side from two nights ago, when she felt the back of his right hand for daring to go against his wishes.

"Yeah?" Kizzy questioned.

"Yeah, man. Seriously irie." His reassurance was filled with confidence as he sought forgiveness for the bruises she had successfully covered with a spread of foundation from the new Iman range.

"Thanks."

Just then, the sound of a horn alerted them. Sure enough, it was Gloria.

"A'right Festus," Kizzy kissed her man. "Me gone yeah?"

"Enjoy yuhself Princess." But he didn't mean it. Just trying hard to fight against his insecurities. They had surfaced again.

"I will," she replied, picking up her bag and squeezing the fingers of her man's right hand. It was a kind of reassurance. She always did this whenever she would go out without him. She always did this. From as far back as she could remember. He had always doubted her virtue, even though she had given him no reason to. His insecurity had overshadowed them both, affecting his ability to function consciously, and hers, the shine to her fullest vibrancy.

She headed for the front door, but suddenly she turned back and ran upstairs, only to find Festus eagerly staring through the kitchen window. Could he have doubted that it was Gloria who was picking her up?

"W'at yuh lef' now?" he asked, feeling slightly embarrassed about being caught spying.

"How could I forget to kiss my son," she answered.

She walked quietly into Fari's room and melted again at his deep, low snoring. His locks flowed majestically around his little face and he smiled as if he was having a pleasant dream. "Oh Fari," Kizzy whispered as she gently prised the toy pistol from his little fingers. Now she couldn't help but hold it in her hand and stare hard at it. She marvelled at how real it looked. Festus had bought it for his seventh birthday and it had become a fixture to his right arm. Playing cops and gangsters with his friends was his newest game. Sometimes he'd be Will Smith, sometimes Wesley Snipes and other times, Samuel L Jackson. He had even managed to get his little friends to persuade their parents to get them all toy pistols like the one he had.

Kizzy placed the toy pistol in Fari's toy box, kissed his forehead and tiptoed out, smiling. Before she could pull Fari's bedroom door shut, another toot from Gloria's car horn alerted her.

"A'right Festus. Me gaan again."

"More time Princess."

"Yuh look irie girl," Gloria told her as she entered the car.

"You too G. If you don't watch it you might pull."

Gloria kissed her teeth playfully, in an attempt to hide the fact that she already had. It was a 'thin ice' situation.

"Listen, G," Kizzy changed the subject, picking up on Gloria's downer. "We're gonna have a good time tonight. I know this t'ing wid Lijah is beating yuh up, but girl, all you need is healing. And it takes time. But I'm here. Jah will work it out. You're not de only one with problems G." She spoke like a trained counsellor.

Gloria was still fighting with her conscience. She had been battling for a long time with the only secret she'd kept from Kizzy since they met years ago. Although she felt justified for her actions, she didn't want her friend thinking badly of her. Making love to another man just to get her own back on Lijah was just something she had done in haste: like the cutting of her locks. The former, recently, to please herself and the latter to please her mother Hortence Fontaine. Now she was feeling bad about herself. Worse that she had taken the guy back to the family house. And in her and Lijah's bed! She didn't know whom she had hurt most now. Herself or Lijah.

As her Corsa hugged the road, she tried to coat over her own guilt by talking about Lijah's nastiness. "The thing is K', that's not just it. I could forgive Lijah if it was jus' de w'ite gyal at his work place. I've been with him too long to mek dat mash us up. But a seventeen year old girl? In my own house? And to think, I was the one who brought de girl inna me house to baby-sit our child. The man was already under suspicion. You'd think he would have tried his hardest to be good."

"Lust G'. Lust. It looks as if it's the hardest of the seven deadly sins to fight. Especially for men." Kizzy offered.

"He lied too, Kizzy. Blatantly. He knew he was checking a white girl, but when I asked him, he denied it totally. And Festus helped him too. And on top of that, he moved into Bernadette's house and started screwing her!"

"Mum! Kizzy! Hi!" the voice of Ikesha interrupted their conversation. They had just pulled into a spot in the car park at the Scratchers Yard and she was parking up in her KA, in an adjacent spot. She loved her little ride, a joint offering from her mum and dad.

They waved and Gloria carried on, "So Lijah gave it all up for lust, right? Still, we'll talk about it another time, Kizzy. I don't talk too much about it in front of Ikesha and Kunta."

She concentrated now on her daughter. It was a rare occasion to see her out and away from her books. She looked absolutely divine. Untouched by any man. And Gloria lived in hope that the man that would eventually take her virginity would be at least 'worthy' of it.

Now a red SAAB pulled up alongside Gloria's Corsa and her heart skipped a beat. *'Oh no!'* she thought, hoping the driver would keep that low profile she had asked him to. She didn't know he would be there tonight. Their eyes met and heat rushed her body. She was pleased that Kizzy did not notice this brotha, or the look in her eyes. He looked trash-an-ready and Gloria wouldn't say no to a piece just then. *Feh real.*

CHAPTER * SIX

What a weepin' an' wailin'... Donga Caymanas Park...
Long Shot kick 'he buckit... Long Shot kick 'he buckit

The song was probably as old as he was. It was his father who first sang it to him years ago. Festus was in one of those moods today. A swing to the right. In fact, outa street, he wore a constant happy-go-lucky front, like a clown wears a smile, letting no one see his fears or his tears. And only the *knowing* could tell that he was a woman beater.

Singing at the top of his voice, he bopped into the bookie shop, cool and easy, lifting his right leg as if there was a *must-be-avoided* snake under every step.

"Whaap'n, Papa Dread?" He stretched a fist out to the sixty-year-old – a wise old owl, if ever there was one. Papa Dread sat comfortably, looking as if he hadn't moved since yesterday. Today he wasn't cutting leather in his little shop, so he figured passing a few hours in the local bookie shop was ok. It was a new and futile hobby he enjoyed. Futile, since his losses almost always outweighed his winnings. And that was ok, as he didn't squander much on the horses. Gambling was never his thing, but Papa Dread enjoyed the atmosphere of the sport more than anything.

"Gimme a good tip nuh Papa. How come yuh jus' a keep all de good tips dem to yuhself?" Festus teased Papa Dread. He leaned *'black-man style'* against the edge of the counter, his racing page sticking out of his back pocket.

Papa Dread smiled, his glazed eyes showing his age, his body trying hard to resist the inevitability of gravity. He was tired. Like an over-worked donkey. But only his *always-young* attitude was staving off a lot more than was going on inside his body. His salt-'n-peppered locks now looked lifeless. More salt than pepper these days. Bald patches were randomly placed over the crown of his head. His appearance was a far cry from his original Handsworth days. Days when he was everyone's mentor. Back in the days, he was one of Selassie's first and most loyal servants this side of the equator. And even now, way into the 21st

century, he managed to maintain a certain level of respect. He had counselled several traumatised youths after the Handsworth riots and lived to tell a tale or two.

A self-taught tailor, even at this age, he held his own in a small section in the Jewellery Quarter, where he transformed plain pieces of leather into master-pieces. Hats, jackets, belts, handbags, eye patches. You want it, Papa Dread could make it. No job too big or too small. Jack and master of his trade.

"Bwoy, me don' know yunnuh, Festus. Paddy gimme dis one earlier. *Sweet Saggle*. Two t'irty." He looked at his watch. "Hurry up an' put it aan before dem stop tekkin' bets."

"Len' me a tenna nuh Papa. Me brok' like daag yaah sah." Festus stretched his hand expectantly towards Papa Dread, who had become used to this by now. He was already reaching into his pocket before Festus had asked. He retrieved his wallet and fished out a ten-pound note. "Nice one, Papa," Festus said as he rushed over to Heidi, an attractive Irish girl. "Ten pound on Sweet Saggle, Heidi. Quick."

"Ok, Festus. Always rushing, aren't you? And d'you mean Sweet *Saddle*?" she joked.

"Cho. Less a de cheek, yuh know weh me mean. But I wouldn't rush *you* though. I'd tend to you nice an' slow," he told her suggestively.

Bongo Dee, a deadly character sat in a corner eavesdropping on Festus flirtatious spiel. He didn't go in for that and kissed his teeth at what he called useless small talk. He was mean. Deadly. With women way down on his line of respect. Secretly, Heidi had a crush on him. Chalk and cheese, but who said the world was perfect?

"Ok, Sweet Talker. I see you haven't changed there, either." She handed Festus his ticket.

"So when am I gonna tek yuh out, Heidi? Yuh know we have lots in common."

"Festus, behave you'self. *Bejesus*. You're a married man. And what might we have in common, I ask you?"

"No I'm not a married man. An' you an' I? We have nuff in common. You know... that *'no blacks, no dogs, no Irish'* t'ing from the immigrating sixties era?"

"I'm not that old, Festus. That's mine and your parents' story, so tell me something else we've got in common."

"Well, the other thing is," he leaned his body close up to the counter and sang seductively, *"ebony and Ivory, la la la la la la la la la, Baby, why can't weeeee? "*

"Festus, stop trying to woo me. You're as good as married."

"As good as? No, man. Far from dat."

"Oh Holy Mother of God. What's the matter with you guys? Can't you be satisfied with what you have at home?"

"Don't lecture me, Heidi. When am I gonna tek yuh out?"

"In your dreams, Festus. D'you think I want your wife beating me up?"

"I haven't got a wife, Heidi. Are you deaf?"

"Your girlfriend then."

"She won't know. Who's gonna tell her? We can just go out for a likkle drink, yunnuh."

"Oh, I'll think about it Festus."

"Sweet. But don' tek too long t'inkin'." He winked seductively at her, then walked away. Her Irish eyes smiled and Bongo Dee caught the tail end. He returned a raw, serious, rugged look that Heidi found appealing.

"Wha' gwaan, Papa!" Now Lijah entered the bookie shop in high spirits.

For a reply, Papa Dread knitted his brows jokingly and asked him in a fatherly tone, "How come yuh so happy when yuh not getting no good food an' Gloria nah gi' yuh no lovin'?"

"What yuh mean, Papa?"

"Yuh not wid Gloria anymore, are yuh? I here yuh livin' wid some vogue type black 'oman. An' messing wid a blonde on top a dat. Here me nuh bredrin, If I were you I would go fin' Gloria an' stop form fool wid yuh life." Lijah would never know, but as Papa Dread spoke, he reflected on Norma, his late queen, who died sadly in childbirth. The baby was already dead and they could not save Norma. Too well, he knew the value of a woman and how fortunate a man is to have his own youth. Some might think he should mind his own business, but only he knew why he had become protective towards everybody's relationship and their youths.

Lijah gave a half smile.

"Jus' mine w'at yuh doin' Lijah. Rememba... pretty rose have nuff thorns. Macca jook t'raas. And rememba seh money an' woman can be the roots of evil sometime. Try an' patch t'ings up wid de woman who have yuh children. Me know w'at me sayin'. Me might be old, but me nuh fool."

The truth punched Lijah slap-bang in his balls and had him thinking harder than before. He wished it were as easy as that. It wasn't down to him. Gloria was calling all shots. He gave Papa Dread his fist, a non-verbal reply that said it all. He knew what the old dread was saying, and had no words to contradict him.

Hardly anything escaped Papa Dead, so the matter of *who* told him about Bernadette and Lucy wasn't an issue to Lijah just then.

"Bwoy, 1 hope dis 'orse win yunnuh Papa!" Festus was back. "Yes Lijah! Wha' gwaan me Lion?" They touched fists. "Wha' de man a seh?" "Su'vivin' Rasta. Yuh done know."

"Bwoy, yuh look tired," Festus told him. "Night work? Or nuff pussy? We all know seh yuh have free pyapa now."

"Is weh yaah talk seh?" Lijah kissed his teeth, wishing Festus wouldn't emphasise anything to do with women just then. Especially not after Papa Dread had just put more than his two pennies in, giving him the third degree. "Me don' know not'n 'bout no pussy. But dis night work shit is doing me whole existence in to rahtid. All I waan do right now, is win de lottery or sop'n." Lijah replied, flashing his locks and displaying a gold-crowned grin.

"Or get a rich raas woman to min' yuh," Festus added. "I man jus' sick a dis whole business of working till yuh sixty-five an' all dat shit. An' den yuh dead before yuh get yuh hands on yuh pension to raas. Is true weh dem seh yaah sah, only fools an' horses work."

But Papa Dread didn't care too much for the *'woman to mind yuh'* bit from in Festus' reasoning, joke or not. He himself was hoping to work way past his sixty-five years, only not for an employer, but for himself. "But still," he stressed, hoping Festus would understand, "we have to be conscious. Yuh 'ear me? *Conscious.*" He had been noticing a change in him for a while. A real cause for concern. But Papa Dread knew when to observe and when to dive in. "I know we all get disillusion from time to time 'bout dis work t'ing," he continued, "but seriously, we have to uplift de name of de rastaman. If yuh know yuh history well, yuh will remba Haile Selassie was a lova of hard work and *I*nity. He used to work for twenty hours a day, with one hour feh pray and t'ree hours feh res'. Nuff a we a wear locks but we lose de responsibility dat goes wid it. We forget de deepa aspec'. One t'ing, for instance... Unnuh done know seh if a man wid locks mess up, de firs' t'ing de Media shout is *'Rastaman!'* Dem t'ings deh condemn de whole movement, bredrin."

"Ah here yuh, Papa," Lijah sounded out, but Festus' *'dying before you can get you hands on your pension'* took him straight to his mother and Gloria's father who did just that. And Gloria's mother who had the most beautiful house in Jamaica wasn't standing in any great stead either. Undoubtedly, with her ill health of late, it was looking as if she wouldn't be living for any length of time, to enjoy it.

Lijah and Festus kissed their teeth, then looked on with despair as Sweet Saddle galloped towards the final fence. *Last.*

"A man cyaan even mek a raas claat dalla on the gee-gees to bombo claat," said Festus, flinging his racing paper in a nearby bin.

"Give de lottery a try Festus. Yuh neva know yuh luck," Lijah advised. "Maybe one day yuh might jus' clap dem six numbas."

"Dat is rubbish, Rasta. Too much people do dat. What chance me an' yuh 'ave?" Festus kissed his teeth again.

"Well bwoy, yuh neva know. I try my luck every week. One day me luck might jus' change. W'at about yuh Papa?"

Papa Dread came back from a daydream. "Wha'?"

"De lottery. Yuh mark it?"

"No, sah. Dat is dead loss. More chance of a Concorde fallin' on yuh head dan winnin' de lottery."

Lijah and Festus laughed.

"Me mekkin' a move," Papa Dread announced.

"Me too," Festus said. "Me have some runnings to do."

"Bwoy, me goin' home," Lijah sounded out.

"Home?" Papa Dread questioned with reason. "Memba w'at me seh Lijah. Fin' yuh queen before it's too late. *Home* is where yuh queen is. Jah know."

"Me know Papa. Serious."

"An' Festus, lis'en," Papa Dread said with a seriousness in his voice, "by the sweat of a man's brow he shall eat his bread. Yuh ovastan'? Serious t'ing."

"True t'ing Papa," Festus agreed as he experienced *déjà vu*. It wasn't the first time Papa Dread scolded him with the teachings of His Majesty.

But Papa dread wasn't convinced of how '*true*' a t'ing, Festus really believed it was, so he added, "Yuh know seh if yuh gonna call upon Selassie I's name, an' yuh not gonna act on his principles, yuh gonna be calling it in vain?"

Lijah looked at Papa Dread's face and saw that familiar seriousness of his warning.

"Yeah, man, Papa. A trut' and rights me a deal wid. Me only a run a likkle joke 'bout de work t'ing."

But Papa dread wasn't convinced. He had realised too, how far back from the true philosophy nuff brothers had slipped.

Before they left the bookie shop, Festus walked over to Heidi. Papa Dread and Lijah watched and worked out what he was up to.

Seconds later, Papa Dread watched the backs of the two men disappearing towards their cars. They made their way past two females and Festus tried the flirting thing. "Whaap'n *Sweet Biscuit?*" he chirped, but when the wrong one turned 'round and smiled at him, he corrected,

"Not you *Mash-up Crackas*."

"Festus, is wha' duh yuh man? Yuh don' have to col' up de lady so. Cho."

"Lady? How yuh know she a lady? She could be a tramp feh all yuh know. Yuh know seh me don't put no raas claat 'oman on no pedestal."

"Easy, Rasta. What if a man call your woman a tramp. You affi gwaan betta dan dat, Festus. Feh real. An' how yuh mean yuh don' put no woman on no pedestal? Wha' 'bout Kizzy?'"

Festus kissed his teeth and reached for the handle of his car door, turning 'round to Lijah, he professed, "Lis'en rasta, de only ladies feh me, are virgins. De sweet untouched. De ones who you can mek yuh mark on. If yuh is de firs' to touch a gyal, yuh can curb ar any how yuh want."

"Yuh feel so?"

"Yeah, man."

"So dat goes feh Kizzy den? Yuh tell me yuh was ar firs'."

Festus ignored Lijah's comment and carried on, "But nuh virgins nuh deh 'bout?... oh... how is Ikesha? Long time me nuh..."

"Wha'?!" Lijah asked as if he was jabbed unexpectedly by a sharp object, "is weh yaah deal wid?" He got jumpy. Didn't know what to think. Why did Festus mention his young virgin daughter in the same breath that he mentioned *virgin, sweet untouched, mek yuh mark* and *touch a gyal?* Of course a father has the right to be paranoid over his young, *'fresh-out-the-kitchen'* daughter, who would have most men *wishing.*

"Weh yuh mean, *'is weh me a deal wid'* bredrin?" Festus quizzed.

"Yuh ask me how Ikesha is, just after fantasising over young virgins bredrin. Me nuh like dat."

Festus laughed. "Nah bredrin, me nuh mean not'n by dat. Ikesha is me likkle goddaughter. How yuh could even t'ing me would even t'ink like dat, blood?"

"Bwoy, anyt'ing is possible dese days yunnuh Festus. Yuh an' I know nuff bredrin who deal wid dem fuckries deh. Yuh know seh Chalice done breed up him woman's teenage daughta. An' Renta is now on his second child wid his woman's young niece. Me is no angel yunnuh rasta, but me nuh deal wid dem t'ings deh." Lijah's eyes showed how serious he was, notwithstanding his little encounter with young Faithlyn. It was no wonder, as he saw Faithlyn in a different light from the regular, 'run-of-the-mill' teenagers. Seriously. The girl had practically raped him! And it was no surprise too, that Festus didn't remind him of her, but he too had seen her as a different kinda teenager. Lijah had already told him in details, how she chucked it on him.

"Bwoy, me cyaan believe seh yuh would t'ink feh one moment dat sop'n like dat would cross me min', Lijah. I used to wipe Ikesha's likkle bottom man, is weh duh yuh?"

"Ah nuh not'n, Festus. I wi' kill feh my daughta. Serious... Anyway, me gaan. Lata star."

"More time, bredrin," Festus said as they touched fists with Lijah, feeling well and truly, 'told'.

Papa Dread trundled in the opposite direction towards his ride, recalling again the first time, on separate occasions, he had met them both.

Festus was just eighteen when he arrived in Birmingham from Bristol. Descending on the second city with nothing but a 'grip': - a square, boring-brown 50's style suitcase smelling of moth balls - one which had reminded Lijah of one that was a permanent fixture on top of his parents' wardrobe. He had met Festus on the front-line, not long after he himself had joined Papa Dread and a few other brothas in a house, which they would share for a while after. Festus had not yet secured a fixed abode, and Papa Dread was soon to his rescue.

Papa Dread had noticed how much of a kindred spirit both Lijah and Festus shared, though only a keen eye could detect it. To him, both brothers seemed to be troubled beings, but whatever their individual problems were, they kept them under wraps. But the Rasta's philosophy soon gave them something to claim. It gave them a sense of belonging, and together they threw the comb away and escaped from themselves and their own individual troubles. Left them behind like footprints on a quiet sea-shore. Only, the tides would not wash them away, and the crevices of their minds held them like seashells held the sounds of the sea. Rastamen's pain, hidden deep within the hard exterior of a 'dread' image.

Papa Dread had been their rock. They shared stories, though choiced ones. They shared misconceptions, preconceptions and truths and rights. But the biggest shock for the dreads was when one day Festus revealed to everyone, that both his parents were killed in a car crash. The brothas didn't have words to express their remorse. Festus had told them too, that he had left Bristol to 'forget' and to 'find himself'. And now, as Papa Dread watched him walk away, he wondered if he had ever done so. *Found himself.* He recalled Lijah telling him, that with all his troubles, he figured they were nothing compared to Festus'. Loosing a parent at any one time is crucial. But to loose both at the same time, is devastation ten-fold.

"Yes Papa! Man cool?" Reds cruised by and pulled him from his thoughts.

"Yeah, man. Me jus' gwine hol' a spliff an' relax, yunnuh?"

"Yeah, man. More time still. Me wi' check yuh lata, yeah?"

"Irie Reds," Papa Dread said, as he entered his car, trying to ignore the pain in his big toe.

CHAPTER * SEVEN

The act of infidelity that drove Lijah to his present situation now seemed like a senseless dream. He himself could not believe it happened to him. Being caught with his pants down was one thing, but how he allowed himself to be led into the trap in the first place, is another. Still, it was the straw that broke the camel's back. It should not have happened. There were other things going on. Bigger things than a quick thing with a seventeen-year-old.

Reasoning with Gloria would have been a no-no, so he didn't attempt to. So that Sunday morning after the Saturday night before, he scraped his belongings off his drive and traded (though reluctantly) the familiar settings of his three-bedroom house for a single bed: surplus to Bernadette's requirement.

Just then, it was good of Bernadette to offer a pillow. There was no question of going to his idrin Festus, although it wouldn't be down to him. Kizzy would have the last say. Besides, letting him rest there would be like upholding his nastiness and working against her best friend Gloria. So it wasn't even worth the contemplation. Lijah wouldn't put the sista on the spot anyway. And there was also his pride to think about.

The sin that cost him the familiar comforts of Gloria's arms? He copulated with Faithlyn, their seventeen-year-old baby-sitter, who offered it on a plate, with a smile and in the comfort of Gloria's settee. Seriously. And although blackmail helped his decision, he simply could not control the urge. *'But only another brother could understand'*, he had thought, justifying himself.

Gloria had walked in from a night out with Kizzy – much earlier than expected and caught him with his pants down, a busy ass and a probing dick. Her untimely presence spread a thick helping of shame over the whole situation, rendering a sudden state of impotence. A state he hoped would not stay for good. Shit, that sort of thing is possible, and the very *thought* of it pained him.

That night, along with the chance of ever babysitting Khamilla, their five-year-old daughter again, Faithlyn lost her voice. *Vocal impotence* you might say. She isn't exactly a coy type, but it didn't help when Gloria, after turning on the light, stood over them in shock. Her loud, palpable silence killed the situation stone dead. Lijah could almost feel the lasers of her eyes, burning deep into the cheeks of his ass, as she stared wide-eyed and open-mouthed, trying to make sense of what she was staring at!

Lijah tried desperately to figure out how he could ever salvage what was left of his pride, while Faithlyn laid beneath him looking like a snail that had just had salt poured on its back. The shock had rendered them both paralysed and unable to move a muscle: slowly shrinking under the shadow of open shame.

"You're screwing our baby-sitter?!" Gloria shouted.

He said nothing.

"Lijah... I asked you a question!"

Well, what did she expect him to say? Christ, it wasn't as if he could deny it. That would have been taking the *'It wasn't me'* thing a bit too far. Besides, the question was hypothetical. So he answered only by letting his locks flow over his eyes, covering the open shame.

"Lijah?" Gloria's voice curdled with hurt, *"She is seventeen years old. She's not that much younger than our daughter Ikesha."*

'With the forwardness of a forty-year-old', Lijah wanted to say.

"I thought I could trust you, Lijah," Gloria sobbed.

Lijah's tongue became heavy and his throat dry. For the first time in his life, he had experienced real shame. Get ketch right in the middle of a session to raas!

Almost as if it was in a dream, Lijah heard the front door click shut and remembered there was a third party in this. Faithlyn had left in the middle of Gloria's shouting and his tangible silence. His mind was still frozen by shock. He couldn't even remember getting up, seeing Faithlyn get dressed, or even her leaving the room. A total *blank-out* must have happened somewhere.

"Mum!" Khamilla's voice entered his ears, alleviating the sound of Gloria's sobs. "Mum!" It came with a difference to his ears now. 'Why didn't Khamilla call *Dad* he wondered. Funny, but it had never bothered him before, and now it seemed that she knew that he had done wrong. "Who's crying, Mum?" she asked, in her sleepy little voice.

Lijah attempted the stairs.

"Leave her alone! Don't even think about putting your hands on my daughter, you bastard! Get out! Get out! I hate the very sight of you!" Gloria almost scraped the skin from the back of her throat. She pushed him out the way and without a doubt; he could feel the hate she had suddenly developed for him.

Lijah knew what she was really hating: the image of what she had just seen. He tried to put his foot in her shoe. But... 'Her daughter?' Lijah asked himself, 'Her daughter?' The feeling of depravity was stifling him already. He knew he was already history, but the thought of his daughter being used as a weapon against him was the worse of all.

He walked to the kitchen and stood in the dark, feeling like a man who had spent one foolish night in a casino and lost his whole life's savings. He knew he should have been stronger and resisted doing the business with Faithlyn - blackmail or not. But she was cute. Cute, facety and fresh from yard. Faithlyn had tried several times to seduce him. Squeezing past him on the stairs, in the passage. Everywhere she got a chance to.

Once, while Lijah was in the shower, Faithlyn pushed the bathroom door open and walked right on in. She stood there with her mouth open, staring at his manhood as if she'd seen a ghost! Then, in an undiluted Jamaican accent, she shouted, *'Jeesas Chris'! Me neva see not'n so big from de day me baan!'* When she'd gotten over the shock, Lijah knew he'd be in more trouble than he had been before. Now Faithlyn would be like a dog that had seen dinner being prepared, and Lijah had better be ready for that *head-up-tail-wagging-gimme-some-a-dat* action. And by the looks of it, throwing her a *one-bone* with a *there-there* pat on the head wouldn't do.

Another time when Gloria was in the bath, getting ready for a night out, Lijah had fallen asleep on the settee. Faithlyn took the opportunity to sit on his lap and started gyrating her young, yet experienced hips, singing, *"Put yuh hog inna me cocoa... Mek 'im root out me mintie!"* Lijah woke in shock and nearly died of a heart attack. He stood up quickly, pushed her off and left the house. Picked her off like ticks to raas.

But men are like babies when it comes to fanny. There's only so much temptation they can resist, and when temptation comes with blackmail, it can be even harder. That night when Gloria caught him in the act, Faithlyn had waved an incriminating photo in front of him. A photo of Lucy and him in his car doing the business! How the hell she got that, he didn't know, but she threatened to tell Gloria if she didn't get her t'ings. Besides, in her determination, she teasingly placed the photo in her knickers and dared him to retrieve it. In his retrieving, fanny magnet held the fingers of his right hand hostage. They tuned her piano, played her song and lost him his queen.

And that wasn't all. Before that, another night when Gloria was out and he was getting ready to leave the house, the facety girl sneaked into the bedroom while he was getting changed. She sneaked up behind him and started groping his balls! He pushed her away in fright and asked, *'What yuh doin', gyal? Yuh mad?!'*

But all she said, with ease, was *'Cho', unnuh English bwoy sof' een sah. All me want yuh feh duh is put yuh wood inna me fire. Gloria nah know not'n. Me piano waan tune'.*

'Faithlyn, yuh mad gyal?' he relented. *'W'at about Rock, yuh Yardie bwoyfrien'? An' anyway, yuh too young.'*

'Me not too young. Me is eighteen nex' year. An' w'at about Rock? He's probably havin' fun right now', she said, rubbing her right hand over Lijah's bare chest.

Lijah managed to escape her again that night, but it was hard going. He was always feeling uneasy and crept around his house like a damn stranger, with Faithlyn winking at him, touching him and all that shit. He wondered how Gloria hadn't noticed, but her suspicions were elsewhere. You see, Faithlyn was the last person she would suspect; as to her face she was a saint. No, Gloria was already watching his every move on the outa-street front. A blonde called Lucy had had him in her clutches, but that's a story in itself. It was hard going trying to convince Gloria that her suspicion was just a figment of her imagination, but with the help of his idrin Festus, he managed to. At least, so he thought.

So in the end he got clobbered for the wrong deed. Sent to jail for the wrong crime.

So Gloria chucked him out. Only he didn't suffer as much as she would have liked. She sent him straight into the arms of another woman. *Bernadette.* He was lost, hurt and vulnerable, so Bernadette's world was his oyster. She was a cushion for his fall. He ran wild with her like an unleashed horse or a newly freed slave. Her 'kin teets' were gleaming smiles. Her glitterings, gold. And soon, her fanny would win his Grammy.

He had forgotten Papa Dread's words, "Rasta, every rose have macca jook."

CHAPTER * EIGHT

The dawn of the New Year caught Gloria unfulfilled, broken-hearted and almost lame – a feeling she had hoped would have now subsided. For her, 2003 had arrived with a bang. Sparks were missing, big time. Earlier she played gooseberry to Kizzy and Festus at an over-hyped, over-priced party that had less kick than a lame flea. It happened every year, and every year they promised to stick to their local club, Fern Gully.

Fern Gully wasn't exactly the Savoy, but security on the door was always tip-top and the girls felt safe. And although it was always filled with men who left their wives or girlfriends at home and came out looking for fresh pussies, the place was always overflowing with vibes. And if Barrier Busta was the DJ in the house, the ladies knew they were guaranteed to rock all night. Give the brother his due; he's a bombastic Selecta. Second to Father Jarvis, he knew just how to choose his music.

But tonight, there was no guarantee that the most kicking of parties would have done Gloria any good. Although they weren't together, she spent the whole night watching the door, scanning the faces of all dreads, and hoping one of them would be Lijah. But the irony of the situation was, she wouldn't have lightened up anyway. Even a one-dance would have been a hard decision. Or even a no-no. That's the trouble with women: cutting their noses off to spite their faces is a scenario that helps them to be strong and independent, but often, in spiting their men, they often spite themselves more.

"Yuh a'right, Gloria?" Festus spent the whole night playing host, making sure she was ok. But he couldn't try hard enough. It was the sista's heart that needed looking after and there wasn't much he could do about that. Besides, he needed to *dance ayard before he could pretend to dance abroad.* His woman needed to be tended to also.

So that morning, Gloria slipped into bed alone at 3am with a bouquet of barbed wire around her heart, swallowed hard and forbade her eyes to cry. She was trying hard not to cry so much of late. But *'Wha' gone bad a morning, cyaan come good a evening'*, she would tell herself. And what was the use of crying anyway?

She told herself she had to maintain an aura of hardness, lest she break down the barrier of strength she had been trying to build and cross the thin line between sanity and insanity. Dying of a broken heart was not on her agenda.

You see, she had allowed herself to love too deep. Or, perhaps, *'allowed herself to love someone more than she loved herself'.* From her reckoning, she had given without receiving. Let in, whilst being shut out. And lied to, whilst she bared her very soul.

Gloria had given Lijah reason to trust her one hundred percent, yet he had hurt her, taking away any hope of trust she may have had. She thought she was his soul mate. His best friend. He lied to her about Lucy even when she begged him to tell her the truth. It was a photo that Faithlyn had accidentally-on-purpose, mislaid, which confirmed her fears.

She cuddled her pillow as her head buzzed with the residue of the two Bacardi Breezers she had sunk earlier. She only drank to be sociable. She could have done without the second, but figured it would help her pain. It hadn't. There she was alone in bed, telling herself that wherever the culprit of her misery was at that precise moment, it wasn't right that he should be *happy, while her heart bled* - a concept that had eluded her. Totally. *'How could Lijah be happy when her heart was threatening to rip itself away from where God had planted it?'*

Prior, she had paced up and down between the lonesome walls of her three-bedroom house wishing Ikesha and Kunta hadn't left home. She needed a cuddle. Now she wished Khamilla was there. Fiona had kindly offered to look after her so Gloria could have a night out.

Now Gloria made cups of tea she didn't really want, and thought of dialling Lijah's number. Earlier she checked for messages on her mobile. Perhaps there would be one that said, *'I know you're still upset with me babes, but Happy New Year anyway'*. But there wasn't any. So how come she was hurting so much? Wasn't that wasted energy? Was she even a thought in the back of his mind?' She had asked herself those familiar questions yet again. She told herself... *'He's a man'*.

You see, Gloria strongly believed that a man could detach himself from his emotions, as easily as he could lie. She reflected again on the trauma of walking into her house, faced with Lijah's busy ass, lashing Faithlyn the baby-sitter. She wondered if he would come to realise that in a way, he had done the same thing to her that his father had done to his mother. The very thing that had poisoned his mind against his father. The thing that hurt him so much, that for a long time he found it hard to tell her in its fullest. It was only after her coaxing him – after him crying in his sleep once too often, that he spilled it all.

It was 3:30am. Her landline phone rang and startled Gloria. It was Kizzy. It was late, but Kizzy had a knack of picking up on her friend's low ebbs. Somehow she knew she would find Gloria still up, sad, pensive and lonely.

"Are you still there torturing yuhself, G?"

"Oh. Kizzy. It's you? Yuh telepathic or sop'n girl? Why aren't you sleeping? Where's Festus?"

"Festus is snoring. Him full up me head wid some shit 'bout 'im not working 'till 'im sixty-five an' all dat. As if he's planning on winning the lottery or something. Then he went off to sleep."

"What? You mean you didn't make love on New Year morning?"

Kizzy kissed her teeth as if Gloria had said an alien thing. "G? I know you've got pride and all that, but aren't you just hurting yourself?"

"Why d'you say that?"

"Well, I was watching you tonight. You really miss Lijah, don't you?"

"I suppose I must do. It's been twenty odd years, Kizzy."

"I think you should give him another chance."

"What?!"

"Hear me out, G. I know he did a slack t'ing, but I can't see you with anyone else. And I don't think there's one couple in this world that has stayed faithful to each other from the day they met, to the end. That is just a man-made wish we all have, G. It doesn't happen. And if so, very rarely. Maybe your father, yes. I couldn't imagine him being unfaithful to your mother. He seemed so loyal. But men like that are few and far between."

"You've always looked up to my father haven't you, K."

"Yes. I must say I do. He's one of those guys who probably wouldn't even consider infidelity, let alone engage in it."

Gloria laughed.

"What's funny?" Kizzy asked.

"Nothing. Has Festus ever screwed out on you, K?" Gloria moved quickly away from the subject of her father's impeccable image. "Would Festus do a thing like that?"

Kizzy laughed cynically. "Funny how we all as individuals, prioritise things differently isn't it, G?"

"Wha' d'you mean?"

"Well, you just asked me if Festus would do 'a thing like that'. G, you probably won't see it my way, but I would think differently of Festus if he fucked out on me, to the way I think of him beating me. I know one hurt is mental and the other is physical, but that's what I mean about how good, bad or average we all see things."

"Mmm," Gloria contemplated.

"I don't know if Festus ever fucked out on me. All I know he's one insecure brother. He's also human and humans have a tendency of not even knowing what they are capable of. I know I personally don't."

"Oh dear," Gloria cut in. "You're in a bit of a philosophical mood tonight, aren't you?"

"G, all I'm saying is, think hard about giving up twenty good years for a mistake made in stupid heat of passion."

"You mean you would forgive him for fucking out on yuh?"

"I don't know, G. When I was younger, I used to say I would never stay with a man who beats me. But you know Festus is violent. He beats me, but..."

"But I thought that was in the past. Kizzy surely Festus don't still...?"

"Yes. Yes, he does. And yes, I know, you'd be gone by now, right?"
"I thought 'im stop doin' dem t'ings." Gloria's voice became angry.
Shock infused. "When was the last time he hit you...?"
"You mean, when was the last time he didn't?"
"Kizzy, we're friends. How could you keep this from...?" Whoops.
She stopped herself. Hypocrisy smacked her around the face. She had
almost forgotten about her secret rendezvous with the SAAB driver, that
she kept so well from Kizzy. "So," she continued, you mean all that *'I
fell in the bath', 'I hit my head on the cupboard door'* and all that, were
excuses?"
"Gloria we all lie from time to time. And some of us might not lie, but
we just don't say anything. We keep certain things away from people we
love the most for whatever reason. Mama Maya did it, I do it."
"You do it?" Gloria asked. "What have you lie about, or what else
haven't you told me?"
"Gloria, sometimes things are left unsaid, for good reasons. But I
know one thing, there's something troubling Lijah, G. Like Festus, he
needs help. I'm not just making excuses for him."
"Are you trying to say there's something troubling all women beaters
and two-timing bastards?" Anger took hold of Gloria even more.
"I d'know. You're the one with the psychology degree. You're the one
who's always using psychology to analyse everything. Now analyse this
one."
Gloria's mind raced. Kizzy got her thinking deep tonight.
"Both our men have problems of their own, G. Like nuff brothas out
there. But try telling a black man he has a problem and there's a reason
or reasons for his actions."
"Yuh right," Gloria agreed, "and I suppose us women have problems
of our own too, when we don't understand that they have problems."
"Irie. And also, it doesn't mean none of us are better than the other, G.
We just have different ways of handling a situation. Women who's never
experienced any of these things, will condemn other women for having
men back after they cheated on them, or beat them, but it's never that
easy to throw away so many valuable years."
"Valuable years?!" Gloria backtracked, just when Kizzy was thinking
she was having a change of heart. "A man beats you and you see *value*?"
Now Gloria was beginning to sound like Fiona. She had never seen this
side to Kizzy and wondered if Festus had been working on her, on
Lijah's behalf. She wondered too, seriously, if Kizzy felt she owed
Festus something. She wondered now, if Kizzy was taking the beating
because she felt she deserved it. At times, it seemed to Gloria, more than

this 'devil I know' theory she had been down with. Or the fact that she thinks he needed help. It puzzled Gloria. Whatever the reason, she knew there was no way she was gonna forgive Lijah, whatever her best mate might say.

"I tried, Kizzy. I tried to forgive and forget but I know it wouldn't work. It would keep coming back. The memories. An' I know I would jus' keep bringing it up every time we argue."

"Jus' have a think, G. No one's perfect. No relationship is perfect. There are nuff t'ings going on outa street dat will mek Lijah's likkle t'ing look like not'n."

"Yuh not dropping yuh standards are yuh, Kizzy?"

"No. Jus' looking at reality."

"Kizzy, Lijah fucked a young gyal inna me house. He was screwing a girl at work. Now he's shacking up with Bernadette. And Festus beats you. Is this *'reality'*? If it is, I'd rather be dreaming."

"G, all I'm saying is, in three months time, you'll be forty, right?"

"Don't remind me," Gloria hastened.

"So the man you're looking for is gonna be around that, right? 'Cos I'm sure yuh not lookin' feh no toy bwoy. If there's a so-called perfect man around that age floating around, it's probably because his woman bitched out on him, or died. If she hasn't just died, dogged him or whatever, then why is he free?"

"Oh please Kizzy, that's taking things to the limit now."

"No, think about it G. I would say he fucked up and she chucked him out. Or he could be a big-time gangster posing to be Mr Right. So one a dem free guys you're gonna meet won't necessarily be no angel. He could have some dark deeds behind him. At least you know Lijah's fault. He's the devil you know."

Gloria was silent. Kizzy wasn't leaving her much scope to trust someone new at all. And now, she couldn't help remembering Yvonne, a sista from work. Yvonne was one of the nicest sistas you could find. She wasn't short of offers, but she just needed someone special to share her dreams with. She had been through hell and back with men and thought her ordeal was ended when she met a guy who just had to be Mr Right: *Marlon*. The sweetest American brother you could ever find. It was perfect. In fact, *too perfect*, come to think of it. A dream relationship. Marlon had alleviated all Yvonne's fears by doing the 'right thing': He introduced her to his mother, sisters - the works. So what could possibly go wrong?

Yvonne and Mr America talked future, marriage, and travel. And she had told her mum, *'This is him, Mum. The man of my dreams. I think he's the man I'm going to marry'*. But one day, no more than two months later, when Gloria asked how things were going, Yvonne emitted, "Don't talk about that shit, Gloria. The only thing that was nice about him was his American accent."

Gloria's mouth fell open. "What?!"

"All I'm saying is, Gloria, be careful who you let into your house, or even your life."

"What d'you mean, Yvonne? Only yesterday you were still so…"

"Ecstatic? Over the moon? Yes, I know. Listen, Gloria, the guy was actually more dangerous than any other guy I had met before. And to think, through trust, I left him alone in my house. I'm shivering at the thought. Looking back now, it feels quite creepy."

"Yvonne, get to the point. What are you talking about? He was talking marriage. Even rushing you to make plans."

Yvonne kissed her teeth. "Well. You know I told you the wonderful treatment he gave me?"

"Yes. You even made me jealous. Lijah had never done anything like that for me."

"Mmm. And you know all the big high-chested promises he made?"

"Yes, yes. Get to the point sista."

"And you know how I told you that he was resting at my house for a while? You know how things gradually build up, a shirt here, a brief there, then before you know it…"

"C'mon Yvonne, suspense is killing me. What happened?"

"Well, I came home one day to find his few belongings gone. No goodbye note. No explanation on my answer phone. Nothing. Just gone. Like a bird. And guess what?"

"What?"

"That gold locket he bought me for my birthday?… He took it with him."

"No! He didn't take back a present he bought you?"

"Damn right."

"But that's stealing. If he bought it for you, it's yours. If he takes it back, especially without telling you, it's stealing."

"Exactly. So he has stolen from my house. But he obviously doesn't think so. Another woman must be wearing that. Or perhaps he sold it." Yvonne laughed. "The thing is, she continued, "because he seemed so open and honest at the beginning, I trusted him with a key to my house. That day I was at work. He sneaked into my house when he was sure there was no way I'd catch him. Like a thief in the night."

"And have you heard from him since?"

"No, but one afternoon, I bumped into him on Corporation Street."

"And what did he have to say for himself?"

"Say? You must be joking girl. The man just gave me a shifty look, then quickly averted his eyes. And I noticed how quickly his forehead sweated too. Dodgy. He was strolling along-side a sista, and without wanting to sound too bitchy, her weave was so long, it was almost laughable. I began to wonder if that was what I was lacking... a record-breaking weave. Anyway, I suppose that shifty glance he gave me was through fear. Perhaps he was worried that I might walk up to his weave queen and say, *'Hey, sista. Do you really know who you're with? Well, let me fill you in... '.*" Yvonne laughed. "But I wouldn't. I was curious to know though, if she was wearing a familiar gold locket."

"But seriously though, Yvonne," Gloria said, "the man gave you no explanation at all?"

"No. Not a dickie-bird. And to think, when I was with him, he had the audacity to be running down some man who was treating his sister bad! But that's no problem. I've escaped. A guy with a character like that would be bad news in my life, Gloria. I'm not even sure if he's told a pack of lies to his family about me. It ended so suddenly, he had to tell them something. I know if that was my brother or my son, I would have to ask him how come it ended so quick. But if my brother had acted like that, I couldn't see him admitting it and tell the whole truth."

"I would have to call his family and say something," Gloria said. "What if he's painted your name black? Make out you're some negative character or something, just to make himself look good?"

"Yes, there's that. And I have the strongest feeling he has painted me black. But no, I won't call them. There's a God. And He will take care of that. By the look of it, he needs God's help, himself, Gloria. He's a troubled soul, but he probably doesn't even know it. Marlon can fool man, but he can't fool God. And talking about God, would you believe the guy hides behind the church?"

"No! He doesn't go to church, does he?!"

"Oh yes. *Brother Marlon.* The well-liked, well-trusted *Brother Marlon.* The *phoney Brother Marlon* who plays women the way he plays his keyboard: one key here, one key there, play them, drop them, then moved right out of tune. Oh yes. Using his American accent as a cunning prop, he is singing *sweet nothings* into the ears of choir members everywhere. I can imagine him giving it that good old *'Hallelujah! And which one of these trusting sistas am I gonna get my eager paws on next?! Aaaamen!'* "

Gloria couldn't believe what she was hearing. "Just one question,

Yvonne," she hastened, "have you changed the lock to your front door?"

"Hell, yes," Yvonne assure her. "The very next day, girl. It's a shame, but if you can't trust a guy in the church, who the hell can you trust?"

Gloria's mind darted back to her dear father, Reverend Fontaine. He wasn't just a guy in the church. He headed it. yet he had picked and eaten fruits from his congregation: at his pleasure and their willingness.

"Oh no. No... No..." Gloria was in shock.

"I'm glad he's gone, though. His leaving is not an issue right now. The issue is Gloria, my passport is missing."

"Yuh wha'?"

"My passport. I can't say he's taken it right now, but it's funny how now that he has left so mysteriously, it's missing."

"But what would he want with your passport?"

"That's big business, you know. Didn't you watch that programme where that man's passport and stuff was stolen and his identity was taken on by a criminal?"

"Yes. I remember."

"I just hope I find mine. It's just not in the place I've always kept it. I don't know who Marlon was, Gloria. He could be anybody. That's why sometimes it's better the devil you know. None of my exes would do that. Marlon was sneaky. In fact, thinking about it now, it sends shivers down my spine, to think that I've spent nights with a guy who... well, I d'know. I'm lost for words."

Now Gloria came back to Kizzy's voice, still rattling on. And now the memory of her new-found acquaintance. An exciting SAAB driver who helped her through a few nights. Who was he? Really? How much did she really know about him? But although she reflected seriously on Yvonne's story, her mysterious friend and Kizzy's advice, she was still determined not to have Lijah back. And she still couldn't understand how understanding Kizzy was about the physical abuse thing she was going through.

"Think about it," Kizzy continued, "A man's woman chucked him out and he's on the prowl. An' a man like that?... Before he settles into another deep relationship again, he's gonna have fun. He's not just gonna settle for you. He's gonna be screwing left right and centre. And more than likely he'll end up with that same woman who'd chucked him out in the first place."

Gloria didn't need Kizzy to tell her that. She had seen so many of that around her, it was unbelievable.

"So trying to find a perfect man to replace Lijah is going to be like finding a needle in a haystack. Or sifting through a bargain basket in the rag market! So girl... *It's better the devil you know."*

"Here we go again, wearing out that dyam phrase, *'betta de devil you know',*" she mimicked her friend. But now, she was well and truly disillusioned. She remained silent for a while, then she started to sob... "How could he, Kizzy? After I gave up the chance of a career and went against my parents' wishes for him?... How could he?"

"Oh G, jus' pull yuhself together man! Everybody gives up something for some reason. At least you know why you did. For love. Why did my real mother give me up? Life's not perfect for no one."

Gloria felt the shake from her friend's voice. This was the fist time Kizzy had ever spoken to her like that. In fact, she even surprised herself. Ever since she started the search for her real mother, everybody else's hard-done-bys seemed somewhat futile.

Gloria realised that the reason for her friend's quest for attention was now greater than hers. She showed her understanding and said, sniffling, "How yuh getting' on wid the search anyway?"

"I've got a lead. But I'll talk to you another day. You need to sort your head out before I fill it with my troubles. Perhaps we all need to sort our heads out. It's the New Year, G. We should be happy. I think one day you'll realise that you should be with Lijah. I just hope it's not too late."

"Kizzy we'll catch up tomorrow." Gloria severed the conversation.

"Irie," Kizzy said, feeling guilty for her little outbursts.

Gloria replaced the receiver and kissed 2002 goodbye. She had already made her resolution – to wash Lijah out of her hair, forever. After all, in less than three months she would be forty and enough was enough. But she knew that if she got any harder, she would be a good match for *Medusa.* She would become almost hardened, with a heart of stone. She didn't want that. She wanted her sensitivity back. But somehow, she knew she couldn't bring herself to forgive Lijah.

Lying there under her duvet as if it was her only friend, Gloria reflected on how it all started. How Lijah came, like a thief in the night, stole her heart and locked it away in his own private cocoon, not knowing that she would be lost without it. Now, she wanted it back. Just so she could be free to love again.

She could not sleep, but she must have sunk deep into her thoughts like a burrowing fox, for when she realised, it was 5am – a whole hour since she had put the phone down from Kizzy. Again, she swallowed hard, this time, with determination and decided that she must live without her heart, like a walking dead. She wouldn't be the only one. Nuff sistas out there are just existing. Living day to day without the men they love, giving their bodies, time and effort to substitutes, mainly through pride: simply not accepting the sharing t'ing or for whatever reason.

But of course Gloria knew she wouldn't rest in peace for a while yet. She saw Lijah every week. He picked Khamilla up every week under this *let's-be-civilised-for-the-sake-of-our-young-daughter* act.   And next week he'd come again, like an interfering spiritualist, to call her soul.

And it's not that she hadn't thought of giving in once or twice, but she had built up a phobia for trusting. She knew that if her heart should rule her head, and she should begin to get comfortable in his arms again, the inevitable heartbreak would show its ugly head – aiming for her heart, like a careless bullet.

Martyr she might be, but she had decided she wasn't going there again. Not with Lijah anyway.

"Oh shit! Who's that?" Gloria perplexed. The doorbell ringing at five in the morning wasn't a usual thing. She looked out but couldn't see a car she recognised. Without turning the light on, she tried to recognise the shadow on her doorstep, but it was hard. *'Lijah'*, she thought to herself, *'it must be Lijah. What is he doing here anyway? And why didn't he ring first? Still, it's the New Year. I suppose being civilise for a while won't hurt.'* As he mind raced, she pulled on her dressing gown and headed downstairs. But as she flicked on the porch light she had second thoughts about opening the front door. It wasn't Lijah at all. It was her mysterious friend. The SAAB driver. She had asked him not to come to the house again until she sorted her head out.

"Yuh gonna let me stand on de doorstep like a begga?" he said with confidence.

"What yuh doin' here?"

"Open up, an' I'll tell yuh," an authentic Jamaican accent wrapped itself around her eardrums.

"But I asked you not to come until…"

"Gloria open de door nuh? Cha. Me jus' waan talk to yuh. New Year an' all dat. If you spen' de New Year night alone, yuh will be lonely feh de res' a de year."

She contemplated. Questioned herself. "I can't…"

"Come aan Gloria man. Me leave a nice dance jus' to come fin' yuh. Yuh know me miss yuh."

"So what if I wasn't here?"

"Well yuh here. Jus' open de door man, cha."

Gloria melted. Reasons began to leave her. Besides, she was lonely. And it wasn't as if she hadn't fallen for Mr Fresh-From-Yard. She opened the door.

"So wha'? Yuh nuh love me again?" he asked, looking into her eyes.

"Yuh don't understand." She locked the front door and walked to the sitting-room. He followed.

"Den tell me, Gloria? Tell me w'at I need to undastan'. Yuh want Lijah back? If yuh want him back, jus' tell me yunnuh. I wi' jus' fin' anadda 'oman. Nuff 'oman out deh. Even dough me love yuh bad."

What was it in this guy that was creeping so quickly into her bones and taking over like a wild forest fire?

He touched her face. Lifted her chin as if she was nothing but a sweet child.

She looked into his eyes and he planted a kiss upon her lips.

She melted even more, yet her conscience pricked. "No. Not here. Not in this house again. It was wrong for me to let you make love to me in here in the first place. It's still Lijah's house..."

"When yuh gonna stop being Likkle Miss Perfec' Gloria? Didn't Lijah fuck a gyal in dis house? Did he t'ink about yuh then?" He kissed her neck. Eased his palms under her dressing gown and caressed her firm breasts. She moaned and scolded herself for wanting it, but it was a New Year, so perhaps this new feeling was just what she could do with.

He roamed.

She hummed.

He delved.

Her body temperature rose. She fought it. "No... no... stop it. Not here. I'm not..."

"You're not what?" he asked, his warm breath brushing her ear lobes alternatively, as he moved his sun-kissed face around hers with more gentleness than a kitten. His moist kisses dancing playfully on her skin, silently pitter-pattering against its surface like warm drizzles of rain.

She sighed, driven by something. The woman in her awoken.

Now, a discarded dressing gown fell gracefully onto the floor of the quiet living-room. Her body tingled with undiluted wanting.

Now, Jamaican muscles lifted a black English sista with mastery. Confidently, he mounted the stairs, carrying her like a newly wed. Soon, her bed met their hot, passionate bodies. And as their heavens came down he commanded, "Say my name... Say my name Gloria." His voice heightened, "Why don't you eva say my name dese days, Gloria? Yuh used to when we firs' met. Me like de way yuh seh it, yunnuh. Wid yuh sweet English tongue. I know why yuh don't seh it anymore. Yuh still holding on to Lijah, right?"

But Gloria said nothing. All she knew was that she was enjoying him inside her. Sweet. Erotic. Ecstasy. Then came the rain. Opened heavens.

Showers of passion.

Soon, they came to rest in each other's arms, his deep snoring dodging and diving the waves of her thoughts. Among other things, she wondered why. Why did she find it so hard to say his name, even when he commanded her to? Will saying it make her little rendezvous real? Will it wash Lijah away? She herself just didn't know.

As she stared at his cute face, she sunk into a deep slumber. It took her to some place else.

Now Gloria stared at the red digits on her clock. 6:30am, still the morning of the New Year. She picked up the receiver of her ringing telephone and wasn't at all surprise to hear Kunta's voice. He was calling from the hospital where Shari was having a tough time. Her waters had broken just under an hour ago and she was, by Kunta's reckoning, in nuff pain. Gloria calmed her son down, crawled out of bed and freshened up. Shari's mother was in London and was most certainly not gonna be there for her. Her career was more important than her daughter and grandchild. Gloria had already told Kunta to call her whatever time of the day she was taken in.

She shook her lover to consciousness and told him he had to go. Besides, she wasn't feeling too comfortable with him leaving in the cold light of day. Neighbours talk.

It wasn't long before Gloria was pulling into the visitor's car park and not long after that, she was hurrying with grave concern towards the maternity section.

"Now w'en we tell yuh to push, yuh have to push, young lady. Or we'll be here all night." The playful voice of a Barbadian woman boomed out of a delivery room, over the distressing sound of a young girl. Gloria knew it was Shari. It brought back memories of when she gave birth to Ikesha.

"Mum!" Kunta was pacing outside with his head in his hand.

"Didn't you wanna go in Kunta?" Gloria asked. "It's your first child."

"Nah," Kunta replied nervously, looking at his mum as if she was crazy.

"Kunta! Get Kunta! Pleeease!" Shari's frightened voice found strength and a nurse raced out to find the teenage dad-to-be.

"Kunta, she wants yuh. Come. Put dis gown on," the Barbadian nurse came at him like a tornado.

Kunta looked at his mum. He was worried to death.

"Can I come in too?" Gloria asked.

"Are you her mother?" the woman sang in her sweet, undiluted Bajan accent.

"No. I'm Kunta's mum."

"Ok. I'll get you a gown."

Gloria wondered who would need her more, her son or his girlfriend. Kunta had no blood left in his cheeks and by the looks of it, Shari had no strength to push.

"Kunta." Shari stretched her hand towards her boyfriend. "It's horrible," she groaned.

"Yuh tek de pleasure, now tek de pain!" the voice of a Jamaican woman countered, in a harsh, unsympathetic tone. But not without a glare from Gloria.

"Don't I know you?" Gloria prolonged her stare and threw the question like a poisoned arrow at the matron-type woman with bosoms like Mount Everest.

"Me know nuff people. Who is yuh parents?" she asked, peering condescendingly over the rims of her glasses, which vexed Gloria even more.

"Who my parents are, is not relevant right now. Besides, I'm not a child."

"What a facety 'oman," the woman mumbled, perturbed.

"Who knows, you might not have been much older than Shari when you had your first child in Jamaica" Gloria said sternly, as if she knew the woman. "So comfort the girl and don't distress her. It's your job. Most of you older people forget that you were young once. And that you did the same t'ing de kids are doin' now. The only difference is, it would probably have been undaneat' a sycamore or mango tree. Or in some coffee grove or somewhere like dat. And in dem days you were marched home to the boy's parents, and he would have to marry yuh! In your case though, any man who got you into trouble would have probably ran miles."

The sweet Barbadian woman's face was a question mark. "A'right. Stop it now. That's enough." She held Gloria around her shoulders as if to comfort her.

The harsh woman glared surprisingly at Gloria, wondering who on earth she was and how come she had the cheek to talk like that to her.

The three white nurses looked at each other questioningly, as the patios feud overshadowed Shari's agony. Gloria had never done anything like that before, but she was tired. Confused. Stressed. Even a little angry with herself for her actions earlier that morning. She was a free woman, yet she felt as if she was cheating on Lijah. Her head was swimming with all sorts. It wouldn't take much to rile her and this self-righteous woman had blown her last fuse.

"Ok ladies. Let's do the only thing that needs doing the most right now. Let's get this baby into the world peacefully, shall we? Or I'll have to ask you both to leave. Shari can do without this." A smartly dressed white nurse took charge and reached for Shari's pulse.

The woman cut her eyes, sucked her teeth long and loud. Now everyone felt the hurricane from her frock-tail.

"Zelda! Where yuh goin?!" The sweet Bajan woman perplexed.

A tall German-looking doctor walked in as Zelda breezed out.

Zelda was still baffled at Gloria's outburst and at who she was. *'How would she know what age I first gave birth? Undaneat' a sycamore or mango tree? Dyam outa aada...'*, she mumbled as she floated down the corridor.

Gloria walked up to Shari and patted her right hand. Kunta rested a trembling hand on her right shoulder as she gripped his hand tight. The ultimate question floated in the air, but later they would ask Gloria all about it. Just then was no time. That outburst was just not Gloria's style.

"I can't do this," Shari moaned.

"Yes you can, Shari," Gloria assured. "I did it three times. Just look at this big young stallion who put you into this situation. I brought him here. He was eight pounds and I was much smaller than you... So you can do it." Gloria's words made Shari half smile. She looked at her boyfriend, who seemed to need more help than her.

"Ok, Shari, push now girl," the German doctor commanded ten minutes later.

Kunta wished he could share the pain. He felt guilty, but in the next few minutes, hopefully, he would become more mature than he ever was.

Shari took deep breaths. Panted. Agonised. Yelled. Pushed and pushed.

Then out slid a scrunched, squashed head covered in blood.

Then a thud. Kunta's knees had given way and he fell to the floor. Cold out. Now he needed the same stretcher that his girlfriend used earlier.

"It's a boy! Well done!" a nurse shouted, while another tended to Kunta.

Shari managed some strength to smile. Her tired eyes met Gloria's. Then she looked across the room at Kunta and raised her eyebrows jokingly. "Men," she said. "One drop a blood and they're out." She was just pleased her ordeal was over.

It wasn't long before a swaddling bundle was laid onto her chest.

When Gloria had had her full fix of her new-born grandchild, she strode slowly into the corridor, her fingers busy typing out a text. It was now 9:30am. Wherever he was, and whoever he was holding, Lijah needed to know that he was a granddad at 38.

Now Zelda hurried sheepishly past Gloria. Gloria paused and decided to put Mrs Self-Righteous even straighter. Her voice followed the escaping woman down the corridor like a herd-man's noose, pulling her back with a jolt, "Zelda?"

Zelda stopped dead in her tracks.

"Don't you have five different children for five different men?"

Her eyes widened, asking all sorts of questions.

"And didn't you copulate with one Reverend Fontaine in Leeds in your young days? When you knew full well he had a wife?"

Zelda eyes cowered now. They begged for mercy. She had tried to run from her past, yet she had not escaped it. Now it was obvious who Gloria was. No mistaking. She was the spitting image of Hortence Fontaine. 'What a small world?' Zelda asked herself. Now self-righteousness must go.

Gloria would see her from time to time on a Sunday morning. Dressed to the nines in her fine apparels, her frock-tails always swinging behind her as if trying to sweep her past away. Swinging, singing and humming like the branches of a willow tree: *'Swish, Swash, MyShitDon'tStink... Swish, Swash, MyShitDon'tStink... Swish, Swash... '*

Zelda turned away and disappeared somewhere down the hospital's corridor.

Gloria felt guilty. She was always taught to 'respect her elders', but at times she would question the 'limit' of 'respect'. She knew too that age doesn't always command respect. Still, she was only human. And had Zelda been as pleasant as the Barbadian woman, she would most certainly not have reacted like that. That was her mother's battle, not hers. An un-fought battle that perhaps should have stayed so. But days later when Gloria looked back and was true to herself, she admitted, *'It felt damn good'*.

After Lijah, Gloria text Ikesha. She would have been out celebrating with her friends the night before and would be sleeping late. Although she wasn't in the least maternal, she would be pleased. *'A New Year's baby boy! Menilek Negus Benjamin!'*

Texting wasn't Lijah's thing, but not long after, he returned one. *'Nice one Empress! Maybe this will have us reasoning again. A toast to being grandparents, my queen!'*

But Gloria didn't return one. *'How could he call me his queen '*, she thought, allowing all sorts of images to cloud her mind again. She wished it wouldn't be so on this special night, but she couldn't help it. She switched her mobile off and headed for Ward 10. There, she found Shari fast asleep and Kunta staring at her. Baby Menilek was being incubated. He had a touch of jaundice.

CHAPTER * NINE

Menilek's Christening Day was pulling with a nice, easy flow. Papa Dread eased pon de corner. A far corner of the marquee, enjoying his specially prepared vegetarian meal. Each to his own, but like several other things true Rastamen didn't do, he didn't eat meat. Sugar sipped on a glass of carrot juice, as he took in Papa Dread's reasoning. Of late, the talk was the black youths of Birmingham, and whether or not there was a gang culture. A strong and respected figure in the community, he always argued that the youths needed strong role models. He argued about the *virtual reality* culture of violence at the outset, where violence is disguised in games. Where at first hand, youths learned only to solve their differences and fight their wars by the use of weapons such as the gun.

"So who you t'ink is filtering guns onto the street for our yout' dem feh get hold of? Who yuh t'ink is filling the streets with crack, cocaine and all dem designer drugs shit? Tek Jamaica for instance. Jamaica manufacture guns? Dem manufacture cocaine? Crack? All dem shit? No... So how dem get into Jamaica?" He kissed his teeth. "We affi wise-up, Rasta. Of course we can't get to de root a de problem, but we cyan try to get to de minds of our yout' dem. They are our future."

Jaro shuffled his feet.

"Tek me for instance," Papa Dread continued. "Look how long I've been burning my lamb's bread an' it don' mess up my head. Yet de first time a yout' man put coke or crack in him body, he's headin' feh disasta! From dem legalise de herbs, clean up de streets of guns an' t'ing, give us back our youth clubs and mek we deal wid we youths, t'ings can work. There are certain things that should be made exceptions. But from what I can see, these evils seem to be rules to raas! I hear guns are being sold on the black-market for around two hundred pounds apiece or less. Not much more than a pair of designer footwear weh de kids are buying dese days. Every day is a gunshot an' anadda yout' drop. These things are like toys to our youths. If we don't do somet'ing, our yout' dem will have no future but de gun an' drugs culture an' de bone yard."

"Is long time me a show yuh dat," Reds gave a sincere aye.

Bunti nodded his head simultaneously, and Jaro hummed a mutual agreement. He wasn't his loud chirpy self today. As well as being under his sensi, he was well and truly under the weather. Some deep shit was troubling him. Apart from the fact that there was a famine and the man couldn't obtain any real lambs-bread, and Rock was crawling too much up his nose, everything was shit.

Papa Dread continued, "Nuff of our yout' dem nuh need nothing but simple direction. The schools fail dem, so dem drop out. An' when dem drop out there's nothing on the street for dem to do but get into badness. Tek nuff a dem yout' out there on the street. Nuff a dem don't have an academic bone in dem body. But dem good at art, music, creative t'ings. But once the system tell dem seh dem fail, dem don't even bother feh show dem true creative potential. Dem jus' feel seh dem is a true failure. So it's up to us as elders to help dem."

Lijah was drawn to the last part of Papa Dread's speech. He had been in deep conversation with Gloria for a while. He caught Jaro's eyes and penetrated them. A nonverbal conversation only they understood. Jaro shuffled. He felt out of place. His spine chilled and he felt he was loosing control. Only he knew how a small fish like Lijah could make him feel as if it was Judgement Day.

Kunta drew nearer, almost taking the words out of Papa Dread's mouth. He had always been one who managed to escape the pressures of his peers and stayed out of the constant mischief that surrounded the youngsters of Birmingham and the world over, for that matter. As he listened, he looked at his three-month-old baby and at his girlfriend Shari as she fed him breast milk, earlier pumped into a bottle.

Kunta turned his eyes in search of his mother and found her in deep conversation with his father. Of late, Kunta, unlike Ikesha, found himself wishing they would resolve their differences and make up. He had a dream that unlike his friends' parents, Lijah and Gloria would stay together, forever. He had even tried reasoning with Lijah, who found it hard, since Kunta didn't know half the story as to why they were really apart. Gloria too had chosen to spare her children the sordid details. As far as Kunta knew, and from what he gathered from unintentionally overhearing a conversation between his parents, the reason for them being apart lies solely with a mysterious blonde. Besides, Kunta and Ikesha would not forgive Lijah for the baby-sitter thing, so that was kept hush-hush - although they wondered about Faithlyn's sudden and mysterious disappearance, which Gloria was quite reluctant to talk about.

"How you doing, bro'?" Ikesha pulled Kunta from his thoughts. "How you enjoying being a dad?"

"Bwoy, Ikesha, nuff sleepless nights sis'. Mum said Menilek is jus' like I was as a baby. Cry-cry."

"How's Shari coping?"

"Ok. I think," Kunta said, looking unsure.

"You think! Kunta, you should *know*. You talk, don't you? She don't seem happy to me man. I hope you're doing your share with the baby."

Kunta held his head for a few seconds, as if his brain ached – a way of asking his sister to chill. She has been known for showing her concern in the form of a full-blown lecture. "Go talk to her, sis'. I think she must be having that post -natal depression t'ing. You are a woman."

"Kunta, I don't need you to tell me I'm a woman, but what do I know about no post-natal depression? Ask Mum to talk to her." Ikesha kept her eyes on Shari as she spoke, and could clearly see that something was wrong.

The marquee was buzzing with old friends of Lijah and Gloria. An old enemy of Lijah's hung close too. For years, Lijah had kept him at hand: an old advice from his father, *'keep your enemies close, it's a good way of watching there every move'*. Kunta's DJ friends and their girlfriends mingled like rivals amongst Ikesha's friends. Toddlers toddled around with no cares. On the surface, everything seemed to be everything.

"So where's my plate a curry-goat!" Sista Scorcha breezed in, wearing next to nothing. She was ready again for another session at The Hurricane and was killing two birds with one stone. Christening party or not, legs, batty cheeks and tits had to be outa door. The hot sista caught all eyes. All except Kunta's. He was on an investigative mission and carried on the conversation with his sister.

"What yuh t'ink Mum and Dad are talking about, Ikesha? It's a long time since they haven't spoken to each other for so long. Yuh t'ink they'll make up?"

"No way." Ikesha sounded sure. As if she knew something nobody else did.

"How you sound so sure, Ikesha?" Kunta perplexed.

"Mum's seeing somebody else," Ikesha said, matter-of-factly, then hurried over to one of her friends and where Scorcha was now exhibiting her new dancehall moves, fresh from yard. Some *'pon de riva, pon de bank'* business.

"Seeing somebody else?! Mum?! Ikesha!" Kunta was shocked. Ten times more shocked than when he had heard about his dad's little affair with another woman. What was good for the goose was never gonna be good for the gander. No way. Luckily the DJ dropped a heavy rhythm, drowning out his alarmed response.

Ikesha was well away, leaving her brother stunned. Now he stared at his parents with a difference, seeing his mother as an alien being. He was almost in a state of trance, but was alerted when Shari placed a screaming baby in his arms. "Take the baby, Kunta. I've burped him already."

The DJ dropped another sudden rhythm and baby Menilek jolted to attention, his little ears pricked up. It wouldn't be surprising if music were his first love. After all he had been hearing a mixture even before he popped out into the world. At Gloria and Lijah's it was reggae, at Kunta and Shari's it was rap, hip-hop, soul and garage and Ikesha's, a little bit of everything. But who knows, by the time he is of age, there might be a new breed of music.

Baby in arms, Kunta's emotions were being pulled left, right and centre. He watched Shari disappearing into the house and didn't need to ask if she was tripping on her post-natal imbalance again. "Oh shit," he stressed, wishing she would be fine on Menilek's Christening Day. Post-natal depression was one thing he didn't bargain for. He had seen the sleepless nights with his mother when she had Khamilla, his little sister. Nappies, colic and all the drawbacks that came with a new baby. But Shari's jangled hormones were certainly not bargained for. "Me should be havin' fun wid me frien's. Not dealin' wid no post-natal shit. No ragin' female hormones rubbish!"

And that wasn't all. Shari was finding it difficult to control her temper. Cooking utensils and other convenient objects have been known to sail past Kunta's head recently. No one knew, but they were both suffering in silence. Kunta felt he couldn't cope. Thought he needed some kind of remedy. An escapism maybe. Something.

"Yuh see what me mean! Hey! Come 'ere Fari!" Papa Dread's voice alerted everyone, tearing Kunta drastically away from his troubles. He was frantically beckoning the seven-year-old. Fari's long locks hid his sweet face, as he walked towards Papa Dread. The small boy looked surprised. "Is who gi' yuh dis t'ing?" Papa Dread reached towards a toy pistol Fari held in his hand.

"Daddy gave it to me." Now he looked frightened. Unsure. Perplexed at what all the fuss was about. He could see that Papa Dread wasn't smiling. He always smiled at him.

Kizzy and Festus were now looking towards their son and Papa Dread. Papa Dread beckoned them over.

"It's de same t'ing me jus' talkin' 'bout, Festus? Yuh don't need feh give de yout' nuh toy gun to play wid man. Look how real de t'ing look. There's other t'ings Fari can play wid!"

Kizzy looked at Festus, taken aback at the seriousness at which Papa

Dread was addressing the simple toy.

"Cho, Papa. It's only a toy man. It's not as if real bullets inna it or not'n." Festus tried to convince the old dread.

"Look, bredrin. Ovastan' me nuh. Me talking about the conditioning of our youth's minds. Yes, dis is a toy, but there are real ones on the streets looking jus like dis. Yuh don' want 'im get used to playing wid no toy gun! What next? Play-crack? Play-cocaine? Play heroin?"

"No, Papa. Yuh goin' too far now, man. A toy is a toy."

Papa Dread kissed his teeth as if to dismiss Festus' light look on a serious scenario.

Jaro got up and stepped sideways like a crab, heading towards the house. Kizzy shuddered just from the breeze of his passing. No one knew, but she hated him. From way back when. Everything about him made her hairs stood on end.

"Yuh a'right?" Festus asked her, as she tensed her body and an uneasy look came over her.

"Yes. I'm fine."

"Why yuh nuh like Jaro? Me notice seh every time 'im get near yuh, yuh cringe. Him do yuh sop'n?"

"No. Him jus' mek me uneasy."

"Still. Nuff people nuh like Jaro. I's like 'im have a bad spirit."

But Festus would never know how much his woman disliked Jaro. And she wasn't alone today. Oh no. She had company.

Papa Dread fixed his eyes on the back of Jaro's head as he walked away. He had sensed a grave uneasiness about Jaro, ever since he started talking about the negative gun and drug culture on the streets. He noticed how little contribution he had put into the conversation. They went back a long way, but now, more than ever, he was beginning to feel that Jaro was an impostor. A traitor. An enemy in the camp. Something just didn't feel right.

Many would condemn him. Tell him he was wrong about the herbs thing. Tell him that drugs is drugs, ganja or not. But to Papa Dread, selling likkle herbs was no crime at all. In fact he couldn't wait to see the day when they legalise it. That was his opinion and he was sticking to it. But this gun culture and the designer drugs that the youth are getting into are no good to anyone. Like he said, '*It will only escalate dis black-on-black violence everyone is talking about. Mash-up de yout' dem brain.*'

"Yuh not going are you, Jaro?" Reds called out, picking up on the same vibes that Papa Dread was.

"Nah, man," he said without looking back. "Me jus gone tek a leak. Look like me drink too much Red Stripe." Sweat oozed out of his forehead. Papa Dread kept his eyes on the back of his head until he disappeared into the house. Until he could prove otherwise, his mind would stay fixed on his suspicions.

"Listen, Festus," Papa Dread relented, "Yuh see dis gun t'ing? It's getting too strong among our yout' man dem. We used to use our fist to sort out our differences. Now an' then man an' man might use a knife. Ok, I'm not sayin' dat is right, but nowadays, it's a gun t'ing. Every man reachin' feh a piece a metal full up a lead. Check out Bingi Man dance las' week. De yout' weh get shoot up is me bredrin son. Even now it's grieving me, man. To de point where if I know who bring dat gun onto de street, I would deal wid him meself! De yout' dem was fighting ova a girl! Now you tell me... a girl! I man feel strong 'bout dis, rasta. It's a serious t'ing."

Papa Dread was always stern, but today he was angry with it. It was meant to be a happy occasion, and he didn't intend to spoil the day, but his mood was becoming contagious. Before long, almost everyone had gathered around him, listening to more of his concerns. It was clearly a labour of love. Mess with the youths, and you've messed with him.

"Oh no!" Kunta shouted. Something else fought for his attention. He had taken his eyes off Papa Dread to find that Menilek had puked all over his clothes. He shouted, Shari!" Then he remembered she had stormed off earlier in a mood. Gloria noticed and came to his rescue.

"Where's Shari?" she asked. But Kunta was only concerned with getting himself cleaned up. He let go of his baby into Gloria's arms and hurried into the house and towards the bathroom, passing Jaro sitting halfway up the stairs. He gave him a nod.

Kunta found Shari sitting on the edge of the bath holding her head. "Shari? What's de matta, man? Menilek sick-up. You didn't burp him properly." That was the least of the young girl's problem. Kunta didn't notice she was crying.

"Leave me alone!" she screamed. "Get out! I hate you!" A bottle of Dark an' Lovely conditioner flew across the bathroom, just missing Kunta's head.

Kunta tried to hold her, realising now how upset she really was. "Wha's wrong, Shari man?"

"I'm pregnant again, Kunta," she sobbed. "We can't even manage to look after Menilek. What we gonna do?"

"Pregnant again? How yuh mek dat happen, Shari? Why yuh neva tek de pill?"

That was all she needed. An array of fists landed simultaneously in Kunta's face, about his head and in his chest. Heels connected vengefully against his ankles. Nails scratched everywhere they could find purchase.

"Shari! Yuh crazy!" The confused young man pushed his girl against the wall and stormed out with a stinging face, a throbbing ankle and his designer garms still decorated with baby's sick. Tears welled in his eyes and he desperately searched his young mind for answers. He was just a child, trying to deal with a man's situation.

"Worries?" Jaro asked, catching him at an all-time low.

Kunta swept his hand across his face and removed showers of tears. He paused and penetrated Jaro's eyes. "I don't know what's wrong wid ar. Post-natal depression or somet'ing. An' she's pregnant again."

"A whole heap a t'ings wrong wid her den, yout'." A classic seeped in from the garden, rode up the stairs on which he sat, and clung to the walls around him: '*Wolves and Leopard are trying to kill the sheep and the shepherd'*. "Woman is worries yout'", Jaro continued. "Worries." And as he spoke, like a demonic Saviour, the brainless elder graced the young man's palm with *something*. No natural herbs, but an alien *something*. A pick-me-up? Lick-me-down? It would surely serve both purposes. For a while at least. The picking-up would send out a message of '*false niceness'*. The licking-down would make him wish he had listened to the rivers and the lakes he was used to. And if he was lucky enough to bounce back, his mother's tears might be ones of joy.

Seconds later, Kunta tripped on a fix of devil food, his nostrils allowing it entrance to his bloodstream. A sure road to hell.

CHAPTER * TEN

Gloria re-laid the long see-through bag, which held the faithful strands of locks in the bottom of her drawer. It seemed bizarre, but each time she contemplated getting rid of them proved harder than the time before. Lijah had despaired the day her mother took a pair of scissors to them. 'An evil act' he had called it, but Hortence stuck to her motive of 'being cruel to be kind'. Gloria had fallen ill with pneumonia and anaemia at the same time. She had already decided she wouldn't go back home, so her mother had travelled down from Leeds to look after her. But this private nursing care came with a crucial condition: the locks had to go. Her mother had come up with her own diagnosis, and decided that it was them that were making her ill. Claimed they were '*sucking her out'*.

"Why d'you keep them, G? Really," Kizzy asked, when she returned to Gloria's bedroom with a steaming cup of cerassie tea, and caught her friend staring reminiscently at the nostalgic relic.

"I don't really know. I just know I can't get rid of them. I enjoyed

growing them, K. I was in love. Would have done anything for Lijah
then. Anything. Grew horns if he had asked me to. Even when I knew
my parents were hurting like hell."

Kizzy sipped her cerassie tea and listened with interest.

"But I allowed my locks to be cut because of love too. Love for my
mum. So I suppose that's it: a symbol of love. That's the reason I can't
get rid of them. *Grown, cut and kept* out of love. You'd keep yours as
well, K. Not that you'd ever cut them."

"Irie. I suppose I would keep them." She looked at her dreads in the
mirror. "Can't imagine myself without dem though. They're too much a
part of me now."

But Kizzy's concern wasn't with locks just then. No one needed to tell
her that her friend was having another one of those painful days. They
come and go. Worse now since she had put Lijah out. She tried to change
the subject. "Did you enjoy last night, G?"

"It was ok. But you know parties aren't like they used to be," she
stressed, her depression filling every corner of the room. She was now
reflecting on Rialto – the night her and Kizzy met the two dreads.

"You're beginning to sound like an old woman," Kizzy told her
jokingly.

Gloria laughed. "I'm seriously thinking of going to live in Jamaica you
know, K," Gloria added, closing the drawer on her locks. "Mum's not
doing too good. She needs me. She's got a helper, but it's not the same. I
want to be with her."

"I thought your mum would want to come back to England."

"No. It's her wish to die there, K. In the country of her birth. I have to
respect that."

"Irie." But Kizzy knew there was more to Gloria's decision.

"You sure about dis, G? I mean living there for good. It's a whole new
way of life in Jamdown yunnuh girl. You know I would live there
tomorrow. I've been giving it a lot of thought. You know Mama Maya
have a beautiful house out dere an' t'ing. I personally love JA. But
rememba... t'ings different out deh. I know you've been visiting a lot
lately, but living there is a different t'ing. From what Mama Maya said,
you need a good income to live like you were in England."

"Everyone's got different views on Jamaica, K. I'm gonna give it a go.
If it doesn't work out, I'm a British citizen. I could always come back."

"An' yuh know the expectations of the men there are different from de
ones dem ova 'ere. They seem to think black English women are rich."

Gloria's mind washed over her lover. "That's just some of them, K.
You can't generalise like that." She was on the defence. "Some black

men in England dig for gold too."

Kizzy looked questioningly at her. There was a time when Gloria would agree without defending or ramming home a comparison.

"And anyway, I don't really give a shit about the expectations of nuh dyam man. Man is de las' t'ing on me min' right now."

Kizzy recognised that sting and knew not to dwell anymore on the subject of men.

"Gloria have you spoken to Lijah about the idea?"

"Lijah don't have no say in what I do or how I run my life anymore. I gave him the best years of it, K, and he did nothing but threw it up against the wall."

"Seen. But how will he feel about you taking Khamilla though? And what will you do with the house?"

"Yeah, well however he's gonna feel about me taking Khamilla will just be tough. She needs her mum and I'm not leaving her. But I suppose there's the issue with the house. He'll have to buy me out. If he can afford to buy a MRS Roadster Sport, he can afford to buy me out. Either that, or we'll sell." Her voice curdled with hurt.

"You know, it's funny... So many times I thought of leaving Festus, but every time I imagine us apart, it just doesn't feel right. I know he's no angel but..." Kizzy stared into space, reached into her inner depth and shook her head. "In fact, I still can't get my head 'round you and Lijah," she continued, "you two are made for each other. I still can't believe you're apart."

"Yeah. So I thought too. Made for each other. Being apart never crossed my mind." Gloria's eyes filled up, but she disguised it perfectly.

Now guilt surfaced again, but she was most certainly not gonna tell Kizzy about her mysterious SAAB lover. The guy she foolishly took back to the house to get back at Lijah. The guy she secretly sees from time to time and was slowly falling for. She knew that Kizzy had always analysed things before she made decisions. And that's without her views on throwing away a long-term relationship because of a few stupid mistakes a guy would make. Among other things, she had always said that Jah had put their brains where their dicks should be, so that's why they're always thinking with their dicks. In Festus' case, it was his fists. But Kizzy was riding on the theory rather than the practical. She hadn't experienced infidelity before. If Festus had ever done the dirty on her, he had certainly managed to keep it under wraps. Along with the pain of physical violence, the only other hurt she felt (the one that stayed at the back of her mind), was her idea of *rejection*. Until she could find her real mother, ask her why she gave her up for adoption, she wouldn't really settle. But she had already decided that if she found her, and if the reason or reasons were good, she would forgive her. She hoped she would find her some day.

"Really though, G... is your mother the real reason you're going to live in Jamaica? Or is it the fact that you're hurting and is running away? Sometime we run out of a frying pan an' straight into a fire, yunnuh."

"To tell yuh de trut', it's everyt'ing. A fresh start will do me good. I know Ikesha will be fine. She's sensible. At least she seems so. But Kunta and Shari? Mmm... I d'know. I'm still a bit worried about them. They have a young baby and Shari is pregnant again and I don't know how they'll manage."

"Shari's pregnant again?! But Menilek is just three months old!" Kizzy was shocked.

"Yeah. And the thing is, it's not like when Lijah and I were young, K. I feel we were much more mature. And it's not as if Shari's mum is around either. And Kunta... He lost his job the other day."

"Oh no!" Kizzy could feel her concerns.

"And health wise," Gloria continued, "I'm not too sure if he's ok. He doesn't seem himself, and try telling Kunta about going to the doctors.... But yes. He's my only concern. He's my baby, Kizzy. He might think he's a man, but he's a child at heart. I don't want him going off the rails. He's a good kid, but there are so much badness outa street dese days, it's so easy for the kids to get drawn into this easy-money culture. Young guys being used as drug mules, delivering drugs from one part a Birmingham to de next for a fee. I'm not saying Kunta is stupid, but with two kids to feed and no job. I just don't know. Lijah an I can only help so much."

"I know how you feel," Kizzy said.

"Shari loves him to bits but they just seem so young. An' you know it takes more than love to bring up a family. I don' wanna sound too much like an old woman, but I still don't think these youngsters have it, K."

"G, you won't be happy in JA with all this on yuh mind. Have another think about going to stay for good. I know you can't live yuh kids' life feh dem, but I think you need to stick around. You also need to be with your mum too, but I don't think you'll be settled living there permanently. Not right now anyway."

Kizzy knew exactly where Gloria was at. She knew she didn't want Kunta chasing any dangerous waterfalls. And that he would listen to the rivers and lakes he was used to. But life has a way of kicking kids' feet from under them, only for the parents to pick up the blame. Parents who have done their utmost best to do the most difficult job in the world. The only job that comes without any form of training whatsoever.

"I know. I'm torn between my son and my mother. They both need me."

"Not just them, G. Lijah and Ikesha too. You know Ikesha how she likes those long chats."

"Ikesha's cool. Anyway, you're her godmother. You're close. She's confided in you many times before. If she's got any problems, she'll come to you. I know it."

"And Lijah?"

Gloria kissed her teeth. "Yuh stay deh feelin' sorry feh Lijah." She switched quickly from Lijah and said, "I haven't mentioned any of this to any of them as yet. I'll wait a bit. I'll watch Kunta and Shari for a while and when I'm good and ready, I'll get them all together. Lijah too. We'll have a good talk at the dinner table. Besides, It'll have to be after Ikesha's graduation." Gloria turned away from Kizzy, trying to hide her tears. Only she knew how much Lijah had hurt her. Enough for her not to want to be in the same country as him – the biggest denial of all, since she still loved him to the bones.

"Good luck, G, whatever you decide." It was almost as if Kizzy had been defeated at trying to persuade her best friend to reconsider. "Thinking about it, I'm gonna need some good luck too. Finding a mother that gave you up thirty odd years ago isn't gonna be easy. So yuh si G, you've got your troubles, I've got mine."

Gloria turned now and looked at her sistren. She thought of her own dad, Pastor Fontaine who had passed on. And again of her mum, now sickly in Jamaica. Lijah's dad Lothan, now in Jamaica with a new wife. His mother Nettie who Lijah reckoned died the loneliest death anyone could ever die: a death that chipped away at Lijah like waves against an eroding rock. Waves he tried to fight, but they were much too strong. Even for a dread.

The sistas reached out and hugged each other, each one wishing the other happiness.

Now, Kizzy's eyes came to rest on a pile of A4 paper on the floor in a corner of the room. This burning novel Gloria had embarked upon used to be the topic of their conversation, but lately, talking about it had taken back-stage. The surprise Lijah had sprung on Gloria and Kizzy's preoccupation with finding her blood mother had taken precedence over everything.

'*A quiet place*', Gloria had thought. '*A quiet place in Jamaica. That's where I'll finish my novel*'.

"So yuh still nuh fin' no job yet, Festus?" Kizzy quizzed in the early hours of Friday morning. "I still think you should have found a job before giving up yuh present one."

Festus kissed his teeth and rolled over. "If I man did fin' a job, me wouldn't be in bed, would I? An' who gives a shit what yuh t'ink?"

"Are you looking though?" she relented, deliberately ignoring his slam.

"What's wid dis blood claat interrogation!" he snapped. "Yes! Me looking! But maybe not as hard as you looking feh yuh fuckin' madda!"

Kizzy was standing in front of the mirror at the time, trying to tuck a few strands of her locks under her wrap. It was 7:30am. Certainly no time for unexpected outbursts like that. Lately, something gave her strength. She couldn't explain it, but a fighting spirit seemed to have landed and was taking precedence over that old passive spirit that had locked her up for years.

She turned to Festus. "What did you say, Festus? Me neva know yuh feel a way 'bout me looking feh me blood madda?"

A long kiss-teet' came from under the duvet.

"Festus?!" She dragged the duvet off his head. *Whooo.* What had gotten into her? That was outright bravery. In their house, that just wasn't the done thing.

Festus raised his head and looked questioningly at her. She never did things like that. He was always the aggressive one. "Is weh yaah deal wid?! Yuh mad?"

"Are you against me looking for my blood mother? Jus' ansa me dat Festus... Your parents sadly died in a car crash, so I thought you would be more sympathetic..."

"Listen, Kizzy, gwaan a work. I'm not in any mood to argue right now. If yuh waan fine yuh madda, fine ar. Me jus' feel seh it wrong. If she wanted you in the firs' place, she would neva give yuh up, would she?"

"Festus? Why yuh so cold? We talk 'bout it before. I thought you were with me on this."

"Well, I have been having second thoughts. I t'ink yuh should leave it. Let sleeping dogs lie. What if yuh go open a nasty cyan of worms to raas? What if she didn't want to be found? De woman might be with a white man who knew nothing of her past. What if shi nuh want her husband to know she even slept wid a black man t'raas. I feel it's dangerous, Kizzy. Trus' me. Yuh diggin' up de past. I t'ink you should put all dem energy deh inna Fari. Not in tryin' to fin' some woman who dumped you in a children's home."

"Festus? Why yuh so heartless. An' don' tell me 'bout how much energy I should put into my Fari. My son is my life! You put more energy inna dat drunken tramp Montie, dan yuh put inna Fari. So don' gimme dat!"

He was puzzled at her retaliation. Her raised voice. Her fighting talk. "Cha. Nuh worry 'bout me, Kizzy. Jus' t'ink 'bout yuhself." He shoved the duvet aside, stormed out of the bed. Kizzy winced as she expected to feel the force of a fist or something. But instead, he headed for the bathroom. He bumped into his son on the landing. It was half an hour before Fari was due to be up, but he was awoken by the high-pitched feud and was walking towards his parents' bedroom, rubbing his eyes, his locks all over the place.

"Mum? Why you and Dad shouting again?" Fari was frightened. He knew what raised voices meant for his mother. A slap. A punch. A held neck. Anything that made his dad feel better. He hated it.

"Nothing, Son. It's ok now. Yuh dad is just a bit upset," Kizzy soothed him. "I'm going to work now. Get washed, have your breakfast and yuh dad will tek yuh to school."

"Where's my gun, Mum? Where did you put it? Can I have it?"

"No, Son. You heard what Papa Dread said the other day."

"Yeah but it's just a toy."

They heard the bathroom door open. "Go have a wash now Fari. See you later." She kissed him.

Fari left reluctantly and Festus re-entered the room. Kizzy picked up her bag and looked at him. He was certainly not himself but neither was she. Of late, expressing his idea of *who* ruled the roost had moved to another level. It frightened her, and she was preparing herself mentally and physically for it. Her sister Fiona's advice was beginning to lodge in her head. Festus was a coward. And like Papa Dread said, only a coward man beats women. She didn't know why she had only just thought of it, but she knew that if she dared to retaliate, he would probably crumble. She had tried for years to try to understand. Attribute his brutality to something psychological, but what was the use? How would it help her?

"Festus?" Kizzy asked when he returned to the bedroom, "what's really bothering you? Cos' I can't really believe you'd feel a way about me wanting to find my mother. Are you sure this hasn't got anything to do with what we talked about the other day? 'Bout yuh fed up of working? Don' wanna work 'till yuh sixty-five?"

He ignored her.

"Well, unless yuh win de lottery, dat's what yuh gonna have to do. Like everybody else," she said daringly.

He ignored her again, then said, "Pick me up a ten poun' draw lata? I'll pay you back." He spoke without looking at her.

"Where from? Yuh know dere's famine. Reds don't have not'n. And I'm not dealin' wid Jaro. I hear Jaro is dealin' wid nastiness. Much more dan de natural herbs."

This was not news to Festus. He already knew. He just didn't mention it to Kizzy.

"A'right. Len' me a tenna 'till lata. I'll get it."

"Jus' be careful, Festus. You could be in the wrong place at the wrong time. I'd rather you didn't go to Jaro. He's just getting greedy. Want more an' more all de time. He's dealin' shit. Before you know it, he starts dealin' it to kids. I neva did like Jaro."

"Yuh seem to have a lot of opinion lately. It looks like dis searchin' t'ing is getting' to yuh head. Anyway, aren't you like Jaro? You want more. Want yuh real madda. More dan Maya yuh adopted madda. Want more an' more all de time." That was clearly sarcasm, but Kizzy felt as if Festus was taking Jaro's side.

"How can you compare that with what I jus' said Festus? Look, somet'ing fresh going on in yuh head. Deal wid it. I'm going to work." She left the bedroom. "Bye Fari! See yuh lata!" She shouted over the sounds of splashing water.

"Bye, Mum!" a tired voice shouted back.

Festus listened to the sound of the closing door, threw his torso across the bed and sighed. Searched his own mind and asked himself a few questions. He had previously told himself, *'I'm not going back to that night work crap again'*. So there he was, thirty-eight with not a cent in the bank. No pension. The house and endowment policy belonged to Kizzy. Some re-mortgage shit he did a few years back to raise some money for a venture that failed. Presently, his share of the house was non-existent. He had nothing. A real pittance of a deal to show for his working life so far. Yes, he should have planned it better, but it was too late. But now he wouldn't dwell too long on it. He had a plan.

But Kizzy had been wondering what was really the matter with Festus of late. Of course he had always been violent. Always raging. But something was making him worse. And was it just that he was fed up of working? Or was it just plain old lazyitis?

"Dad! I'm ready!" Fari jolted Festus from his thoughts.

"Ok, Son. Me comin'. Yuh 'ave yuh breakfast?"

"Yes."

Festus pulled on a Nike top, wrapped an elastic band around his locks and reached for his car keys. But before he headed downstairs, he was pulled, through curiosity, towards the spare room. He lifted the base of the mattress and felt. "Safe," he mumbled as he patted the spot. His mind was satisfied.

"Come, Dad. I'll be late," said Fari, but only after he had stepped away from the door of the spare room, smiling. Now he knew where his dad had hidden his toy gun. He saw it. The black handle and the silver barrel were in clear view when his dad lifted the mattress. He loved his little toy gun. Later when his dad wasn't looking, he would sneak it out and play with his friends. Papa Dread would never know. And his dad would never know either, for he would put it back before he realised it was missing.

CHAPTER * ELEVEN

Gloria cooked dinner for her family. It was almost like a last farewell, as the stereo hummed in the background, cutting through the strange atmosphere that was beginning to creep in.

Lijah held Khamilla on one hip and his grandson Menilek on the other. A proud dad and granddad, but with a troubled mind. He knew what Gloria had called them there to say. He knew how she was with her telling songs, and knew she had only just begun.

The table was divine. Gloria dropped it like her mother Hortence used to. Way back when in Leeds. Before she met Lijah. Manish water for starters. Grilled plantains, fried dumplings, fritters, fried snappers garnished with onions and red peppers. Jerk chicken, rice an' peas, sexy juice and mounds of vegetables. The whole shebang.

Lijah watched her like a hawk. She looked fit. Obviously, she was still keeping up her visits to the gym. What could he do to convince her not to leave?

"Ok, it's ready!" Gloria shouted for the sake of Kunta and Shari. They were in the back garden, reasoning fervently about something ominous.

Ikesha placed a bookmark in Patrick Augustus' 'Baby Father', laid it on the coffee table and headed for the dining room. "We're like a proper family again," she said, with deep meaning, as she pulled out her chair, "this looks lovely, Mum."

"Yeah, but we're not, are we? We're not a propa family...we used to be," Kunta gave his opinion, "we're a dysfunctional family now."

The comment alerted everyone. Dysfunctional? It wasn't his style to use descriptions like that.

"No we're not, Kunta!" Gloria felt attacked. "What yuh mean by dat?" She stared questioningly at Kunta. It was the most he'd said to the family, in one sentence, for days. "And don't spoil the day. I spent a lot of time preparing this meal."

Lijah's eyes pierced Gloria's. Almost in affiliation. Gloria averted hers and rested them on Ikesha.

And as if by fate, the stereo cued:

I had to meet you here today, There's so many things to say
Please don't stop me till I'm through, I guess this is the thing to do...

Lijah's heart jabbed as she reached him again with those telling lyrics. It was almost as if she had lined up the tape just so. The irony was, she felt it too. A silent torture. Why do people do it to themselves?

Menilek cried and Shari fussed. She was now four months into her second pregnancy; only it was looking more like six.

Kunta looked spaced out. As if he needed a year's sleep. Lately, he didn't say much, so Gloria was shocked at his *'dysfunctional'* comment. He just sniffled a lot. Sniffle, sniffle, sniffle. As if he had a constant cold.

"Yuh a'right, Kunta?" Gloria asked.

"Yeah. I'm cool, Mum." He was surely on another planet.

"Yuh sure, son? Yuh look like yuh sick. Got a job yet?" Lijah knew more than what Gloria knew, but he wouldn't bother her with the problem. He figured it wasn't anything that a father-and-son-chat couldn't fix.

"Nah. Can't even live on what they give yuh on de dole. Pittance man. By the time you buy food and clothes feh de baby..." He kissed his teeth, as if life had failed him already.

"What about doing a few hours wid Papa Dread? He could teach you how to cut leather. How to stitch. It's not a bad trade, Kunta. If yuh want, I'll talk to him feh yuh. Papa Dread check feh yuh, yuh done know. He's yuh godfaada. You'll be ok until you find yuh feet. It won't be no big money, but it betta dan not'n. Top up yuh dole money." Lijah eased a jerked-chicken breast onto his plate.

"Talk to 'im den, Dad," Kunta murmured, half-caring, "see if he'll help me out."

"I will, Son. Plus 'im t'inking 'bout starting up dat yout' club in Moseley. You could help him. Yuh know w'at de yout' dem want."

Gloria passed the gravy to Lijah. Their fingers touched. Tangled. They both felt it. A sweet volt of electricity seeping to and from each other. Gloria stiffened up and pretended it didn't happen. Lijah looked at her. It was almost like making telepathic love. Virtual reality. Or something.

Spaced out or not, Kunta noticed. "Are you two gonna get back togedda? Look how long you've been togedda. Doesn't anybody stay togedda any more? All me friends parents split up, man. I thought my parents were different." He placed a snapper fish on a mound of rice an' peas. Inwardly he meditated on what Ikesha had said about his mum *'seeing somebody else'*. It didn't seem real. He felt let down. Weakened. Like an insecure branch, watching the roots of the tree he had sprouted from, dying. The root that he once drew his strength from. If that root was weakened, how could he stay strong enough to pass strength to Menilek and his unborn child? And if they were reared weak, without strong parental roots, then where will future generations be?

All eyes were now on Gloria and Lijah. Their eyes were on each other. No one answered. Kunta seemed somewhat agitated. His parents' *'getting back together'* seemed more important to him than they had thought. He was still a baby, having babies. He had frightened himself and needed help to deal with an unsure future, but he simply did not know how to convey his feelings, directly. *'How come my grandparents stayed together?'* he wondered. *'Didn't they have problems?'* But the disillusioned young man knew only of the half that was forever being told. Not about the half that was forever withheld.

"Well, Kunta," Gloria addressed her son, as if he was the only one sitting at the table. "I'm definitely going to live in Jamaica. Mum's not well. She's not asked me to come, but I know she needs me. She doesn't want to come back to England, so I'm going. But only when I'm sure you have settled, found a job an' can look after Shari an' de kids."

"And what about me?" Ikesha asked, smiling. But Gloria knew she was joking. Although she would miss her mum, she seemed like a born survivor. Gloria thought she would be fine. Kunta, however, was like his father. Under his hard exterior was a marsh mallow centre. He couldn't help it. Things bothered him. If he weren't in control, he could go to pieces. But Lijah had always had Gloria. A solid woman. Although she doubted whether Lijah would agree, since some men's idea of a *solid* woman is one who stayed even after she had caught him, or even heard of him, time and time again, humping pieces of skirts.

Gloria wasn't so sure Shari would be a solid rock on which her son would stand. After all, she herself was just a baby, having babies. A young girl whose mother had abandoned her. Left her to fend for herself, like a bird would, its fledgling: before it had learned to fly. A young girl who didn't even know who her father was.

"An' w'at about me?" Lijah asked sarcastically. "Notice I man don't count. An' what about Khamilla? Was my baby girl asked if she wanted to leave her dad?"

Khamilla sat staring, swinging her legs, as little girls do, and staring at her dad, as she had prior stared at everyone as they spoke. She was taking it all in. This could wait until after dinner, but Lijah couldn't help it. It was almost as if he was hoping Gloria wouldn't confirm his fears: that she was 'checking out'. He didn't want her to go. But even if she stayed, what would change? She would still be hard towards him. Besides, it was a catch-twenty-two situation. He had to deal with Lucy, the persistent blonde, once and for all. Her offerings were much too tempting to give up. Perhaps it would be better if Gloria goes. At least, for long enough for him to *collect*. He wasn't sure. Gloria could stay on the back burner for a bit, even though she would always be at the front of his mind. But there was a little consolation: she would be away from that mysterious SAAB driver.

"So unnuh gwine spoil me dinna? Can we eat firs', den we discuss dis?"

"I always t'ink a dinna table is de bes' place feh a family to discuss family mattas," Lijah said assertively, not letting up.

"But not if it's gonna get heated, Lijah. An' I can see this will. We'll choke," Gloria finished off cynically, filing Khamilla's plate.

"But yuh tekkin' Khamilla all de way to Jamaica, G. Me don't have nuh seh inna de matta?"

"Lijah... feh God's sake... mek we eat in peace nuh. Please. Without yuh sarcasm. I'm going to Jamaica whether yuh like it or not. An' yuh couldn't keep Khamilla anyway. She's a girl, she needs her mother. And anyway, I don't want her hanging around your women. Yuh *Bernadette*, or even dat w'ite girl yuh sleeping wid? An' who knows, yuh might even tek up wid dat Fait'lyn again," Gloria snapped.

Kunta, Ikesha and Shari looked at each other simultaneously.

Lines of perplexity formed around Khamilla's little eyes.

"Yeah, G. Gwaan. Yuh cyarry aan. Mek me look bad in front a de pickney dem. Why don't you tell dem 'bout de SAAB driva after you chucked me out? An' by de way, where did yuh tek him? Inna me bed?" He was fighting fire with fire and the heat from the furnace could be felt.

Mouths were opened every-which-way and Gloria could have stabbed his heart out.

"SAAB driva?" Kunta perked up, "SAAB driva?"

Gloria stared daggers at Lijah.

"Let's eat, man!" Ikesha took the upper hand, proving the solid rock of the family.

"A family that eats together stays together. That's what Gra'ma Fontaine used to say." Philosophical shit poured from Kunta's intoxicated head. "But it's not true, is it?" he continued, looking at his mum, then his dad as if he wanted an answer.

But they averted their eyes.

Shari looked at her man.

Disappointment came to roost in Kunta's already sick-looking eyes.

"Jerk chicken, anyone?" Ikesha tried to break the uncomfortable silence that followed, but it was hard.

They ate almost in silence. A loud palpable silence, with only sounds from Khamilla and Menilek's gurgling.

"Is it true, Mum?" Kunta asked, not long after dinner.

Gloria hoped it wouldn't come, but it had to. Funny, but they were standing in the same spot in the garden, where Lijah and Gloria stood talking, on Menilek's christening. Shari and Ikesha had volunteered to do the washing-up. Lijah was perched on the settee, looking out at his queen and his six-feet-tall son. Khamilla played with her nephew Menilek.

"Is *what* true, son? That a family that *eats* together *stays* together?" Gloria asked, as if she didn't know exactly what her son was talking about.

"No, not that. That you're seeing somebody else?"

"Kunta, You're ready to judge me now, right? How come yuh neva ask yuh dad about all his little escapades? Are you taking on that mentality that men can do what they want, and women should remain saints?"

"Nah, man, Mum, but *you*? You're my mum. How could you? Anadda man?... Did you bring him in the house like dad said? And in his bed?"

"Ok Kunta, that's enough! I'm not havin' dis! I'm yuh madda! Don't come talking to me as if I'm the child around here, yuh 'ear me? Yuh might have woman an' pickney, but I'm still yuh mum! It seem like it was only yestodeh, I was wipin' yuh ass!" Gloria paused and stared in through the patio glass at Lijah, who was hearing every word, scolded him with a cut-eye, then she turned, giving him her back. Kunta took her outburst as a *'Yes'. 'Yes, I've slept with someone else'.*

"Oh no, Mum... I can't see you an' Dad getting back now?"

"But you could see us getting back if I didn't sleep wid anadda man, Kunta?" She kissed her teeth. "Kunta, don't be such male chauvinist. What about what yuh dad did? What you're saying is dat it's a'right for your dad to do his nastiness and I forgive him, but it would be out of the question if it were the other way around. Kunta, I walked in on yuh dad and Faithlyn! In my living-room! On my settee!... And now he's living with Bernadette." She dropped her voice at the end, as if she was tired, "and seeing a white girl at the same time. So Kunta, don't think that the only reason me an' yuh dad won't get back, is because I did one thing. I wouldn't get back with him anyway."

Her words raced in through the slightly opened patio door and jabbed Lijah right where it hurt. "G," Gloria and Kunta turned quickly, and saw him there, "I'll buy you out. If that's what you want." He sounded like a wounded puppy. He knew she was too, but it looked as if things were irretrievable. Damaged beyond repair. "I'll talk to the bank an' sort sop'n out."

But there was a burning question in Kunta's eyes, and he had to voice it, "Fait'lyn? Yuh don't mean Fait'lyn de baby-sitta, do yuh?"

Lijah passed over his son's question and addressed Gloria again, "Jus' promise me one t'ing, G."

"And what's that, Lijah?"

"Jus' mek sure seh yuh nuh mek no man put dem han' on Khamilla. An' mek sure seh she don't call no adda man Daddy! Yuh 'ear me?!"

Kunta jumped, then he gathered himself. "You two need to talk. Propa. Yuh get me? Propa," he told them, walking briskly towards the house, letting them know he was giving them space. "Shari, come on. We're goin'." Shari and Ikesha soon caught on to what was going on. Kunta rounded up his family, bade his sisters goodbye and did an exodus. Ikesha took her little sister with her to give her parents even more space.

It wasn't long before Gloria and Lijah were alone. They both occupied patio-chairs, a good distance from each other, fighting against their bodies' desire. They had been talking for a long while, Lijah trying to make amends, Gloria repelling him, relentlessly. The lion roared. The Empress chanted. But to no avail.

Soon, they noticed a sharp chill, as the warm day turned suddenly into a chilly evening. They both retired inside. Lijah leant his back against the kitchen sink and Gloria sat at the dining table facing him, the stereo was still playing in the background.

If love's so nice
Tell him why it hurt so bad...

"Wha' yuh have feh drink, G? Sop'n strong... If it's not too much feh ask?" Lijah tried to make himself comfortable.

"Diamon' W'ite? Special Brew? Tennant?" Gloria asked.

"Mek me have a Tennant nuh?"

"Rememba, yuh drivin'," Gloria said, as she walked to the fridge.

"For a moment there, G, I thought you cared."

She kissed her teeth and returned with a Super T.

"So dis SAAB man... Is a serious t'ing, G?" Lijah asked, remembering that he was Gloria's first. The thought laid thick on his mind.

"What does it matter, Lijah? Serious or not, you and I are not together anymore."

His heart pricked with a dull ache.

"Yuh serious with any of your women?" she continued. "Your only concern right now should be that Khamilla might call another man Dad. An' that won't happen, so don't worry."

"That's not my only concern, G. How about the concern that anadda man is fucking my queen?" He jabbed his remark home, with his eyes fixed on her, then sipped his Tennant. His right leg shook. Agitation crept in and anger and frustration raised their ugly heads again.

Gloria knew what came with his anger. She could not get her breath around his snide remark. *'Who was he to talk?'* Gloria wondered.

"And you're not fucking anybody, Lijah? Listen," she kissed her teeth, "I can't stand this double-standard thing. One rule feh yuh an' one rule feh me." She was getting angry too, but she tried to control it. "Remember Lijah, *you* fucked up in the first place. Yes, *you*. Don't ever forget it." She poured herself a brandy, her back towards him.

"And remember, *you* chucked me out. None a dese women yuh keep mentioning means not'n to me, G. No other woman could ever come in here an' trouble yuh. Yuh a de wife. Yuh done know. It's just sex with other women. You are the only woman I eva mek love to. But you don't want him back, G. I'm a man. I have to relieve myself from time to time. Dat is one t'ing unnuh woman cyaan understan'. Unnuh chuck unnuh man out, an' expect dem feh stay celibate. How dat go? Bombo cl..."

"Don't gimme dat shit, Lijah! Yuh was relievin' yuhself wid adda women long before me chuck yuh out!"

He couldn't answer. The truth had got him good and proper. His leg shook as he leaned into his Tennant for rescue.

Gloria was crying inside. A deep silent cry. She stood, still with her back towards him as he spoke, trying to hide her tears.

And the most uncanny cue from her stereo. Gloria's song:
Take the ribbon from your hair, Shake it loose and let it fall
Lijah felt a heavy pang of something, and now, *déjà vu* smacked them both about the head.

Lay it soft against my skin, Like the shadows on the wall
He felt he had to hold her, so he shuffled, unsure, towards her, and did. Held her tight. It felt good. Oh my God, it felt good. Like the first shower of rain, after a drought.

But Gloria winced away, her emotions fighting with her pride – *'love yuh, hate yuh, love yuh, hate yuh...'*

He gripped her tight, turned her face and tasted her tears.
Come and lay down by my side, Till the early morning light
The ice around her heart began to melt and she lightened up. She
allowed him to spread his locks around her, for old times' sake. And now
she trembled as she allowed his warm, moist lips to caress hers,
devouring her tongue, like the first time. He paused and stared a non-
verbal question into her eyes. She looked away. Gently, he coupled her
face in his palms; spread them around her shoulders, and down her back.
Now he caressed her waist. Her breasts. Her firm ass. Kissed her neck.
She wanted him. Badly. But her pride forbade her wanting.
All I'm taking is your time, So help me make it through the night
Her juices flowed. He knew her too well, and reached now for her inner
thighs and remembered again, the first time. She was his queen.
"Oh, G... I missed you so much."
"No!" She pushed him away. "No Lijah! No!"
He stared bafflingly at the side of her face as she turned away from
him. "What is it, G? We love each other. Why yuh fightin' it?"
"Go! Go, Lijah! Please! Go!" She was in floods of tears.
"Ok.... Ok.... I'll go, G... If that's what you want... I'll go."
Perplexed, he put his palms up and stepped back slowly, as if to stave off
a fight, or even to show her he had given in.
He picked up his jacket and headed for the door, reaching into his
pocket for his keys, his mind puzzled.
Gloria didn't watch his back disappearing as she always did. Her eyes
were filled with tears and her mind with the vivid image of Lijah's ass,
moving busily between Faithlyn's young thighs. He was her Emperor
and she, his Empress. Infidelity wasn't in the game they decided on
playing.
As Lijah pulled away from the house, he noticed that infamous red
SAAB pulling into the spot he'd just pulled out of. With its dark tinted
windows, unless he hung around, he was never gonna get a glance of the
driver. He told himself that perhaps it was a good thing he didn't know
who his rival was. Every man has it in him to kill, but it wouldn't be
worth it.
'Dodgy', he thought as he pulled away, *'only people who had
something to hide, blacked out the windows of their rides'.*
After leaving Gloria's, Lijah didn't head straight home. He knew
Bernadette would be home, but he wanted to chill. Air his mind a bit. So
he drove up to Cannon Hill Park and settled his MRS Roadster Sports
into a parking spot in a far corner. He got thinking about Gloria – in fact,
she had never left his head: the way she rejected him earlier. And that

mysterious guy in the red SAAB that was, most probably, now kindling the fire that he had started. His belly churned. He picked up his mobile from the dash and dialled Gloria.

"Hello," Gloria answered in a sleepy voice. A sleepy, sex-filled voice.

"Hello, G',"

"Lijah. Hi. What is it?"

He paused. "I didn't get a chance to say it... Thanks for the dinner."

"Oh. It's ok." Her heart swung like a pendulum.

"More time, Yeah?"

"Bye, Lijah."

Oh Girl, his stereo mocked, *I'll be in trouble if you leave me now,*
        Cos I don' know where to look for love...

Lijah quickly ejected the tape before the damn thing devoured him emotionally.

Lijah must have dosed for a while, for when he woke up, it was 8pm. A couple in the car beside him was having a serious foreplay session. He pulled himself together, started his engine and headed for his rented abode.

"You look stressed, Lijah," Bernadette told him as he walked through the door. She had always allowed him to talk freely about anything, and tonight she would be all ears. He flopped in the settee and began to talk. She poured him a brandy, listened and soothed him with her usual massage. But today she was filled with questions, and it was almost as if he were on trial. Therapeutic trial.

"Would you say you were in-tune with Gloria before your break-up?" she asked.

He hated being put on the spot. "What d'you mean?" he asked.

"Well, I know you lived together for a long time, but how much time did you spend to find out what she really liked. I mean sexually, sensually and spiritually?"

Lijah was baffled. On the whole, now that Bernadette had put it like that, he knew little about his queen, and it showed.

"For instance, do you really know what turns her on?"

He chuckled. A way of throwing her off the scent of his *ignorance*.

"Would you know how or where to find her G-spot?" she relented, as she moulded his shoulder.

Finding his way back into Gloria's arms was gonna be a task. Taking up another, of finding G-spots, wasn't on his agenda. Besides, knowing what the hell a G-spot was, would help.

"Lijah, a woman's G-spot is half to two thirds in, on the front of the vagina. If pressed firmly with either the penis or the finger, it can trigger an erotic sensation." She massaged as she spoke.

"Yeah?" he said, half intrigued, half wondering if this woman was so obsessed with sex; she had devoted time to research the damn thing.

"Don't tell me your woman could have a wickedly healthy G-spot that she had not had the pleasure of enjoying? Still, Solomon was the wisest man, but even he didn't know the secret of a woman."

This woman is full of mystery', he thought. *'A force, it seemed, not to be reckoned with. And a force, nonetheless, driven by sex'.*

"Then again, she could not have one. Not all women have a G-spot. But like they say, 'No seek, no find'," she said cynically.

"Have you?" he asked, feeling good he could contribute to her one-sided spiel.

"You damn right. And I'm gonna show you how to find it. C'mon. Let's go take a shower."

The honest truth was, just then, Lijah would have preferred to find out what was going on in Gloria's head. All he could imagine was this guy's hands all over her.

"So, do us guys have the pleasure of having an equivalent of a G-spot?" he asked, to fill time as Bernadette led him upstairs.

"Don't tell me you don't know where a man's G-spot lies," she asked, matter-of-factly.

She saw the perplexity in his eyes and said, "Second thoughts, perhaps you wouldn't want to know... it's up your..."

"Enough, Bernadette! Enough... some things are just too disgusting for words." Lijah turned an ashy grey and sweat sprang quickly to his brows.

"Lijah? Are you ok? You look as if you've seen a ghost."

Bernadette hadn't the slightest clue, but she had taken him to that place in his mind where homophobic devils feared to tread. "Just talk about more pleasant t'ings, man."

They were now in the shower.

"Ok. Let's talk about... orgasms."

'Oh no', Lijah thought. Not that he didn't like talking about sex - after all, it was the whole reason for climbing those stairs and climbing into the shower.

"Can you remember your first orgasm?" she asked him as he rubbed soap over her body.

"Yes I can," he replied. I was just sixteen. The girl was eighteen. I was a friend of her brother's. Her mum was a nurse and worked nights. I can't remember how it really started, but I ended up in her bedroom, while her brother had her friend downstairs."

"I was thirteen," Bernadette told him, cutting him off as if she wasn't interested in the whole of his story.

"Thirteen!" he gasped, "that's sick. That guy should be done for child molesting."

"Oh no. It wasn't like that. It happened on the swing in my garden."

"What?"

"One minute my friend was pushing me, the next, I felt this jelly-like sensation around my pelvic area. Well, that was the only way I could explain it to the doctor. You see, I blacked clean out, giving my friend the fright of her life. Needless to say, I was rather embarrassed when the doctor told my mum that I had had an enormous orgasm."

As she spoke, Bernadette administered her infamous tactility, yet Lijah's mind was on Gloria. There he was with Bernadette, but his mind was on the other side of town. The thought of that other guy wouldn't leave his head. And why was she crying? Why did she lead him on, then blanked him at the penultimate moment?

"Wha'?" He came back to Bernadette's story. "You must be the only girl to experience that," he suggested. "No wonder you're so horny. You were born horny, I think."

She laughed out loud.

The telephone interrupted their little chat. Lijah noticed a strange familiarity in the tone of the voice that filled the answer phone, but it was hard to detect over the sprinkling sounds of the shower.

"Who's that?" he asked, flying slightly past his nest.

"A friend," she told him, a slight scolding in her tone.

Bernadette hadn't promised him anything, but somehow, Lijah couldn't help the streak of jealousy that crept up inside his head. It was most unexpected and he felt he was losing control. Now, he wanted to hold something that was his. He realised that he was tangling with a few women, but not one he could call his own. It didn't feel right. Gloria didn't want him back, Bernadette didn't want to be serious and he only wanted Lucy's money.

"Anyway," Bernadette continued, without the slightest clue to his concerns, "my second such orgasm was at sixteen. I was in a lift, and by that time, I didn't need anyone telling me what was happening. It was going down rather fast and I could not help expressing my pleasure in an ecstatic moan. The old lady next to me smiled, almost as if she understood what I had just experienced."

As her conversation got more intriguing, she captured his undivided attention. And now that jealousy was creeping in, he began to see her in a different light: more than just a casual thing.

"Who was he, really, Bernadette?"

"Who was *who*?" she asked, totally forgetting the phone call earlier.

"The guy on the phone." Anger surfaced, and he gripped her like a possession that was about to be stolen, forgetting his own strength.

"Lijah?" she must have felt his anger.

"I ask you, who the fuck is he?"

"Are you getting jealous?" she perplexed.

He ignored her verbally, but spoke to her through his might, lifting her left leg and resting it on the edge of the bath. Eagerly, he eased his manhood into her.

"Lijah?" she said again, still puzzled at his erotic anger.

"Is he fucking you?" he asked, ignoring her call.

"What?!" she gasped.

"I said! Is the guy on the telephone fucking you?!"

"Lijah, what is this?"

"Answer me, Bernadette!"

"That is none of your business," she groaned. "Don't you start getting possessive with me."

"Ansa me!"

She tensed her body and stared at him.

"I said, ansa me!" he shouted, as he fucked like a newly released prisoner.

"Yes! Yes! He is! He's fucking me real good, you bastard! So now what?!"

Suddenly, like he hated the SAAB driver. He hated the guy on the telephone. He hated Bernadette's past and Gloria's present, and wished he were the only one that had ever touched them. The need to be in control spread over him again. His rage was like madness and he could not control that either. 'What can I control?' he asked himself inwardly, as his heart raced. '*Shit*'. *I couldn't even control my father's emotionally killing my mother*'.

Anger gripped him.

"No... No... You're...You're..." Bernadette agonised.

But he had mistaken her pain for pleasure, until she shouted above the ripples of his thoughts, "Stop it! Stop it! You're hurting me! Stop it, you bastard!"

But he stopped only when he had burst his bank. It was too late and now, the feeling that he had violated her, pulled at his brain, causing to wonder, '*who*' or even '*what*' he had become.

But he knew one thing: he had fallen dangerously in love with

Bernadette. A dangerous, possessive love that was now threatening to devour his very soul. Now he was confused. Totally confused. Is it possible to love two people at the same time? What had suddenly leapt into his head, his body, his senses?

It was all eating him up now: confusion, frustration, obsession with money and now, this jealousy thing: one of the seven deadly sins. Was he bordering on the edge of Festus' problem? Whatever else he needed, he most certainly needed help. Feh real.

CHAPTER * TWELVE

Time had really flown by since Gloria left for Jamaica. Not that Lijah was having fun without her – he was missing her like crazy. He killed time the best he could. When he wasn't tangled with Lucy or Bernadette, he found himself cooling out at some dancehall session or other. Luckily, he nearly always had a free Saturday night.

Tonight it was *'History in the Making'*. He and his idrin Festus took a trip over to Bilston. Vibes Injection was his favourite sound, so it was their force that had brought him out. He settled for a cosy corner in the Million Dollar nightclub, taking in some of the most exclusive sound systems around. Saxon Studio from London was in the house. V-Rocket from Nottingham, Kebra Negus from Wolverhampton. Heavy or what?

Although the guys were oblivious to Lijah's presence, he was standing within yards of Birmingham's own, Vibes Injection's sound crew. Federal G, Rin-Tin-Tin, Skankie and the one Cyclone Quality were doing their thing: injecting nuff niceness inna de place. The vibe was wicked. Even Father Jarvis, Country Bwoy and Mr Chat 'Bout eased in looking as cool as ice, followed by DJ Clashington and Rankin Trustus. Lady Mutiny and Sandra Irie graced the place with their presence too. The hot chicks turned heads as they moved through the crowd: female connection of all times, there would be no Benny Hill Awards for those two dejaying divas. So the vintage collection of DJ's was in the house - oblivious to the happenings in the lives of the ravers they mingled with, they held their own corners, and rocked away.

Lijah touched fists and gave a warm welcome to an old friend. Conteh. Conteh Egyptian. Mr Vibes Injection himself. The original *Mr Soon Come* himself. Yes. The boy was back in town. Released from Her Majesty's grip. Standing there remembering how some woman he had messed with, called Mena, had set him up with a vengeance: planted evidence from a robbery in his shop and got him on the wrong side of the law. Revenge taken to its limit that was. *Evil bitch?* Or a *'good-on-you' switch?* Debatable.

"Whaap'n, Egyptian?" Lijah asked, not knowing the Supa was released. Bwoy, me glad feh see yuh, yunnuh, Star. Dat bird t'ing is no joke."

"Tell me about it, man. Still. Me glad to be here again. Yuh know seh music is me life. Cyaan do widout it. Inna me bones. It was maddening widout it inna dat place."

"So how come dem let yuh out so quick?"

"Bwoy, dem prove seh w'at me was sayin' in de firs' place was right. At de time, de security camera inna me shop was playing up. Me try show dem seh it was a woman who planted dem shit from dat robbery on me, but…"

"So dem prove it now?"

"Yeah, man. Me madda Gladys always used to seh, *'Only believe. All t'ings are possible'.* Me do nuff prayin' when I was inside, still. Nasty place. Nuff batty-man. One bwoy all try a t'ing pon me een deh. Me jus t'ump out 'im blood claat teet dem. A man affi kill me firs' before 'im do me dat, bredrin. Kill me. Serious."

Lijah cringed. Why must everyone remind him of that shit?

"Bwoy, praise Jah. Glad to know yuh deh 'bout," Lijah told him.

"Yes me frien'. Man de pon street again. Feh real," Conteh said in his ever-prevailing cool tone as he touched Lijah's fist.

"Live up, yeah?" Lijah said sincerely, eased into a nice corner.

Security was always tight. Propa. There was nothing like a sweet ital lick halfway through, or even during a mellow dancehall session, but Lijah had taken no chances. Before he had left his yard, he had soothed his head with a nice, mellow draw. That would set him up feh de night. With just the right amount of herbs in his head and music to keep him rocking, he was cruising. The woman he held onto could almost be called a mampie, but he liked it. She kept him warm – something to hold on to for that moment. She was in his arm, (or he in hers) his dick hard against her groin, and it went without saying, she had high hopes - but as always, it was Gloria that was on his mind.

Time flew by. Vibes Injection was mashing up de place, but Lijah had to make a move. He hadn't really had his fill of music, but he was unsettled and needed to be in the arms of someone. He was missing Gloria, Khamilla – his whole family. He was basically missing life the way it was, but it wouldn't be that easy to ease back, so tonight he needed a substitute. The mampie was out. He wasn't into too much working tonight. He had already touched fist with Festus, Bunti, and Sugar and gave Jaro a stiff nod. The foursome was in some deep reasoning. Reds was resting by a speaker box as if he was sizing up a situation.

As Lijah squeezed through the crowd towards the exit, someone gripped his fingers. It felt like more than just a simple *hello*. It was Novellette, a long time chick he used to check, when Gloria was still commuting to and from Leeds. The grip said *'me still like yuh'* but she was with her man, who was holding onto her from behind, without the slightest clue of this tactile gesture. So not'n couldn't gwaan desso.

Bernadette was on one of her London trips, so that was out too. Where would Lucy be? Things had been a bit heavy lately. Nuff things were going down. More than he could take. He had his family to think about. Ikesha was ok, but Kunta was beginning to be a worry, and what with Gloria taking Khamilla away, his mind was working overtime.

Lucy. Yeah. It was his only hope. He flicked her a text. It was only 3am. Early for her. If she wasn't entertaining Baby Face Glen, he could pop over. She had convinced him they were just friends, so she should know.

Lucy returned his text within seconds, giving him the ok, so he headed out to the country to her mansion.

As he drove down winding country lanes, he was lost in thoughts as he reflected on how it all started with Lucy:

The night-work t'ing was doing his head in. Couldn't do a whole stretch without a huge spliff. So here he was on his break, sitting in his car inhaling some ital, when the door handle clicked. Freaked out, he chucked the damn spliff out the window, thinking it was a Babylon. When he checked, it was a blonde from the tyre-testing section. Lucy. He knew, because he had always marvelled over how much she looked like Madonna. And she always wore a gold, personalised pendant, saying, *Lucy.*

The car park was secluded and for some reason, there was no security camera and no probe lighting: something that had puzzled Lijah, from the start. Like pay rises, these were things that were forever coming, but this was his second year at the plant and none of them had yet materialised. Still, he wasn't complaining. It gave him the privacy to spend his break with his own thoughts, being away from the huge slave-driving building with his ital stick.

Before he could ask her what her game was, Lucy was sitting in his car, skirt up, showing him more flesh than he cared to see just then.

A more subtle introduction would have been nice, but he soon realised he wasn't gonna have it. Her pum-pum was literally in his face and he needed to know what had got into her head, since it was already quite obvious what she wanted to get *inside* her.

That was the first time anything like that had ever happened to Lijah. Apart from Faithlyn the baby-sitter, he always did the approaching, so being approached like that freaked him out. He had heard about 'women's lib' and 'twenty-first century' shit, but that took the biscuit.

But anyway, here was Lucy, hugging the car seat where his woman Gloria always sat. The thought of what Gloria would say, knocked him out for a second.

"Hello," she said, practically giving it away. Well, the woman had what she thought was a skirt on beneath her overalls, but she didn't need to tell him she had no knickers on. "Do I need to say anything?" Her upper-class accent contrasted totally with any woman Lijah had ever met, let alone touched. "I'm sure you've read the signs, *Lijah.*" Seemed she liked the sound of his name on her tongue – the way she emphasised both syllables. "You know... with me giving you the eyes and all that. Ever since I first saw you..."

Cat must have got his tongue, because really and truly, he couldn't speak. The woman was all up in his face, playing with his locks, kissing his neck, and asking: "How d'you get your hair like this? I've always wanted so much to touch real locks. Believe me, it took a lot of courage," she panted, like a hot dog.

'*So what made you think that my locks would be easy access, like some 'try me' sample from the body shop?*' he thought to himself.

All this time, he stared at this woman, wondering if it was some kind of a dream, or even a set-up or something. What if she called rape? What was her game? *Really.*

She pulled down the zip on his overalls and his body froze.

"Lucy?" He didn't know where the word came from, since seconds before, cat had got him tongue. "Lucy?" he said it again. He was in a state of semi-shock. You see, now the head of his dick was pushing sweetly against the back of her throat.

"Yes, Lijah?" the woman asked casually, taking a second out.

"What the hell yuh doin'?"

"Come now, Lijah," she whispered, lifting her head again, "surely you would have worked it out by now." she patronised. "Complaining?" she asked, resuming seconds later, her job of oral pleasure.

"Well... er... yeah... er... no... er... Oh fuck!" he exclaimed in pleasure, as he relaxed into the taking. '*Bombo claat',* he thought, '*is dere anyt'ing sweeta dan dis shit?*' Though it would be embarrassing to admit, it was his first head! Gloria was a conscious sista who wouldn't entertain such a t'ing. And the women before? Well... It just didn't happen. That was considered a thing that devil women do.

Lucy worked his organ like a dream, and as he responded by running his fingers through her blonde hair, he thought of Gloria. Everything was in juxtaposition. Everything, including the way she worked his ring-ting-ting!

Then panic set in. *'Shit! Gloria! My queen! She'll kill me!'* he had thought.

"Lucy," he fought with his conscience.

She replied by moving her head faster and faster up and down his shaft.

Then, "Jah-hah-hah!" he shouted, as he burst his bank.

Seconds later, Lucy came up for air, pulling her hair off her forehead and giving him teeth. Lijah was speechless again. He wanted to search for the spliff he had thrown out the window earlier t'raas.

Lucy started to wind back Gloria's seat, speaking to him with her eyes. When the seat was to her desired setting, she lay there saying, "C'mon, Lijah. What are you waiting for?"

"Lucy, shouldn't there be some kind of conversation before…"

"Before you fuck me?"

"Do you always find it so easy to…"

"Are you gonna fuck me or not, Lijah?"

Her demanding tone aroused him, giving life to his wood. 'Shit', he thought. 'Protection!' There was none, so he pulled at the glove compartment and reached for some used cling-film, a now crumpled piece of plastic Gloria had wrapped his sandwiches in earlier. Well? What was he supposed to do? Ride bare-backed? What if Lucy did this with most of the night shift?

It was the best he could do. He wrapped Gloria's dick in the piece of cling-film and proceeded to cool the heat in Lucy. As she howled like Lassie, he knew he would be in trouble. This would simply be a starter. Game soup to raas. Stag juice an' t'ing. Surely, she would be back for more.

But as time went by, Lucy had proven more and more strange. But in a way, he thought they both held each other at ransom. Seemingly, she wanted his dick and he wanted her dosh. Before, he had always delighted in the chase. Now he was about to be chased. Feh real.

Lash for cash was fair dos from where he was standing.

So that was that: his first encounter with Lucy. And as he cruised down the narrow country lanes, he thought more of this dog-eat-dog world we all swim around in, like starved sharks, all hungry for different things.

When Lijah arrived at the mansion, Lucy was standing at the door waiting for him. This posh country residence stood in remoteness, looking like Amityville. As he pulled up, his headlights shone on her and through her thin silk baby-doll nightdress. She held her pure white tabby cat in her hand, stroking it with passion. It looked like a scene from a horror movie. Lucy was knickerless and her nipples protruded firmly and invitingly at him. He decided, *'tonight, she will do'*.

It had been a long time since Lijah slept so deeply. In the near dawn, he thought the voices he heard were in his dream. Lucy was in conversation with a male. A black male, with an uncut Jamaican accent. When he came to consciousness, he listened with intent, feeling rather vulnerable. She seemed to be having an argument with this guy about the fact that he was there!

"Calm down, Glen," Lucy was saying, trying to pacify the irate brotha.

Then Lijah realised it had to be *the* Baby Face Glen.

"Dis is a raas claat passa-passa, Lucy! Is yuh me come from Jamaica feh see. Now yuh have anadda man inna yuh bed! Is wha' kin' a bombo claat fuckries dat! A feel like jus' t'ump up yuh raas, an' den go upstairs an pop a gun unda 'im bombo claat!"

Lijah freaked. Then he heard footsteps. What was best for him to do? There he was, nude, unarmed with nowhere to hide, with an angry brotha on his tail. Why did Lucy let this guy in anyway? Why did she put him in a situation like that?

Before Lijah could get dressed, Baby Face was in the room, in a stinking mood, and in his face.

"Get dressed, Rasta an' ease out. Me wi' deal wid Lucy lata. Me affi protect my meal ticket. Me nuh business a bombo claat. Is she bring me 'ere."

Lijah hated the gun to his head. In fact, he needed to check his underwear. He was sure he had filled it. *Literally.* He didn't argue with Baby Face, and neither did Lucy.

As he eased his MRS Roadster Sports off Lucy's drive in the early hours of the morning, he couldn't help but noticing that the red SAAB that was parked there, look just like the one that was parked, from time to time, outside Gloria's house. It was almost as if red SAABs were beginning to haunt him.

Two weeks later, Baby Face was deported on some *'possession of a fire arms'* shit and some additional drug charge. Getting into details about it with Lucy wasn't on Lijah's agenda. Besides, she didn't know much more than the surface bit. So instead, he listened to her cooing apologetically, and pawing him all over. Yes. In normal circumstances, he would have told her to take a hike, but money talks. Loud too. Is wha' duh yuh?

Lijah was planning on moving wholly and solely back to his house, but first he needed to talk to Bernadette. Sometimes he would go to the house, lie across the bed in the dark and reminisce. But not tonight. Bernadette was due back from another one of her disappearing acts and he was waiting for her. Besides, he was still freaked from the Baby Face encounter and could do with her therapy.

It was Thursday and nearly a week since she left a note on the kitchen table, telling Lijah she was off to London for a while. It wasn't a note like one would leave a husband, a boyfriend, or even a lover. It was just a courtesy note. One you'd leave for a lodger. And however he felt about her, that was exactly what he must have been to Bernadette: sweet love-making or not.

'Was she with that guy on the telephone?' he asked himself. She had told him that this guy lived in London. And although in the shower she had told him that he was a lover, later she swore he was just a friend. What made her changed her tune? After all, she was a free woman. But of course, it was none of his business. She had promised him nothing but sexual healing.

Now he recalled the silence after the shower thing. Then the strange conversation the day after: *'Lijah'*, she had said, *"what was all that about last night? That wasn't lovemaking. That was practical rape. You were rough and selfish, and by the look of things you are becoming possessive. You are my lodger, and yes, a lover, but we have no hold on each other. In fact, I thought you were taking a trip to Jamaica to see if you could patch things up with Gloria? I think you're losing your true perspective, Lijah. You know I'm not one for dictating, but this thing with Lucy too – I know you're holding out for her money, but weigh up the situation. She's kept you dangling for a while now. If you want your family back, go after Gloria. Don't ever get sex or money confused with a substitute for real love. The Lucy thing is becoming stupid and you're reading more into what you and I have. We're just having fun. Never forget that'.*

And Lijah had stared at her, speechless, as more mystery oozed from her. He had always wanted to find out what exactly happened between Bernadette and Jacques, but by the look of things, she was never gonna be forthcoming. She was most definitely a completely different person from the one that left for France, years ago. However, *'Carefree'* was his first description opinion of her when her had first tangled with her on her return. But lately, *'ruthless'* seemed more appropriate. She had a game, but he couldn't put his finger on it. Luckily, although he had fallen deeply in love with her, she wasn't the only thing occupying his mind just then.

'Lijah, don't ever try to control me... Ever!' was her command that sealed her lecture that day.

The confrontation stayed vivid in his head.

He ripped the note and threw it in the bin. She was right. He just hated not being in control. As far as he could see, everyone around him was taking control of their own destiny, while he was pussyfooting around, fucking out his fears and his frustrations. The way he saw it, he had gone too far with the Lucy thing now, not to *collect* now. He was nearing the end of the road. It was then that he decided that he would soon have to take that trip to Jamaica. Talk to the old man. Look up Gloria and Khamilla. Dust down his head, so to speak.

CHAPTER * THIRTEEN

Papa Dread stood over Kunta, watching attentively as the youth tried carefully to cut a strip he had marked out for him, from the bail of leather. The order he was given for leather hats a month ago was due out in a week, so it made sense to utilise his godson. When Lijah had asked him to help Kunta out with a little earner, there was no hesitation. But after the first few minutes of being around him, Papa Dread didn't need telling that all wasn't well with the once bright young man.

"Everyt'ing cool, Kunta?" Papa Dread asked.

"Yeah Papa, everyt'ing cool," Kunta's hands shook and he was sniffling frantically, yet he didn't have a cold.

"Everyt'ing a'right wid yuh madda when you heard from her?" Papa Dread watched even closer with concern, as if it was his own son. After all, that's what godfathers are for. He remembered when Kunta was first born. Just a day old in fact. Gloria had placed the tiny bundle in his hand and it made him nervous. Like Ikesha before him, Kunta's cries used to keep him up, as his room was just across the corridor from Lijah and Gloria's.

Papa Dread regretted never having children of his own. Not that he couldn't, but although he never talked about it, he was deeply affected by the death of his queen, Norma. She died in childbirth. And his son, stillborn. It was him that asked Lijah to name his son Kunta. That was what he was planning on naming his son. He had never taken another woman serious, but respected the unity of the family, to the max.

Papa Dread was born with a nature to care. Everybody's children were his own. Sadly, his strong desire to protect them from harm was much stronger than his ability to do so - unless he was Superman of course. Guaranteed, if Papa Dread lost his temper or got aggravated, it would be over a yout' getting into trouble and giving Babylon a cause to handle them. Likewise, the unnecessary loss of a young life or anything stunting a youth's ability to progress. And if an adult who should know better would have a hand in it, he or she would know about it.

Back in the day, he ran one of the most successful youth clubs in Birmingham. But funding and other political shit had everything to do with everything, and soon, even that became another struggle.

"Yeah," Kunta replied, "Mum's fine. It's jus' Gra'ma Fontaine. She's really ill now."

"An' wha' bout yuh, Kunta? Really. Wha' 'bout yuh? You seem to have dat cold for a long time. Sniffing a lot. Tremblin' as well. Yuh tekkin' anyt'ing feh it?" Papa Dread was *'playing fool to ketch wise'*.

"Me don't have a cold."

"So how come yuh sniffing an' tremblin' soh?" Papa Dread fixed his eyes, more firmly on the youth.

Kunta kept his eyes on the strip of leather, knowing full well that Papa Dread had sussed him.

"Kunta, look pon me." For the first time Papa Dread had a chance to perform his godfather role.

Kunta pushed the strip of leather aside and looked at his godfather, frustration creeping in: the *'Leave me alone-I hate authority-Let me live my life as I please'* things were clogging his head.

Papa Dread looked him in the eyes. "Yuh messing wid any shit outa street, Kunta?"

Silence. Eyes averted.

"Kunta... yuh have a woman, a baby an' anadda chile on de way. Now is not de time to be getting spaced out on shit. What yuh t'ink will happen to yuh family when dem shit drugs mash up yuh head? Dem tings cause anxiety, Kunta. Paranoia. Tu'n yuh fool! Yuh see it on TV. Yuh know w'at it cyan duh. Why yuh waan touch dem cullu-cullu deh? Dem t'ings cause anxiety, Kunta. Paranoia. Tu'n yuh fool. Yuh eva see yuh dad touch dem t'ings deh? Yuh eva hear seh herbs mash up anybody's head?"

Silence. Agitation.

"A'right. Yuh not talking. Jus' tell me w'at yuh tekkin' an' where yuh get it from."

"I can't, Papa. I can't tell you."

"Yuh can't tell me?!... Kunta, yuh care more about de people dat is mashing up yuh brain dan yuh care 'bout yuhself an' yuh family?"

Silence. The *'get me out of here'* body language.

"What yuh tekkin', Kunta? Dis is a serious t'ing."

Silence.

"Me seh w'at yuh tekkin'?

Silence.

"Kunta, tell me sop'n. How yuh get mixed up in dem t'ings deh anyway? Lijah and Gloria are not bad parents. Dat is de firs' t'ing de media an' people who don't know will be saying when t'ings go wrong."

"It's..." Kunta attempted to spill his troubles, but Papa Dread's mobile interrupted the flow.

"Hol' on a minute, Kunta." He turned and faced the window as if he needed light to talk. Besides he didn't want Kunta to see the tears of frustration in his eyes.

"Whaap'n, Reds? T'ings cool? A'right. Listen, call me back lata, me 'ave a crisis pon me hands right now."

But when he turned, the crisis had turned into a calamity. Kunta had made a speedy exit, with Papa Dread only managing to catch a slight gust of his wind. The young man was in turmoil and conveniently breezed out. He was in torment.

"Kunta!" But Papa Dread may as well have been speaking to his shadow.

Papa Dread needed to get to the bottom of this. Seriously. In a way, Kunta was left in his care. Gloria was in Jamaica and although Lijah was around, he himself could do with assistance on the mentoring front. Papa Dread wasn't even sure if any of them had the slightest idea of what was going on, since Lijah had not mentioned anything untoward.

Papa Dread dialled Reds, who himself had lost his son in a mad shoot up years ago. The yout' had simply pulled with the wrong crowd, got caught up in some shit and consequently, he was used as a drugs mule, for the value of a few pounds, a quick fix and the promise of a fast motor. Now he was on a ghost train, ten feet under. It was no joke. "Whaap'n Reds?... Man cool?... Wha' yuh did want earlier?... Eeh heh? A'right... Dat cool. Anyway, bredrin, me waan yuh duh me a fava. Keep yuh ears to de groun' on a likkle matta feh me. Pass 'roun' lata nuh.... Yeah, man.... Cool." He clicked off, scratching his grey, patchy locks as he did when he was thinking. *'Wolves an' leopards are trying to kill the sheep and the shepherd'*, he hummed in an almost mournful tone, as he examined the bit of leather that Kunta was cutting earlier. Then he tuned into the pain in his big toe, which had become another bane in his life.

Buying Gloria's share and keeping the house was a good move for Lijah. Now that she was in Jamaica, and when Bernadette would do her disappearing act, and Lucy would grate on his brain, he would rest by himself in the bedroom Gloria and he once shared. Though the whole place had a cold emptiness about it, Lijah could recall certain moments. Good memorable times. But sometimes the bad times would creep up on him whether he liked it or not. Like the other night when he remembered how Gloria nearly had him cornered. Before the Faithlyn shit that was. He had sat running it through his head along with a stick of sensi and the voice of Father Jarvis on Sting FM:

"What the fuck is that on your neck?!" Gloria had said, looking at his neck, as if some demonic *'thing'* was clinging to it.

"What?!" He clammed up.

"Dat nastiness!" She pointed with disdain to the spot, poking it with her fierce fingernails. "Like some dyam vampire was sucking yuh blood or somet'ing!"

Then Lijah vaguely remembered Lucy doing some sucking serious thing on his neck the night before. Yes, vaguely. Well, his mind was filled with that little *'gift'* she so matter-of-factly offered when she got back from Jamaica, it made his contribution to her pleasure, bountiful.

In his recollection, he walked over to the mirror – getting as far as ever from Gloria, consciously protecting his head at the same time. Well, everyone knows that hell hath no fury like a woman scorned. And that night, Gloria was seriously scorned.

Lijah wanted to kill Lucy. *'Fuck!'* he thought when he saw the bruise on his neck, *'if she didn't draw blood, I'll cut my locks off to rahtid!'* He felt like some silly teenager with this purple-looking bruise on his neck. He was a big man and those things just didn't look right. What on earth was she thinking of? Surely she knew he had to go home to his queen?

"Oh, that?" he said, turning now to Gloria, "some idiot bwoy was messing around last night wid some bits a tyre. Tossing dem around like a fool, jus' because the supervisor wasn't around. A piece a de dyam t'ing caught me on me neck. Tell yuh de trut', I didn't even realise seh it bruise me so. Yuh wait 'till a ketch dat likkle w'ite bwoy tonight. Cho."

He in his thinking that he had convinced Gloria, he had let his guard down. To his surprise, she came at him with more fury than hell's fire and it was too late for him to defend himself. The mop broom she wheeled at his head connected with his right temple, and before he hit the floor, his head met the banister with brute force. She threw the mop on top of his body, picked up her bag and went to work, fuming.

By the look of things, Gloria could not have cared less if Lijah was dead. When she walked in that night, all she did was cut her eyes, and looked at him like something that had just crawled out from under a stone.

But Lijah had a plan. Things were getting real serious and it needed some drastic measures. Gloria had never been violent towards him, so he knew he had fuelled a serious fire. A call to his bredrin Festus was necessary. Festus agreed to back him up on the tyre-tossing thing and that evening he called and spoke to Gloria. Lijah sat listening to Gloria's side, and from her narrative, he could only assume what Festus might have been saying:

"Listen Festus," Gloria spoke with her hands as if Festus could see, "if you think I'm stupid, yuh an' yuh bredrin have anadda t'ing coming... Mmm... Mmm... An' it caused that mark on his Lijah's neck, Festus?... So you're telling me dat is not some nasty love bite on Lijah's neck?... Mmm... Mmm... Listen Festus, I'll tek yuh word for it. I don't know why, but I will. But bruised neck aside, there's something funny going on with Lijah. Even if *you* don't know it. I'm a woman Festus. Remember I've known this man for over twenty years... Mmm... Mmm... A'right Festus. More time."

That night, for the first time in months, Lijah rang in sick. Gloria showed a little remorse about the mop broom t'ing and he played into it and into Gloria's arms. That was still a bit surprising, as she had told Festus she was convinced there was still something funny going on with him. But it was almost as if she felt she owed him some affection for nearly killing him, so that night he held her again. It was like making love to a new woman.

After that, Gloria and Lijah made sweeter love than ever before and Lijah was beginning to be convinced that this 'extra affair' was really adding spice to his love life. But he would be lying if he said he wasn't counting the days to Lucy's return. He knew the old lady would turn in her grave, but money was doing something to his brain. And to him, it wasn't dirty money. It wasn't like robbing a bank, or stealing from the poor. Fact was, he felt he was working for his pay.

Yes, this little gift was haunting him in a big way.

In the meantime, seemingly, Gloria became her old self again. Of course she didn't give up her beauty regime, or her regular visits to the gym, but she cooked him yard food, groomed his locks, ironed his clothes and rubbed him down with cocoa butter after his bath. T'ings were sweet again, and he loved that. But still, Gloria watched. A good watchdog never sleeps.

But that was all Lijah did lately. Think. Wish. Reminisce about Gloria and the way they were.

He had come to the end of yet another shift. Sunday afternoons are quiet times anyway, but today seemed extra lonely. Kunta had not long left, and he spent the whole afternoon vegetating and feeling sorry for himself. Lucy was in his head again. All he could think of was the first time she told him about bringing Baby Face over from Jamaica. She didn't know jack about this guy. But Lijah's concerns were more about his 'territory', than any kind of sentiment towards Lucy's welfare.

That particular night stuck vividly in his head. When Gloria was around, he was foolish enough to give Lucy his mobile number. He made it his utmost duty to set the ringer on silent, whenever he was in his yard. From stories his idrins had told me, lonely lovers had no qualm about calling their men whenever the mood would take them.

A bredrin once told him that once in the middle of making love to his woman, a young t'ing he was touching, called his mobile, which was sitting at the head of the bed, nearer to his woman's head. It was when the phone rang that he remembered that he didn't turn it off. When his woman picked it up, which he didn't think she would, least of all, in the middle of their lovemaking, he froze and was turned right off from the look she gave him. He took the phone and listened. Well, let's say, his hard-on died. Immediately. The young girl was out with her mates and had had a bit too much to drink. All Marcus could hear was *'Marcus baby, I need to see you tonight. Twice a week is not enough. Are you coming to see me? ... I need you...'*

Marcus clicked the phone off, fuming, as he watched his woman ejecting his garms from the wardrobe. No explanation under the sun could help him. She chucked him clean out. And that was after kneading his dick tight. Like a wad of corn-meal dough!

'So yuh see, *Rasta*', Marcus had said in finishing off his little story, *'Mobile phones aren't always saviours'*.

So now, Lijah never underestimates the dangers of mobile phones, like he never underestimates their usefulness.

Anyway, one night, just over a month after Lucy left for Jamaica, he kissed Gloria, picked up his mobile and headed for the door. He noticed a *'3 missed calls'* message on his mobile. He checked and found the number was Lucy's. She had also left a message: *'Baby, me reach back'*, in a strange Jamaican accent. At first he didn't realise it was she. *'Call me as soon as yuh get dis message'*. Along with this new accent, he wondered what else she had acquired.

Somehow, he thought Lucy would have called from Jamaica at least once, but she didn't. Still, if he were in JA with his idrins, he probably wouldn't have time to call anyone.

Before he started his engine, he returned Lucy's call. She told him how much she loved Jamaica, the food, the beaches – in fact, there wasn't much about Jamaica that she didn't like. "Would live dere tomorrow Lijah," she assured him, in her imitated patio.

"Hey, w'at's wid dis new accent?" he asked her.

"I bet I could match you now, Lijah? Word for word."

"It would tek yuh more dan a month to even try. Anyway, when am I seeing you again?"

"Working tonight?" she asked.

"Yeah. I man have to work. We're not all as rich as you, Lucy," he mimicked the upper-class accent she was trying seemingly to discard.

"Listen, I'll come up and see you tonight. I'll be there before your break," she assured him.

Luckily, he was owed an extended break. Tonight he would need more time to talk to Lucy. There was only one thing on his mind, and he wanted to know how close he was to it. Yes, he had no doubt that the damn thing makes the world go 'round. Seriously. *Money*.

That night, Lijah leant back in his car, feeling somewhat apprehensive. Or was it nerves? He wasn't sure. It was the first time he would see Lucy after her trip to Jamaica. You could call it a bit of both; apprehension and nerves. Apprehensive, since Gloria and he were getting on so great for the past four weeks, and nerves, since anything could change with Lucy in four weeks. But he had nearly lost his woman over her, so he figured he might as well follow this tempting rainbow. With a bit of luck, there might be a big pot of gold at the end.

So there he was, waiting, sensi in his brain, when déjà vu: like the first time Lucy had pulled on his door handle, only this time, he saw her coming, though he could hardly recognise her, for the most golden tan she had acquired.

"Whaap'n?" Lucy asked.

It was strange and Lijah didn't like it. He didn't know why, but he just couldn't get used to it. He would rather Lucy stayed the way she was, with her upper-class tongue.

"New tongue?" he asked.

"Yeah, man. Babylon leave... Ras-ta-man alone," she sang in carefree patois, mimicking some advert she had seen on TV.

"Lucy, I see you're in high spirits."

"So would you, Lijah, if you'd just had de wickedest time of yuh life."

She was trying hard, but the mixture of the Queen's English and Jamaican patois just didn't go. Unlike other English girls Lijah had heard, it just didn't flow easily off Lucy's tongue.

"Get it right, Lucy," Lijah snapped, "or don't try at all." Something niggled him, and he couldn't help it.

"What's up with you? I hope you're not going to be miserable tonight," she said, reaching over to play with his locks and wasted no time fumbling his dick.

Lijah restrained her left hand like a heartfelt protest.

She stared puzzlingly at him. "What's the matter, Lijah? Didn't you miss me?" she asked. But there was mischief in her eyes. Undiluted mischief, and he could see it. He now felt sure she had met someone in JA.

"Did you have a good time, Lucy?" he asked, avoiding her question.

She paused and stared at him again, then she started: "Oh, Jamaica is so, absolutely beautiful. Puzzles me how anyone could leave such a beautiful Island for such a cold, boring country like England. Like I said, Lijah, I'd live there tomorrow..."

"So... did you give it away?" he asked, keeping his eyes on her.

"Give *what* away?"

"De pussy, what else?" He was stern.

Lucy paused, with questions in her eyes. "What right have you got to ask me that, Lijah? You've got Gloria. You should be asking her those questions, not me."

"I asked you, did you give it away?!"

"No," she said looking away, but then looking back at him again, as if she found a new game to play, "but I met this guy though. Baby Face Glen. Just a friend. Showed me around the Island like only a well-trained guide could. We did Ochi Rios, Nigril... the lot. We even went to Point Hill and Watermount in St Catherine. Two very humble places in the country.

"You went to Point Hill, St. Catherine?! That's where my old man is. Real *country*. Didn't think a toffee-nosed woman like you could manage dem parts?"

"Yeah. I managed. We had a Land Rover. It was very nice. Different from the tourist side of the country, but nice. Glen and I became real good friends. I think every tourist should have a good buddy, Lijah. And Baby Face Glen was just that. Said he wants to come over to England for a holiday. I think I'll send him an invitation letter. I figure I owe him. He really took time out for me."

He couldn't stop staring at Lucy. "You're not telling me you're gonna send this guy an invitation letter, Lucy."

"Why not? He's a friend?"

The first thing Lijah thought was, 'what else did this Baby Face Glen show her? His good buddy? And he imagined, the first thing the brotha would have thought when she saw Lucy, was, '*See boops deh! Me a go eat ar out!*'

For the first time, Lucy's seemingly naïvety struck him and he seriously wanted to protect her from Baby Face Glen. Even though he didn't know the brotha, something was fishy. If not Lucy, he had to protect his just deserves.

"Lucy, you can't just go away for four weeks, meet some guy and decide to bring him to England."

"Oh dear, Lijah. If I didn't know you, I'd say you were jealous."

Lijah kissed his teeth.

"Lijah. Look. Baby Face is a friend. He'll be good for me. Fresh from Jamaica. I want to learn more about black culture, and something tells me you don't approve of that. And in the long run, I want a proper relationship with a black guy. You know how you freaked out that time I told you how I felt about you. What we have will always be restricted. Gloria, remember? Your family and your commitment towards them. You could never really commit to me, could you? Eventually, me want to be comin' home to a black man." She flicked her hair and kissed his lips.

Lijah couldn't believe it. One month in Jamaica and Lucy was talking with *hot roast breadfruit* in her mouth, to raas. Something was seriously telling him that Baby Face Glen was much more than 'just a friend'.

"Lijah, have you ever driven one of those MRS Roadster Sports? I think you'd really like them. Baby Face was telling me how much he would love to drive one. Either that or a SAAB," she said, now in her upper-class tongue. It was laced with sarcasm. Lucy switched from patois to the Queen's English when it suited her. "I don't know whether to wait until he gets here to look, or to start now."

"Lucy, are you serious? Are you really gonna bring this guy up? Like I said, you don't even know him."

"I have spent more hours with Baby Face than I have with you, so who do you suppose I know best? 'Course, I'd like to know *you* better, but we both know it means commitment. And I couldn't ask you for that, could I, Lijah?"

"Are you gonna wear that word 'commitment' out, Lucy? How many times have you talked about that since you sat down?"

"Well, I'm right, aren't I? You are already committed. Four hundred thousand is a lot of money, Lijah. I could do with a good head to help me sort things out. Preferably a dread with a good head. You'd be grand, but if not, I'll have to settle for Baby Face. He seems…"

Lijah was puzzled. "So you're trying to tell me, you don't know any other *'good heads'* than some guy you bumped into a month ago in Jamaica, Lucy?"

"What's the matter, Lijah, don't you trust my judgement?"

He glanced at his watch and realised that he had already used up twenty minutes of his break, and all he heard from Lucy was *'Baby Face this, Baby Face that'*… He had another twenty minutes extension and was gonna use it, his way.

He could feel a slight anger erupting. "Listen Lucy, jus' ease up on dis Baby Face guy, yeah? At least feh now. All you did for the past twenty minutes was sang this guy's praises. I thought you missed me."

"You know I did." She took that as a cue and started fumbling his dick again.

As she touched him, Lijah kept getting flashes of this Baby Face guy crouching on his patch. Now the anger raced in like a tornado, making him horny. He took Lucy firm by her shoulders and pulled her close to him. He couldn't help it. He was losing himself. The night was hot and Lucy barely had any clothes on. Lijah was like a hungry dog – considering he wasn't really hungry. Gloria had seen to that earlier.

Now, he damned near swallowed Lucy's thin lips. He raged at her neck and her firm pink breasts. And when he entered her, he had forgotten his own strength.

"Lijah! Stop, you're hurting me!"

But he ignored her, pinning her down like a beast-man would a criminal, and now she was gasping for breath.

"Fuck dis Baby Face guy! *I* need a fucking MRS Roadster Sports and everything else you may be planning on giving him!"

And now, in a fit of anger and rage, Lijah burst his bank.

Lucy laid there, still, the sweat from his forehead, dripping into her blonde hair. He eased up, adjusted himself and relaxed into his seat, wondering what he had become. Who was he? What was overtaking his head? What was turning him into a madman, almost a rapist? But the answer didn't take long to come back – *Money: the root of some evil.* And it was there and then, that Lijah denounced his rastaman status. He was not worthy of it. No. Not in the least.

And later, much later, his denunciation would make more sense. This moment was simply the tip of a huge iceberg.

"You've got it Lucy," he told her, in an almost beaten voice.

"Got what?" Lucy asked in her Delilah's voice.

"Commitment. You want commitment don't you?"

She stared at him, speechless.

"Well, you've got it."

"But what about Glo...?"

"I said!... you've got it! Is there any fucking pleasing you?!"

"Lijah," she said, pulling on his locks, as if she was petting her cat, "I love you."

Shit. Who told her to say that? Her words did something to him and he suddenly lost it. "Fix up yuhself gyal, an' cum outa me cyar! Now!" Lijah was one confused brotha.

Lucy was startled. She most certainly didn't expect that. She turned and looked at him, perplexed.

"What is it, Lijah?"

He kissed his teeth. If she could only read my thoughts: *'Gloria loves me and I love her, so don't come wid dat shit. 'Bout yuh love me. Don't love me, love my dick. As of now, it's the key to your daddy's Will'.*

"Ok Lucy, I have to go back to work now," he said, leaving his soul on a *'tick'*, remembering his mother's words:

'The man that chases silver and gold,

Shall lose his soul,

And fade away'...

And he had known too, that it would not only be Nettie that would turn in her grave, but Haile Selassie would too.

Lijah's next encounter with Lucy wasn't a pleasant one, since it goes without saying that the *last* one was far from great. That night, she couldn't understand his coldness and walked away sheepishly, leaving Lijah wondering if some women confused a good, sweet screw with love.

Well anyway, here we were again, *'diet fuck break'*, her giving him some coy attitude shit.

"What's up, Lucy?" he asked, as if he didn't know.

"I should be asking you that, Lijah. Your attitude last time, telling me to get out your car like that. You treated me like a piece of shit or something. I see you enjoy rejecting people. I wonder if things like that are hereditary. You know... like looks. Or certain illnesses? What do you think, Lijah?"

"Lucy, I don't know what yuh talking about, but the other night you told him you loved me. I'm sorry, but it's not in the equation, girl. Accept that."

"But you told me I have commitment, Lijah."

"That's different, Lucy. Totally different."

"So what do you suggest I do now, take my heart out and wash it? I've fallen in love with you, and you or I can't change that."

She looked at him with her big blue eyes, pouted her thin, pink lips, then reached for his dick. This woman was pressing some buttons, yet Lijah had nothing for her but a hard dick.

As if she had planned her strategy, she lifted her head, cheating him of the ultimate pleasure, flashed her long blonde hair and said, "My mother has sorted out my share of Daddy's Will. I won't be here much longer." It still puzzled him why she was there in the first place anyway. Regardless. When he had first seen Lucy, she seemed more like a spy sent to secretly scrutinise the work force, rather than someone who was employed in the plant.

But it hit him. Shit. It was as if, along with the great heads she gave, he was about to loose his hard earned legacy too! No fucking way. Tonight Lucy would get it real sweet – and with one bag a lies.

He squeezed her right, held her tight, and gave her all he had.

"I would never ask you to leave your woman Lijah," she panted. "I'll just have to find myself another big... black... sexy rastaman to share daddy's money with... or of course... Baby Face Glen." Her toffee-nosed accent was almost mocking.

Again, he felt that surging sense of loss as never before. A rush of stupidity filled his head, and money made him utter total rubbish. "I love you, Lucy. You know that babes." Now it felt as if his soul was totally sold. Sold on a promise.

"You do?" she sighed, flashing her lashes like Falene in Bambi.

"Yes," he said, rocking her with brute force. A force she relished.

"Yes! Yes! Yes!" she screamed.

Naturally, the woman was a nymphomaniac. Seriously. But he was simply working for his pay. Yet there was no certainty of getting this cash. And how could he demand it? Did this make him a male-prostitute? 'After all', he thought, 'prostitution is simply *a favour for a favour*'. What the hell has really gotten into me? Gloria would have a field day. She had already called me a *'Fallen Rasta'*. Questions flooded his head and he felt like shit. His father's words rushed in: *'a man dat stretch out 'im han' an' tek money from a woman is no man at all'*. Yet, something was holding Lijah. Grasping him in fact. Why couldn't he just walk away? Lucy was a meal ticket and he wanted it badly. Her money could do wonders for him, and it wasn't as if she wasn't getting what she wanted. He told himself that it was ok, but a strange anger did not elude him. It erupted in him again and as he entered her again, more strange new thoughts entered his head, with Lucy's agonising moans acting as a backdrop for them.

CHAPTER * FOURTEEN

Of all the other things on his mind, the thought that dominated Lijah's head was the first time he had noticed Gloria's deliberate *'dissing'*, which, whenever he would think about it, Lucy would always come into it.

As he recalled, he had arrived home from work one morning and noticed that Gloria was already up, dressed and sat reading The Voice newspaper. She hadn't waited in bed for him like she always did. Said she suspected he was sleeping with someone else, and that she was convinced that when he claimed he was doing the nightshift, he was in someone's bed, and that it wouldn't be long before she proved her suspicion right.

To convince her she was wrong, Lijah showed her his payslips. "How d'you work this out then, G? If I was doin' de dirty on yuh, babes, and not really working, how come me get full pay?"

Gloria scanned the payslips, satisfied herself that he had been putting in the hours, but she threw them down on the table in defiance, letting him know that regardless, her intuitions were right about his infidelity. He was simply guilty until proven innocent. And now, he would do his utmost endeavour to convince her otherwise.

'The original black woman' Lijah's friends used to call Gloria. *'A woman who knows just how to look after her man'*. Gloria was simply *born domesticated*, with housework being more of a therapy than a chore. If Lijah came home once and found a bit of dust had settled anywhere, guaranteed, Gloria would not be feeling well. If a pillowcase were left un-ironed, it would bug her. She would cook him, Kunta, Ikesha and Khamilla fresh food every day. And when the time was right, she would wash, dry and pamper his locks as if he were a newborn baby. As far as Lijah could see, the most time Gloria spent for herself was whenever she had the urge to write. When she did, she would spend hours on some imaginary stuff that was going on in her head. Stuff she never showed to anyone, except, occasionally, Kizzy. Mostly, she had kept her work secretly to herself, until one day Lijah stumbled upon a manuscript she had hidden at the bottom of the wardrobe. That was the first time he had come to realise that he was living with a serious writer. Gloria was seriously talented, but she went wild when he mentioned that he had seen her work. She freaked out. It was as if he had caught her

masturbating or something.

"Gloria, this is good stuff. What good is it in the wardrobe? Why don't you send it off to some publishers?" But Gloria simply folded it to her chest as if she was trying to hide an open shame. But that was another matter.

So she continued to diss him, big time. Pum-pum privilege seemingly, gone for good. The more he denied infidelity, the more she called him a liar. He would finish a nightshift, sleep all day, and wake with a hard-on, with no hope of getting anything from Gloria. Consequently, it became harder to refuse Lucy, so he would accept her offerings. But Lucy would not be spared his anger. He was angry with her for being the cause of Gloria's upset with him. Still, the fault wasn't entirely hers, since he could have refused, but it was on a plate. With dividends too! And which man would refuse that? Besides, he had convinced himself that he had come too near to a small fortune, to turn back now. He just couldn't wait for the time when Lucy would *free up* the dosh.

Deep down, Lijah felt sure that Gloria would never leave him. Lost in the confidence that love was locked too tight. He also felt she wasn't an irrational person and wouldn't do anything drastic. Not without concrete evidence, anyway. But from what he could see, she had found a new passion. She had taken up permanent residence at the local gym, and whatever miracle diet she was on, it was working like magic. It was as if she was on some kind of a mission, and her first task was to get fit.

One morning, through pure accident, he caught a glimpse of her in a black leotard; as she was getting ready to go to yet another keep fit class. The truth was, he damn near committed rape - something that is most certainly not in him. He had never taken what was not given to him. Seriously though, Gloria's waistline was creeping back like a victorious hide-and-seek winner. Her hips looked as if she had had some suction business going on. Her hair was cut into some cheek, sexy style and her skin was as pretty as an African princess'. Her dimples, that were once lost with her waistline, were visible again. Her face had taken its old chiselled shape, and she walked about the house with a difference Lijah could not comprehend. He felt she was up to something all right, but nothing serious enough to really leave him.

Yes, that morning he almost committed rape, but instead, his dick bulged in protest against a serious urge. And in trying to break hard ice, he sang, in jest: '*Tings a gwaan feh yuh, honey!*'

But Gloria simply cut her eyes scornfully at him and carried on packing her gym bag.

"Gloria, mek we talk nuh," he stressed, "ho' yuh jus' a diss me suh?"

She ignored him, picked up her gym bag, mumbled something abusive and hurried down the stairs, leaving Lijah confused as to what to think. It was clear that she was becoming a different person and her assertiveness worried him somewhat. Not that being assertive is negative, but something told him he had better brace himself for a storm. A storm that he had summoned himself. Still, he would stand his ground. She had no proof of his affair and he would stick by his story. But not without due care and attention.

In all this, Lucy didn't help, and the stronger Gloria's dissing became, the more Lijah reflected on Lucy's ultimatum. He didn't want to rush things, but this rich English rose was rushing him some ways. Her words were, '*Lijah, if you're not prepared to move in with me after I've renovated the house just how I want it, I will seriously have to think about getting to know Baby Face Glen better. You and I could always remain friends.*'

Lijah hated ultimatums and besides, there was no room for any. He simply couldn't move in with her.

The situation was getting sticky, and again, Papa Dread and the old man's words were haunting him like hell: '*Woman an' money is de root of all evil*', they had said. And like a test, he had them both, wrapped up it seemed, in one package.

He thought of how hard it would be to lose Gloria, the love of a lifetime, but likewise, it wouldn't be easy to give up the chance of a lifetime. The thought though, of how he'd explain to Gloria about his little fortune would be another hurdle. But, where there was a will, there'd be a way.

Lijah weighed up the choice over and over in his head. Love or money. Love or money. Shit. He juggled the damn things around in his head so much, it damned near sent him crazy. He felt he was a bastard to even contemplate a comparison, but it would take a wickedly strong man to give up a MRS Roadster and nuff dollars. '*Money an' material t'ings isn't everyt'ing*', his old man's voice challenged him again.

That morning, in his recollection, Lucy's voice ricocheted against the surface of his brain like an echo. "Let's drive over to the country to see the house," she had causally said one day when he promised to meet her for a secret rendezvous, in broad daylight, one Sunday afternoon. That was when the subtle ultimatum blurted into his head like a misfired archery arrow. "The workmen are there right now," she told him, "I'm paying them well, so they don't mind working on Sundays. They sometimes do the nightshift too."

Nightshift. Such a painful word for Lijah of late. The fact was, he minded doing the nightshift. He was sick of it. To him, it was nothing to do with not being a man or anything like that, but like he had always said, there had to be more to life than working his fingers to the bone, well into retirement, and as soon as the time would come for him to enjoy the fruits of his toil, arthritis, diabetes, blood pressure, heart attack or some cheating illness would kick him down, trample on his sorry ass and laugh in his face. *Damn.*

Lucy's mansion was a far cry from the humble Edgbaston abode he shared with his queen, and an even farther cry from the serenity of the front seat of his car, in a secluded car park, with a stick of sensi.

She had held his hand firmly, as they waded through a host of red-faced workmen in white overalls, countless cans of paint and as many questioning eyes. He tried to find an end to the ceiling with his eyes, but it was like climbing Everest. The stairs were never-ending - he imagined, like the ones the ghosts of noble Englishmen climbed, in ancient times.

"Let's go see our bedroom, Lijah," Lucy said, pulling him up an everlasting staircase. But like the time she had used the *'love'* word, one word hit a surge of *'fear'* home to him. *'Our'.* As far as he could remember, he couldn't recall saying yes to Lucy's little *'moving in'* idea, but he assumed she must have taken the word *'commitment'* for yes.

As he climbed the stairs, Lijah thought of Gloria at home; perhaps at that moment, sitting, relaxing in *'their'* bedroom. He knew that if she could see him then, she would die of a brain eruption, or even commit murder.

He must have thought long, for without remembering the remainder of the journey there, he found himself standing in a room so huge, *'cosy'* was hard to imagine.

"Do you like chandeliers?" Lucy asked, looking up at the skied ceiling.

He thought of his mediocre, but adequate lampshade from Argos and said, "Yeah, yeah," trying to sound enthusiastic, "love them."

"Daddy's ghost won't recognise this place when I'm done," she said, swirling like a ballerina. "Lijah, we will be really happy here." She cuddled up to him and smothered him with a big kiss. But, for the first time since meeting Lucy, Lijah felt trapped. Shit. The woman was making plans. Big plans! And it felt as if he couldn't back out. But perhaps *'didn't want to'* were the operative words: not for the want of Lucy, but for early retirement.

But something just didn't feel right. Maybe it was the vastness of the room. Or the fact that there was no bed, no adjustable car seat, and no curtains. Just a vast stretch of floorboards, covered at its corners by dustsheets.

And now, in the middle of this huge open room, Lucy attacked the buttons on the shirt Gloria had bought him for Christmas, opening them with speed. The sound of the workmen marinating with her heavy breathing, gave Lijah a confused, unsafe feeling. He wanted a place to be private. A cornered wall. A curtained room. Something. He stood motionless, as Lucy (uncaring or unconcerned about the fact that they were not totally alone in the house) helped herself to his inside 'foot'.

Rolling his weapon out from his Calvin Klein underwear like a thick, sturdy black pudding she had needed to curve her hunger, she engulfed him. Now he needed a corner desperately, but Lucy (who seemed to enjoy spacious naughtiness) had him firmly in her grip. In the cold light of that strange Sunday afternoon, it felt different. Strange. Incomparable. Even weird.

He thought of Gloria again. He was reminded how much he loved her and became angry at the whole situation. Yes, anger crept in and took a hold of him. As always, it made him horny, though he couldn't be sure of the order of its appearance - before or after the guilt. Anger, guilt, horny? Or guilt, anger, horny?

Mercilessly, he grabbed Lucy by her hair, plucked her up from the floor like a lion seizing its prey, and headed for the nearest corner he longed for. It seemed Lucy had become susceptible to his anger. As if it turned her on. She smiled cunningly, as he pushed her, face-up and spread-eagled against the wall, like a mean police officer.

The skirt she wore was similar to the one she wore on their first encounter: hardly anything to it. And she was knickerless too! Her strapless boob-tube type top was easy. He covered her back with his stout body and grasped her left breast with his left hand. Now, in his own troubled silence, he helped his angry, hungry weapon inside her hungry woman. He had no mercy on her. The Irish moss and Guinness punch Gloria had fed him for years, were talking, and Lucy was answering loud and clear.

"Lucy! Are you alright?" A burly, blonde workman rushed to her rescue. Her agonising yells must have told him she needed help, but instead, he was confronted by the rigorous movement of Lijah's firm black ass, and the thankful *Yes! Yes! Yes!* from Lucy. Without stopping, Lijah stared his voyeur in the eyes. Strangely enough, the guy stood there, looking, as if he needed to be convinced that he was seeing right. Or even stranger, as if he wanted to join in, but with an interest for Lijah, rather than Lucy. It chilled Lijah. To the bones.

For a second or two, their eyes locked: Lijah looking a scolding 'piss off now' look into his, and he, an inexplicable one into Lijah's.

All Lijah knew, was that this guy looked familiar. Very familiar. A familiarity that made him angry. He didn't let up on Lucy, who herself didn't give a damn about this guy's presence.

After what seemed like much too long, the burly blonde retreated with an emphasised perplexity on his face. This look that went way beyond the activity at hand.

"Lijah! I love you! I love you!" It seemed she had forgotten his reaction to those words.

And now, nympho or not, she would wish she hadn't said that. He remembered the first time she had said those words. And he remembered his thoughts too: *'Gloria loves me and I love her, so don't come wid dat shit. 'Bout yuh love me. Don't love me, love my dick. As of now, it's the key to your daddy's will'.* He damned nearly killed her with it.

Later, downstairs, of all the workmen, Lijah could feel the thick atmosphere that oozed from the perverted voyeur. The one who had that wishful look in his eyes earlier, as he stared at his ass. He kept his eyes firmly on the wall he was painting, stroking it with a chilling strangeness and Lijah felt it. But he simply told himself this guy was a racist and was obviously hating the fact that he had been where he most probably wanted to go.

"Missed a bit," Lijah said, in an upper-class English tongue.

The guy, around forty-five years old, looked around, and if looks could kill, Lijah would be dead.

"Lighten up mate, it's the 21st century. The taboo is gone from this sort a thing. Where have you been?" Lijah said, mimicking an even more aristocratic tongue.

This time, the guy turned again and gave him an anger-filled stare. Lijah stared back. And then, he really saw his eyes for what they were. Something in this guy's eyes took him back to a time and a place he'd rather not be. This guy had the eyes of an old cellmate he wanted to kill as a youth. He was just nineteen years old, naïve and weedy, and this guy, a twenty-four year old, tattooed, skin-head with more muscles than Rocky Marciano.

Lijah's stomach now began to churn. "C'mon Lucy. Let's get outa here," he urged suddenly, almost shaking.

Lucy seemed to be amused with the *to*ing and *fro*ing of verbal and nonverbal teasing between her worker and Lijah. In an almost rebellious gesture, she gripped his fingers tighter. To Lijah, it was like waving a red cloth in front of bulls.

"See you later, guys," Lucy shouted on her way out.

Among other things, Lijah thought again about the situation he was in. He knew things wouldn't be as easy as they seemed, or as he would like it to be. He was giving what Lucy craved, but the time was drawing near when it would almost be certain that it wouldn't be enough. It got him wondering about the strength of his collateral. Baby Face Glen was waiting in the wings of a Jamaican seaport. Fresh from yard, the brother might have more to offer on the slamming front. Rough, raw and always ready. Doing hungry tourists who would escape from their boring English boyfriends every year, to taste forbidden fruits (home-grown style) was probably what Baby Face did for a living - hoping to make that one big break. That big break every tourist would offer him after he would lace their pearly asses with his length of black, desired flesh. Who hadn't seen *Jamaica Uncut?* No messing. *Feh real.*

But for Lijah, the break made with Lucy would be all the break he would need. And for him, losing that break would be one defeat that would not be easily acceptable, but what could he do? Lucy had already laid her ultimatum on the line. She may be a nymphomaniac, but she most certainly wasn't stupid. She knew he loved Gloria, but the offer of a MRS Roadster Sports, a tidy sum and a designer wardrobe were seriously tempting.

For now, he would play her game. But he could almost feel Gloria's hands around his neck, squeezing hard.

"Let's go, Darling," Lucy said, assertively, pulling on his arm. But as he followed her out, so did the evil gaze of that strange, yet familiar looking guy. His eyes pierced his soul, and sent another chilling sensation down his spine.

But that was then. Now, Gloria was in Jamaica and although he had his MRS Roadster Sport, he was still holding out for his dollars. There were other crucial things on his mind too, so he sunk deep into his thoughts and drifted, surfing the low-ways of his mind.

CHAPTER * FIFTEEN

'Let he without sin cast the first stone', Lijah thought to himself as he gazed out the window of the Lexus as it glided through Fern Gully in Jamaica. He knew that he himself was far from *'sinless'*, so he had not come to judge. Just to bury a few ghosts.

He was on his way to *country*. Lothan, his old man, had taken himself out of the *country* for forty odd years, but the love for *country* could not be taken out of him. Kingston and tourist-infested parts of the island could stay. He wanted to relax where he grew up as a boy. Finish his life in peace. Lijah thought hard about that *'finish his life in peace'* bit. He didn't know how much peace his old man would have after the questions he had come to ask. It would be a *make or break* situation. Lijah was thinking about number one. Taking control of his life depended on it. Only Gloria knew how much certain things controlled the way he flexed. The sins of his father were manifesting in him. He was feeling it. Yet he was no third or fourth generation, like the Bible says.

"Yuh is a English man?" the taxi driver asked.

"Nah, man. Me is a Jamaican. Me born a Inglan, but me is a Jamaican." He said it with pride. Years ago, when asked the same question in England, he had said, *'Me is an African'*. Perhaps for him, the question was a contextual one.

"So is how often yuh come home?"

"Bwoy... not as often as I should."

"Yeah? Yuh feh come of'n, man. Jamaica nice, yunnuh. De only problem, dallaz nah run. PJ Patterson tryin' 'im bes' but bwoy... it's gonna tek years to turn t'ings 'roun'. Me feel seh de people dem who live inna de countryside betta dan de people dem weh live inna de town. From dem 'ave dem likkle farm, wid dem yam, green bananas, coconut, breadfruit, sweet potatoes... all dem t'ings deh, t'ings cyan run cool," the Dennis Brown look-alike professed.

"Yeah? But most young people nuh waan badda wid de farming no more," Lijah surmised.

"Dat is a true t'ing, bredrin. Nobody nuh waan get dem hands dirty nuh more. Everybody waan live inna town or go a foreign. An' den w'en de foreigner dem come, dem complain 'bout foreign. Nobody nuh happy. Jah cyaan seem to please everybody."

"Dere is problem everywhere, my frien'. Is true weh yuh seh. No one is eva satisfied. Nuh matta weh yuh deh."

"Me 'ere de bes' t'ing feh do is to get yuhself a rich w'ite 'oman an' marry ar."

"Yeah? Is who tell yuh dat?" Lijah asked.

"Yeah, man. Nuff Jamaican go a foreign an' do dat. Dem seh it's hard feh get a black 'oman feh tek dem serious an' marry dem like dat."

Lijah laughed. "Well yuh see *me,* is one black 'oman me waan feh marry. An' she's right here in JA."

"So yuh love Jamaican 'oman?"

"Bwoy, she's like me, yunnuh. Born in Inglan, but love Jamdown."

"She live in de country like yuh ole man?"

"Nah. Kingston. She an' me likkle girl. Her mother died three months ago. Yuh see... Dat is one a de problem with living in foreign. Yuh work all yuh days till yuh sixty-five, den as soon as yuh come to enjoy yuh retirement yuh dead to t'raas. Don't even live feh enjoy de fruits a yuh labour."

"Is a serious t'ing!" the taxi driver agreed, "me observe dat nuff time. Bwoy if me come to Inglan, me would definitely get a rich w'ite 'oman. Me 'ere seh dem love black man. Me 'ere seh de w'ite man dem dick likkle. A true?" He laughed, ending the whole conversation flippantly.

Lijah laughed. At the same time he thought about Lucy. The taxi driver would love to hear about Lucy, but Lijah had better things to talk, or even think about. "Bwoy, me nuh know if dem dick big, likkle or in between, yunnuh sah. All me know is dat dere has always been this thing as to why white women love black men. Only dem could tell yuh dat. An' I suppose each one would 'ave their own different reason." He eased back, smiling at the taxi driver's haughty laugh, the sounds of barking dogs, tooting of horns and the playful noises of children as they cruised past scattered splashes of houses in tiny villages.

Lijah must have had a long doze, for when he woke up, the car was cruising through Watermount Square, and heading for Point Hill. *'St. Catherine is truly a nice place to live if you try to accept greenery, as opposed to the concrete-jungle life style England has got us all accustomed to'*, he thought.

As the taxi climbed the difficult road to Point Hill, Lijah took in the sights, both of the countryside and of a few sexy asses he had fancied a romp with on a few of his visits. One thing he learnt was that unlike Faithlyn, not all Jamaican girls free-up so easily. After all, *'horse is horse and class is class'*. There are still some facety, virtuous ones at large. Ones that held it down like precious stones.

Judd, Dorr, Dawn and Paula stepped aside to make way for the passing Lexus. Lijah fantasised at the thought of passing a few hours with the girls. Remembering him from last year, they smiled and waved.

"Easy nuh, driva," Lijah requested.

The girls came closer. "Whaap'n Lijah. Is weh yaah seh?" Judd asked with a smile.

"Tell me nuh, Sweetness? Is weh de action deh lata?" Lijah asked, tripping on testosterone. He couldn't help it. The girls were hot and the heat didn't help.

"We goin' to a Vibes Injection dance uppa Point Hill, lata," Dorr said.

"Vibes Injection? Yuh have a Vibes Injection in Jamaica?"

"No… Vibes Injection from Birmingham, Inglan' man," they said almost in unison, "dem playing against we own, *King Sonic,*" Judd finished off.

"King *who?* "

"King Sonic man, dem is a boss soun'," Judd assured him.

"Me neva 'ear 'bout dem," Lijah said.

"Yeah, man, a guy call Teddy T run t'ings. Dem wicked me a tell yuh. Dere's Coco, a boss selecta, but he's in foreign now. Den yuh have Jubbie, Aircraft, Bagga, Riley, Fedda Mop, Rizzla, Spragga an' Paubo-Hype. Yuh see w'en dah crew deh get togedda?" she kissed her teeth, sealing an endorsement, "pure niceness gwaan."

"Yeah?" Lijah smiled. "Me wi' check it out, yes. But me still don' t'ink King Sonic cyan beat Vibes Injection dough," he bantered. Still... neva min' dat. Is which one a yuh girls gonna tek me to dis dance?"

"Yuh outa luck," Paula assured him, "we 'ave we man. But nuff girls will be dere. Yuh wi' a'right. Anyway, yunnuh lef' yuh girl inna Inglan'?" Dawn asked, hand akimbo, giving off a facety attitude.

"Ah hope yuh nuh come feh bad-out pan ar yunnuh?" Dorr scolded playfully.

"Yeah," Paula added, "is dat me waan know. You Inglan' men always come out for a few weeks, have fun with the Jamaican girls an' lef' dem. Yuh women in Inglan' don't even know anyt'ing 'bout it."

Lijah chuckled, and wiped the perspiration from his brows. "A'right. Me wi' see unnuh lata. But my girl is right 'ere in Jamaica," he said as the car laboured up the hill. He kept his eyes on the girls through the rear view mirror until they disappeared out of view.

When the car pulled up outside his old man's house, Lijah could not help resenting the fact that the woman who sat on the veranda of this beautiful house, was not Nettie, his dear mother.

He paid the taxi driver and fixed his eyes on his old man, sitting there as if he was waiting for God. He had sorry eyes. Sorrow swam in a watery distance that Lijah pitied. He could see it a mile off. White strands of hair mingled mischievously amidst an unruly mop of salt-n'-pepper curls. Lijah thought it strange. He had not seen grey hairs on his old man before.

It was obvious Lothan wanted to help his son with his bags, but he couldn't. Willing heart, weak flesh. And that set Lijah's mind racing down another road. Does the nasty *'thief of youth'* take everything? All abilities, leaving only will and weakness? The question was, *'Could his old man still make love?'* For some reason, Lijah thought of Ronnie Biggs: the great train robber who, in his prime, managed to out-run and out-smart all authorities. Yet, in the end, he had to surrender to age and illness.

He remembered the times he and Festus reasoned about old people and sex. Is it shameful to *do it* at seventy? Why should age dictate one's pleasure, anyway? But Lijah was in fact thinking about himself. Worried about losing his appetite. Although he would not admit it, the ageing process frightened him.

"So how is life, Pops?" Lijah asked, an hour after he had greeted his dad and Dora, and settled down. He didn't come to make Dora feel awkward, but it was obvious she was. Although he wanted to ask her a burning question, what was done, was done, and the clock could not be turned. It was his old man's life. She was his wife now. Nettie was buried and Lijah hoped his old man could bury the hatchet by solving the mystery that was threatening to butcher his very soul. It had chopped for too long at his inner peace. Only his old man could help: he, with all his righteous teachings: *'Be a real man, work for your living, never take money from a woman, prepare for old age...'* and the rest. Lothan had spoken with such convictions; it was as if he had experienced it for himself. And it wasn't to say Lothan was wrong, but there were things Lijah could see in his teachings that didn't add up.

Nettie died at no age. Fifty years. Even the thought of her plight would kill Lijah inside, every time he would allow himself to think about her. She was everybody's wings, legs and soul. She always reminded him of the strings you couldn't see in a theatre. The invisible strings that invisible people pulled on puppets. The strings you only managed to see in a crisis, when the lighting would be wrong or something so. She was the wind beneath all wings. With all her shortcomings at such a young age, Lijah was convinced that she didn't die from the nasty stroke, or the fierce diabetes that stole both her legs, leaving her with two undignified stubs, nor the high blood pressure that needed to be watched like a hawk. No. He was convinced his mother died of a broken heart. And she, with health, was the most beautiful woman he had ever seen.

They (Nettie, Dora and Lothan) had lived in Britain for most of their lives. Things didn't work to plan. The plan was that Lothan and Nettie would return to Jamaica after retiring. They would sell up, gather every penny of their savings, pensions, pack every bit of their earthly belongings and make their final exodus to Jamaica. Instead, Lothan did it with Dora, a black nurse, who paid homely visits to a legless, speechless, broken Nettie, who could emit nothing but hums, tears and sighs. A black nurse she had once called, *'her best friend'.*

To Lijah's understanding of what went down, if Dora was Nettie's best friend, she needed no enemies.

Nettie had such strength up until at least forty-five; it was hard to watch her die at fifty. So Lijah didn't. Watch her die that is. He left home to escape the hurt that only *born-to-care* women could cope with. Besides, he could see what was coming, and his leaving home prevented him from committing murder.

Killing his old man would have been easy. So instead Lijah took up the banner of the *peaceful* rastaman. He spent most of his energy chanting down Babylon's philosophy: visiting Nyabinghi sessions, trying to live with the laws of nature, reflecting on the different interpretation of the Bible and the history of Africa. Serious t'ing. Feh real.

Lijah needed salvation, so he looked to repatriation. Though to him, he didn't see it as a physical return to Africa, but to become aware of his African identity. He had tried to change his reality, right here in Birmingham. But as time went on, the Covenant would prove not so much heavy, but hard to maintain, inna Babylon.

But Dora was another story. One that hurt even a dread like Lijah to tell. And now, as she busied herself about the place, trying her best to please, Lijah's thoughts were, *'the axe forgets, the tree remembers'*.

Lothan sat on the veranda, almost lifeless, his gold watch: a golden handshake from the railways sat proud on his shaking wrist. Words came slowly from his mouth, the odd ones here and there, reminding Lijah of those days (before Dora was an issue) when he and his old lady would argue silently about some white woman he had had an affair with. A woman whose name seemed to fail them both. Consciously, they avoided it like the plague, as if its mention would turn them both, into pillars of salt.

Lothan was young then. In his prime. Now he was seventy years old, lucky for him. Or perhaps not so lucky – (Nettie never lived that long). An age he must have looked forward to, since to him, it must have warranted the end to a journey, when he would quench his thirst happily, lounging in a deck chair daily, watching happy days go by.

But now his health was failing. The fingers of his right hand were stiff from a stroke, the ones on his left and also his knees pained constantly from arthritis, his eyes glazed and watery, the way most old black men's looked: as if the years of restricted tears could no longer be forced back, and had come to swim above their black pupils, like oil on the surface of a once-blocked river.

Only, Lothan's eyes had a strange distance in them. A telling distance. One Lijah never saw in other old men's eyes. Perhaps because he never really looked.

As Lijah looked at his old man, he recalled him at around forty years old – *'good if he could have retired then, he and the old lady'*, Lijah thought. But of course that would have been impossible. *The system* would not have allowed that. It wanted your blood. No one gets an easy ride – unless of course, you come into money, either by winning some, or if you're lucky enough to have inherited some. For Lothan, both options seemed impossible. He didn't do the horses, he didn't mark the pools, or the lottery. And as for inheritance... well, it goes without saying.

And if the system didn't get you, something else would. Like blood pressure, diabetes, cancer or heart disease.

Or the broken heart that got poor old Nettie.

But that wasn't all that Lijah recalled. Uncle Stan. As Lothan got older, he seemed to look more and more like his younger brother, or vice versa. Only, Uncle Stan was still cruising around Birmingham, looking a bill of health. Lijah couldn't help wondering again why they had no longer spoken to each other.

"So 'ow is Inglan'?" Lothan asked, staring off into the distance over the heads of several coffee trees at the bottom of his yard, and at the sinking sun. The distance in his eyes made Lijah wonder if he cared at all how England was.

A donkey brayed in the distance, interrupting his response. Lijah looked towards the sound and answered, "Jus' as you lef' it, Dad. No change. Well... apart from the changes in industry, all aimed towards more and better production. You know. Glorified slavery. The railway is privatised now, though. A bit different from when you worked for them."

The old man chuckled, but found it hard to do that. Hard on his chest. Lijah felt a sense of pity and it made him wish he could invent a way to cheat the ageing process. Stay the age he was forever. Forty and fit. But ironically, for some reason, he envied his old man also. Not for his oldness, or his state of health, but for the quiet place where he was sitting. His situation of *rest*. The daily sunshine. The no-mortgage situation. Home.

" 'ow is Gloria an' de kids?"

"They're ok, Dad. She's here in Jamaica, yunnuh. Her mum died."

"Hortence dead?!"

"Yeah, Dad. Neither she nor Pastor Fontaine lived to reap wha' dem sow. All de hard work inna Inglan'. De house is Gloria's now."

"Is weh yaah seh?"

But Lijah didn't know how to tell the whole story: that he and Gloria were really apart.

Dora came out to the veranda with a cool jug of cool-aid. Before she laid it down on the small table between the old man and Lijah, she wiped a paraffin-damped cloth over its surface. "Keep de flies away," she said, as if she knew Lijah was about to ask her why.

She walked back into the house, then quickly followed with two long thin glasses from England. To Lijah's surprise, they were Nettie's glasses. He remembered them from way back when. *'Doesn't this woman respect anything?'* he thought. *'Like the ageing process, she takes every damn thing'.*

Dora averted her eyes. Guilt, Lijah could only assume, was gripping her. He supposed, for her, it would be nice if she didn't set eyes on Roy, Faye or him again. Leaving England was a form of escape. She had run, but she couldn't hide. *'Did she think it would be so easy? Every herring must hang by its own gill'.* Lijah's thought echoed again.

Dora busied herself around the place like the annoying mosquitoes that buzzed around Lijah's ears, or the odd fly or two, that mockingly pitched anywhere they could not detect paraffin. It was as if she could hear the silent snap of Lothan's pained fingers. It was her business to please.

Lijah looked deep into everything. Perhaps it was the naturalness of the countryside or even the difference in the rays of the sun.

A donkey strolled by slowly. In its own language, the beast complained, unnoticed, of the heat. It's owner's weight, it seemed, too much for it to bear. But what choice did the dumb beast have? What easy way out was there? None. Nettie sprung to his mind again. What choice did she have, when her only voice laid in a cursed walking stick that failed to hammer out the adulterous affair between her husband and her best friend?

A mangy dog followed at the tired beast's heels, growling, perhaps at the sight of Lijah. Or perhaps the smell of 'Foreign'.

Lothan's yard dog retaliated over the sounds of the greetings between him and the passer-by. The man, old and tired-looking, was obviously coming from his yam field. The donkey's hamper was laden with what seemed like a whole crop of yellow yams. The man, though dilapidated, looked much healthier than Lothan, who had spent most of his life in the Motherland.

Lijah drifted into his own thoughts again, and they consumed him, until his father's voice summoned him, "Lijah, leave 'oman alone an' sort out yuh life wid Gloria," he said, as if he was waiting for his visit to tell him that.

After wondering what his old man knew, Lijah stared at him and thought, *'Let him without sin cast the first stone'.* How could his old man say that? What about him and Dora? And that mysterious white woman?

Ok, so Lothan knew something. But what? About Bernadette? Or about Lucy? And why should Lijah listen to him, of all people. He, who made Nettie suffer at the hands of his now so-called wife.

"Wha' yuh mean, Dad?" Lijah asked.

"Jus' be careful, Son. If yuh don' stan' strong, woman wi' pull yuh dong. Us men are weak. Strong in muscles but weak in de flesh an' de mind. I suppose dat is why God mek women have children."

"Oh Dad, cut de parables. W'at yuh trying to seh?"

"Jus' be careful, Son. Jus' be careful," he replied, as if he really knew something Lijah didn't. "Dem seh *'a bird in the hand is worth two in de bush'*. See de value of what you have, before t'rowing it away and chasing w'at yuh don't have." There was a strange chastising in Lothan's voice and Lijah felt somewhat victimised. Now he was intrigued. For the first time in his life he had realised that his father wasn't just a difficult disciplinarian, like he, Faye and Roy all thought. A disciplinarian who, in his later life, needed to discipline himself. All they had seen, was this sturdy man; a Paul Robson look-alike, dishing out nothing but strict discipline. And they respected him to the max. But that respect soon disappeared when his true persona had shown.

"A'right," Lothan continued. "Me know seh yuh still resent me feh yuh madda's death. But me cyaan turn de clock back, Lijah. All me can do is pray an' ask God's forgiveness. Dere is adda t'ings me need forgiveness for as well."

The old man had never spoken openly to Lijah about anything in his life before, and Lijah had never asked him. So, this woman that nearly *pulled him down*, remained a mystery.

The odd words he and his sister Faye had strained their ears to catch through key-holes, the nooks of slightly opened doors, or the ones the wind would carry in from the pretentious harmony of *'gardening together'*, could never sum the whole thing up. All these odd words seemed to have *'this woman'* dashed, sprinkled or even carelessly *'thrown in'*. But of course, Lijah and Faye weren't fools. They already knew this was no black woman. Nettie's words were choiced. Descriptive. Tinged with bitterness too. She was, most certainly, a woman scorned. Her words were ones that did not relate to a black woman. Like *'De dyam pale 'kin bakra'*, and some Lijah can hardly remember now. But he was old enough to know they were describing a white woman. Words that would perhaps have branded Nettie a racist. But none different to those that a bitter white woman would use to describe a black woman who was stealing love on the side, with her dear husband.

"Who is the woman you and Mum always used to argue about when us kids were young, Dad? I feel seh all dem worries made her ill too."

"Aye sah," Lothan sighed. "Son, don't yuh eva leave anyt'ing alone?" He paused as if his brain needed intervals between words. *"Elijah Zephaniah Benjamin"*... she chose yuh name, yunnuh. Yuh was ar favourite. Broke her heart when yuh did dat off-licence t'ing. An' worse when yuh lef' home an' tek up wid dat Rastafari t'ing." Lothan kept his eyes on the golden sun, as if his peace lay in its sinking and the fluffy gold clouds that gathered over it.

Dora came out again and her breeze told Lijah she felt a way about him quizzing the old man.

"We had a child," Lothan emitted out of the blue.

"Who?! We who?! Yuh an' dis woman?!"

"Yes."

"Bombo cl..." Lijah held his tongue. No matter what, it was his father. Pastor Fontaine's words hit him, *'Honour thy mother and thy father, that thy days may be long upon the land which the Lord thy God giveth thee'*.

"Yuh madda knew about it. She mek it worry ar mind too much. Before she lose her speech, she used to seh it was de memory of it, dat gave her de stroke."

"An' what do you t'ink, Dad?" Lijah asked.

"Lijah, I don't know. Could be. But Lijah, dere were adda t'ings dat went aan in our lives."

"Adda t'ings?"

Lothan ignored him. "But it badda me... de chile. Me couldn't sleep at nights, knowing seh me have a chile in a children's home, somewhere."

"In a children's home?"

"Yes, Lijah, she gave her up. Gave up de pickney. She must be around thirty-eight years old now. Born in 1965. Pretty likkle girl."

"Why she give ar up?"

"Lijah, she was a white 'oman, married to a white man. Rich white man."

"What?!"

Lothan ignored Lijah's outburst and carried on, "How could she explain a black child? Especially in dose days. It was bad enough when single white woman tek up wid a black man. Dose women were brave. But a married one?! Jeeesas C'ris'." He kissed his teeth, drumming his point home.

"Yuh was seriously messin' wid a married 'oman?"

"Working feh deh railway wasn't enough. I needed extra money. We had all you chil'ren to feed. I was the odd job man feh her husban',"

Lothan continued.

For the first time, apart from when his mother died, Lijah detected some kind of regret in his father's voice.

"Dem was high society people. De husban' used to own a textile business in Dudley. She neva work. She had a likkle bwoy around six years old. Conrad. Funny likkle bwoy he was. Right likkle Hitler. Blonde 'air, blue yie. Used to gwaan like a likkle girl. I wouldn' be surprise if 'im don' turn out gay. And a likkle girl around t'ree years old. I can't remember her name." He scratched his head.

Lijah listened hard.

"Dat woman could neva leave me alone, Lijah. I'm sure she was addicted to sex. All me waan to do was to keep de garden tidy like ar husban' was paying me to do. But all she waan to do was to get me inna bed, in de shed... anywhere she could."

Lijah chuckled although he knew it wasn't funny.

"Sometime," Lothan relented, "de likkle girl would ketch we! Yes! Ketch we! Good t'ing she was too young. One time she wake from ar likkle nap an' come into de bedroom. She jus' stood dere an' stare an' stare. Like she was tryin' to work out w'at we was doin'. It was as if she knew it was wrong. She was small, but I neva like de look in dat likkle girl's eyes. Yuh know how yuh can get some evil likkle pickney." Lothan paused and looked towards the kitchen from where Dora rattled cutlery. The rattling seemed exaggerated. As if to distract them from her own silence or to tell of her disapproval of Lothan's 'telling'. Then Lothan looked out across the Jamaican skies again. "She always gimme money," he stated. "Like she was paying me feh sex. She used to shove it inna me pocket when we finish doing it. Push it inna me pocket, widout sayin' a word."

"Bwoy," Lijah said, sounding shocked, and seeing his father through different eyes now. "I see dat as disguised prostitution, Dad." Then he remembered part of his father's lecture years ago back in England, '*a man dat stretch out 'im han' an' tek money from a woman is no man at all'*. Did his old man see himself as less of a man for accepting this woman's money? Or perhaps he didn't see it as '*stretching out his hand*', since it was always '*shoved into his pocket*'.

"I couldn't understan' it," Lothan continued, "her husban' loved her so much. Treated her like a queen. Seem to me if she kill 'im an' 'im come alive again, he would forgive her."

"But not for fucking a black man, Dad. No way. Not in dem days. An' de gardener at dat! Who she t'ink she was? Lady Chatterley?" Lijah said, seeing a funny side to it all.

"No. Not in dem days," Lothan said. "Dat would be like a deadly sin!" His eyes opened wide, to allow a laugh that came as a surprise. "Anyway," he resumed, "it gwaan an' gwaan 'till me could neva look ar husban' in de face. Me tell ar it had to stop. Heh! Who tell me to seh dat?! She get vex wid me!... Threaten to tell her husban seh me rape ar, if me stop givin' her ar t'ings. Lijah, I didn't know *what* to do."

"Wha?! Rape?" Lijah exclaimed. "Dat would have been a definite jail sentence."

"Of course. So dat is why me carry aan. An' on top a dat, every night yuh madda would turn her back to me. Would neva mek me touch ar. So since she wasn't giving me not'ing, I just carried on wid *her*."

Lijah laughed a cynical laugh through his nose. Its intonation said, *'Yeah, right'*. Just then, he didn't care that he wasn't in a position to 'judge'. This was his mother they were talking about.

"De first time she try feh seduce me, me frighten till a didn't know wha' feh do. Seh she was curious. Seh she jus' waan experience how a black man tas'e." It made Lothan laugh at the top of his voice, but seconds later he went serious again. "I didn't believe her. I t'ought it was a trick. Nuff black man get ketch like dat before, yunnuh. Woman entice dem, den dem call rape."

Dora made her presence felt again. The smell of cooking wafted a *'ready'* smell in the air.

"De first time she mek me tek all me clothes off. Stared at me. I felt like a slave being examined. Then she started to touch me all over. When me wood stan' up she sigh. Like she just discover somet'ing strange. She neva 'top teasing me till I had to tek ar. Dat night I couldn't touch yuh madda. Guilt nearly kill me. It's true. A guilty conscience needs no accuser."

"So where is dis woman now, Dad?"

"A don't know. But when she left her husban' it was a big scandal. From she fin' out seh she pregnant, she pack up an' leave. She tell me seh she try dat gin t'ing. Yuh no. Dem call it mother's ruin. Tell me seh she drink nuff gin an' sit inna hot bath, tryin' to get rid a de baby, but it neva work.   Me fret, me fret, me fret so till! Dat is when I t'ought she would tell her husban' seh me rape her. But she didn't. She jus' pack up an' leave her husban, de likkle bwoy an' de likkle girl. And a note."

"So how did you see the baby?"

"One night, about t'ree months afta de baby born, she turn up on me door-step. Yuh madda was on night work – she knew what night she used to work. She come wid de likkle girl wrap up inna one likkle bundle. All you chil'ren were sittin' in de front room. She seh she come to show me de child before she give it up. She seh she love me. An' if me run away wid her she wouldn't give up de chile. But how I do dat, Lijah? Can yuh imagine how me did feel? Me couldn't tek de chile, me didn't wan' it to be given away an' as feh leavin' yuh madda an' you kids? Well, it was outa de question. I didn't love her. It was jus' a sex t'ing."

Lijah was mesmerised. This was his old man. Havin' it off with Dora in his mother's front room was one thing, but knocking off his boss's wife in those days, when the consequences were so serious... Well...

"Me cry de livin' eye-wata w'en she leave wid de baby. Dat was de last me see of her an' de chile."

Lijah swallowed mouthfuls of the ice cold cool-aid Dora had made him. Listening to his dad seemed to have made him extra thirsty. Much more thirsty than the sweltering heat had.

"Yuh mean she jus' run off suh?"

"Jus like dat. All dem lives messed up. Me, yuh madda, hers, her husban', de two kids she lef wid her husban... an' me likkle girl. She give ar 'way like a bag a sugar." He paused and wiped a tear from his flooded eyes.

Lijah didn't expect this. He had never seen his old man cry.

"I know you kids resent Dora," he blew his nose in a starched, white hanky. "Roy hate ar. 'im tell me seh 'im would neva come to Jamaica to visit us. Seh Dora kill Nettie. Faye mus' feel de same. Dat mus' be why she neva come back to England. I know *you* do as well, Lijah. But dere is more to it dan dat. T'ings you chil'ren don't know."

Lijah knew there were always two sides to every story. Unfortunately, people sometimes go to their graves, with only the side that matters most to them. It just hurt to think he would never hear how his mother really felt in those times. Hear it from her own mouth, rather than the badly written note she tried desperately to scribble for him. One that was cleverly concealed, avoiding confiscation. The note Lijah kept for some strange reason.

"Lijah, like me seh, yuh madda neva stop cussing me 'bout dis w'ite 'oman," Lothan continued, ignoring Dora's call for dinner. "She neva mek me touch ar afta she fin' out. Feh years. Long, long before she fell sick, me nuh get not'n. Even dough we sleep inna de same bed..."

Lothan's pauses between sentences got longer now and Lijah suspected something about the sharpness of his memory. He would get dates way out and even put one of his own children's name where another should be.

He continued, "Lijah, yuh madda would tu'n ar back gimme all de time. Dat was from you were two years old. Mmmm... yes... neva touched yuh madda since yuh was about two years old..." he paused again, now, as if in deep reminiscence.

Lijah was sure now that his father's memory was wavering. He knew he meant since *Faye* was two years old, since Faye was the youngest, but it was ok. That was minor. He wouldn't correct him. Besides, that might interrupt the flow and he might miss out on crucial information.

"Lijah, yuh madda neva fo'gave me... neva... But I fo'gave her, dough. Yes. I fo'gave her. Fo'gave her for what she did. I deserved it. But it hurt me, Lijah... hurt me... Hurt me bad."

"What, Dad? What did you forgive Mum for? Not lettin' yuh touch her? Is dat w'at hurt you so much? Don' talk in parables, man."

"No, Son... no." Lothan's tone gave Lijah the feeling that there was something much more detrimental to his story.

"Den w'at, Dad?"

But Lothan ignored Lijah's pressing questions and continued, "But me neva leave ar, Lijah. I stayed wid yuh madda all de way t'rough. Mmmm. All de way..." he paused again, then said, "Faye... Faye... yuh hear anyt'ing from Faye, Lijah?"

Lijah was worried now. The old man had jumped from telling him about life in the bedroom with his mother, to reminiscing about his last daughter, Faye. Was senility really beginning to set in?

"No, Dad. Not'n. Faye an' Roy act as if dem nuh have nuh family. Anyway, cyarry aan, Dad. Yuh was sayin' yuh haven't touch Mum since... an' yuh forgave her for..."

"Yuh should understan', Lijah," Lothan cut in, "I am a man. All men need to be satisfied sexually. Women t'ink dem spitin' yuh w'en dem tek it weh, but men cyan always fin' anadda 'oman... Could you stay dat long widout sex, Lijah?" He had double-backed to the part before the 'forgiving'.

Lijah answered with a smirk.

"I was a young man as well," the old man continued. "Hot-blooded too. An' I'm sure I was sufferin' from some illness. Me faada before me had de same t'ing. Wid all de research nowadays, some scientist or de adda will soon come up wid an ansa feh it. Wheneva me used to get vex... angry... really upset. A real hot sexual urge used to tek me. Me was like an animal. Sometime dis w'ite 'oman used to suffa. Sometime she bawl so loud, me frighten!... de likkle girl used to run come... But sometime she like it."

Lijah couldn't help but chuckle, as he looked to see where Dora was. It was funny, but he found himself affiliating with his old man. Could this sexual urge, triggered by anger, really be a hereditary illness? He got thinking and most certainly would not rule it out. At least he knew it was passed down. He wasn't alone. His father and grandfather before him had experienced it. If nothing else, his trip to Jamaica revealed that much. He wondered if it was the same for Uncle Stan.

Now, from his father's story, he was beginning to see, not necessary justification, but a clearer picture. That was what he came for. But now he wanted to know one thing. *'Why did his old man make his mother hear him and Dora making love in her living-room, while she lay helpless in her sick-bed?'* And maybe, just maybe, if the flow was right, he might ask why his old man and his Uncle Stan (a brother that looked almost identical to him) just didn't see eye-to-eye.

As it seemed, Dora was meant to be Nettie's best friend. On her sick-bed, before her health had really deteriorated, she managed to get her friend Dora as a permanent bank-nurse. But as time went on, she asked for bread and got stone. Asked for love and got nothing but mental torture. Asked for food, and got with it: with heavy doses of sleeping pills which were always mixed in with the Milo she loved so much. And at times, ironically, she would be saved by those doses: when mentally torturing sounds would seep up from her living-room, through the cracks of her bedroom floor and into the crevices of her mind. Yes, part way through, sleep would rescue her.

Dora didn't see it as evil. To her, she was being kind. What Nettie couldn't hear, wouldn't hurt her. But if only they could have held on. Waited patiently. Checked to see if Nettie was fast asleep. But passion is like fire. When it blazes its trail inside a lustful couple, patience has no say.

For a while Nettie had not realised what was happening. But time is longer than rope, and anything one does in the dark, will sure come out in the light. It had only been a matter of time before she detected her husband's betrayal with her best friend. She couldn't voice her feelings vocally, since the stroke had taken her voice. But the carpet on her bedroom floor held the telltale wear, as she would hammer in protest. Hammer hard against its pile, with a once-faithful walking stick. A walking stick that had no other use to her, but to bang out infidelity and heartless selfishness. No use but to drown out the sound of her husband and best friend doing what she could only dream of. She would bang frantically with the little strength she had, miming *'Stop it! Stop it!'* But in the heat of their passion, Lothan and Dora hadn't listened. They were taken up by their own pleasure. And by the time they had finished, Dora's nurse's uniform crumpled, and Lothan's desires satisfied, the strong dose of sleeping pills Dora had administered to Nettie's Milo, had taken her to another planet. Until the next time round.

"I know Mum was sick and couldn't satisfy you, Dad, but couldn't you have gone to Dora's house?" Lijah asked.

"Her husban' was around den."

"Dora had a husban'?!"

"Yes. Nasty c'aracta he was. Always drunk. He used to beat 'ar terribly, Lijah. She ran away from Bristol an' lef' 'im. But 'im fin' ar. She gave 'im a chance, but once a beater, always a beater. Dora an' yuh madda worked together at the hospital. Dem become friends. She used to tell Nettie all ar troubles."

But Lijah was biased. No story at all from Dora was ever gonna convince him. "Dad, there are two sides to every story. Have you heard the side of dis 'nasty c'aracta' of a husban' Dora told you about?"

"Son, I don' t'ink she was lyin'. But, yes. Dere is two sides to every story. True."

Lijah was intrigued, even though his dad had not yet answered his question. Besides, apart from the burning one about Uncle Stan, there was the critical other: *'Sweetie'*. Who was *Sweetie?* He remembered his mother's wailing one day, before she lost her speech. He had paid her a well-overdue visit and was not expecting this: *'I shouldn't have done it to Sweetie'*, she had wailed, *'she was my friend. I'm being punished. Forgive me, Sweetie. Forgive me'*. She had begged for Sweetie's earthly forgiveness. And Lijah had hoped, that whoever this Sweetie was, and whatever his mother had done to her, she would be forgiven.

But what did his mother do to this *Sweetie?*

"No, we couldn't go to Dora's house," Lothan continued. "De living-room was de only place. We try to be quiet but... well...." Lothan seemed all talked out. There were enough gaps in his conversation to warrant concern. His slurring became more noticeable too. "Son, I tried wid yuh madda before she became ill. Me beg ar feh life inna de bedroom again. She jus develop a hate feh me. It was either me become a monk, or get somet'ing. Afta she became ill, Dora became a shoulda to cry on. You chil'ren wasn't dere when I was sad. Couldn't bear to see Nettie like dat. She was too young to end up like dat. I was sad. Angry. Frustrated. I needed love an' comfort. One day Dora see me crying. She comfort me. Lijah, yuh should know. Dere's not'ing like de bosom of a woman to comfort a broken man. Dat day, we mek love on de settee. It became a pattern afta dat. Each time she finish seeing to Nettie, we would do we t'ings. I wish I could turn de clock back, so she didn't hear."

"But Dad, she used to knock! Wid her stick! I rememba dat day I came..."

How could Lothan forget it? He was almost caught in the act by his son.

"I wondered what the knocking was," Lijah relented. "Couldn't yuh jus'...! Jus'! Jus'!" He flashed his locks and wiped an unexpected tear from his manly eyes.

Dora was listening in her own torturing silence. Her dinner was getting cold. The smell of boiled breadfruit, yellow yam, cornmeal dumplings and ackee an' salt fish mingled amongst the air of a hard-hitting story from England. She shuffled her feet. Clinked the edge of her Dutch-pot. Tried to cover the sound. Make it stop. But somehow, she knew it had to be aired. She wouldn't ask for earthly forgiveness, but hoped her Heavenly Father, would listen. She had told herself she didn't deserve it. She herself had a story to tell. A secret to reveal. Everyone has. Years ago, back in Birmingham, she had divorced a man she married in Bristol. He found comfort in whiskey bottles, the streets of Handsworth and a hiding place in his forever spaced-out brain. But now, she had Lothan. Her meat, Nettie's poison.

Lijah thought of the situation of him and Gloria. How he begged her forgiveness. How she chucked him out. How she rejected him the last time he tried to make love to her. He meditated over his parents' life and knew how deep infidelity affected people. How that kind of forgiveness must be one of the hardest to render. It was almost as if his life had taken on the same path as his father. Was it fate? Was history really repeating itself? He decided to try with all he had, to get Gloria back. Face his fears. Exorcise a few more ghosts and take a real good look at himself.

He would spend a few days with his old man. Tek een de Vibes Injection verses King Sonic dance, then he'd make his way over to Kingston.

But this burning question came when Lothan was least expecting it. "Dad... who is Sweetie? Along with everything, I should have asked you long ago. Mum cried. Said she was being punished. Shouldn't have done it to Sweetie. What did she..."

"She told you about Sweetie?"

Dora stepped briskly out onto the veranda and picked up the used glasses.

"No, Dad. Not in details. She didn't tell me who Sweetie was."

"Sweetie was the girl I was supposed to marry, Lijah. She was my sweetheart. She was Nettie's bes' frien'. I came to Englan' wid de intention to send feh Sweetie. Nettie's father sent for her before I could send for Sweetie. Nettie's faada died in a terrible accident at a foundry he was working. Nettie shared the same rented house with me and a few others. In those days, we who came, were all lonely, Lijah. All lonely. I was lonely an' Nettie was lonely. Plus, she was grievin' ova de deat' of ar faada. Well... all an' all... one t'ing led to de adda. We couldn't stop ourselves. We fell in love. She fell pregnant with Roy in 1957. I decided to do de right t'ing. Marry her."

"What?!" So what about Sweetie?"

"I couldn't even tell her myself. Not even in a letter. I had to let her hear it through de grapevine."

"Isn't that a bit low, Dad?" Here he was again. Judging. After he had promised himself he wouldn't.

"All of us do low t'ings in our lives, Son. Is your life perfec'?" Lothan settled his eyes on his son with purpose, as if he wanted an answer, but he got none.

"Son, when yuh live inna glass-house, yuh should neva t'row stones."

Lijah shrunk. His third eye kicked in revealing a too-bright picture of his own life. "Far from it, Dad. My life is far from perfect."

"Well, gimme a chance feh explain. Yuh is de one who come to Jamaica wid yuh whole heap a question dem...." He paused, kissed his teeth, then said, "Sweetie's faada sent for her a year later. I saw her from time to time in Handsworth. De firs' time me try to speak to her, she cuss me like a dog. An' she neva spoke to Nettie. Have us up inna ar heart. Bitta. If she see Nettie coming towards ar on the same side a de road, she would cross to de adda side. I t'ink she went off men completely... she neva married."

"Sweetie lived in Birmingham?"

"Yes, Son. Sweetie is closer dan yuh t'ink."

"Wha' d'you mean, closer than I think? Do I know her?"

"Son. I've suffered enough. I'm old now. None of us are perfect. Let me just have me last days in peace. Don't ask me any more questions. I hope God has forgiven me, Nettie, Dora... everybody. De Bible seh He is a merciful God." Lothan sounded more and more tired.

Dora showed her presence again. A kind of *'Leave him alone now'* presence.

"So... Dad, yuh not gonna tell me who Sw..."

"Lijah, yuh faada is tired now. Let bygones be bygones," Dora showed she had a voice.

But Lijah couldn't help wondering why it was such a big thing to say *who* Sweetie was. After all, his old man had told him pretty much everything else. Could that be any worse than the rest?

"Yuh see yuh uncle Stan lately?" Lothan asked out of the blue.

"No. Not lately," Lijah replied, a little surprised at his father's question.

Lothan stared off into the distance again and could have drifted far, was it not for Dora's voice that alerted him to dinner, once again.

"Thank heavens for microwaves," Lijah said, as they sat, eventually, to eat. Eating cold boiled breadfruit would certainly not be his favourite thing. Regardless of what he might claim to be, he was a born English man.

As he laid in his bed that night, finding it hard to go to sleep after that long chat with his old man, mosquitoes singing in his ears, Lijah started thinking again, about his mother. She had done a human thing. Immoral maybe, but human just the same. Hard to believe, but she had taken her best friend's man. Now, Lijah saw her not as Nettie, the sick, bed-ridden and hard-done-by, but as Nettie, the young woman who was lonely in a country that was not her own, grieving her deceased father. Both her and the old man had a choice. A choice of where their loyalties lie. She was Sweetie's best friend, and Lothan, Sweetie's sweetheart. Both their loyalties should have been with Sweetie, but they were adults. They made their choices. And they chose.

Lijah had stopped judging now. It was easier. Easier not to judge. Easier when he realised that his mother was simply a human being, with a need. A need so strong, she took her best friend's man. And his old man was human too. He had needs. Needs so strong, he made love to his wife's new best friend, immediately beneath her sick-bed.

But how did his mum first suspect his old man? Perhaps he'll ask him how she first found out about this white woman. But he'll never know how she felt when she made the decision never to make his old man touch her again? Did *she* sleep with another man?

Now, Lijah recalled when he came home the morning after his first encounter with Lucy. He didn't walk into the bedroom and kiss Gloria like he used to. His conscience was digging at his soul. Conscience *after the deed*, but conscience, nevertheless. That morning he sat downstairs watching early morning TV. An hour later Gloria got up for work. The sound of her footsteps on the landing and her flushing the loo, brushing her teeth and showering, beat him up. *'She must be thinking something'*, he had thought. You see, he always had a shower and fell into bed with her for an hour or so, every morning before she was due to get out. It was routine. Like a wake-up call. And if it didn't happen, there had to be a good reason.

Gloria's footsteps back to the bedroom held a message: *'Something's up, Lijah. How come you haven't come upstairs this morning?'*

She came downstairs and walked to the kitchen. Lijah could feel her thoughts: so thick on the air they both shared, and it was as cruel as torture. Even the flicking-on of the kettle and the sound of the spoon against her cup beat him up.

Then she walked into the sitting-room and he felt sure she could see, or even smell Lucy on him. Women had that kind of bloodhound instinct: the ability to sniff out other females.

"You a'right?" she asked, looking him up and down with nuff questions in her eyes.

"Yeah, man. Me cool." But he couldn't even look his queen in the eyes.

"How come you didn't come upstairs?" she said under her breath, holding her cup of tea like a friend.

"Oh Babes, by de time I realised what de time was, you were up. I didn't want you to be late," he lied.

"Lijah, please. Don't gimme dat. An' how come yuh sitting on the settee with your overalls. Yuh neva do dat before? You're all nervy. W'at's wrong?" She spoke with a sharp tongue and looked him up and down again.

'Shit. A woman's intuition is like hypnosis. Mek yuh want to come clean to raas', he thought. He knew Gloria had convinced herself that something wasn't right, because she didn't even bring him a cup of tea. That wasn't like her. She was never selfish like that.

"Sorry, G', I'm not meself dis morning. Had a rough night. Yuh know 'ow dem w'ite man cyan work yuh hard. T'ink it's still slavery days to rahtid."

She gave him a long, questioning look, then turned and headed back to the kitchen, turning her fears over and over in her head. And he had heard the force of the cup connecting with the sink, his heart leapt. "See you later," she said, and the sound of the door pulling shut jabbed his heart.

The old lady would most probably handle things different from Gloria, but he would have liked to know how. He knew he hadn't got to know her much. What was she really feeling all those years before she died? Had she ever retaliated like Gloria had? Then he remembered the guy in the red SAAB. It busted his brain. He tried to sleep, but it was hard.

"Shoo fly don't bother me, shoo fly don't bother me..." Khamilla's voice was music to Lijah's ears. He had not seen her yet. The house had more burglar bars than it had bricks. Nonetheless it was a beautiful house. The garden was well kept. Humming birds busied themselves, stealing nectar from the healthy border of horseshoes. Lignum vitae dashed in random corners. The airwaves boomed:

Boom bye bye inna batty bwoy head
Rude bwoy nah promote nuh batty bwoy dem affi dead...

A lazy dog slept on the front step, heat rising in a wavering haze around it.

'*One man's poison is another man's meat*', Lijah thought, but he knew Gloria wasn't looking at it like that. It would have been nice if her parents had the chance to enjoy their life savings. Their blood, sweat and tears in Britain. The house they'd spent their lives wishing to retire in.

Lijah had turned up the same time as Nathan, the odd job guy who was helping the Fontaines the last time he was in JA. Nathan held a bag of shopping in one hand and a jelly-coconut in the other. Lijah followed him through. He was pleased at the sound of his daughter, shouting Daddy! But the smile was soon wiped off his face, when he realised that Khamilla could not have been calling *him* daddy, since she had not yet seen him.

He spotted his little girl playing with a gold knuckle-dustered hand. '*Who is dis brotha?*' he wondered. 'Some kinda gold-display stand or sop'n?'

Khamilla seemed fascinated by the spread of gold rings on this guy's hand. She was playing, but stopped at intervals, to play with it. A black Kangol hat tilted backwards on this man's head as he lay, swinging lazily on a hammock, his back towards Lijah. A woman lay with ease on top of him, her head resting on his chest.

"Miss G! Lijah is here," Nathan announced, in a sweet, uncut Jamaican accent.

"Daddy!" Khamilla shouted, running towards him. Lijah felt better, but not over the moon. She could only have one daddy. Feh real.

Gloria lifted her head and turned to face Nathan and Lijah. "Lijah?" her voice lazy from the heat. "I didn't know yuh were coming?" She rose and walked towards him.

Lijah penetrated her eyes, the knitted lines in his forehead asking the question, '*So yuh have man?*' Now he knew the idea of getting her back would have to be reconsidered. Gloria looked too cosy.

"Who was Khamilla calling Dad earlier, G? It certainly wasn't me."

Gloria looked sheepish.

"Dat was the firs' t'ing I said to you when you told Kunta you wouldn't get back wid me," Lijah said, only loud enough for Gloria to hear, avoiding eye contact with his rival. "I don't want me daughta calling anadda man daddy, G. Is jus' so." He raised his voice now.

" *'Hello G'*, would have been nice," Gloria said cynically. Lijah, dis is Glen. Glen, dis is Lijah." She took the shopping from Nathan and headed towards the veranda. "What yuh wan' feh drink, Lijah?" she asked as she walked.

"Yuh 'ave any cool-aid? Please." He remembered the last time Gloria got him a drink. The day she got the family together to tell them she had decided to live in Jamaica. He had sunk Super T, and she, a brandy. He had reached the inside of her thighs when she rejected him. Point blank. He still felt like a wounded dog. Worse when he knew Baby Face Glen had gone clear.

The men looked at each other. And now, the slow-motion gesture for a handshake gave them time to take a stock. Collect their thoughts. Then came the shock. Their last encounter in England not so long ago was much different from this. Baby Face Glen knitted his brows. Lijah gulped on his breath. *'Fuck! Of all de people Khamilla could be calling Daddy!'* His worse nightmare had just come true. Worse than he had ever expected. Perhaps he would wake up in a minute.

"Whaap'n pussy bwoy," Baby Face Glen asked assertively, stretching his words, yard style. "So yuh is de same Lijah...? Bombo claat. De las' time me see yuh, yuh did affi run to raas." He laughed mockingly. "Bwoy... it look like seh me an yuh 'ave a few t'ings in common. Feh one, we have de same taste in women: black an' w'ite. By de way... how is Lucy? A feel seh is yuh why me neva get more dan me SAAB, yunnuh." He gestured to the red SAAB parked in the garage and the whole jigsaw fitted. Now, Lijah's contempt for red SAAB would stay for good. "My girl Gloria pay feh de shipping-down," he continued. Me jus' affi mek sure seh me keep ar sweet inna bed. Unnuh English man cyaan fuck." He lifted his head and emitted a mocking laugh.

Lijah ground his teeth.

"She cook me up some good food an..." Baby Face took the opportunity to taunt Lijah. After all, he was on his territory now. "Feh a English 'oman, she come een like real Jamaican... By de way, me 'ere seh yuh get ketch grin'ing de baby-sitta. A true?" Baby Face laughed out loud again, exhibited a pack of oversized gold crowns, but there was no doubt as to what Lijah was thinking. *'Twenty-four-carrot-shit'*. "So is weh yuh did seh when she ketch yuh? *'It wasn't me'?"* He imitated Shaggy's voice, then another grating laugh. "A nuh not'n. You 'ave Lucy, me 'ave yuh queen." He spread the five fingers of his right hand and jabbed the air.

'This man isn't Gloria's type,' Lijah told himself. *'Weh she doing wid dis man? Why is Khamilla calling dis man daddy? Dere mus' be nuff betta men inna Jamaica she could have?'*

"Listen Rasta," Baby Face's eyes darkened with an evil cloud of threat, and the intimidation could be felt, immediately. "Yuh see if yuh tell Gloria anyt'ing 'bout me. Like if me see she mekin' any funny moves... like she waan lef' me? I will mek sure seh me fin' yuh an lick two shot unda yuh bombo claat... Yuh know how long me wait feh a meal ticket like dis. Yuh t'ink me is idiot like yuh? Work feh w'ite man till yuh sixty-five an all dat. Nah, man. Me nuh stupid. Me fin' boops."

Lijah was seething. Now he started to blame himself. He knew if he hadn't messed up, Gloria wouldn't be shacking up with this guy. He knew he had to do something. There was no way he could be at peace in Birmingham, knowing that Gloria and his daughter were with this guy. No way.

But what could he do?

Gloria appeared with a tray containing two glasses of cool-aid.

"Is what we 'aving feh dinna, Baby?" Baby Face twisted the knife a bit more. He rubbed his hand over Gloria's ass. An ass that had become sexier than before. It was obvious she had kept up her gym regime in JA.

"Yellow yam, green bananas, cornmeal dumplings and snappa fish," Gloria said, placing the tray on the small garden table. She knew it was Lijah's favourite meal.

"Nice. Gimme a box juice nuh, G. Me nuh want nuh Cool-aid." One-upmanship was being pushed to a pathetic limit now.

Lijah seethed even more. *'She used to be my girl'*, he sang inwardly, gritting his teeth and remembering the times he first made love to Gloria. Imagining this man's hands all over her was pulling at the meal he ate earlier, at his dad's.

Meanwhile, hours ahead in Birmingham, the unthinkable was going down. A deadly predator prowled in search of fresh meat. He liked them young. Vulnerable.

He held her tight, his groin against her ass.

The palm of his hands almost clutching her breasts.

She moved like an amateur against his hard dick.

Synchronized foreplay.

His woman (although the term was used loosely) was heavily pregnant and home, alone. *Stupid-ass-bitch*, his reference to her, summed up their relationship a treat. He had first used this term of disaffection when she first told him she was pregnant. They had made no promises to each other, so no loyalties lay with her. So tonight, as she nursed her belly in a sorry one-bedroom flat (abandoned by a distant cousin) in Alum Rock, he nursed his need for sex, drugs, guns and a whole lot more. It had happened all too quickly. They had simply met on their *marks* in a dance hall and got *set* to turn up the heat of the night. Little Miss Rough-it was *ready* to lay her body down, and there was nothing left for this dude to do, but to *go* crazy at it.

Tonight, like several other nights, if there were fresh meat to be had, he would have it.

"Yuh want a drink, Baby Girl?" This smooth-talking dude figured his fix from this *fresh-out-the-kitchen* lady was a sure one, and warranted a drink.

"Sweet white wine, please," Ikesha told him.

"A'right. Me soon come." He slithered across the crowded room to the bar, almost leaving a silvery trail behind.

Ikesha looked around for Sista Scorcha. It was her who had persuaded her to let her hair down at The Hurricane nightclub, once again, and now she was shocking out with a *'blinger'* from Jamaica. Or was it America? Or Canada, even? Regardless, he wasn't her type. Far from it. But she figured tonight, she would take a walk on the wild side. Stick her feet into this big pool of excitement, then pull it out again, real quick. But how was she to know that he had left his pregnant woman at home? How was she to know he had a woman at all? In fact, how was she to know that this was a globetrotting gangster, who had dabbled in almost anything, through sheer ruthlessness? Travelled to almost anywhere, through sheer pressure, from the law? In fact, what did it matter? It was only a dance.

Now, Sista Scorcha was by her side. She watched as the smooth operator handed Ikesha her sweet white wine. The mean dancehall queen gave him a warning look. *She* herself might be a dancehall tigress, but Ikesha, although not exactly naïve, was no reckoning for this guy's force. Scorcha had heard rumours of what he was capable of, and it was most certainly, not good. But it was only a dance; so filling Ikesha in wasn't necessary just then. "Just be careful, Ikesha," she whispered into her cousin's ears, then she headed over to the other side of the room to talk to Screech, a wanna-be dancehall queen. But Ikesha was used to those words. Scorcha nearly always told her that, as, no matter how many times Ikesha came out, she always seemed so green. New to the scene. Scorcha always felt the need to protect.

Ikesha was having a good time. The DJ licked out *Renegade*, the infamous rhythm, and the need for her dancing partner to be nasty, heightened. He jabbed her young ass with a brand new dance, "Yuh ready feh dis?" he asked, in a rough-and-ready tone.

Ikesha answered with a smile. But was she really beginning to like it?

An hour or so must have passed and the sweats of their foreheads flowed like a warm familiarity, onto each other's, mixing, mingling and flowing.

"Yuh want to come an' talk to me in me car?" He had picked up on the heat that was overcoming her. That was surely a long foreplay.

"Why?" Her body tingled under his spell: that strange, new, raw-edged, un-cut approach. It felt like the wild side she wanted to walk on for a while. But this was Ikesha. Young, *street-foolish*, but *'sensible'* Ikesha. How could this happen? Could she not feel the trouble he oozed?

"Me jus' waan talk to yuh, Baby Girl."

"You can talk here." She felt slightly light-headed.

"Nah, man." He held her hand and began to lead her.

"I have to tell Scorcha that I'm going. I came with her."

"But yuh jus' going outside. Yuh not leavin'."

"But I still want to tell her."

"How yuh ac' like baby so? Yuh is a big 'oman now. Look how yuh body good. Hot an' fresh-out-de-kitchen," he told her, his lecherous lips now brushing her left ear lobe.

"A'right. But jus' for a bit."

Ikesha couldn't deny it. She wanted to go. Live a little. After all, what could be wrong with sitting in a brother's car having a little conversation?

They walked to his black BM, where conversation came to life in a different kinda way. Switching accents like a maniac switched lanes on a busy highway; the brother talked of Jamaica, Canada, The Bronx, London and Birmingham. And yes, good old dance moves.

His adventurous life intrigued Ikesha, but still, she talked of books, living, travel and eventually finding not necessarily Mr Right, but a worthy guy.

"How old are you, Baby Girl?" he asked, reaching across and putting his arm around her.

"Twenty one... so, why do they call you...?"

But he had pounced like a hungry dog catching a piece of food, from mid air. His tongue was halfway down her throat. His right arm eagerly fumbled her raised nipples through her blouse and thin, laced bra.

"No. Stop it." She tried to push him off, though half serious, half playful.

He restrained her arms and kissed her neck, moving swiftly to her chest.

"No! You can't..." She got a little sterner, now.

"It's ok, Baby Girl... it's ok." He kissed her lips again. "You're so sweet... so nice. Yuh have a good body." His American accent did something for her. In fact, she didn't know which accent she liked more: the uncut Yankee dialect or the ready *yard* tongue.

Now, his right hand had found its way up her blouse and had gained access to her young, bare, tender breasts.

The sensation was good, but she was confused and doubted her own sense of responsibility. *Hotcoldhotcoldhot...* what did she want? His words were convincing. He knew his game well. And never before had she been touched so intimately.

Now, his tongue was moving slowly inside her belly button. It felt good, but surely, it had to be wrong. It wasn't her style. She had waited too long to end up giving it away in the cluster phobic confines of a BMW.

"Stop it! No! I'm not ready for..."

For the first time, she was having her nipples sucked. Warm moist lips pulled sweetly at her virgin breasts. Her whole body tingled.

"I want to make love to you, Baby Girl. You feel so nice." He fumbled her vagina through her trousers. "Can I come home with you tonight?"

"I don't... think... so."

"I want you, Baby Girl. Badly." He helped her right hand towards his hard dick, to prove how much.

Never before had she touched a man. No. Not at the ripe old age of twenty-one. Unlike most young ladies her age, she had no practical idea. "Take me back to the club. Scorcha will be worried."

"So, you gonna let me come home with you tonight? I won't do anything you don't want me to do. I just really like you. The way you move," he kissed her lips. "The softness of your lips... the firmness of your breasts..."

She felt like a woman, but still she told him, "Take me back."

"Only if you promise to let me talk to you at your place," he faked a feline playfulness.

"I came with Scorcha. I have to go with her."

"No problem. Jus' give me your number and your address. I'll come after she's taken you home."

There were no doubts as to how worried Scorcha was. When Ikesha walked back into the club, she was nearly having a fit. "Where did you go, Ikesha?! Me was lookin' all ova feh yuh. I know you're a big girl now, but…" Scorcha knew what she was talking about. Her own days as a scholar may have passed her by, and although she was always the one to encourage her cousin to let her hair down from time to time, she wanted to see her dream to become a newsreader materialise.

"It's ok. Just needed some fresh air." Ikesha wasn't even good at lying. She jittered. Felt hot. And the fact that she had decided to invite Mr Hot Stuff over for coffee, made it worse.

"You should have said. I would have come wid yuh. Anyway, me ready now. Yuh enjoy yuhself tonight?"

"Yes. It was good."

"Hope yuh neva tek dat bwoy serious. Dat one dat was dancin' wid yuh. Is weh 'im deh? 'im gone?… He's not yuh type. But me know yuh sensible anyway." Scorcha said, as she walked through the exit of The Hurricane once again.

"Did *you* enjoy yourself, Scorcha?" Ikesha asked her.

"Yeah, man. As always. Wicked night."

It was strange. This was the first man with any kind of lustful desire, to walk through Ikesha's door. And her choice for the *first* couldn't be more wrong. Before now, some would have called her sensible. A young lady with her head screwed on. And some would have said she was just a late developer, whose peers had left her way behind. Shari for one, had wished she had been just a little like Ikesha.

It was just over half an hour since Scorcha had dropped her off. He had called, disguising his eager intentions, and she had invited him over.

"Dis is a nice likkle place you have here, Baby Girl." It was his American accent that was now in role. "Looks like books are your first love."

"Yes. I've just finished my Media degree. I'm gonna make the most of my life before I'm old." She was sat nervously on the end of her settee.

"C'mover here and sit by me. Let's talk… oh. Waid a minute. Cain I gedda caffee or sop'n?" Admittedly, Ikesha was impressed with his versatility in American and Jamaican. He couldn't do the English one too tough, so he had left it alone.

"Yes. Sorry, I forgot to ask," she almost panicked.

"Tell you what?" the cool operator suggested, as he rose to his feet, "I'll make it." He was forward. "Just show me where things are. I'll make you one while I'm at it. I make a mean coffee, Baby Girl. That's providing you like coffee."

Ikesha chuckled. "Ok." She led him to the kitchen.

She hadn't asked before, so, as the kettle hummed to a boil, she asked,

"So how come you've lived in so many countries? Jamaica, America, Canada...?"

"Oh, it's a long story. I wanna talk about you. How many men have you had?"

She looked sheepishly at him. "None."

"None?! You're never a virgin?"

"Yes. And I want it to stay that way until I'm sure."

"Until you're sure of what?"

"That the person is... well... I shouldn't really say Mr Right, because I don't think many people meet Mr Right, settle down and live happily ever after. But the person who will take my virginity will be special. And it won't be for now, that's for sure."

"Me hear yuh, Baby Girl," he said, holding her in check. The message was clear. She would be game for a grope, but there won't be no fucking. There would be teasing, but no pleasing. Foreplay, yes, but the afters could stay.

But was he worried? *No*. He had a will. And with this *will*, came a gruesome, deadly, horrific *way*.

Coffee was served.

Hot and fresh out the kitchen... R Kelly's *Ignition* seeped out from the living-room and into the kitchen.

"I feel so comfortable with you, Baby Girl. It's as if I knew you before." The statement was delivered with a mixture of accents.

"Really?" She was flattered.

They were back in the living-room now, on the settee, sitting at a very close distance to each other. *Dip her feet in, then pull them out again, quickly. Take a walk on the wild side.* That was all she wanted. But *who* was he? Not just his name. What monster? What manner of man had she let into her flat?

Mama rollin' that body...

"Yeah, man. Me like yuh."

Bounce, bounce, bounce, bounce, bounce, bounce... R Kelly was doing his thing.

Of all the nice guys in Birmingham, what character had crossed this undeserving, young girl's doorstep? She was alone. Vulnerable. Nobody knew she had him there. Not even her cousin, Scorcha, who was now in snooze land. As far as she was concerned, she had dropped Ikesha home, and watched her close her front door, before she drove off again.

"You feel so good, Baby Girl," he whispered, kissing the smooth skin of her sweet face and the memories of their earlier encounter in his car filled her head. "It's gonna be a lucky guy who gets to de-flower you."

She chuckled, choking on flattery, not knowing how rehearsed it was.

"Hey, what time is it?" He faked a concern to rush. Like a ravenous man would fake his desire to walk away from a pot of bubbling peas soup.

"Four o'clock," she assured him.

He reached for his coffee and sipped it. "I hope you're not gonna waste dat nice cup a coffee I made you. I don't make coffee for everyone, you know. Only a sweet girl like you could get a man like me inna de kitchen."

She laughed.

"Drink yuh coffee, man," he almost commanded, "you haven't touched it," he ended in a cunning banter.

"I almost forgot," she said, reaching over for the specially made cup of beverage. It was lukewarm now, so big sips were taken between lines of conversation. Soon, the cup was empty.

"So, why do they call you R...?"

"...Four o'clock, hey?" he cut in quick and purposefully, before she could finish her question. Almost as if to avoid the ugly task of explaining.

"Five past four, now," she reminded him, then relented, "They usually give names like that to people that are hard. Solid. You know, like bad boys and gangsters. Like there's a guy around call Bongo Dee. From what I heard, he's deadly, man. But you're not like that, are you?"

He laughed, and as the rapturous sounds ended in a significant calm, he looked a devilish look into her eyes. A look she had not detected. All she could see in his dilated pupils was the same magnetised look she had seen back at The Hurricane nightclub. The look that had tempted her to take that walk on the wild side. *Dip her feet in, then pull them out again, real quick.*

"Oh, right. Soon I have to make tracks. Hit the pillows in my own crib."

But, before he had suggested that, Ikesha found that her conversation had began to wane into an uncontrollable slur. She felt dizzy, as if there was something more than coffee and milk in her cup. An overwhelming sleepiness had overcome her. She couldn't control it. And soon, it would take her, like the effect of an administered dose of anaesthetic.

"Baby Girl?" He was simply checking for the slightest morsel of consciousness. She heard his call through her semi-consciousness, but could not reply. She slumped onto the settee, and was fast falling into total unconsciousness. For a few seconds, she was aware of being undressed. His hands on her breasts. Between her thighs.

Bounce, bounce, bounce, bounce, bounce, bounce…

"Ikesha?" he checked again.

But that was it. All she heard. All she felt. She was gone. Out of it and into a world of deep unconsciousness.

And now, the one-man show had really begun.

Now it's like murder she wrote…

Busy, uninvited hands fumbled her outer and inner thighs.

Once I get you out them clothes…

His lips were on hers, and his hot breath all over her face. Eager fingers parted her lower lips.

I'm about to take my key…

Was he sick? Had the world gone totally mad? Was this a man that would say no to necrophilia? Debatable.

Stick it in the ignition…

And now, the strange treading of un-tread path.

Uncovered, disdain feet treading virgin snow.

The unfelt pain.

Violation.

A fading wish.

Bounce, bounce, bounce, bounce, bounce, bounce…

The rape drug GHB cruised through her bloodstream like a hungry shark, while her molester breathed sighs of satisfying relief.

A rose and a thorn.

He was a dangerous hunter. And she? Just another kill.

So gimme that toot toot…

And I'll give you that beep beep…

Ikesha woke and found herself lying awkwardly on her living-room floor. The pain in her back and the sensation from carpet burns made her panic. Her head thumped and she felt sick.

And what was that feeling? That weird, stinging, tingling, achy feeling… down below? She panicked even more now. Then she touched it. Her flower that was so well preserved.

'Oh my God'.

Blood.

She sobbed.

Blood that flowed from a broken lining.

'Oh… my… God'.

A stolen purity.

Another virginity profanely taken.

Another fallen victim, who will remain tight-lipped, forced to do so, by the threatening prospect of *shame*.

Another chosen sperm had long gone danced towards a waiting egg.

Another ambitious dream threatened.

Yes, another victim who would not cry *RAPE* for the sake of 'saving face'.

"Muuuuuum! Muuuuuum!" But Gloria would not hear her daughter's cry. She was countless miles away across the Caribbean Sea. "Mum!" Now, hysteria was setting in, "Mum! Mum!..." And never before had the word been infused with such meaning.

Shower.

Hot steaming shower.

The strong force of its boiling torrents. Surely that would help. Wash it all away. *BeatWashBeatWash...* Surely.

Then came the calm. The setting-in of a harsh reality. The *'no choice'* acceptance. It came with the breaking of a strange new morning, hugging her like a forced bonding.

The birds sang. They too, seemed confused. Or perhaps they weren't. Perhaps they were perfectly clued-up. You see, the dawn had long gone. And it was much too late for birds to sing.

CHAPTER * SIXTEEN

'Perhaps I should have listened to Festus, and let sleeping dogs lie', Kizzy thought as she sat nervously outside the house, trying to stop her hands from shaking. The final pieces to her jigsaw had come to light and now she was sat outside the front door wondering if this was one big mistake. But she knew she couldn't turn back now. If she did, she would always be on the flip side of the coin, wishing she had gone all the way.

The old lady had said she didn't want to be found. Didn't want to be confronted. But selfish as it may be, Kizzy was angry, and came anyway. She did a back-door thing and got access to her mother's name and address. To be rejected once in your life was bad enough. But twice? No. She wasn't having it.

'She didn't think about my feelings then, so why should I think about hers, now?' Kizzy thought, as she played nervously with the tips of her dreads, Bob Marley's *'Redemption Song'* seeping, like a prayer, into her head.

It was much closer to home than she had bargained for. Good old Moseley Village. Just around the corner. A place she visited at least twice a week, without the slightest idea that on numerous occasions, she had driven past the residence of the woman who had given birth to her.

She could not imagine what type of person could be behind that big white door. The house was intimidating: perhaps because of her fears. And there was no one, or nothing that could allay them. *'If only Gloria was here,'* she thought.

"Do or die," Kizzy said as she walked up the gravelled path to the front door. Before knocking, she peered in through the netless window, and saw nothing but a pack of dogs.

The knocker chilled her. A lion's head. Its opened mouth gaping out at her. Differing thoughts flooded her head. *'Perhaps the woman, hearing her footsteps on the gravel, would peer out, see a mixed race girl and choose not to answer the door. Or perhaps curiosity would get the better of her, and make her want to see again, the child she had carried inside her for nine months, now grown'.*

A perfectly groomed poodle spotted her and became unsettled. It didn't bark and Kizzy was grateful.

'My locks', she thought. *'Would my locks frighten her?'*

She counted the dogs. Six at least. Five corgis and a poodle. Now, before she could knock, one of them barked and alerted the occupier. An old lady manoeuvred her wheelchair towards the window and looked out. Kizzy eased back to prevent a premature decision on the old lady's part. She was assuming that that was her mother.

"Who's there?" a voice came through the letterbox.

Kizzy hesitated. She wasn't expecting that. Before she could think of an answer, she heard hurried footsteps descending the stairs. A blonde woman in her thirties opened the front door. She was a dead ringer for Madonna.

"Yes?" she asked in a toffee-nosed accent.

"I'm... er..." Kizzy stuttered, "is this where...?"

"You are?" the woman rushed her. Stunted her flow.

"I'm looking..."

"Searching for your mother?" she answered her own question with a question, keeping her eyes purposefully on Kizzy's birthmark.

"How did you...?"

"Well...? Are you?" She was abrupt. Bordering on rude, to be exact. It was as if she was expecting her.

"Er... Yes... I..." Kizzy peered over the woman's shoulder at the woman sitting in the wheelchair. The woman stared back at her, terrified.

" I know who you are. Come in," the old woman said.

Kizzy, who had so much to say, had drawn a blank. Her tongue felt heavy as she stepped in, and past the younger woman that held onto the doorknob, like an anchor.

The smell of mothballs struggled to prevail over the smell of dogs. Judging by the front of the house, she had imagined *Jasmine&Lavender* air freshener. Freshly cut fuchsias in old ceramic vases. Priceless, wooden old-fashioned furniture.

The old woman's eyes were glazed. She kept them on the extra-dark birthmark, just above Kizzy's left collarbone as she wheeled herself back into the living-room, laying her stick across her lap.

"Coffee?" the young blonde woman asked, almost rubbing her hands together in a *'getting down to business'* manner. Kizzy found her strange. Very strange.

"No... no thank you." Kizzy wanted answers, not English hospitality in a cup.

"Are you Tracy?" the old woman asked. "I told them I didn't want you coming."

"No... No... I'm not Tracy. I'm... Kizzy." I'm... sorry. I think there's been some mistake. I must have been given the wrong..."

"But you must be. You have her birthmark." The old lady became agitated. "It's the map of Jamaica," she continued, "he was homesick, your father. He said that was why you had that birthmark." Kizzy was a bit puzzled. Mama Maya had always told her that that sort of thing affected pregnant women. Not expectant fathers. And besides, she hadn't heard any white person talking like that. They would more likely be cynical about black people's explanation of birthmarks.

"Mine is liver," the old woman continued. "My mother used to love liver. Just above my left thigh... Yes... I loved him... your father." She stroked one of her corgis as if it were a child.

"Are you Beatrice, then? Beatrice Langford?" Kizzy wondered why she hadn't asked that before, but who does all the right things in sequence, in situations like this?

"Yes. I am."

Somehow Kizzy expected a much younger woman. Around sixty. But Beatrice looked much older. Must have had her late. But that was the least of her worry. She looked at the young blonde woman. *Her* name didn't seem to matter. She must be the helper. "I think I'll have that coffee now... can I sit down?" she asked, politely.

"Yes. Of course. How rude of us," the old lady said, shushing a well-groomed poodle from its resting-place. "I've seen you before. Yes. So many times in the village. Never dreamt it was you. Only your birthmark would have confirmed. Looked at every mixed race female I saw. All through the years I looked. But I would never confront my fears... Would never try to find you. Just looked."

Kizzy stared at her, almost with disbelief.

"You turned out nice. Your hair. Like Bob Marley's... S'pose you're a bit like your father."

Now, she watched the old lady's eyes fill up. She felt for her, but not as a daughter would. There were no heartfelt happy-sad feelings here. Not like she had with Mama Maya, her adopted mother.

"But why did you give me up? Where's my father? Is he dead?"

"Tea!" the blonde entered the room with a tray, breaking into the most crucial moment as if she was announcing the winning of a prize or something.

"You two might as well get acquainted. After all, you are half-sisters. We have so much to talk about. I haven't got long to live, you see. And I can't leave my money to dogs now, can I?"

"We're... sisters?" Kizzy stared at the cocky blonde.

"Yes. Sisters," the blonde answered, as if it was a jeer. "You have a brother too. If you stay long enough, you might meet him."

Not long after, there was a jingling of keys. A blonde white man pushed his head 'round the door. He had shifty eyes. The 'burly blonde' swept one hello across the room, then rested his eyes on Kizzy. "You must be Tracy," he said, fixing his eyes on her birthmark: everybody's landmark.

"She's Kizzy now," the old lady corrected. "They've changed her name."

He walked over to the fireplace, seemingly, ignoring the old woman's explanation. He picked up a bottle of Emporio Armani and sprayed it wastefully on himself, everyone else in the room catching a share of the squirt. Burly he might have been, but there was something about him that made Kizzy think '*camp*'.

"So why did you give me up?" Kizzy got back to business. That's what she was there for. Not to be acquainted with siblings.

Today was Fari's eighth birthday and he wouldn't be happy if he didn't have a party. A week ago, Kizzy spent some time in Jolly's, choosing a special card for him. The table was packed with presents, the majority brought by his ten friends who came to celebrate with him. They all huddled round the table anxiously waiting for the moment when Fari would blow out the candles and they could tuck into all the goodies. Uncle Lijah was on his way over. He had rung to say he was running late. It was a pity Auntie Gloria couldn't be there. Fari knew they weren't blood-related as such, but they were his godparents and as good as real auntie/uncle relatives, so the auntie/uncle term came almost naturally. He had always addressed them so.

Kunta was perched on the bottom stairs, sniffling frantically: an action he couldn't control of late. He looked ill, and under the weather. Along with the lining of his nostrils, the young man was losing it, slowly. But he had never failed to be with Fari on his birthday. He was like the big brother Fari never had. In fact, for a while, it was thought that Kizzy couldn't conceive. But by rights, if Festus wasn't supposedly firing blanks, she should have had children as old as Ikesha and Kunta. So when she fell pregnant with Fari, everyone sighed with relief.

Shari sat on the stairs above Kunta. She was almost fit to drop. Their second child was due in a month.

Eleven-month-old Menilek amused his auntie, Ikesha. Besides, she needed to be amused. Having an abortion was a tough one, but with her mother across the sea, it was a double-whammy. And for such a young girl too. But even if Gloria were here, would Ikesha have told her? And the rape? Would she have shared that with Gloria? Sista Scorcha thought everything was fine. So the secret lay only with the troubled young girl, and a shifty Mr Black BM.

In fact, how many black women had cried rape? Brought their offenders to justice? How many have, or will, bravely throw back the veil of pride, look shame in the eye and cry rape? Not many. No. If there's one thing sistas cannot take, it's shame. Shame of any sort. Pointing fingers. Whispers behind palms. Sussu-sussu. So the thought of anyone saying, *'See her? She was raped, yunnuh'*, would most certainly not do.

Kizzy scanned the front of the house frantically, as soon as a car would pull up. She would never forgive Festus if he missed Fari's birthday. With all his misgivings – the regular beatings that Kizzy took, for whatever reason, Festus had never missed his son's birthday party before. Lately though, his behaviour had taken another strangeness not even Kizzy could understand. Of course she knew he was pissed off about her wanting to search for her real mother, but that couldn't be all. Still, it was a sore subject since that morning he had that strange outburst, so Kizzy kept any pursuit proceedings to herself. Eventually, she would find a way of telling him that she had found her. *'Let's get Fari's birthday out the way'*, was her thought.

"Just hold on another few minutes, Darling," Kizzy said to Fari. "Your dad will be here in a minute. We'll sing happy birthday then and you can blow out your candles."

It was hard. Try stalling a bunch of seven and eight year olds when there is a mouth-watering selection of food to be had. Luckily Fari had already opened all his presents.

Kizzy looked up to the sound of a car pulling up. It was Lijah. She wished it were Festus.

"Irie," Kizzy said as she opened the door.

Lijah walked in and gave her a kiss. "Yes sistren," he said.

He spotted Kunta and Shari on the stairs. He gave Kunta his fist and kissed Shari. Now, he paused and looked questioningly at his son. A pang of concern bubbled in his belly. He would talk to him later.

"Yo! Ikesha!" She was coming towards him in the passage. He kissed her and his grandson.

"Hiyah, Dad," Ikesha said in a down tone.

Lijah noticed the low key in his daughter's voice. They hadn't spoken for a while, as there had been too much going on lately. Lijah had lots to say too, but all would come later.

"Where's the birt'day bwoy?" Lijah shouted, putting his head 'round the dining-room door. A bunch of oversized seven and eight-year-olds looked at him.

"Uncle Lijah!" Fari shouted, giving Lijah his fist.

"Bwoy, yuh have nuff presents. Here. Auntie Gloria sen' dis, an' dis is from me." He handed Fari the packages simultaneously.

"Thank you, Uncle Lijah... And Auntie Gloria in Jamaica!" he shouted amusingly, as if Gloria could hear. "Is she coming back, Uncle Lijah?" Fari asked.

Kizzy looked at Lijah.

"I hope so, Fari." He looked at Kizzy. "I hope so." There were things he would have liked to tell Kizzy. But more so, there were things he would have liked to tell Gloria. But he never had the chance to tell her anything. Baby Face was constantly by her side. Like ticks on a cow's behind t'raas. But he knew one thing. He felt guilty for leaving his daughter to an unsure fate.

Kizzy lightened up. Festus had just pulled up. "Yuh dad's here now, Fari." She rushed to the front door and opened it. Festus hurried up the drive knowing he was late.

"Weh yuh was, Festus?" Kizzy dared to ask.

"Cho Kizzy, me's a big man. Me's no pickney. Don' ask me dem t'ings deh." He seemed harassed.

The point was taken and Kizzy was clocking him. Hard.

"Kunta!" Festus shouted, and the whole fist-touching, cheek-kissing, baby-petting was on again.

"Whaap'n, Ikesha?" Festus leered sneakily at her ass.

"Cool, Uncle Festus."

Lijah and Festus did the knuckle-wrapping thing – the non-verbal gesture worth more than any words could say.

"Yuh did go pon de front-line?" Lijah asked him.

"Yeah. Me jus' lef' dem man deh."

"Who?" Lijah asked.

"Jaro, Sugar an' Bunti dem."

Lijah took a stock. He knew how the front-line had changed, lately. Besides Festus seemed a bit too wrapped up. T'ings had changed from back in de days when a likkle herbs was the worse anyone could ever possess. Festus had become too preoccupied with certain crowd individuals. Especially after he himself alerted Lijah about certain dealings outa street: another ride Lijah assigned himself to watch. He and Festus had flexed for the longest time, and he had always seen him as a deep brotha, much deeper than any of the others. But even from the early years, Lijah had detected that his bredrin hardly talked about emotional things. Like the death of his mother, for instance. After the first telling, he seemed to have clammed up. All he would say was '*my madda dead years ago, Rasta. Me don't even waan feh talk 'bout it.*'

His attitude used to surprise Lijah. Even though he himself didn't talk too much about his own mother, the nasty nurse and his old man, he had always felt that the car crash that took two parents at once was a much nastier fatality. But like him, Festus just soaked himself in Rastafarianism. Talking about his family was like walking on hot coal. Lijah never pried, but he knew Festus had a problem. Like he knew he had *his*.

Although, of late, everyone thought it had stopped, there was hardly a month that Kizzy never had a beating. In the beginning though, they all wondered why she stayed. She had this 'better the devil I know' theory that didn't cut with bruises, bad enough to make a rebellious slave look good. It was a dying shame, but it had become a norm for poor little Fari. And that was not good at all.

Festus was seriously insecure. And to him, the only way to deal with it was by his might.

"Yuh get anyt'ing?" Lijah asked.

"Yeah, man. Me 'ave a nice draw. Expensive still. Yuh know how it go, famine an t'ing?" Festus handed Fari his present: a brand new leather hat made by Papa Dread's own hands. It would secure his locks just fine. Papa Dread sent him a leather jacket made specially, but he himself couldn't make it: his big toe had begun to play up again. In fact, the pain seemed to have moved up his leg, and was now settling in his right hip. And his own concoction of herbal remedy seemed to be failing.

"A'right Son?" Happy Birt'day!" Festus touched his son's fist.

"Dad, I thought you were neva gonna come."

"Nah, man. 'Ow me feh do dat? Yuh mad?" Festus said.

"Ok everybody!" Kizzy initiated, *"Happy Birthday to you! Happy Birthday to you! Happy Birthday Dear Fari! Happy Birthday tooo yooou!"*

"Hip Hip! Hooray! Hip Hip! Hooray!" the room echoed.

In one puff, Fari blew all his eight candles out.

It didn't seem long before the grown-ups found themselves in the living-room talking about varying subjects. Kunta and Shari had left. The kids made use of the garden. Everyone was missing Gloria.

Fari ran in from the garden and whispered in his mum's ear, "Mum, is Dad and Uncle Lijah going out later?"

"Why?" She whispered back.

"Because I wanna play with my toy gun."

"Oh Fari. I don't know. I told you he hid it. I only took it out the other day because you pestered me so much. He wouldn't like it. Plus what if Papa Dread finds out?"

"It's rude to whisper," Ikesha joked.

Fari looked at her, smiled, then proceeded to whisper.

"He won't find out. I'll make sure I put it back in its hiding place."

"Hey?! How yuh know where the hiding place is?" Kizzy whispered, jokingly.

Fari looked sheepish.

"Well," Kizzy whispered, "since you know where it is, when he's gone, you go get it, play, then put it back, ok?"

"Ok, Mum. Thank you… every time he's not here I'll do that, yeah?"

Fari hurried back to his friends.

"Yuh nuh know seh bwoy pickney nuh feh whispa-whispa like girl?" Festus shouted jokingly at his son and they all laughed.

"Fari's got everything for you, Auntie Kizzy?" Ikesha stated. "As he gets older, he's looking more and more like you. He's got nothing for Uncle Festus. Your genes are obviously stronger."

"I know," Kizzy agreed.

"I reckon she gimme a jacket, to raas," Festus joked, with a naked disrespect.

"Festus, nuh mek dem joke deh, bredrin," Lijah told him. "Is wha' duh yuh?"

But Kizzy simply held her head down in embarrassment.

"So wha'? Dat possible yunnuh bredrin. Is 'oman we a deal wid

178

yunnuh, star. Me nuh trus' dem a raas."

Ikesha didn't know how to take this. She hadn't heard Festus talk like that before. She changed the subject.

The evening was drawing in and a slight chill spread a blanket of gloom over a so far happy day. The trickling of kids whose parents had not arrived to pick them up, played cops and gangsters, using their fingers as guns, playing dead and doing all the things little boys do when imitating gangster movies.

Lijah shook himself together and announced he was making a move. It was contagious and Ikesha soon followed.

Now Festus and Kizzy were alone in the living-room. Words were scanty. Conversation dry. They had kept up some sort of charade for their guests.

A few more parents arrived. Tobias, Tobijah and Nomiah's mums all rang to say they were running late. Fari didn't care. All the better for him, he could play longer.

"Listen. Me soon come," Festus addressed Kizzy without looking at her. "Me jus' aggo check Rock. 'im owe me some money." Festus pulled on his spliff and handed it to Kizzy. It was almost like the *'cooking-you-dinner'* or *'bringing-you-flowers-cause-I'm-guilty'* gesture. He had always been mean with his spliff. Worse when there's a famine. He surprised Kizzy. "If Jaro rings, tell 'im feh call me mobile."

But Kizzy hoped Jaro wouldn't call. If there was one person who made her uneasy, it was Jaro - with Rock following close behind. She took the spliff and said nothing. She was hoping Festus would stay the whole hog with Fari, but there was no point labouring even trying to persuade him. She just hoped he would loosen up soon, so she could share the news of finding her mother with him.

"Fari!" Festus shouted down the garden. "Me soon come!"

It was music to Fari's ears. He knew his dad's *'Soon come'* was more like 'Nah come', and he would have nuff time to play with his toy gun.

He watched his dad's car disappear, then took the stairs two at a time, heading for the spare room to reach his gun. The mattress was heavy but he managed to lift it up. 'Yes!' he said. There it was. Just where he had seen it that morning when his dad had checked. All he had to do was to make sure it was there the next time he checked.

Little Fari thought he recognised a little more weight in his toy gun. He also thought there was a slight difference in its look, too, but thought there had to be an explanation.

"Mum, can we play out the front?" Fari asked. "I've got my gun. We wanna play cops and gangsters."

"Yeah. Not too far though, Fari. Tobijah dem mum soon come."

"Ok, Mum... Tobias! Tobijah! Nomiah! We're playing out the front. It's betta!"

"Where I can see you, Fari!" Kizzy shouted.

"Yes, Mum!"

His friends came running in, through the house and out the front door. Fari squeezed his gun into the waist of his jeans.

"Oh no!" Fari sighed in disappointment. He looked over towards the house and saw not one, or two, but all three mums pulling up. Playing cops and gangsters on his own would be no fun at all. Soon the boys said goodbye and walked towards their mothers' cars.

Fari asked their mums if they could come back another day. They all promised.

Minutes later, as the convoy of cars pulled off, Fari pulled his gun from his waist and aimed playfully at them. But before he could press the trigger, he saw his dad's car pulling up. The eight-year-old had never shifted so fast. The gun needed to be replaced. *Like yesterday.*

CHAPTER * SEVENTEEN

The next day, Kizzy woke with butterflies in her belly. In fact she could hardly sleep the night before. She had already broken the ice with her mother, and had discovered she had a half-sister and a half-brother, yet the notion of meeting them again made her nervous. She didn't feel Lucy was a half-sister she would miss. And as for her half-brother? He made Kizzy cringe. She had a strong spirit, and something told her, this brother lived a dirty life. The thought of it all made her want to change her mind.

Beatrice wanted to sort out her will. All three of them were about to come into a fortune. Lucy was already bathing in what her daddy had left her, and now it was time to hold her basket under her mother's cherry tree. But Kizzy wasn't used to this. Wealth. She had worked hard for the little she had. And of course Festus would not be expecting anything like this. If so, he would not have minded about Kizzy trying to find her mother. He would not have worried too much about working nine-to-five-till-sixty-five. Everybody would like an easy life. Money may not be everything, but it's certainly a big *'something'*. Kizzy herself even wondered if it might bring Festus a little happiness. Help whatever it is that's been troubling him. Stop the brutality that she had come so accustomed to.

"Hi, Fiona," Kizzy spoke apprehensively down the telephone line. "Yuh cool?... I just rang to ask you a favour... Could you have Fari for me this evening?... Remember I told you I'm going back to see her?... My blood mother... I feel so funny, though. As if I'm only after her money."

"Why shouldn't you be after her money, Kizzy?" Fiona had told her. "She gave you up for thirty odd years. If it weren't for Mama Maya, who knows where you'd be. Still, at least you found her. I could be sitting next to *my* mother on a bus and don't know it's her."

"True... so will you be able to have Fari?"

"Yes. 'Course I will. He can stop over until Saturday if he wants to."

"Great, Fi', that will be even better. Thanks. He'll love that. Plus I want to talk to Festus later about me finding my mother, but you know how he reacts sometimes. There's never gonna be a good time, but I don't want Fari seeing any more violence."

"And what about you, Kizzy? Do you want to see any more? Have you decided to stop taking that crap? That's the only way Fari is gonna stop seeing it. He's been seeing it for too long, K'. I just hope my little nephew don't grow up thinking that that kinda thing is normal. Never mind Festus being *'De devil yuh know'*. He's the devil no one wants to know. Kizzy, no woman in her right mind should be taking any beating from any man in the 21st century. People see you as some strong sista. Wid yuh long flowing locks an' all dat, an' yuh still tekkin' licks from man? Nah, man. Dat nuh right."

Fiona and Festus had never seen eye to eye ever since the first time he laid his hand on her sister. She had so much pent-up anger towards him, it wouldn't be worth his while to give her the chance to let rip at him.

Kizzy and Fiona were opposites. Kizzy was petite, too tolerant and looked beyond the immediate problem. Her strengths, it seemed, lay on the inside: analysing, justifying and forgiving, rendering her *weak* on the outside. Fiona, however, could outwardly challenge any man who dared to try to use her as a punch bag. Her tolerance went out the window with Winston, aka *Bush Tea*. And as for analysing the reason why a man becomes a woman beater, you'd do better sending her to fetch water in a basket.

The day had stretched much longer than Kizzy had expected. Her head was buzzing with things she didn't expect. Talking to Beatrice in such depth was a real eye-opener. She was overwhelmed and wanted so much to talk to Festus, even though she had gone against his wishes, and disturbed a sleeping dog. Luckily, the dog didn't bite.

She pulled up outside her house to see a host of familiar cars. A Jeep, two Golfs and a Beema. She was tired and laden with the guilt of not telling Festus what she had been up to. It was the second secret she had kept from him and she had intended not to keep any more, no matter how small. The first one was big enough. But the way he was had given her no choice.

Lately she had been sneaking around rather stealthily. Like a burglar in an alarmed building. He had been giving her suspicious looks, and somehow, she knew he was thinking something that wasn't so. If only he would ask. Or even talk to her. Instead, he had let his preoccupation take him over and it was getting to her in a big way.

Tonight she didn't want to play at being polite; hosting a gang of *itally* charged domino players. Besides, Kizzy had lost respect for a few guys in the once-faithful pack. Having them gather in her house had lost the easy edge it once had. One member of the bunch, in particular, she could do without. *Period.*

'Why should I feel guilty for seeking out my real mother?' she asked herself as she tried to find a place to park. *'Festus makes me feel as if I'm having an affair.'* She managed to find parking several yards from her usual spot. She parked up and ejected Gladys Knight's *'Misty Blue'* from her stereo.

"What's happening, K?" A slow *charged* voice penetrated the windows of her car. She looked towards the sound, easing down her window at the same time.

"Yuh comin,' I'm goin', yeah?' Reds stated the obvious.

"Reds! What's happening?"

"Tell me nuh, Sweetness?" He was now standing with his elbows against the roof of her car. "Nice night?"

"Er... Yeah... Yeah. It was ok... I see Festus' got a house-full."

"Yeah. Bwoy I had to ease out. Think I've been losing my touch aroun' de domino table, lately. An' I man don' like losing, yunnuh. Still, just as long as I don't lose me touch wid me queen. Or as long as we don' lose anadda yout' to drugs, yaah 'ear me?"

His latter statement seemed out of place, but Reds was mysterious like that and something told Kizzy he wasn't here tonight for the sake of banging a few dominoes on a table.

"I hear yuh, Reds. True t'ing."

"A'right, Empress. Gwaan go hol'-up yuh man. Communicate. Yeah? Communication is good."

Kizzy smiled. It was hard to believe that Reds could be as deadly as sin, yet, on the other hand, he could be as charming as ever. Like Papa Dread, if the cause is a just one, Reds is not to be messed with. Both men were the only ones Kizzy had some respect left for and felt comfortable with.

"Well, Sweetness, me gone, yeah?" He touched her right shoulder and walked away, leaving a stretched-out hand behind, a trademark unique to his persona.

"See you, Reds," Kizzy said, as she looked across to the illuminating square of her downstairs window. She checked her watch. Time had flown, only, she wasn't having fun. The busy silhouette of her other half showed either a break from their game, or that his guests were leaving. She finally emerged from her car and walked nervously up the path.

She didn't need to push her key. Festus' guests were leaving, and the front door was wide open.

"Something I said, guys?" she forced a joke.

"Whaap'n, Babes?" Bunti said.

"Yuh know it's pas' yuh bedtime?" Sugar bantered. "Yuh shouldn't be out dem time a night yah."

But all Kizzy's attention was on her man. She watched his eyes. She could feel his mood. It was as sliceable as a tight duccunnuh pudding. She felt naked. Vulnerable. If only she could beam herself upstairs. Away. Anywhere. Anywhere up and out of this gathering.

"Festus, more time, Bredrin. Ketch yuh lata," Jaro sounded out. His voice grated on Kizzy. He was the last to go. On top of her present fear, the hairs at the back of Kizzy's neck stood up. 'Why was he here anyway?' she asked herself. 'In my house. My space. Why does he still come? Does he have a short memory? Or is he simply nerveless?'

But now, as she felt Festus' silent persecution, Kizzy wished someone would stay. Anyone, apart from Jaro. Anyone who could protect her from her pending fate. Yes. She could almost feel the licks already.

"Yeah, man," Festus replied, touching fists with Jaro, "more time."

She was now inside, and making her way fast, upstairs. To wipe the guilt away, maybe. The guilt of defiance. The guilt of seeing her mother, against her man's wish.

The front door slammed and she shuddered. Her blood chilled and hairs stood on end, all over her body.

Now, the silence was stifling. She hated it.

"Where's Fari, Kizzy?" Festus' voice jabbed, ready for his premeditated fight.

"He's with Fiona." She continued her ascent.

"Why?" He followed.

"Because I was going out. I wasn't sure you'd be in." She didn't look back. Bravery and fear fought for possession in her throat.

"Did yuh ask me if I was goin' to be in? Yuh know me nuh like me son wid dat gyal."

"I wouldn't want Fari being here tonight anyway, Festus. I don't like the company you're keeping, anymore. An' anyway, *dat gyal* happens to be my sista. Fari's auntie." Fear was winning, but she wouldn't show it. Instead, she gave as much as she was getting, and it riled him.

Women should know their place. Yes. Even in the 21st century.

"Yeah? What about de friends you're keeping, Kizzy? An' by de way... Fiona is *not* yuh blood sista, so derefore, *not* Fari's blood auntie, seen? Me nuh like ar, Kizzy. Me sure she is a dyam dyke, to rahtid."

Kizzy gave him a daggered look. "Festus, my sister isn't gay. Don't go throwing wild accusations around."

"She is, Kizzy. You must be the only one who can't see dat. And anyway..." the antagonist continued, "seem to me, you fin' some man. You've been acting kinda strange, lately." He sat on the bed, looking questioningly at her. His left foot shook: like a bull would scratch the ground, in readiness for a charge.

"Not as strange as you've been acting, Festus. Had a good evening, did yuh? Wid all yuh fas' lane frien' dem?" she placed her ass on the bed.

He kissed his teeth as he stood up, now watching her harder than before. Today, her strength to argue back puzzled him. And what did she mean by *'his fast-lane friends?'* What did she know?

Kizzy stood now, as the atmosphere in the room stiffened, viewing him through the full-length mirror. She could feel his eyes digging through her flesh. The moment felt wild. More than ever before, she felt cornered. Unsafe. She didn't want him there at all. But still, she wouldn't show it.

"You couldn't make us a cup of tea, could you Fes'? I'm dying for one." Perhaps changing the vibe would help, she thought.

"Yeah. Afta a kiss." He was testing. "Didn't you miss me?" he bantered, a cunning reason behind it. She didn't like it. Felt she was on trial.

" 'Course I did. But you didn't miss me. All yuh bredrin dem was here."

"Yeah, right. Like I could mek love to me bredrin dem." Now he came towards her and groped her breasts, his hands, eyes and body working like litmus paper, looking for a result. An expected reaction. A clue. A host of off-the-beaten-track suspicions rushing around in his head and crawling up the strands of his locks like an army of disturbed ants. He was, most certainly, putting her to the test. Flashbacks of his parents entered his head and played havoc with his brain cells.

She turned her head away from him. "Festus, just make us a cup a tea, will yah."

"Wait a minute... are you begrudging me a kiss, Kizzy?"

" 'Course not." She turned towards him again, and kissed his lips. She wanted to try and wade off brutality.

He responded with more passion than she could cope with just then. Confusion gripped him. The thought of another man should have repelled him, but it didn't. Instead, it wrapped itself in jealousy, possession, rejection and memories. Yes, old memories. Memories of things Kizzy didn't know, and would never have dreamt of.

"Hol' aan a minute... what fragrance am I detecting?" He paused.

"Wha' yuh mean, Festus?" she bemused.

"The strange fragrance. I can't place it."

"DKNY, you silly." Fear filled her. What on earth could he be thinking? You've smelt DKNY before. Festus, stop talkin' nonsense."

"Nah, man. Dat is no DKNY a bombo claat. DKNY an' somet'ing else, maybe? Emporio Armani? Yes. Dat's it."

Shit. She remembered. Her half-brother was always showering in the thing, unintentionally obliging everyone with squirts of it. It wasn't even any good trying to tell him the truth.

Now, she saw the familiar rage in her man's eyes and knew this was the pivotal moment.

He loosened his grip on her. Deep obsession and jealousy were devouring him. The only way he knew best was to punish her with his might; his brand of 'ownership' lay in the buckle of his belt, the force of his fists, the sole of his shoes. And yes, the angry lump of flesh that hung from the meeting of his thighs.

Now he must intimidate her. Brutally. Dis-empower her, just a little bit more. Show her who is boss. Then, came again, the flashbacks of his parents, a confusing signal he had read wrongly. No room for reasoning. No heart for compassion. No ability to love her. To look within himself, or beyond the realms of his might.

"What are you talking about, Festus?"

"Ahhh... I see... It's *Festus* all of a sudden is it? Not *Fes'?*" How petty? The brother needed help. Seriously. A slave to insecurity and the rhythm of a gruesome past.

She looked deeper into his eyes. "Festus, if yuh have sop'n feh seh, den seh it! Yuh accusing me of sop'n?!"

"Where were you tonight, K'?" He flashed his locks as he became more agitated.

"I went to see a friend."

"I said... Where... the fuck... were you, Kizzy?!"

"I'm not listening to this." She attempted an exit, but was pulled back by her left arm.

"Who is he, Kizzy?... Fed up wid me now, yuh gone fin' man? All yuh 'oman is de same, yunnuh!"

"Festus, let me go! You're hurting me!"

"You haven't answered my question, Kizzy!" Whap! The force of his hand across her face sent her flying, and her head met with the frame of the door, leaving her dazed.

"Are you fucking around on me, K?" Whap! Another blow met her left cheek.

"Festus, for God's sake!" she screamed at the top of her voice. "Weh yuh get dat stupid idea from?!" she protested, as she was pushed to the floor.

"Stupid idea?!" Thud! Now the boot was in. "Stupid idea?!"

"Festus!" She held her belly, winded.

"How could you, Kizzy?!" He picked her up and pounded her onto the bed. "How could yuh mek anadda man touch yuh?! Yuh t'ink I don't notice de way yuh sneaking 'round feh weeks, now? Who de fuck is he?!" A slap to her precious face.

Now, he released the studded button on his jeans.

"Festus... Please!" she pleaded.

"Who *is* he, Bitch?!"

She felt her brain shake inside her scull from the force of his fist.

Rip! There goes that little dress she loved so much. Whack! The buckled end of his belt greeted her left thigh.

"Festus! Stop it! Stop it!"

Now his body overpowered hers, crushing her breasts, as he stretched her arms beyond their capabilities. And like a mad man, his teeth descended deep into her right breast, biting mercilessly into her tender flesh. She needed help. But God help *him*. He needed it most. A monster had been created for the longest time.

"Yuh jus' like me fuckin' madda, Dora!" he babbled between gasps of air. "Dat is exactly what she used to do! She used to tek adda man! Dress up inna dat nurse's uniform every night, pretending she's some saint, w'en all de time she was fuckin' out on me ole man! Dat is w'at turned him into a fuckin' drunken tramp, walking de streets of Birmingham like a dog, to raas! Woman! Dem is de root of all fuckin' evil!"

And now... the intrusive entering. The ruthless hammering.

He did not see Kizzy. Just a 'fallen' woman. In his eyes, she was a *whore*. A *slut*. A *prostitute*. Everything she wasn't. His corrupted mind had already devalued her, and now, his body must.

"De root of all fuckin' evil! No wonder he used to beat the hell out of her!"

The fierce hammering of jealousy heightened.

"Now she is livin' in Jamaica wid a new man! Retiring in style! Soaking up de sun, while me ole man walk de streets of Handsworth, lifting de lids of every bin he can fin'!"

"Festus! Stop it! What yuh talking about!"

The violating of her flesh, prolonged. Like madness, anger gave him strength ten-fold.

He had tarred her with his mother's brush, and his attempt to punish her came with his sexual might, his rod of correction having no mercy on his woman who had no part in his messed up past.

"Festus... I thought... your... parents... died in a car crash." Kizzy was now dazed, but had to ask.

Festus ignored her question. "I had to run away!" His anger became amplified. "Leave Bristol to bombo claat! I was only a yout'. I couldn't take it any longer! The root of all evil! Woman! Ugh! Woman! Ugh! Woman! Ugh! Ugh! Ugh!" The *fierce, angry coming of a man, juxtaposed* with *the tears of a frightened little boy.*

His sick temperament.

Her unexplainable hurt.

Merciless, uninvited protruding.

The ripping of her depth that came with a force her abuser himself didn't even know he had possessed.

Her now '*broken*' spirit.

Her no-avail tears.

Old memories surfaced.

And now, their deadly silence.

This abuser was not born, but made. The heights of a misguided manhood, reached and kept, attained by years of watching, hearing, feeling. And he, while his father abused, without realising, soaked up every bit: *'The power of a man is in his might! The weapon of control is in his fists! The power of a man! The power! The power! The power!'*

But Fari. Yes, sweet little Fari. What about him? Was he being a sponge? Or a duck's back? Would history repeat itself? Was another monster being created? Only time would tell. Yes. *Only time.*

Should Festus have sympathised with his mother, and not empathised with his father? Whatever he should or should not have done, he had empathised wrongfully, identifying himself mentally with his father's plight, whilst apathetic to his mother's pain. And now, the only outlet for his anger was the woman he loved.

This was not Deep South America in the 1800s, where white men raped black women for economic and psychological gain. No... it was inner city Birmingham, 21st century England, where a brother violates his woman to gain *'control'*.

Now, the reason for their deadly silence, coupled. Entwined. Danced like evil shadows against the walls of their minds. Kizzy baffled, Festus confused. Both wanting to know. *She* wanted to know what shark had been swimming around in her man's head. *He* wanted to know how to deal with his emotions, and seek help. But his pride wouldn't let him seek the help he needed. It was much bigger than his need. Yes. Good old *Pride*. It cometh before a fall.

Kizzy's echoing sobs, mixed with the knowledge of the lie she had lived for so many years with a man she loved to the core, spread a blanket of horrible *'truth'* over her body. Her body, which was now a spiritual levitation. In her moment of realisation, she had tried to disown it. Step out of it, like a pissed up nightdress, at dawn. She detested her beautiful body. To her, it was ugly again. As ugly as she had thought it to be, eight years ago. Eight years ago when she was *raped*. Yes. A well kept secret. A secret she could never tell Festus. He would have only accused her of instigating it. Wanting it. She knew him well.

But that was different. Festus was her man. He raped her brutally. Back then, although by force, it was more on the sly. A deadly character with an evil, lustful wanting. A wanting that had manifested itself into an unauthorised *'taking'*.

Kizzy didn't need to ask. She now knew that Montie, the drunken tramp, was Festus' father. The father who she, and everyone else, was led to believe had died, years ago. All was revealed to her, now. All, including the emphasis of the fact that you can never really *'know'* anyone, completely. Everybody wears a mask. Big or small, everybody has a secret.

'But his mother? Who is his mother?' she thought, as her insides throbbed like a stubborn toothache. *'Is she alive?'*

Festus fixed up. The *too-far-gone* contempt he had for women, triggered by the belief he had of his mother's action, had made his queen a victim. Convicted her a whore before proving her one. He was a product of his parents' lives. He had physically run from Bristol, to a big city, but he couldn't hide. No man can hide from himself.

But it didn't stop there. His earlier recognition of the need to seek help had diminished, and now, remorse wasn't even a speck in his turmoiled head. It was lost. Lost in the black clouds of a deadly wish. The ultimate wish, to find and kill the man he thought had dared to touch his woman. Kizzy dragged herself to the phone like a dope-head and struggled to remember her own sister's telephone number. She was one frightened sista. More frightened than she could ever remember being.

"Fi'... Get over here, will you?" she despaired. Now..."

"Kizzy?!" Fiona's perplexed voice floated over Kizzy's thoughts. "Are you ok?! What's wrong?!"

"He's beaten me up again, Fi'. *Raped* me dis time."

"He what?!"

"Fi', Festus thinks I'm having an affair. I'm in a bad state, sis."

"Kizzy?... Festus *RAPED* you?!"

"Yes... Just get here quick, will you."

"Kizzy, yuh call de police?!"

"No!... No!... No police, Fiona. No police... He'd probably kill me."

Fiona turned up to find Festus sitting at the wheel of his car, his right foot onto the pavement, Bob Marley's *'No woman no cry'* blaring out. *'Was that of any significance to his woman's state?'* Fiona wondered, *'or was it pure coincidence?'*

Festus pulled on a spliff, looking spaced out, as if he was at a place in his head where maybe drug addicts go to *'forget'*. Or even where death lives.

Fiona tried to analyse the situation. She looked at the front door. It was wide open. A nosy next-door neighbour stood, arms folded, and looking at her. She had obviously heard the commotion yet again, and was hoping gossip would flow towards her, in the wind.

Fiona slammed her car door and hurried past Festus, towards the path leading to the house, giving him nothing but a silent, *promising* glance. It said *'Yuh dead bwoy.'*

"Kizzy?!" she shouted from the bottom of the stairs, after checking the living-room.

"Up here, Fi'!"

Fiona ascended the stairs in tiers of four.

"What the f...!" She saw red. *Scarlet red.*

"Where's Fari?" Kizzy had hoped Fiona hadn't brought him.

"He's ok. He's over at the house with Grace."

"Grace?" Kizzy didn't like Fari being with strangers.

"Grace is my friend. Don't worry. Fari's fine," Fiona reassured her. "Grace is that lady I told you I read about in a magazine. You know, the one whose face was damaged by her boyfriend through jealousy."

"So how did you meet her? You read about her and she appeared?"

Kizzy found a second to front a little joviality.

"Kizzy, there's no time for jokes. Your state is more important right now, but if you really want to know, I met Grace at the Leeds Carnival. I remembered her from the magazine, and you know I'm not shy. I approached her and we became friends. She was living in London at the time, but her family is from Leeds," Fiona stated at speed. "Anyway, why did Festus do dis to you dis time, Kizzy? That's the question," she finished off.

"I told you, he thinks I'm having an affair. I didn't even tell him that I've just been searching for my mother. I probably would still have got battered anyway."

"Oh my God! Have you seen your face, girl!" Fiona shouted, as if she had only just seen it.

Kizzy's eyes were but two slits, and her jaws looked as if she had just had a stubborn wisdom tooth plucked by an amateur dentist. It was swollen beyond recognition. It had never been that bad. How could she allow Fari to see her like that?

"That's nothing, girl," she mumbled, "Good thing you can't see my insides."

"Kizzy… He *seriously* raped you?"

"Yes. Seriously. He was like an animal, Fi'. How does anyone prove that they've been raped by their *live-in-boyfriend - the man they love?"*

"*Love* Kizzy?! *Love*?! Don't tell me rubbish 'bout *love*. Wha' yuh call *love*? Don' tell me rubbish 'bout love! It's about time we all examine dis t'ing we all call *love!* I suppose yuh gonna tell me Festus *love* yuh as well! *Love* yuh when he's bus'in' yuh ass! *Love* yuh when him rapin' yuh! Yes?! Is dat *love?!"*

Festus was now in the room like a damp, mouldy cloth, He must have crept upstairs, since neither of the women had heard him approaching. His presence was ghostly. Airy.

"How do you prove it to *who*, Kizzy?" His voice was low. Threatening. Deliberately, he ignored Fiona's strong speech, (of which he had heard every word) and concerned himself only with his woman's.

"How could you do this, Festus? Yuh fuckin' heap a shit! Yuh on drugs or sop'n?!" Fiona voiced her opinion, a foul woman-beating stench crawling nastily up her nose, making her angry at the world. Angry at women for not shouting rape. For accepting abuse once too many times. For letting men off too lightly. For putting up with shit.

"You keep de fuck outa dis, Fiona." He kept his eyes on Kizzy, his stare demanding an answer to his pert question.

"Keep outa dis?" Fiona was enraged to a pivot that would shock even herself. "She is me sista! My fuckin' sista! Keep outa dis?! Are you sick?!" she relented, begging for confrontation. Up in his face. Eyes bulging. Heart pumping. Muscles tensing.

"Festus repeated, "I said... keep outa dis, gyal! Yuh t'ink yuh bad!" But she was still in his face. Staring him out. Puckering her lips. Breathing like a bull.

"So wha'?!... Yuh deaf?!"

"Yuh see if dat was *me*, Festus?... Yuh dead." Now, her index finger was too close to his left cheek. Speckles of spittle raced, uncontrolled from her frothing mouth, and settled on his top lip, with unease.

"But it wouldn't be *you*, would it, Bitch?! I wouldn't be with you, would I? I don't make love to men, an' yuh is like a fuckin' man, to rahtid. Yuh too dyam butch, gya..."

But before he could end his little speech, she floored his ass with a *'butch'* leg sweep. "So how about tangling with this butch lady then, *Mighty Mouse*?! Or do you just batter the sweet, feline types, like Kizzy?... And by the way," she lowered her voice and whispered in a vengeful tone, "since you will never know the meaning of *'love'*, you could never *'make love'* to anyone: man, woman or beast."

And before he could grasp what had hit him, she picked him up by the scruff of his neck. Whack! A classic uppercut punch startled him. He fell to the floor again. "What was that you were saying?" she asked, mockingly.

"What de fuck! Jeeesas C'ris'!... Listen gyal," he gasped, spitting a tooth and tasting his own blood. "Yuh come inna me yard an' attack me?!"

"*Your* yard, Festus? *Your* yard? Aren't you forgetting something? Dis is Kizzy's yard. Didn't you re-mortgage an' tek your share not so long ago? Or have your feet been under the table so long after it should have been kicked out from under it, you've forgotten?"

He lay there, perplexed, looking up at her, hating the power of a woman, over him. The deadly power of a woman scorned. For a moment, it was as if Kizzy was not there. The shock of her sister's ability to defend herself had taken her breath away. The beef Fiona had with her man, had to be cooked. *Period.* It had been left to simmer for far too long.

She stepped away from him, still fuming. He found his feet, but his pride was slipping. Fast.

"Ever experienced the Yoko Geri, Mr Mighty Mouse?" Kizzy relented. Duff! The deadly Side Thrust Kick immobilised him.

"Fi'?!" Kizzy spoke, now. "Stop it now! Stop it! You'll kill 'im!" How easy she had forgotten. Pity was creeping in. From what Fiona could see, her sister had simply become a creature of habit. A habit that had become stuck to the corner of her brain, like years of over-laid wallpaper. Stuck with love glue.

"I'll kill him before he kills you, Kiz'? Not a bad idea, is it?...Well, what are you gonna do about it, Kizzy? Are you gonna report this assault? Or are you gonna hang in there for more like you've been doing feh years? The phone's there. All you have to do is dial 999."

Kizzy's reply was nothing but a spate of uncontrollable sobs.

"Listen sis, the decision is yours. I can't force you to report your man for assault and rape. But I know one t'ing... Yuh *not* staying here tonight."

"*Ohhhhhh*," Festus grumbled, emerging from a state of semi-consciousness.

"You won't be going to any ball for a while," Fiona continued, ignoring Festus' grunts, "so let me just grab a few casual stuff." She spoke into the wardrobe, quickly grabbing a few things and throwing them into a case she had found at the top. "C'mon." She lifted her sister, bodily, and took her down the stairs and out to the car. The nosy next-door-neighbour stood her ground, now leaning against her gate, her non-verbal statement palpable.

"The bastard!" Fiona muttered, still not believing Kizzy had allowed this to happen to her.

"Kizzy! Weh yuh going?!" Festus had managed to scramble downstairs. "Going to yuh bwoyfrien'? It doesn't end here, Kizzy! It nuh en' yasso a raas claat. An' as feh *you*, Miss Karate Queen! Yuh dead, to rahtid!"

"Whaddaff!" Fiona was back with more vengeance. The Mae Tobi Geri caught Festus, unawares. Duff! The Jumping Front Snap Kick was a goodnight kiss. She didn't think she'd see the day when she'd use her karate moves, seriously. She was loving it. "In your dreams, you fucking woman-beating, peanut-brain, rapist shit!"

Festus was helpless.

"And if I were you," Fiona relented, "I'd cut dem locks off. Yuh giving true Rastamen a bad name. Rastamen are *peaceful* men. Not shits like yuh!" she whispered vengefully in his ears, her lips sweeping his earlobes with waves of wrath.

Fiona pulled up the front door after swinging Festus' hanging legs inside it, like a lump of dead, contemptuous carcass: that was a goodwill gesture. Luckily for him, she had not left them there, while she slammed the heavy, wooden front door.

"I miss Gloria so much," Kizzy was sobbing, holding her stomach, when Fiona returned to the car. "She must be having such a fun time, while I'm being used as a beating stick." She coughed. Blood splattered all over Fiona's dashboard.

"Shit! You're going straight to the hospital. Now!" Fiona started the engine, and put her foot down.

Luckily, Kizzy's brain was intact, but she needed to pay another visit to the dentist. The doctor had asked her if she wanted to press charges, but his question was simply as routine as the notes he wrote. He had seen enough of that situation, and knew she wouldn't. Statistics had shown that last year, alone, 19,000 women were physically abused in Britain. Nevertheless, the proportion that actually pressed charges, were considerably lower. So, as always, women-beaters were laughing. Cooking on gas. *Feh real!*

But it was tricky turning up at Fiona's, after the hospital trip. They had already surmised that trying to hide Kizzy's bruises from Fari was no less than impossible. It would be a while before her face would be back to normal.

"Mummy! What's wrong with your face?! Has Daddy been hitting you again?!" Fari had discarded the computer game he was earlier engrossed in, and accosted his mother and auntie in the passageway.

"Don't worry, Fari. Mum is gonna be fine," Fiona answered for her sister, who could do nothing for her son. She simply spoke through the nonverbal gesture of a tight hug, and her everlasting love.

"You wait 'till a get my gun!" the naïve little boy said, "I'm gonna shoot Daddy! Shoot him! Shoot him! Shoot him!" Hysteria was setting in. This was the worse he had seen his mother's face and it was playing havoc with his little mind.

"Fari!" Kizzy covered her son's mouth and hugged tighter, to control his temper. "Don't *ever* talk about shooting anyone! D'you hear me?! *Ever!*"

Fiona's face showed a grave concern. Her expression spelt, *'I told you so'*. And although she wouldn't say it just then, Kizzy knew how many times she had warned her about the making of monsters.

'Oh my God', Kizzy thought now, to herself. *'What have I done? Have I allowed my son's mind to become violently corrupted? Have I exposed him to one too many scenes of violence?'*

Fari hiccupped as he tried to force his temper back. He caught his breath. His mother's broken silence and the fierceness in the way she unleashed her chastising, frightened him. She had never shouted at him with such passion before.

"But when will he stop beating you, Mum?" His question was calm, now. "When, Mum? I want him to stop. I hate it. One day, you might die." He kept his sad, brown eyes on his mother's bruised face.

Kizzy's heart skipped a beat. She looked up to catch Fiona's scolding gaze. A gaze that chastised, and asked for answers to the very same question. *When? When will it stop?*

She averted her eyes and rested them now on her son. She loved him so much. He was the spitting image of her. Now, her mind went on a crucial journey. It raced back to a time, approximately eight years, nine months and some weeks back. Another cruel emotion devoured her. Fari didn't have the slightest resemblance to his *father*. And Kizzy thanked God for that. But only she knew why. Yes. Only she knew why it was good that her only son didn't inherit the genes that formed his facial features, from his father. And she hoped too, that he would not inherit his evil ways. But that was another story. And although it had raised its ugly head, it had no place in that moment and time. "When I make it happen, Son," she told Fari. "The beating will stop when I make it happen. And I will. Trus' me."

Footsteps were heard descending the stairs. They broke the stiffness of the moment. Embarrassed about her face, Kizzy cowered as she looked up towards the sound. She had momentarily forgotten what her sister had said earlier: that Fari was over at the house with *Grace*. She figured this was her. She beheld an attractive black woman, wearing a short nightshirt. Funny, but for a split second, she reminded Kizzy of Gloria. The shape and contours of her face were remarkably like her best mate's. Now, like earlier, Kizzy missed her, like a severed right arm.

Unlike Gloria though, Grace's beauty was tainted by a long, upraised scar, leading from her right temple to the top of her right cheek. She looked sleepy, as though she had been disturbed from a well-needed nap.

"Hi," Grace said, with a cynical look on her face. "You must be Kizzy." She was there when Fiona had the distressed call from Kizzy and rushed out.

"Irie," Kizzy replied, not enjoying the fact that Grace stared at her from an upward viewpoint. Regardless of Grace's almighty scar and the short history Fiona had given her on this lady who had up-rooted from Leeds, and come to lose herself in the second city, Kizzy still felt intimidated. Belittled. Beneath her. Both physically and mentally. It would perhaps feel better if she would come down. Stand with them in the hallway. On the same level. But instead, she stood there, at the top of the stairs, staring long, hard and condescendingly, down at Kizzy: burning a seemingly un-apologetic stare into her very soul.

But Kizzy had read her wrongly. Grace was simply in a state of emphatic shock.

"Oh. Sorry," Fiona butted with a quick intro. "Kizzy, this is Grace. Grace, this is my sister, Kizzy." Grace understood what both women were feeling. No need for explanation. They were now, all four, standing in the passageway. Still, Fari stared, trance-like and pitifully at his mother's battered face, his little mind slowly twisting, raging. Stealing his youth.

Now, Kizzy looked perplexed, from Fiona to Grace consecutively, the ultimate question in her eyes. Her mind had averted from her own situation and had come to roost on the one at hand. Surely, this could never be what she was thinking? No... surely... not.

"Yes, sis. Let me put you out of your misery, sis. We're lovers. An don' gimme none a dat third degree shit."

Kizzy swallowed hard. "L... L... Lovers?! Fi'... you're... gay?"

"Yes... I am."

"Fari, go play in the living-room, Darling. I'll be there in a bit." Kizzy gently eased her son towards the living-room door. When he was in, she pulled it shut, then turned to face her sister and Grace.

"Oh, for God's sake, Fiona, you're not gay. You're following a trend. It's like a fashion t'ing. It's been all over the TV of late, everyone is wearing this thing like a label. Don't be silly... Yuh crazy?"

"No, sis. Not crazy... Just gay."

"Oh... my... G..." Kizzy felt a tingling in her throat. It was as if someone had put her in a cement mixer and rotated it at an unbelievable speed.

"And don't even think about judging me," Fiona told her. "Jus' check yuh face and yuh last fix from Festus, before yuh judge me. At least Grace won't beat or rape me." Fiona walked quickly into the kitchen. She was on the defence. Maybe a bit too much. Kizzy was at a tender stage just then, and a little cotton-wool treatment wouldn't go amiss. Besides, a shock like that was not what she was expecting.

"Whoa... who said I was judging you?" Kizzy said, putting her hands up and following her sister into the kitchen.

"Your words and actions said it all, Kizzy," Grace butted in, smiling. "Yuh see this?' she pointed to the scar on her face, when Kizzy turned 'round to face her. "This is after eight years of beating. Hoping it would stop. Listening to him telling me he *loved* me. You see Kizzy, I must admit, after a good old beating, sex used to be sweet. The making up was passionate. The tears he would cry convinced me that he loved me deeply and dearly. The *'Baby I won't do it again'*. The *'I do it because I love you'*... Yes. I fell for it all. I thought that jealousy, possessiveness and a good old ass-beating followed by his tears, equalled love. And you'd be surprised the number of women that do. Still... I'm lucky to be alive." She fished a cigarette from a small pocket on her nightshirt and continued, "I used to be a model. Great potential. That went out the window years ago. Yes... For good."

"Yeah, but... couldn't you...?"

"Find another man?" I did. In fact, six of them. One every year, since I left him. *Rebound queen,* me. Drawn to the same type, like bees to a honey pot. The same old jealous, possessive, obsessive, women-beating, controlling freaks. The last one had it for all of the rest. He should have been dead. Born lucky I guess. Now he sports a sexy stub for a right arm." With that, Grace walked to the sitting-room to talk to Fari.

Kizzy winced at the thought of a severed right arm. It forced her to reflect again on Fiona's Dutch-pot attack on Winston, aka *Bush Tea,* some years back.

"Yeah," Fiona added, as if she knew what her sister was thinking. "We're two of a kind. Only, Grace took too many years to learn. And *you,* K? When will *you* learn? Maybe never."

"Yeah... but another woman, Fi'?! Nah, man. If I leave Festus it's not gonna be for no woman." She kissed her teeth. And anyway, what will Mama Maya think?"

Fiona chuckled, "I thought you weren't judging me?"

Kizzy averted her eyes.

"And what can Mama Maya think?" Fiona asked. "Kizzy, you're so naïve."

"Me? Naïve? Why? Wha' yuh mean?"

"Mama Maya is gay herself, Kizzy. Her and Aunt Patricia."

"Fiona! What yuh talkin' about?! Are you crazy?! What gave you the right to be talkin' like dat about them?! What evidence have you got?!"

Fiona chuckled again. "Chill, sis. You'll add a soaring blood pressure to those injuries... Have you ever seen one intimate gentleman caller come to the house? One man that meant anything to Mama Maya?"

"Well, no... but..."

"And who was Aunt Patricia? Really? She wasn't a blood relation. All that whispering, chuckling in the dead of the night whenever she'd come. Didn't you think something was funny?"

"No. Not really. They're just very close friends. In the past, Gloria and I sat up in bed chatting for hours. Nothing like that crossed our minds. I

think you're thinking like that, Fiona, because you're that way inclined...
or at least you *think* so."

"Dream on, Kizzy. Close your eyes to reality."

Kizzy paused now, to reflect. "So is that evidence enough for you to
make such assumptions, Fiona? Because two women whispered and
chuckled in bed? Women all over the world are doing that now, but it
doesn't make them..."

"Ok," Fiona cut in. "Look deep into yourself and tell me that you
don't think Mama Maya and Aunt Patricia were lovers."

"No. I still think you're making false accusations, Fiona. It's wrong.
And it's sick to think that."

"Ok, Kizzy," Fiona told her, "Mama Maya and Aunt Patricia aren't
gay. We weren't adopted. The Pope isn't catholic. A vast majority of the
population of Birmingham has got AIDS. Gays won't be eventually
ordained to head churches... and Festus hasn't just beaten and raped
your sorry ass."

Oh dear. Was she on a roll or what? This lady made no bones when
she needed to drum home a point.

"That wasn't called for, Fiona. Just because I don't believe that the
two people that showed us the most love, are gay, don't mean that you
have to..."

"Ok, Sis. Let's end this little conversation now. You don't need to be
getting upset right now. You need TLC after what just happened to you,"
Fiona said, "but I still think you should press charges against Festus."

Fiona and Grace walked slowly down Kings Heath High Street, Grace's
right arm looping through Fiona's left. Earlier they had browsed the
gleaming selection of gold under the display counter of *The Golden
Touch*, an extension to the main branch in Town. Grace had seen the
good life, and was partial to the quality of her jewellery, so when she had
discovered this fine outlet, she had wasted no time in returning to support
the owner: besides, she had a crush on him. The first time Fiona had
taken her to this branch that stood it's ground in the Kings Heath
shopping centre, she had melted. *Seriously.* This fine specimen of a
brotha had served her with style. He had smiled with his eyes: a unique
cluster of designer wrinkles rushing in to cove them, throwing out a
sprinkling of subtle seduction. But he knew nothing of it. It was just him.
He really didn't mean to. Just born that way. And to top it all, this
spontaneous reaction emphasised the cutest dimples you ever did see –
his nice, white teeth, innocently calling her women to flirt. Grace had
told herself, *'This brotha must have invented the phrase, 'Service with a*

smile'.' Feh real.

There was no harm in fantasising, but at the end of the day, someone should tell Grace that *Smiler* was particular. Very. And a bisexual female was never gonna be his cup of tea. *No way.* But there was no charge for fantasising, so she had allowed her mind to take her to wherever it wanted to. Why not? People do that shit all the time. But everyone knows that looking at a Diamond doesn't necessarily mean that one will get the chance to wear it. *Period.*

A brother wearing locks cruised slowly by, in a Suzuki Jeep. '*I love you Selassie, I... I love you...*' booming out of his stereo, the thick Saturday traffic not allowing him to go more than ten miles an hour. A red, gold and green dice dangled from behind his rear-view mirror. His crown, made from the finest leather and by Papa Dread's own hand, secured his vintage locks.

Fiona recognised him, and for a few seconds, the hairs at the back of her neck stood up.

He nodded his head at her as he cruised by.

A subtle, unsure gesture.

This brotha once had Africa on his brain.

Repatriation was once high on his to-do list.

He once had a queen and shared Sizzler's dream. '*Black woman an' chile'.* But, as the years rolled by, he had lost the will to carry the banner of the '*true rastaman'* with pride. Lost it somewhere, in the topsy-turvy arms of *Babylon.*

Back in the day, he had a black woman who had no designs on being used as a beating stick. A black woman, who knew that a real rastaman didn't beat his queen, but cherished her.

As the brotha cruised, he kept his eyes on Fiona, almost as if he wanted to say, '*Long time no see. An' who's yuh frien'?*' But instead, he spoke with his unshaken stare, not seeing the linking of the sistas arms for what it was.

His stereo now boomed '*Come Ethiopians come, I've got a message for you...*'

A Dutch-pot mark held a steadfast claim to his temple.

Old memories swam in his head: they don't leave like people do.

"That's Winston," Fiona put Grace out of her misery. "Winston, aka *Bush Tea.* I told you, remember? Like Festus, he's got nimble hands. Another lost soul. Fallen from the Majestic grace of a *true* rastaman. Giving Rastafarians a bad name. I say big-up de true rastamen, forever.

Graced looked at him now, with interest. A blonde sat proud at his side. She was the spitting image of Madonna. She wore a gold, personalised pendant around her neck. It caught the light and without care, Grace read it: *Lucy.*

The traffic let up and Winston put his foot down.

CHAPTER * EIGHTEEN

Lijah was trying hard to relax when Kizzy knocked. It was strange: the state of her face and the fact that she was on his doorstep without prior notice. Kizzy always called before she turned up, even when Gloria was there. She and Lijah got on well together. She didn't take sides, but ever since Gloria left and he had moved back into the house, Kizzy called, but hadn't visited.

"Kizzy?!... Jeeesas C'ris'!... Whaap'n to yuh face?" Asking why she was there could wait. Lijah was seeing old bruises. All the swelling had gone down. This was a week after her last ordeal with Festus, so what would Lijah have said if he had seen her then?

Kizzy stepped in.

"Don' tell me Festus is still up to 'im tricks again."

"What do you think," Kizzy said, walking to the living-room and helping herself to her favourite armchair.

"Is weh Festus a deal wid, Kizzy?"

"I don't know, Lijah. I don't know what Festus is dealin' wid. Really."

"Nah, man. Me affi have words wid Festus. De bredrin cyaan still a deal wid dem t'ing inna dis yah time. We need consciousness right now. Not dis. Me t'ink 'im stop dem t'ings deh. Serious."

"Lijah... he thinks I'm having an affair. He beat me up and raped me."

"Him what?!... *RAPE?* But you own man cyaan *rape* yuh?... Is weh yaah seh?"

"Well, let's put it this way, Lijah, I didn't consent. And I don't mean I was tired and didn't want sex. I mean it was taken by force. Brute force. Festus is being eaten away by something. He's getting worse. I can't take it anymore, Lijah. I know I have this 'Devil I know' approach to life, but... I d'know. I gave Festus lots of chances. I suppose I stayed with him because I feel I owe him."

"You owe him? Wha' yuh owe him?"

"Oh. Neva mind, Lijah."

'What does she mean?' Lijah asked himself. *'She owe him? Owe him the right to beat her ass?'* He moved the conversation on. "When did he do dis?"

"About a week ago. It was different from the other times he hit me, Lijah." He was like an animal. A stranger. Rough and ruthless. And it was the things he was saying…" She paused. "That's the main reason I'm here."

"What t'ings?" Lijah was perplexed.

"Lijah, what has Festus told you about his parents?"

"The same t'ing he told you, I suppose. They died in a car crash. Fact is de bredrin don' even like talking 'bout it, too tough. From he told me years ago, he hardly mentioned it. So w'at brought dis on?"

"Well it's not true."

"Yuh mean it wasn't a car crash?"

"No. I mean… they're not dead at all. His father is Montie. The drunken tramp."

"Wait a minute… run dat by me again." Lijah sat down. "Montie?… De Handsworth tramp?… Is Festus ole man?"

"Uh huh." Kizzy lit a spliff.

"Is weh yaah seh? Who tell yuh dat, Kizzy?"

"He did…when he was ra…" Kizzy started to cry. Not even the best spliff in the world could soothe that.

Lijah panicked. Of all her domestic problems over the years, Lijah had never, personally, seen her cry.

"Nuh cry, man. Is a'right. Me know how yuh feel."

"No you don't, Lijah! No! No! No! How could you know how I feel? Have you ever been raped? Violated? I know he was my man but that's not the point. It was rape." Kizzy needed this outlet, like a car needs a good run. And the memory of the first time invaded her mind, too. The first time she was *taken*. Man-handled. *Raped.*

"That's a consolation, Kizzy."

"Consolation!"

"Feh de want of a betta word. He was yuh man. And yes, I have been ra…" He stopped suddenly in his tracks. Clammed up. Turned in on himself like shama-macca in a Jamaican bush. What was he doing? He had confided in Papa Dread, but he had pledged that was as far as it would go. Between him, an evil sodomite and Papa Dread.

"Lijah?"

He was getting angry now.

He remembered it clearly, and it was devouring him.

Now, he could almost feel it.

The forced restriction of his burly, blonde cellmate.

His hard restraint.

Forbidden to cry.

To tell the warden.

Now, his skin crawled as he relived his youth. And now he wanted to kill. Not only that perverted cellmate, but the brotha who had got him in that position in the first place. The brotha who had pulled him on a robbery, way over his youthful head and told him, *"I don't tek kindly to grass. If yuh get ketch, don' call me name... or yuh is dead meat'.* The brotha whose secret he had kept, not even breathing a word to Festus, Papa Dread or Gloria. A brother who managed to churn his stomach, even now.

"You... have... been... what, Lijah?" Kizzy stopped crying. She knew what he was about to say. But *Lijah?* How could *Lijah* be raped? He's a man. And as far as she knew, he had never done a bird. Gloria had never mentioned it.

Now she saw his brown eyes like she had never seen them before. Tears filled them. Only Gloria had ever seen him cry. "Lijah?... Who raped...?"

"Stop it! Nuh ask me not'n! Jus' done it right Yasso! Now! Done de fucking convasation!"

She shied away from his fury. He had never sworn to her before. In fact, she had never seen him angry. She only knew what Gloria had told her.

He calmed, slightly. His eyes apologised, and now, he looked to her for comfort. It was Gloria that he needed, but she wasn't there.

Now, they spoke with their eyes. Kizzy understood. *'It must be so',* she thought. *'Yes. He was raped. Oh my God'.* She reached out and stroked his locks. Kissed his tears. Eased her fingers over his full, dark lips. Cupped his cheeks. Reached forward and kissed his warm, trembling mouth.

Thoughts crossing.

Minds locking.

Gestures synchronised.

And now, the inevitable. They rose to their feet, his dick, to the occasion, and her nipples to his touch. They needed each other. TLC. He was angry, and like hand and glove, it came with 'horny'.

They ascended the stairs, ridding each other of their clothes.

Inner thighs touching.

Fingers gripping.

Pleasure giving.

Pleasure receiving.

It would be the dawning of a new moment.

The world was locked out.

Who they were, blocked out.

The morality of *dos* and *don'ts,* sidestepped. At least... until their heavens came down.

Panic set in when Kizzy had come to realise what they had done, but the horse had already bolted. "Oh my God... Oh my God... what will Gloria think of me?"

"And Festus? What will he think of me?" Lijah seconded her emotion, cynically. "Who's gonna tell them, Kizzy? Don't go beating up yuhself because a dis now. We were two human beings in need of a little TLC. We both gave and received. Gloria has left me. Yes, I want her back, but she's not coming back. She's got a new man in Jamaica now. You and I aren't making promises. Just giving in to the weakness of the flesh, in a time of need."

"We've deceived them, Lijah! I don't care what you say! It shouldn't happen! We were long-time friends." Tears were flowing again.

But Lijah wouldn't let it be. He hated tears. Sorrow. He wanted to kiss them away. Make them better.

And she herself could not resist.

Now *he* kissed her.

Tasted her salty tears.

Reached again for her firm breasts.

Her inner thighs.

Kissed her hard nipples.

The sink of her navel.

The span of her arms.

And when he had convinced her that it wasn't wrong, he took her again, to the land of ecstasy.

Lijah didn't know why, but he panicked when he woke from his slumber. He rose and fixed himself up. He watched Kizzy as she dosed, then proceeded downstairs.

Minutes later, as he heard splashes from the bathroom, as Kizzy took a shower, for just one absent-minded second he thought it was Gloria. He turned and looked at her picture and remembered how she used to sing to him. Play records, cassettes, and CD's *to* or *at* him. She always spoke through music. And now he sang:

I've got your picture, Still hanging on the wall
You know my heart cries out, To know that you were gone
And you've got to be there, still hanging, Hanging on the wall.

He must have been meditating for the longest time, when Kizzy walked slowly into the room. She had caught the sadness in his voice, and now, seeing him look up at Gloria's picture, confirmed she was just a substitute. But so was he, so she comforted herself with Lijah's words:

'We are two human beings in need of a little TLC. Just giving in to the weakness of the flesh, in a time of need'.

"It's like incest," Kizzy said, at the end of Lijah's heartfelt song.

"What is?"

"What we just did. Gloria is like my sister. You and Festus are like brothers. We are too close. Like family. Lijah I had never dreamt…"

Lijah's index finger sealed her lips.

"Don't use dat word, Kizzy. It wasn't *incest*. We're not *blood* family. Guilt and regrets are no good now. We've done it. The milk is spilt. The horse has bolted."

"How can I look her in the eye…?"

"What were you saying about Festus' parents?" Lijah deliberately cut her off. "Montie isn't really his dad, is he?"

"So he said."

"I noticed the way he always used to be concerned about him. Talking to him, giving him money. Telling him to stop rummaging in the bins. One day 'im nearly cry to raas. I t'ought de man was just doin' de Good Samaritan t'ing. So now me know. No wonder."

"Yes. I know," Kizzy stared into space. "But his mother. I wonder who she is? All I know, she is a nurse. Said something about her dressing up in a nurse's uniform every night… pretending she's a saint…when all de time she was fuckin' out on his ole man… He said that is what turned his old man into a drunken tramp, walking de streets of Birmingham like a dog."

"So, did Montie come to Birmingham and left her in Bristol? 'Cause yuh know seh is Bristol Festus come from."

"I didn't get that much information. All I know is that she's in Jamaica with a new man. Retiring in style. Soaking up de sun."

Lijah had a wild thought. A shot in the dark thought. But of course it could never be. "He didn't say her name, did he?"

"Yes, he did. *Dora*. He said, *'You're just like me fuckin' madda Dora!'*

Lijah nearly choked on his own breath. *Dora*. His old man's new wife. Her nurse's uniform. Could it be her? "Oh no! Not *Dora!*"

"You know her?" Kizzy perplexed.

"Let's say, I'll be making a courtesy call to Jamaica later. Could be coincidence, but I doubt it. There are just a couple more questions I'd like to ask de ole man."

"Your old man?" Kizzy paused to think. "It's never *that* Dora. Your old man's new wife?!"

"Listen Kizzy, the world is smaller than we think."

Kizzy's mouth was wide open, her chin nearly touching her chest.

Now, she wanted to ask Lijah what he meant earlier. About him being raped. But another predicament had just appeared on his stack pile, so she decided to hold fire. Tomorrow would be another day.

Gloria had always known that solitude isn't always a bad thing. It isn't a crime to be alone. Now she sat, swinging in her hammock, soaking up the Jamaican sun. She spoke to, questioned and listened to her inner self. The warm rain poured, fighting for reign with the sun. Gloria loved the rain and didn't run for shelter. It reminded her of a certain day in Birmingham, England. In Cannon Hill Park, when she had soaked up torrents, John Holt seeping into her head. But now, it wasn't John Holt. It was George Nookes, doing his version of:

> *When you've got troubles, don't cry*
> *Just remember, God is standing by...*

Gloria thought too about the day she decided to leave her parents' home in Leeds. It wasn't about rebellion. She had grown her own wings and decided it was time to fly. But Mrs Hortence Fontaine had thought the skies of Birmingham were too high. Too high and polluted with all things strange. And with her chastising scissors, she tried to clip her daughter's wings. But it didn't work. Her verbal scissors had grown blunt from constant forbidding. They were exhausted: their serrated edges cutting no dash on Gloria's ears. Besides, Gloria had that strong determination about her. So, with curt resoluteness in her eyes, love prevailed, and Lijah had won.

She thought of her parents and the life they had led. For the marriage, she was the only child. Could Hortence have any more? She had never asked. But her father did. Had several. Good old *Reverend* Fontaine. Hid behind his title like warriors behind their shields. Moved through his congregation in mysterious ways, his lustful wonders, to perform. Yes. He had spread his seed and scattered his eager seeds upon the lands of several women. Seeds that had grown into trees that Gloria didn't even know. Only rumours of their scattering. Hopefully, they would have been fed and watered by God's almighty hands. Grown into prosperous trees. But that wasn't her problem. She had her own life to think about.

Only days ago, she had visited their graves in Watermount, St Catherine. It had always been their wish to be buried there. She hoped they were *'resting in peace'*.

But it was against her father's well-kept tombstone that she had leant, thinking about the meaning of friendship. *'A 'best friend'*, she had thought. *'What is that? How many people can honestly put their hands on their hearts and say, 'I have a 'best friend'?'* She was thinking of

Kizzy. She was a friend all right. But *'best'?* You see, someone had once suggested to her, that a *friend* is a person who knows just a few things about you. But a *'best friend'* is a person who knows your deepest secrets. A person who could write a book about you. Although she loved Kizzy, and although they went way back, Gloria knew that wasn't so, for them. Not in the least. The secrets they had each in turn kept from each other would have a domino effect on their lives, if exposed. From every exposed action, there would be a most devastating reaction.

Secrets. Necessary or unnecessary evils? The answer is contextual.

Now there were fresh thoughts too. Like the number of police she had called upon to remove Baby Face Glen from her house. Lijah had never raised his hand to her. Never. Unlike Festus to Kizzy. But she had been frightened for her and Khamilla's life, as she waited for the police. Of all the upright, ambitious and up-standing Jamaican men, she had to bump into Baby Face. He carried a gun. He was as deadly as sin. Her escape was so narrow, she couldn't even begin to realise how much. She had left Lijah and climbed obliviously into a dangerous existence.

At first, Lijah didn't recognise the voice at the end of the telephone line. The person shouted. Not rudely, but as she were fooled by the fact that a long-distance call commanded a high decibels.

"Hello! Lijah! It's me! I'm callin' from Jamaica!"

"Who is *me*?"

"Dora! Yuh faada's wife!"

Lijah panicked, "Is he ok?!"

"Yes. He's ok. Everyt'ing's a'right. I've been meanin' to call feh a while, really."

"What is it, Dora? Sop'n wrong?"

"Well, aaam. Lijah, me don't even know where to start."

"Tek yuh time, Dora."

"Festus eva tell not'ing 'bout me, Lijah?"

"Festus? Like w'at, Dora?"

"Well, I don't t'ink he did. Or you woulda mention it when you came out to Jamaica las' time an' ask yuh faada dem w'ole heap a question deh."

"What should Festus tell me 'bout yuh Dora?" He played dumb. In fact, he had intended to call and ask his father if that was the same Dora Festus told Kizzy about, but Dora had saved him a phone call.

"Dis is not easy feh me, Lijah, but... well... de ting is..."

"W'at is it, Dora?"

"Well, Lijah... dis might be a bit of a shock to yuh... but I'm Festus' madda. It's a long story, but me an' yuh faada are sorting out mekkin' our will. We left it a bit late. Yuh know we not getting' any younga... Lijah? Are yuh dere?"

"Yes, Dora. I'm here."

"Lijah, I know Festus wrote me off as dead. I heard he told people his parents are dead, but it isn't so. It's too long a story to tell ova de telephone. Festus hates me because of the lies his faada told him about me. I know he wouldn't even want to talk to me, but if de worse should happen, I want yuh to let him know dat he's in my will."

"But Dora, dis isn't de way, is it? It don' seem right. I t'ink yuh should call Festus yuhself."

"Yuh didn't act su'prise, Lijah. It looks as if yuh knew all along."

"Dora, it's not important. What is, is dat yuh an' Festus mek peace before de worse happen."

"Lijah. I'm not as bad as Festus would have mek me out to be. Festus' faada was cruel. He used to beat me. When I used to go to work, he used to t'ink I was cyarrying aan wid anadda man. I wasn't doin' anyt'ing like dat."

"Dora, dat is feh yuh an' Festus to discuss... but let me jus' ask yuh one t'ing."

"What?"

"Why did you do it to Mum? Yuh was meant to be her frien'."

"Lijah, yuh faada explain it all to yuh. Why yuh askin' me again?"

"I jus' waan to hear your side, Dora. Why?"

"Lijah, Nettie always said to me, "Dora, if anyt'ing happen to me, look afta Lothan.""

"But Dora, she didn't mean you should screw him in her livin' room! Where she could hear!" Lijah was doing a u-turn. He thought he understood when his father explained, but Dora's voice erupted something in him.

"Lijah, yuh madda was my frien', but she was no saint herself." Dora was stern.

"Weh yuh seh?" It was as if she had wrenched his insides out. "Ok. She might have taken Dad off dis Sweetie, but she was lonely. I know it wasn't right, but she was lonely. She was in a strange and cold country. Just lost her father too. But you... you could have found someone else. And to be fuckin' him in her living-room!"

"Lijah, yuh cyan disrespec' me all yuh want, but dere are two sides to every story. An' dere is always a half dat is neva told. Maybe one day you'll hear the w'ole story."

"Listen, Dora. Do you want Festus' telephone number? You can tell him yuhself 'bout yuh will."

"No, Lijah. Just tell 'im feh me."

"Ok. But me still t'ink yuh should talk before the worse happens."

"If it's God's will He will let me know if we should talk, Lijah. But I don't feel that I should push him. I tried before. But Festus made his mind up. He's dead set against me."

"A'right, Dora. I'll tell Festus what yuh seh. But whatever you t'ink, I don't t'ink it will ever be God's will, for you to go to your grave before you make peace with your son." Lijah didn't want to prolong the conversation another second. "Say hello to de ole man feh me. I won't keep yuh any longa. It's expensive."

"Mmmm." Dora had no words left.

Lijah put the phone down and took a few deep breaths. *'Strange world'*, he thought, *'strange world'*.

CHAPTER * NINETEEN
Fire deh a muss-muss tail, 'im t'ink a cool breeze...

The journey over to Lucy's mansion was a troubled one. Lijah's mind was filled with all sorts, but when he got there, he found more trouble than that in his mind. The burly blonde guy that had caught him the middle of the act with Lucy was just pulling off in a silver BM. *'Why does that guy look so much like that guy in prison?'* he asked himself.

"Who's that?" he asked, perplexed.

"That's my brother."

"Your brother? You never said you had a brother."

"I never said a lot of things, Lijah. But that doesn't mean that a lot isn't happen." She sounded sarcastic.

They were in Lucy's bedroom now. She had led him there purposefully.

"Ok. I see your mood is a bit ruffled, Lucy... Listen... I need some cash. I know you bought me the Roadster an' set me up some ways a' ready, but a whole heap a shit has crashed around me. My son is on some shit. I need some money to put him in some proper place to dry out. Private. If I don't, I'm gonna lose him, Lucy. I'm in a heap a shit right now."

Lucy stroked Lijah's chest as she pretended to listen. They were lying in an exquisitely dressed four-poster bed, in the middle of a room about the size of all the rooms in Lijah and Gloria's house.

Today, Lucy seemed different. Ruthless. Desperate diseases need desperate remedies, and now, it seemed they both had desperate needs. Yes. So desperate their needs, they could be likened to diseases.

'Justify... Justify... Justify my love...' The voice of Madonna filled the room.

"Lucy, yuh listenin' to me?"

"Of course. As much as you listen to me when I talk, Lijah."

She was busy. More preoccupied with the act of 'control' than anything else, and soon Lijah found himself succumbing to bondage and wondered if she went to the same sex school as Bernadette. He had willingly given himself up to Lucy's antics. The 'do with me what you wish' attitude was clear. *A nuh not'n.* Just as long as he got what he wanted in the end. Besides, he was enjoying the sweet torment, but his mind was only partly there. It was every-which-way. Gloria. Kunta. Ikesha. Festus. His mother. His old man. Papa Dread. Everything. Nothing seemed to be going well around him. He searched his mind and tried to find a positive happening of late. It was hard. The most pleasure he'd had, was that of the carnal flesh. He needed to put his life in order.

Everything, it seemed, was driven by money. He had not set his financial house in order and now he found himself almost prostituting himself to come up with some ready cash.

It was already a half-hearted thing, but now, his mind was beginning to drift from the idea of sex. And besides, he wished Lucy would answer him. Instead, she had his big toe in her mouth, sucking on it like it was a damn lollipop. *'Is there a limit as to what part of the anatomy people will use for sex?'* he thought to himself. Sweeping her hands over the inside of his thighs, Lucy stroked his stiff manhood. She licked his nipples. Her mission, it seemed, was to torment him sexually, only he couldn't see her. He was blindfolded and his other senses were heightened. He could hear her seductive whispers, smell her perfume, feel her fingertips and taste her. He came for money: a quick-fix remedy to his troubled life, she was offering sex, a heat-of-the-moment solution to a burning desire.

"Lucy..."

"Relax, Lijah. You're a black man. Black men are supposed to be cool... or was I misled?" A strange joviality filled her voice.

But if only he could see her eyes.

Evil filled them.

Like a scene from a horror movie.

"You want my money, *Lijah...?*" she paused, easing her warm tongue over his eager manhood, "but you don't... want... me, right?' she added drama to his name. Evil drama.

Lijah winced pensively, as he detected the change in her tone.

"Remind you of anyone you know, *Lijah Boy?* Well... I don't suppose you would see that side of him, would you...? Your father...? You're a bit like him, aren't you, *Lijah?*"

"Lucy... w'at yuh talkin' 'bout?" thoughts spinning around in his head like a whirlpool. *'Who is this woman? Am I in danger?'*

"Like father, like son... Yes...you're like your fucking father, aren't you?!" *SLAP!*

Oh my God. Was another hell about to break loose for Lijah? Was another disaster waiting to happen? He had come to milk his cash cow, but it seemed she was about to milk his ass for her own, sweet revenge. *Pandemonium.*

"What the f...? Lucy! Yuh mad, gyal!?"

Now he felt her warm vagina devouring his dick. She gripped him, like Bernadette did. *Déjà vu* was drowning him. Memories from Bernadette's bedroom. Only this was Lucy. Lucy with bitter-sweet kisses. And he was frightened. Of course he was. He was wrapped, tied and tangled, lying beneath a woman who was administering blows to his face and talking about his father! Shit.

"Lucy? What's all dis about?! Untie me. Get dis blind-fold off... C'mon... Let's talk. What's my old man's got to do with you?" He tried to be calm.

"The difference is, *Lijah...*" she bit his left nipple, hard, and the touch of cold metal danced across his chest. *'What was it?'* he wondered. It was her gold pendant. The one that held her name. *Lucy.* It was as cold as the lady who wore it.

"Raas claat! Lucy! Yuh mad, gyal?! Bombo claat! Yuh should be in a fucking straight jacket, to raas!" And he hadn't seen anything yet. Who the hell said sexual pain was pleasure. Some sadistic perverts, no doubt.

"Like I was saying... the difference is... Unlike my mother... I have no rich, white husband. No little blonde son. No little blonde daughter. No garden that needs tending. And you...? You have no wife and kids to get home to. She's left you...Yes. Gloria has left you... And me...? I won't be pushing no cash into your pocket, like my mother did to your father." As she spoke, she fucked him, as if that was part of the punishment.

"Bombo claat! Lucy!" Lijah put two and two together and came up with the score. He recalled his father's story. *'Could Lucy really be that little girl that used to walk in on his old man and her mother? The little blonde girl that stared and stared and stared at the old man and her mother when she caught them in a compromising position',* he wondered.

"She left me, Lijah. Left me, my brother and my father. Upt and ran away... as if we didn't exist. And d'you know he never stopped loving her... the old fool. Loved her so much, he left her a fortune in his Will. After all that. Isn't that what you call *'unconditional'* love?"

"Get to the point, Lucy." Lijah's anxiety was close to the limit.

"Get to the point? You want me to get to the point?" she reached for a dodgy-looking object with a point that should not be anywhere near a bedroom, let alone in a bed!

"Ohhhhh! Jesus! What de fuck was dat?!" Lijah got the *point* alright. The sharpest *point*. Right up against the entrance to his forbidden zone, as he lay there, like a giant *X*, helpless and at the mercy of Lucy.

If heaven was missing angels, a mental home somewhere in Birmingham was missing Lucy.

"As I was saying," she calmly continued, "my father loved my mother to the max... but he hated all black men. They were like a phobia to him. The whole thing wrecked his life, Lijah. He was such a sweet man. I promised I'd get his revenge for him. The sins of the fathers?! You know all about that don't you, Lijah?! You black people know the Bible inside out.... Yes?"

She bit.

Lashed.

Twisted.

Fucked.

"Lucy! Jeesas C'ris'! Help!"

"No, *Lijah*... Jeesas C'ris' won't help you."

Lijah tried desperately to free himself from the tight knots that he had so freely allowed Lucy to tie. "Untie me blood claat han' dem Lucy!"

"I swear I'd hunt you down. Avenge my father. My mother. My brother. Myself," she said with deadly venom.

"But Lucy, how can you blame me?! It was my father! Not me! Why should I pay for my father's mess ups?!"

"The sins of the father, remember? Something about it descending onto the third and fourth generation." She laughed mockingly, throwing her head back and wildly flashing her hair all over her face.

"Well, feh one t'ing, yuh cyaan count," Lijah said, "an' it don' mean dat anyway! Untie me, gyal!"

"Pardon? What did you say?"

"You crazy bitch! Yuh mental! Twisted!"

"Lijah. You're not by any chance abusing me verbally, are you?" Her voice got calmer and calmer all the time. "Are you forgetting something? You are in bondage. Wrapped, tied and tangled." She kissed his earlobes. "I've got you in my grip. Are you sure you want to abuse me, verbally? I have the handle, Lijah. Don't forget. So... feel the sharpness of the blade, you bastard!" *WHAP!*

Lijah's manhood would not die. He was *angry.* Anger and frustration always gave him an erection. He needed no Spanish fly. No sexual aid. Only, today he could do without it. His wrists and ankles were bruised from the constant pulling, kicking and tugging.

There was a calm. A frightening calm. He didn't like it. What was she up to?

The strike of a match.

The smell of burning candles.

Lavender.

He remembered Bernadette. She burnt them. Always.

But now, this deadly, evil female had taken it to another level. Lijah screamed when drips of hot liquid made contact with his chest, his navel, and his groin.

"Lucy! Yuh fucka! W'at yuh doin', gyal?!"

More slaps connected with his thighs.

Hot liquid from the burning candle greeted him again.

"Woooie! Woooie! Jeeesas C'ris'! Lucy! Gyal, yuh need to see a psychiatrist, man! Serious! Me seh, untie me to blood claat!"

"And how is he doing now, Lijah?" she asked calmly. "Your... dear... father, Lothan...? How did I know his name? I hear you ask. Well... you see... my mother never stopped calling it. Never stopped loving him, I suppose. In a way, I can see why. Forbidden fruits. Sweet." Now this time her laugh was the haughtiest. A digging cackle. A deranged jeer.

"Lucy... Untie me, please."

She ignored him. "Having fun in the sun, is he? Good old Lothan. You see, Lijah, if there's one thing I do well, apart from taking *Revenge,* it's *Research.*"

"Wha' yuh mean?"

"I have a sister too, you know. Mixed race. Your father's daughter. Taken to a children's home. Given away like some *'thing'.* All because of your father. Now...? My mother puts all her energy into her dogs. Her curiosity to taste a black man killed her will to love any man again. Apart from your father, of course."

Another drip of hot, liquid candle hit the tip of his manhood, followed by a familiar encounter of Lucy's woman.

"Lucy! Are you a fucking sadist or something?! Yuh don' waan mess wid a black man like dis, yunnuh gyal!"

"But me messing wid a black man. So what?" SLAP!

"How much did you say you want, Lijah?" she taunted.

He couldn't answer. Mouth full a chow-chow. Force-fed chow-chow.

"Didn't hear yah!"

"Luphcphyphyuhphmadphgyalphurghph!!" Muffled utterance.

"I know... that's more like it... I'll decide what you deserve. After all, your performance today has been *priceless."* She whispered the latter.

Lijah's body was black and blue when Lucy had finished with him. She had taken the blind-fold from his eyes and stood over him like the enemy. *Nude.* His eyes were filled with questions. Tears. Hate. Hurt. Resentment. And vengeance. Right then, he could kill. "Untie me, Lucy! Fuck you! Untie me! You bitch!"

"Don't order, Lijah... Manners... Where are your manners?... Beg... C'mon... Let me hear you beg, you bastard!"

Now she produced a gun and held it to his head. He freaked.

"I said... Beg! You bastard!"

"Pleeeeese, Lucy, Pleeeeese. Untie me. Pleeeeese. Me a beg yuh."

But the gun connected with brute force against his temple.

He was concussed.

Knocked out. Cold.

He drifted away with the image of Lucy's evil face in his subconscious.

"Liiiijah... Liiiijah... we've got company." Lucy's voice came like an echo chamber to his ears. *"I wonder who that could be?"* she asked. *"Maybe it's Baby Face Glen. Wouldn't that be a turn up for the books? You just stay right there. I'll be right back."* He watched as Lucy walked nude down the winding staircase and to the door. Even her footsteps sounded weird to Lijah.

'Is she really gonna answer the door in the nude?' Lijah asked himself. Why did he feel so strange? Kinda floaty. Like one would imagine a fluffy cloud to feel.

"Conrad! Hi! You're just in time. Got you some exotic delight. Come upstairs." Lucy's voice rattled in Lijah's eardrum, like the beating of a tin can. *"Just what you have always wanted. A real blackhole. Get his gash, before I give him his cash."*

Lijah freaked when a burly, blonde guy popped his head around the door and stared at his nude body. *'Right little Hitler,'* he thought. Lijah recognised him. He was the workman that had rushed to Lucy's rescue when they first made love in her mansion. But most terrifying of all, he could have sworn he was an older version of the guy who had buggered him up in prison.

"*What the fuck! Lucy... Ok... Enough is enough. Who is dis bombo claat pussy bwoy!*"

"*Enough is enough for me, Lijah. But Conrad hasn't had his fun yet. You see... Conrad is my brother. Conrad is a bad, bad boy. He's even done time. Armed robbery to him is peanuts. Head's all messed up.*"

"*A bit like you, wouldn't you say? And why are you telling me all this?*"

"*Don' matter, does it? Dead man tells no tale.*"

Lijah felt his heart beat faster.

"*Like I was saying,*" she continued, "*I think my mother had a lot to do with Conrad being mental. And your father, of course. Lost faith in women. When my mother left, it affected him. He too wanted revenge. Bent his gender too, I think.*"

"*Gays are born, Lucy! Not fucking made!*" The voice of his father strangely came to him: '*She had a little boy around six. Conrad. Funny likkle bwoy he was. Right likkle Hitler. Blonde 'air, blue yie. Used to gwaan like a likkle girl. I wouldn' be surprise if 'im don' turn gay*',

Conrad was saying nothing. Just unbuckling. Undressing. Rising.

"*This is sick! Sick! Sick! Lucy! Don't let dis fucking chi-chi man near me! Pleeease!*"

"*Chi-chi man? Me t'ought it was batty-man?*" Conrad tried his tongue at patois. "*New name? Where do you Jamaicans ged'em from? Well... no matter... Different name, same entry. And let's see who is the pussy bwoy now.*" He drew closer to Lijah. Closer... Closer... Closer.

Lijah's fear was about to manifest.

His greatest phobia thrust upon him.

His mind was about to be blown.

Conrad grinned in his face.

A weird airy silence echoed around him. The arm of panic strangled him. And there was nothing he could do. Nothing. Nothing but scream. A scream that at first seemed to stay buckled in his throat. It had failed to come out, until: '*L... L... Lucy! No! No! No! Noooooooo!!!...*"

Lijah screamed himself to consciousness.

Woke to reality.

The reality of Lucy's face.

No Conrad.

It wasn't just a dream, but a deadly nightmare.

But it was much too real for his liking. Much too real.

He couldn't tell how long he was out for, but all he knew, he was pleased that the second part of his ordeal was just his subconscious running wild.

And he was pleased too that the dream had ended before Conrad could touch him. He couldn't stand being taken down that road again. Not even in a dream. The memories of his prison cell years ago were still a fixture in his head.

"What's the matter, Lijah?" the voice of evil met his eardrums again. "Looks like you had a nasty dream."

"Lucy, how do you expect to get away with this?" The throbbing in his head heightened.

"I don't expect anything, Lijah. In fact, I've already fulfilled my one expectation. Seeing you suffer. Take your father's punishment. You didn't really think our meeting was by chance, did you? *You fool.*"

"Lucy...you mean you searched me out... started all this... made Gloria leave me... and then...?"

"Yes.... Searched you out. To revenge my father. Revenge is sweet Lijah. Sweet... Sweet."

"No, Lucy. Revenge is for bitter, twisted people."

"Yes. I'm bitter. Bitter at how your father affected my life."

"Lucy, you're a rich woman. Why couldn't you just go on living your life and leave things alone?"

"Maybe because I'm twisted." Evil sprung to her eyes again.

He changed the subject, slightly. "So... the MRS Roadster... How come you let me have that? What's the catch?"

"Just thought a nice rastaman like you would like a prestigious ride like that."

"Lucy, I'm *not* a rastaman. I *used to* be, but not anymore. I'm no longer worthy. I've long gone stopped trying to live up to the upstanding characteristics of a true rastaman. Gone are the days..." *'An' if we should live up in dah hills'...* the words of a vintage track hit him mid-speech. "Cha. You wouldn't ovastan."

"*Ovastan'?*" Her blue eyes were question marks.

"Leave de subjec', Lucy. What's the real reason for you letting me have the MRS?"

"Didn't it keep you sweet for a while? How else could I have pulled you in? Kept you where I wanted you, until my mission was accomplished? Material things draw materialistic people, Lijah." She laughed and said, *"Fooled yah!"*

Lijah didn't try to understand. He was tired. Drained out. All he knew, Lucy was one mad, mixed-up, confused woman and hoped she would untie him and that would be the last he would see of her.

"Ok, Lucy. You have a gun. I can't challenge you. Could you untie me now? Let me go."

"Why not? I'll let you go. Killing you won't prove much."

"So what did torturing me prove?" It still seemed weird. Was Lucy really fulfilled by doing that shit?

She glared at him in reply. "Just don't try anything, or you're dead." As she spoke, she untied him.

He couldn't think straight, but it was worth a try. His thoughts raced away with him, *'The gun. Get the gun by any means necessary.'*

"And don't... even... think about it." It was as if she had read his thoughts.

But he did. Thought passionately about it good and proper. Now he tried it, and succeeded. It was dangerous, but he was angry. As soon as he got free, he overpowered her. Slapped her down like a hooker that had failed to deliver. Twisted her wrist into a painful position. *'Bad bitches deserve bad treatment,'* he justified himself.

And she had no choice but to release the nasty lump of metal into his hand.

"Ok!" Now he awkwardly pointed the deadly weapon at her head, emitting shit he had heard only in movies. He didn't even know if the damn thing was real, but it must have been. Lucy was freaking. "Money, Lucy, money. Have you got any in the house?!" But it wasn't comfortable. It transported him back to his youth. That infamous off-licence stunt, when his accomplice left him in the shit. When he did the crime and then the time. When he took the wrap, alone.

"There's no money in the house."

"Looks like you're dead meat then, aren't you, Lucy? You see. Right now I feel like shit. Don't care about much now. I'll do time again. This time, for your sorry ass."

"Again?" she nosed.

"Yes! I'll go back to jail for you, yuh bitch!" But he lied. He cared for his family. His future. His life. And after his sodomite experience, he wouldn't want to go back in a hurry. But Lucy wouldn't know, so he tried the spiel. The tough-guy shit. With a false, improvised sincerity in his eyes.

"There's no money in..." The mouth of the gun kissed her left cheek and stopped her lying tongue.

"I'll ask you again, Lucy. Just once! Then you're dead."

She took it as gospel. Now that the shoe was on the other foot, the handle in his hand and she at his mercy, it was mighty uncomfortable. Her intention was not to give him a penny, but in a situation like this, money is no match to the value of life. "Er...you ...wouldn't... kill me would you, Lijah?" She cooed.

"Don't fuck wid me, Lucy! Don't gimme dat shit!" The gun butted her left temple. "You don't think I would fall feh dat shit, do you? Is there any money in the house?!"

"In there! In there!... In... there." She pointed to her bottom drawer. "Take it. All of it. Fifty grand. Just don't kill me. Please."

"Fifty... grand?" Lijah pulled out the drawer with the big toe of his right foot, still pointing the gun at Lucy. He glanced down and nearly crapped himself. "Is dis what fifty grand looks like?" He took a few seconds to catch his breath, and then he grabbed a convenient holdall that was lying in the corner of the room. "Fill it up, you crazy bitch!"

Lucy trotted over, staring now at the gun. Shaking, she filled the bag with every last note.

"Are they real? How come you have so much money lying around? You betta not gimme no fake shit?" He felt like the bad guy in a movie and wondered if he had not slipped back into a dream.

"It's not my money," Lucy said, "It's Conrad's. My brother's."

"Where the fuck did he get it from? I know you're rich bastards, but this looks suspicious."

"Remember that bank job on Crime Watch last week?" Lucy said, still shaking.

"Shit," Lijah said, "but why does your brother need to rob banks?"

"He has always been like that, my brother. Took the wrong road. I told you, I think Mum's leaving us has affected him." As she spoke, she filled the bag. "Not even with his inheritance, I don't think he'll ever be satisfied."

"Well, now, it's mine. As compensation for that torture shit yuh jus' put me through." It was as if Lijah had flipped. Turned into a strange being. An alien or something. Just then, the notion that Conrad might just want his money back eluded him just then.

The country house was remote. As remote as Daddy's money once was when Lucy had first taunted Lijah with it.

Lijah got dressed. His head buzzed. It was just after 1am. He hated the winding country roads at night. Lucy was securely tied to the bedpost, so he discarded the gun by the side of the bed and descended the winding staircase. But halfway down, he stopped in his tracks: '*the gun*'. He figured he would need it. He didn't know why, but something had sent a message to his brain: '*It got me out of a situation, so who knows, it might get me out of another.*' He darted back up the stairs and for a few seconds, he rested his eyes on the face of a pitiful Lucy.

"I knew you wouldn't leave me, Lijah. You're not the evil type. Ok, untie me."

He laughed. "Beg Lucy, beg. Where's your manners?" he tormented her with her own words.

"Please, Lijah."

"Beg, you bitch!"

She juddered. Now he retrieved the gun from the side of her bed and held it again to her head. Now, *she* freaked.

"Say your last prayer, Lucy," he taunted.

"You're not going to kill me...?"

"Why not... after three... One... Two... Three." But he did nothing of the sort. Instead, he teased her venomous nipples with the mouth of the gun. *"Fooled yah!"* he mocked, stepping back onto something hard beneath his feet. He looked down to see her gold pendant. *Lucy. 'Just for a split second',* he thought, *'LUCY was something, under my shoe'.* He picked it up and hung it on her left nipple.

Lijah left the room, negotiated the stairs in leaps and bounds and breathed a semi sigh of relief when he hit the cool morning air. A pure white cat jumped off his Roadster, scaring the life out of him. He flashed his locks and said, *"Why worry, when I can pray?"* And he did. There and then. Prayed to Jah.

But his answer came in the form of banging. Banging from the inside of Lucy's front door. She must have broken free. But why was she banging? Why didn't she just open the door and come after him? He wouldn't hang around to find out.

But he hated it. The banging that is. Brought back the infamous memory of his mother. His mother who couldn't voice her feelings. Now the imaginary banging of her walking stick, pounding hopelessly against the carpet on her bedroom floor, taunted Lijah. And now it engulfed him. Her song. The song she loved so much to sing, before she lost her speech:

I see the stars, I hear the rolling thunder
Thy power throughout the universe displayed.

"Lijah! Help me!" Lucy's voice cut through his thought. "I think I'm going crazy!" The desperate voice forced its way through the keyhole and the crease of the door, grabbing viciously at his sanity. "I'm sorry! This thing has eaten me up. Destroyed my personality. If anyone, it should have been your father who paid for this. Not you!"

'But why was she talking from behind the door?' Lijah wondered. He was confused.

Then sing my soul, My Saviour God to Thee
How great Thou art, How great thou art

Why didn't he drive off? Pull out and away from that madhouse?

He gripped his temple, then paused to cry. *"Jah, I'm only human. So was my mother. So is my father. Beatrice. Dora. Festus. Kizzy. Kunta. Ikesha. Gloria. Oh Gloria. My queen."* The brother was in pain. Torment. *"Good, bad or indifferent, Jah, yuh know we're all human. What a confused world this is. What is 'real?' What isn't? Tell me nuh, Jah! Tell me... tell me... tell me."*

But the drumming again. Lucy. Dear, obliging Lucy. He couldn't take it any longer, and turned his stereo up to drown her out. It was Jacob Miller that helped him:

Tired feh lick weed inna gully
Tired feh lick weed inna bush...

Nevertheless, Lijah's head was exploding. He flashed his locks, then *'A man is just a man'* kicked in and took precedence over Jacob Miller.

But then, suddenly, the tape ended.

The banging stopped.

Silence.

A choking, stifling silence.

He had wanted it, but now he had it, it scared him.

Twirled him around like a speck of dust in the centre of a ruthless tornado.

It was all too good to be true. There's no way he could just simply 'get away' with fifty grand's worth of used notes. Lucy, the fly in his soup would still be at large. It didn't feel right. She must be up to something, despite her remorseful pleading.

He started his engine and turned his main beam on. Glaring back at him was a pair of scary looking cat's eyes. *'Shit! English duppy to raas!'* His heart beat like a drum and as he revved his engine the cat scampered.

Lijah moved off, slowly, cautiously, easing his way out of *no-black-man's-land*, hoping he wouldn't pass any blue flashing lights coming from the opposite direction.

He thought about her. *Lucy.* If he could see her then. Helpless. She had freed herself from the bedpost alright, but in a strange kinda way, the knot that held her two hands together had stayed solid, making it impossible for her to open the door. So instead, she banged profusely with her elbows.

The memory of the gun under Lijah's seat chilled him, as the country road took him home. Home to urban Birmingham.

CHAPTER * TWENTY

Lijah sat sprawled out in the middle of his settee with his head in his hand. He had been bu'ning calli-weed from dawn, and it was now nearly dusk. The man could hold his ital, but now, his head didn't belong to him. It was swimming. But with all that, he found space to think. With a mint of marijuana in his brain, a suitcase filled with no less than fifty grand's worth of used notes, sitting precariously at the bottom of his wardrobe, he had to think. He was extra cautious and had stuffed the holdall that was once Lucy's, into a suitcase that Gloria seemed to have left behind when she went to Jamaica. He had temporarily emptied its contents on the bed in the spare room, and made use of the spacious suitcase. Like Lijah, it seemed like another *'thing'* she didn't want.

He needed to meditate long and hard, but chance would be a fine think. He was alerted by a knock on the door. *'Who could it be now, knocking on his door? Was it Festus? Papa Dread?'* He wished it could be either. But the second knock sounded too much like a visit from a beast-man. "Shit!" he muttered, perturbed, convinced that he had been rumbled. Lucy had spilled the beans. Grassed him up. But then again, maybe not. She would have to tell them where it came from, in the first place.

He stood up quickly, flashed his locks and headed for the kitchen, where he could access a clear view of the unexpected caller.

He was puzzled. It was Faithlyn. Shit. *'A bad penny always turns up'*, he thought. *'What the hell could Faithlyn be doing here?'* Lijah perplexed. *'How could she have the balls to turn up on Gloria's doorstep after what happened?'* Now, he took in the brother that sat waiting in the black BM. It was Rock, her roaming boyfriend. No one was really sure what he was: Yardie? Yankee? Canadian? He was a roamer, alright. Another blot on Birmingham's landscape. Roaming Romeo, if you like. But Rock seemed to have wafted here, more from the ghettos of New York, than from anywhere 'ah yard'.

Lijah splashed cold water over his face and went to the front door.

Faithlyn stood there with a cheeky grin, her eyes filled with mystery, as always.

"Whaap'n, Lijah? Yuh look charge. Gimme some a dat nice draw deh nuh?" She was as bright as ever.

"Faithlyn? Whaap'n? I thought you went back to Jamaica."

"Me shoulda gaan long time. Me visa run out but... yunnuh. A so it go. Me outstay me time. Me neva really mek enough dallaz ova 'ere. Life is not as easy in Great Britain as everybody mek out." Her undiluted Jamaican accent echoed in his already charged head, and now he remembered how she had taunted him, her words seeping through the marijuana in his brain, *'Cho'*, *'Unnuh English bwoy sof' een sah. All me want is feh yuh feh put yuh wood inna me fire. Gloria nah know not'n. Me piano waan tune'*.

"Life nuh easy anywhere, Faithlyn. I've been workin' feh years, an' still me nuh mek enough dallaz."

"Me sista jus' come up from Jamaica de adda day. She come feh study. She 'ave de brain. Me affi hustle my way t'rough life. I jus' waan to fin' a way to get some money. Me waan go back a Jamaica. If me mek enough money, me would be on de plane tomorrow." Faithlyn talked like a woman in her forties. Someone who had seen life. Lived it to the fullest. The hardest way.

But Lijah's attention was drawn now to the baby that sat gurgling in the pushchair Faithlyn was holding casually and uncaringly onto. It couldn't have been more than three months old.

"Whose baby is dis, Fait'lyn?" he asked, wondering what couple was stupid enough to trust her with another baby-sitting job. Whose man had she seduced?

"Neva min' *whose baby?* Yuh not gonna ask me in? Where is Gloria? Me know seh she did lef' yuh. But yuh know how we women fool-fool. She might tek yuh back."

"So what if I tell yuh she's inside, now?" Lijah tested.

"Dat's a'right. A come to see both a yuh."

"Gloria inna Jamaica. Come een." Lijah widened the opening and helped Faithlyn with her pushchair, "So Rock not comin' in?" It was a sweeping statement. Rock wasn't exactly welcome. He was a negative force on the streets of Birmingham, doing his best to pull in and contaminate all positive youth, if they weren't strong. He wouldn't wish Rock on anyone's daughter, but Faithlyn seem rude enough to look after herself.

"No. We not stoppin'. Me jus' come feh get me suitcase. Me hope it is still here…"

Lijah kept his eyes on the cute little baby, Faithlyn's voice now like a mere echo in his head.

"…I left it on the bottom of Gloria's wardrobe. I hope she didn't take it to Jamaica." She eased the pushchair into the kitchen and made her way upstairs. The girl was bold. Brave. She opened the wardrobe where she had left her suitcase and found it still there. She assumed the junk she had left in it was still there. It felt the same weight, so she picked it up and headed downstairs, only to find Lijah still looking at the sweet child.

"Yuh fin' it?" Lijah asked, paying more attention to the baby than he was to Faithlyn.

"Yeah. Me fin' it."

Lijah was more charged than he had thought, yet he played happily with the bouncing baby girl.

"Lijah, me jus' rememba, me affi go somewhere. Me don' waan tek de baby. Me cyan jus' leave ar wid yuh feh about half an hour?" Faithlyn, spieled.

"Bwoy, me mash up yunnuh, Faithlyn. Me not in any fit state to look afta any baby. But whose baby is it anyway? If yuh baby-sitting, yuh cyaan jus' leave de people dem pickney wid a total stranga?"

"Jus' half an hour Lijah. Me soon come." She ignored the latter question.

"So why yuh cyaan tek de pickney wid yuh? Or mek Rock look afta her?"

"Please, Lijah." She batted her eyelids. "The baby likes you," she perfected an English accent.

The baby was smiling up at Lijah and it reminded him of Khamilla when she was about that age. Now he missed his little girl badly, but Jamaica was too far away.

"A'right. But not more dan half hour, Fait'lyn. Me affi get some sleep. Please, don't be long."

"No, man. Den me nuh tell yuh seh me soon come." She turned towards the front door, picking up the suitcase that was left there, out of sight, as she spoke to Lijah.

"What's her name?" Lijah shouted.

"Me call ar Shanique," she slammed the front door and continued, shouting though the letter-box, "her full name is Shanique Zephine Benjamin!"

Lijah played with the beautiful baby. *"Shanique. Shanique Benjamin... Benjamin? Benjamin?"* Wha'? We could be related yunnuh likkle girl. Yuh daddy 'ave de same name as me?" He tweaked her rosy cheeks. Gently pierced her dimples. Then Shanique began to fuss. A familiar smell hit his nostrils. She had poo'd! He was no stranger to changing nappies, but he was in no mood for things like that.

Shanique's cries were becoming more piercing and the smell more stench. He had to change her. He reached for the bag Faithlyn had conveniently left and retrieved a nappy. He loosened her pushchair and lifted her out, pressing her soft cheeks against his. Tiny fingers pulled at his locks. He ascended upstairs to change her.

On entering the bedroom, Lijah couldn't help noticing the wardrobe door wide open. It was unusual. If there was one thing he hated, it was a wardrobe door that was opened for no reason at all, so he wouldn't have done it himself. Besides, he had left his stash there and could remember specifically closing it!

Then he looked and saw an empty space where a suitcase was supposed to be. *'Shit! Suitcase! Faithlyn came for her suitcase! Was that Faithlyn's suitcase?! Oh fuck!'* The wild thought raced through head.

The baby cried. His mind raced faster. Tormented. Faithlyn... but where exactly was Faithlyn? He had no contact for her. Would she look in the case before she made it back in half an hour? He hoped she wouldn't.

He told himself to stop worrying and lay Shanique on a towel on the bed. As he removed a mound of stool from her soft bottom, Khamilla filled his mind again. Then Ikesha. He remembered changing their nappies. Then he thought he hadn't seen Ikesha much lately. And the last time she phoned, she didn't sound herself. He hoped she was ok. Now, he wanted his family. *Like breath.*

He cleaned up the baby and decided to put her back in her pushchair. She was sleepy and so was he. He proceeded downstairs, his mind on his fifty grand. Time had flown. Lijah looked at his watch and could not believe that an hour had passed since Faithlyn had left. As he reached to put Shanique back in her pushchair, he couldn't help but notice a letter in the middle of its seat. It had *'Lijah'* written bold as brass on its back.

'For me?' he asked himself. He picked it up and after placing the baby in the pushchair, he opened it. It read, *'Elijah Zephaniah Benjamin, You're the baby's father. Yes, this is your child, Shanique, Zephine Benjamin. Remember twelve months ago when we fucked? I cannot look after her. She'll have a much better life here in England than in Jamaica. Plus I'm here illegally. You are in a better position than I am. I know you may think I'm heartless, but men do it all the time. Drop dem seed an' turn dem back. Now you'll see how it feels being a one-parent-family. I love her. Don't think I don't. Look after her... Faithlyn."*

Lijah's ass hit the nearest chair in the kitchen. He stared at the child, now, with a difference. He remembered the night Gloria had walked in on him as he lashed Faithlyn's 'fresh-from-Jamaica' ass. Yes. The reason his queen chucked him out.

Now his stereo hummed *'I was born a loser'*.

And he was totally convinced it was true to him. That he was a total loser. Everyone and everything around him was winning. Baby Face Glen had won his queen, drugs had won over his son, Lucy was gonna be a constant bane in his life and now Faithlyn had taken his fifty grand and was threatening to take his freedom. He felt pretty sure she wouldn't be coming back.

He peered down at the sleeping angel in her pushchair. Was it really his daughter? The Benjamins had a specific look. The double-jointed bone structure, nose like Marvin Gaye, the cute dimples and those cute, slitty, Chinese eyes. The baby had nothing for him, but she was still young. It could develop.

He needed to rest his brain, but just then the doorbell went again. He rushed towards it thinking Faithlyn had had a change of heart, but it was Ikesha.

"Ikesha? Whaap'n? Yuh a'right?"

"Yeah, Dad," I'm fine."

"Yuh sure? How come yuh...?"

"Dad? Does Faithlyn's boyfriend drive a black BM?" The question seemed burning. Like she *had to know.* Earlier, they sped past her going the opposite direction.

"Yeah. Why?"

"What's his name?"

"Rock. Nasty piece a work. Dat is one bwoy I wouldn't wish on my worse enemy's daughter. Him an' Fait'lyn deserve each adda still."

Ikesha's face turned grey, "Why wouldn't you wish...?"

"Ikesha, you've always lived in your books. You don't have a clue what's going on outa street, too tough. You jus' keep yuh books yuh, 'ear babes?"

"Why wouldn't you wish Rock on...?"

"Why you asking 'bout Rock, Ikesha? He's not even in yuh league."

"No... A friend of mine was..."

"Listen, Ikesha. You tell any frien' of yours to keep away from Rock. He's just bad news. Trus' me. Neva min' de details, jus' tell dem to leave well alone. Yaah 'ear me?"

And now Ikesha's head buzzed with the memories of that sordid night, as she stepped out of The Hurricane nightclub with Rock and into his black BM. But more so, the event that followed back at her place.

"Ikesha? What's bothering you?" Lijah alerted her. "I know things haven't been too good with the family lately, but..."

"Nothing, Dad. I'm ok..." But she drifted back to that dark place again. She had liked him. Trusted him. How wrong? How very wrong? But he had known she would not have let him go all the way. So he took it. How must it have been? She didn't know. She was asleep. She imagined it. *'His fumbling hands! Her once-virgin thighs! His lips on hers! His breath all over her face! His eager fingers parted her lower lips! Entrance without permission! How was it?!... How was it?! And from the*

settee onto the carpet... how did she get there? Rolled? Pushed? Or
lifted gently?'... "I'm ok! I'm ok!"

"Ikesha? Is wha' wrong? Why yuh shouting? I heard you the first
time."

"Oh... Sorry, Dad. I'm fine, honest."

He stared deep into his daughter's soul, wishing she would let him
know where her mind was at.

That weird, stinging, tingling achy feeling, down below.
The panic as she touched her flower that was so well preserved.
Blood.
Sobbing.
Blood that flowed from a broken lining.
A stolen purity.
And the falling torrents from the hot shower could not cure.
The pain.
Violation.
Shame.
And birds that had missed the dawn... and sang too late.

And all because she wanted to *live a little.*

"Ikesha?"

"It's ok, Dad... Whose baby is this?"

Lijah sat down and handed his daughter the letter Faithlyn had left. It
would make it much easier for him, after she had read it. But as she
read, he wondered what was really troubling her.

A young woman with more money than sense, made her way towards the
entrance to Heathrow Airport. She was destined for sunny Jamaica. With
a head full of hope, desperation and wishful thinking, she floated on a
cloud of *fear.*

CHAPTER * TWENTY-ONE

It was now three days since Faithlyn had left the baby with Lijah.
Luckily, he was on two weeks' leave from work. He had already
convinced himself that she wasn't coming back. He had taken to the
child in a paternal kind of way, but this didn't happen in the real world.
Social workers needed to be contacted. Of course he couldn't just keep
the baby like that. If that was to be the case, papers need to be sorted.
Red tapes. Formalities. The works.

For the first time in three days, Lijah ventured outa street and onto the
front-line. He had to find Rock. He knew where he flexed, but where did

he live? Only Rock would know where Faithlyn could be found.

He had tried to secure the baby the best he could in the passenger seat of his Roadster, with the help of a temporary strap and a cushion. Totally illegal, he knew. He knew also, that if her stay with him must stretch for any length of time, he had to invest in much more than a car seat. A bigger ride was top of his list.

Lijah spotted Papa Dread leaning against Jaro's Beema. He looked angry. Jaro's face was like a cluster of storm clouds. Reds was standing close by. His face was set. Bunti and Sugar sat in a car opposite. Storm clouds were raging all around their heads, yet in a quiet, still way. It was obvious that something wasn't right.

Lijah eased his Roadster onto the pavement nearby and jumped out. Papa Dread's voice greeted his ears. "Jaro, me cyaan believe yuh dealing in dem shit deh! We all know seh de herbs is a natural substance. I feel seh dem wi' soon legalise it. Yuh nuh need to be dealing out no cocaine, crack an' all dem designer shit! Dat is w'at is mashin' up de yout' dem brain! Man like yuh should know betta! Look at Lijah's yout' Kunta. 'Dat yout' is supposed to look up to yuh, Jaro!"

Look up to? Lijah knew better. He didn't think so.

"I man neva dish Kunta not'n, Rasta! Me nah tek de blame feh dat!" Jaro defended himself.

Lijah was now standing next to Papa Dread and Jaro. "Is whaa' gwaan, bredrin? What's all dis? Me hear Kunta name a call."

Jaro averted his eyes from Lijah's. He saw the anger in them.

Rock cruised in a gleaming Mercedes. Was it his? And what had he done with the black BM he cruised in earlier? He slowed up, intrigued by the vintage gathering. The narrowness of that section of the road allowed him to touch fists with Bunti and Sugar. He had already made eye contact with Jaro. Reds gave him a standoffish nod.

"Hey, Rock!" Lijah turned his attention to the reason he was outa street in the first place. "Is weh Faithlyn deh?"

"Faithlyn? Faithlyn suppose to be on her way to Jamaica right now," he smirked. "She fly dis mornin'."

"Jamaica?! But she lef' de baby, bredrin. How she feh...?"

"Den is nuh your baby, star," Rock said before Lijah could finish, now speeding off down towards Soho Road, some chi-chi man song booming out of his stereo, leaving Lijah shocked and wondering if he was enjoying any of his fifty grand. The Mercedes was brand new.

Lijah could do nothing about that situation, so now he turned his attention to the one at hand. He would cross the *'Faithlyn'* bridge later.

"Bwoy, it look like we have some traitor inna we midst, Lijah. Me did waan' feh show yuh dat long time. Man like Jaro nuh s'pose to be dealing wid shit like dat!" Papa Dread protested, throwing his hands up in the air.

Lijah looked at Papa Dread, then at Jaro. Sugar and Bunti had their heads down. Reds stood against the wall, saying nothing. Lijah recalled the conversation in the bookie shop with Festus a while back. The one surrounding the rumour about Jaro dealing the *forbidden*.

"Bwoy, me hope yuh nuh have not'n feh do wid my son getting hooked on dat shit, yunnuh, Jaro. Yuh have your yout' dem. Whatever we touch, we neva touch dem t'ings deh. So how yuh can be dishing it out to our yout' dem? If yuh dealing wid dem t'ings, it would only be feh financial gains!"

Jaro kept his head down. He was dreading what was coming. Yes. Even the wickedest man have fear.

"Yeah," Lijah continued, "yuh know all about dat, don't yuh? *Financial gains*. From getting innocent youths to rob off-licence an' tekkin' de wrap! To dishin' their sons shit, hey?!" Lijah's eyes reddened. He had never found it in him to speak like that to Jaro. No. Not since the day he led him down the wrong path when he didn't have a mind of his own and told him, '*I don't tek kindly to grass. If yuh get ketch, don' call me name... or yuh is dead meat*'. But today he didn't seem to give a damn. It was his youth, Kunta, they were talking about now.

Papa Dread's eyes widened, then quickly narrowed again. His brows knitted. Perplexity cupped his face. Reds' body jolted to a regimented alertness. Even Sugar and Bunti looked shocked.

"Is wha' dis, Lijah?.... Wha' yuh mean?... Wha'?... Weh yaah talk 'bout?" Papa Dread jumped on it.

A storm rushed Jaro's face.

"Lijah? Tell me dis is not what me t'inkin', to bombo claat."

Lijah didn't need words. His eyes said it all.

The baby cried, alerting everyone to the tiny body that sat wriggling in Lijah's passenger seat. All eyes and attention turned towards the sound, minds pricked questioningly, but there were more important matters to attend to.

Papa Dread understood. He continued, "It's a sad state of affairs, an' a dying shame too, when man like us can mek money tu'n we fool! An' it look like it did tu'n yuh fool from long time, Jaro! Lijah have sop'n feh tell me. Looks like I've been missing out big time. Still... if Kunta don't clean up himself an' anyt'ing happen to him... an' if me fin' out seh yuh have anyt'ing feh do wid it, Jaro... me a tell yuh... I will mek sure I tek yuh out meself. Rasta don't work feh no CIA, but I wi' kill feh de yout' dem. Especially Kunta! Blood an' fire feh yuh, Jaro! Blood an' fire!"

Papa Dread knew that two wrongs could never make a right, but he was angry beyond recognition.

"So wha'! Is t'reaten yaah t'reaten me, Papa?" Jaro asked.

"T'reaten? Nah sah... No t'reats. It's a raas claat promise... Yaah 'ear me?! A raas claat promise!"

Papa Dread followed Lijah over to his Roadster, limping. The problem with his right leg didn't seem to be getting any better. With all his consciousness and wisdom, Papa Dread hated doctors. It had been at least three years now since his big toe had posed a little problem, but now, the problem seemed to be slowly consuming the whole of his right side. But Papa Dread was a fighter, and when his natural herbal medicine would not work over the traditional, *Babylon medicine*, he would try self-hypnosis to heal himself.

But no one really knew the extent of Papa Dread's illness. He didn't talk much about it. Only when the pain would lick so hard, the expression on his face would 'talk' for him, giving Reds (who saw it most) cause for concern.

"Dat foot don't seem to be getting' any betta, Papa. Yuh shouldn't still be limping like dat?" But Lijah didn't know the half.

"Nah, man. Me a'right. De welfare of de yout' dem is more important dan a troublesome foot on an old dread like me. Jaro is just one big, troublesome foot dat's about to contaminate de whole body a de community to raas."

Lijah knew that when Papa Dread spoke in parables, he was serious. He knew he meant business. There was something up his sleeve. The last thing Lijah, Papa Dread or anyone had ever wanted, was any more black-on-black violence. It was already tearing through the community like fire in a forest. But Papa Dread's disillusionment with the situation had reached a desperate stage. It had gone beyond reasoning. He had seen Kunta and where he was heading. The youth had a family. A future. But what good was all that, with all that shit in his veins and in his brain.

"Whose baby is dis, Lijah?" Papa Dread asked, taking in the features of the tiny baby. He squeezed in to allow an entourage of vehicles to go by. The brothers were moving out. Despite the earlier confrontation, Jaro tooted his horn giving a *'more time'* gesture. But they all knew where they stood with each other.

"Bwoy, de baby is a long story yunnuh, Papa. Come 'roun' a de house nuh. Me waan talk to yuh. Worries. Nuff worries."

Papa Dread was the only person Lijah could tell his troubles to right now. The Dread had already warned him of the perils of woman and money, but he had to share this with someone. The Lucy thing. It was eating rapidly at the front of his brain, with Kunta's situation just behind. And now he was in charge of a young baby.

Papa Dread shouldn't have been driving. All the way to Lijah's house, the pain licked him so hard, it brought tears to his eyes, and only when the effect of a handful the pain-killers kicked in, could he relax.

At Lijah's house they talked, touching on new and old things, but Papa Dread wanted to know mostly about the subject Lijah brought up outa street. The one he had stunned them all with.

"Lijah, dis is 2003. Yuh was jus' a yout' when yuh went to prison feh dat robbery. Yuh neva tell a soul who yuh accomplice was. All de time it was Jaro, an' all dem years yuh hol' dat down, bredrin? Why? Jaro wasn't supposed to be flexin' amongst us bredrin. It look like him was comfortable wid de situation. Like 'im sure yuh wasn't goin' to talk... Lijah, tell me somet'ing... yuh owe Jaro sop'n?"

"Nah, man. Like wha'?"

"Me nuh know. Me a try work out why yuh waan keep a secret like dat, feh a man like Jaro. Yuh keep 'im secret, an' it look like it back-fire. If yuh did expose Jaro, 'im couldn't touch Kunta. Yuh should have at leas' mek me know, Lijah. Yeah, man." Papa Dread still could not believe what had just been revealed to him.

"Papa, I suppose I took dis 'keep yuh enemy close' ting a bit too deep. I suppose dis t'ing about being a grass played on me conscience as well."

"Lijah, Jaro destroyed a part of yuh young life. I know yuh probably don't want me to mention dis, but look what happen to yuh in jail. Dat batty-man t'ng. Dem t'ings deh shouldn't happen to none a Jah's children. A Jaro cause dat, yunnuh Lijah. Man like dat cyaan prospa? An' now, 'im mash up Kunta."

Lijah stared into space. Wondering. Why? What's Jaro's motive for being so evil? "Why yuh t'ink Jaro flex dem way deh, Papa? Years ago, maybe, but now?... 2003? Kunta. De young yout' dem. How many more yout' 'im mash up by dealin' shit feh a likkle profit?"

"Lijah. Some man no need no motive to be evil, yunnuh. Some man is *evil* itself. *Satan. Anti Chris'.* Born feh wicked. Nuff a dem deh 'bout, Lijah. Dis world will neva be rid of evil. Wickedness. Corruption. Believe me. T'ings dread pon eart'."

Now, Lijah had another layer of guilt to stack on his already high pile. Kunta. It's true what Papa Dread had said. If he had at least told his son the true story, maybe it would have opened his eyes to Jaro's wicked ways. Instead, his silence caused history to repeat itself, and allowed Jaro to strike again, at another member of the Benjamin family.

"Jaro feh get drop, Lijah! Tek 'im affa Jah Jah Lan'!"

"But Papa, dis black-on-black violence t'ing is..."

"Lijah. Mek me tell yuh sop'n. Jah mek us all perfec'. We become corrupt. Greedy. Evil an' wicked. Yuh t'ink Jah please wid what's goin' aan pon 'im lan'? Is who sing dah song deh?... *'Come down Faada, come down?...*

"Me a 'ear yuh, Papa. But we cyaan play God. Vengeance is His. He'll know how to deal wid man like Jaro."

Papa Dread kissed his teeth, as if he was disheartened with Lijah. He eased back into the settee and made himself more comfortable. The pain in his leg was threatening to lick him again.

Lijah was mentally pained and needed that outlet. A one-to-one with Papa Dread always helped. Ikesha had helped him to get a few baby things in: bottles, food etc. When she had first learnt of her dad's situation, she was shocked, but she had problems of her own.

He needed no help in making up bottles. Shanique was fed, bathed, changed and had fallen asleep. Lijah himself was hungry but couldn't eat. Papa Dread had earlier feasted on bun an' cheese and a few cups of cerassie tea, sealed with a huge spliff. He was now fast asleep.

Lijah relaxed in the settee and looked closely and deeply at Papa Dread, one of the only true Rastamen that was left. But now he got thinking how things had changed. Papa Dread had always looked at peaceful solutions for other situations in the past. He had always been firm, but violence? No. So had things got that bad, that it had ripped at the core of a good man?

Lijah recalled again when he had first told Papa Dread that he was about to ease out of Handsworth. Papa Dread's words were legendary. Lijah would remember them every time he would meditate. But tonight they were more vivid than ever. *'It nuh matta w'ere yuh bring up yuh pickney dem, Rasta. If dem gwine bad, dem gwine bad. Give de yout' dem de teachings of His Majesty. Leggo all devil's philosophy. Dat is all yuh cyan do. What we sew, we shall reap'.*

'So what went wrong?' Lijah wondered, *'what bad seed did he sow? Why wasn't Kunta a'right? Were he and Gloria to blame? Did Kunta really think they were a dysfunctional family?'* His thoughts pulled him into a dose.

It was the sound of the Channel 4 news that woke Lijah. Not even Papa Dread's snoring could have shaken him. The baby slept peacefully. He homed in on the TV screen when he recognised Faithlyn's face, and like a gush of cold water, it wiped the sleep clean from his eyes. The reporter blurted, *'A young Jamaican woman was held for questioning*

early this morning by police at Heathrow Airport. Eighteen-year-old
Faithlyn Jackson who was travelling alone was overcome with nerves
when x-ray cameras picked up images of an extortionate amount of cash
in her suitcase. She refused to give an account as to how she came by the
money'.

The newsreader could not read fast enough for Lijah. Papa Dread had
come alive too, catching the tail end of it all.

"Isn't dat yuh baby-sitta, Lijah? Weh she get all dat money from?
Business must be good feh Rock. Me notice seh him a drive Mercedes
now. A bet is 'im sen' Fait'lyn home wid dat money?"

"Is my money, Papa."

"Wha' yuh seh?"

"Is my money. Well... Lucy's money... Well, bwoy it look like I have
to start from de beginning."

"Yeah," Papa Dread got ready, "start from de beginning, Lijah. Is how
much more secret yuh have, bredrin?"

Lijah started at the beginning and talked for England.

Papa Dread listened.

Shanique slept.

"How did a conscious man like meself get mixed up in sop'n like dis,
Papa? Me whole life seems to be falling apart. Gloria lef' me and now
she's wid some gangster bwoy a yard. Kunta is touching cocaine, an'
bwoy... What's going on, Papa Dread?"

"Bwoy, I wish I knew. If I did I'd weed it out. Whatever the force is, it
seems to be stronger than our consciousness." Papa Dread scratched his
patchy, greying locks as if that would bring out the answer. He rubbed
his hand over his face and sighed. "Jus watch yuh back, Lijah. I don' feel
seh dat Conrad bwoy is about to give up fifty grand so easy. An' dis
Lucy girl mus' want ar cyar back. It nuh done. Trus' me."

Lijah wasn't surprised. He had thought of all that way before Papa
dread had mentioned it.

"As far as de front-line is concerned," Papa Dread continued, "I'm
keeping me ears close to the ground. Listen to de grapevine. Jaro, Bunti,
Sugar an' Rock up to sop'n."

"Yuh sure, Papa?"

"Look, Lijah. Me might be old, but me not fool. From what I hear they
have started somet'ing that's gonna spread like wild fire. Spread out into
our community. Mash up de likkle yout' dem head. None of us cyan
guarantee that our yout' dem will be strong enough to say 'No'. Tek
Kunta for instance. Who could have told you that Kunta could be so
stupid?"

"Yeah. Me know. Gloria doesn't even know. I can't tell her. It would kill her. I was hoping he wouldn't get too deep. See sense. Pull out. But it look like once they smell dis cocaine shit, they're hooked."

Papa Dread's eyes bulged with frustration. He wanted an answer. He needed to do something. Someone needed to protect the young black youths. The root of the problem needed to be destroyed. But how?

Shanique stirred.

"Lijah, try not to worry too much. T'ings will work out. Jus' cool." He paused. "So how yuh gwine cope wid dis baby, anyway? Man like yuh s'pose to relax now. Tek t'ings easy. Not lumbered wid a young baby. An' how yuh know is your baby, anyway? Some woman ginnal, yunnuh. Yuh tek blood tes'?"

"Not yet," Lijah said, looking with more interest now, at the baby.

"But bwoy, it can't be easy. Why don't you call social services an' explain to dem wha' happen? Fait'lyn was jus' on de news. They'll believe yuh."

"Yeah, man. Me affi sort sop'n out tomorrow. Firs' t'ing." But he looked at the baby and something told him he couldn't do it. It hadn't been long, but he was becoming attached. He was beginning to convince himself the child was really his.

Ever since the day Fiona had dealt viciously with Festus, Kizzy had not faced him. He had called. Apologised. Pleaded. Begged. But to no avail. Kizzy's mind was well and truly made up. But her stay at Fiona's was only temporary, and from time to time, she needed clothes for her and Fari. To pick up her mail. Oddments. And they were all there at the house with Festus. So she had mastered the art of sneaking back, from time to time, whenever he wasn't there.

Today, as she snuck back into the house, the adrenalin rush nearly killed her. *'Get my gun, Mum'*, Fari's had told her before she left Fiona's. *'It's under the mattress in the spare room'*. And after wondering whether or not she should, (considering his little hysterical outbreak and his naïve promise of *'shooting'* Festus) she had promised she would bring it back. *'It's only a toy'*, she reminded herself again.

But as she entered the house, she didn't need telling: she could smell her: another woman all over her house. The urge to pry overcame her. She couldn't help it. A woman's curiosity, and all that. She climbed the stairs, walked purposely into the bedroom and peeled back the sheets. No messing. *Yeap.* Just as she had thought. Strands of blonde hair all over his pillow and top sheet. She re-laid the sheets, then proceeded to carry out her main mission.

But suddenly! The turning of keys in the lock!

The urgent closing of the front door.

Oh my God! Quick! Hide!

The wardrobe! Inside the wardrobe!

She could hear him now. Festus. In the room. In her head. His shadow now making the inside of her refuge even darker. It was maddening. Her heart was beating. Fast.

Rustle… rustle… rustle. Shit! He opened the wardrobe. Just his side. She was sure he was looking at her feet. Had to be. She could feel it. His eyes piercing her knuckles that were tightly gripping her knees.

He grabbed a shirt. Wardrobe door shut. Quick shower. Dressed. Down the stairs and out the front door again. *Phew*. Luckily, he was on a mission and didn't hang around.

Now, Kizzy breathed again, and only when she had heard the disappearing sound of his engine, had she emerged from her hiding-place. She quickly grabbed what she came for, and threw them into a bag. Then she remembered Fari's gun.

"But this isn't the toy gun Fari had?" Kizzy questioned herself as she stared at the frightening metal piece she had picked up from the bottom of the mattress. "It's… heavy…. This thing looks real."

She dropped it.

Nerves held her rigid. "That's a real gun… for sure. Could that really be the gun my son played with not so long ago?"

Lijah. She had to talk to Lijah. Why? She didn't know. After all, what could he do? All she knew, she wanted to talk to him.

She called a taxi and thanked God it arrived when it did. For no sooner had she placed her ass on the seat and shut the door, Festus turned up again. He must have forgotten something.

He spotted her. Shit. Pulled right up along-side the taxi and locked his gaze within hers. She turned away as the taxi moved off.

"Kizzy? Yuh a'right?" Lijah asked, surprised at the sight of her on his doorstep. After their last encounter, and what with her beating herself up about their little dirty deed, she was the last person he was expecting.

"Yes. Fine… Er… Lijah, can I come in?"

" 'Course yuh cyan," he was bemused. "Problem?" Deep inside, he thought, *'Oh no. Not another one pregnant'*.

"Lijah, have you ever seen a real gun?" Kizzy asked anxiously, as she walked to the sitting-room.

"No," he lied. "Only on that amnesty thing on TV, why?"

"Lijah… I think Festus has a gun. I'm sure…" Panic set in.

"Calm down, Kizzy. How yuh know dis?"

"I saw it. Picked it up. It's under the mattress in the spare room. I thought it was Fari's toy gun but…"

"Kizzy, dere must be some mistake. Toy guns look real nowadays yunnuh."

"But Lijah… the weight. It was heavy. And there was something about it that made me think it's real. And to think, Fari played with it!"

"Cho. Nuh panic, man. Weh Festus feh get gun from? 'Im is bad man?" Lijah kissed his teeth, playing the game of ignorance well. The gun he himself had taken from Lucy, was hidden somewhere in his bedroom. However, he couldn't help but wonder about the possibility of Festus having one.

But Kizzy's attention was drawn now, for the first time, to the sight of the sleeping baby in its pushchair. "Whose baby is this, Lijah?"

"Oh… You haven't heard. I thought bad news travelled fast. The baby is a legacy from Faithlyn. I'm sure Gloria filled you in already on the beginning. One of the reasons why she left me."

"This is *your* baby? With Faithlyn?"

"So she seh. Me nuh know. I fucked her, so…"

"So… yuh baby-sitting?"

"No. She's lef' de baby, Kizzy. Dumped the baby on me, and left. Tek off to raas."

"… Yuh joking." Kizzy's response was slow coming. She couldn't comprehend how a woman could have given birth to a child, dumped it on the father and left, with no intention of coming back. Not after being attached to the child for nine months. Inside her. Moving. Kicking. Feeding. *How could she?* She wondered.

"Anyway, dat's my problem," Lijah told her. "We yaah seh 'bout Festus?"

"Listen, Lijah, I have to go. It's probably me being paranoid. It's true, Festus is no bad man."

She got up and Lijah walked her to the front door. The narrowness of the porch made closeness impossible. The memory of the lustful moment they shared, rushed them both.

"See yuh, Lijah," Kizzy said, running away from the awkward moment.

"More time, Kizzy, yeah?" Lijah said, watching her ass disappear.

CHAPTER * TWENTY-TWO

Ikesha wasn't strong enough to carry the pain and guilt of a hidden rape and worse of all, an abortion. Although she was close to her mum, if there were anything she couldn't talk to her about, she'd talk to Auntie Kizzy, her godmother. She hadn't seen her for a while, not since Fari's birthday party. She should have kept in contact more, but there is always a reason for everything.

There was more Ikesha should have known about the life of Kizzy and Festus, but Gloria didn't practise to tell her everything. Ikesha thought things were ok. Not brilliant, but ok. And it was simply what she *didn't* know that had influenced the way she saw their relationship. Today though, it would have been good if she had at least known that Auntie Kizzy and Fari were staying with Fiona.

She pulled up outside her Godparents' house and told herself, 'I should have phoned first'. Their car was parked up, so that was a good sign: someone at least, was in.

She settled her KA behind their car, locked up and proceeded up the drive. She needed this talk with Auntie Kizzy badly. Although abortion was a no-no in the tribal faith, she knew Auntie Kizzy would not judge her or see her as a lesser person.

"Whaap'n, Ikesha?" Festus seemed surprised to see her.

"Hello, Uncle Festus. Is Auntie Kizzy here?"

"Er... No, Ikesha, she..."

"Is she gone to town?"

He felt awkward. He realised there and then that Ikesha didn't know that Kizzy had left him. He knew how the family flexed too, and knew that Gloria and Lijah didn't always divulge their business to their children.

"Yes. What did you want her for?"

"Just for a chat."

"Aaam. Come een, Ikesha. Yuh know seh yuh can chat to yuh godfaada as well. Unless it's one a dem woman talk t'ings." He chuckled.

"When will Auntie Kizzy be back? I'll wait if she won't be long."

"Yeah. Come een an' wait. She shouldn't be long."

Ikesha was comfortable with him. He was her godfather. Her Uncle Festus. A nuh not'n.

"How's Gloria, Ikesha? She likin' it in Jamaica?" His talk couldn't be smaller.

"Yes. I think so." She noticed a strange untidiness about the house, that just wasn't Kizzy's style, but people get busy and standards sometimes drop. "Where's Fari?" she asked, curiously, remembering that Fari wasn't fund of crowds and the hustle and bustle of Birmingham city centre.

"He's with his Auntie Fiona. Sit down, Ikesha." He shouldn't be looking at her the way he was. To him, she was a mere baby. Half his age.

"Yuh still goin' on dat back-packin' trip I hear yuh was planning?" There were other seats, but he sat close to her on the settee. But it didn't feel strange. It was Uncle Festus. And besides, she had sat next to him before on numerous occasions.

"No. I've changed my mind. I've applied for a job at the BBC."

He sprawled out beside her now, making himself comfortable and playing idly with the remote. And, as if a most uncanny turn of fate had planned it so, the TV screen came to rest on a rape scene in some movie, throwing Ikesha's emotions all over the place. She felt uneasy. "Turn it over, Uncle Festus! Turn it over!"

"Wha' wrong, Ikesha? Yuh a'right?" He got jumpy and wondered now if she had heard about his attack on Kizzy. That unjustified rape. The assault he could not control.

Ikesha started to cry. She got up to go. "Sorry, Uncle Festus, it reminds me of…"

"Of what? It's only a movie. Wha' it remin' yuh of?"

"It reminds me of Rock!"

"Rock? How de movie remind yuh of Rock and upset yuh so?"

"He raped me."

"Rock raped you?"

"Yes… he did."

Festus knew that he of all people couldn't talk. He was no saint, considering what he had done to Kizzy.

"Yuh tell yuh dad?"

"No. I haven't told anyone. That's what I came to tell Auntie Kizzy," she sobbed, "I just have to talk to someone."

Festus rose to his feet in an attempt to show some kind of emotion towards his goddaughter. Maybe he would tell her the truth that Kizzy won't be coming back. How could he not? This was a Princess. A 'homemade' Princess. One he had watched grow from a baby girl with twinkling eyes, to a fine young lady, with honourable wishes. One that had men, including himself, *wishing*.

He held her close and she cried in his arms.

"Hush, Ikesha. It's gonna be a'right." The caring cuddle brought both their warm necks together, and the compelling urge to kiss her was so strong, he was almost shaking from its force.

"Can I use your phone to call Auntie Kizzy? I've got no credit at the moment. I just wanna see if she will be here soon."

"Ikesha, she…"

She pulled away and now Festus could see the deep sorrow in her eyes. She might have been raped, but her innocence drew him. *'Innocence breeds no room for betrayal'*, he thought. An innocent person like Ikesha couldn't hurt him. He felt they needed each other.

"She what, Uncle Festus?"

She looked into his eyes for an answer, but he looked for consent to touch her. And whatever he thought he saw in her eyes, he had interpreted it for *'yes'*, so he pulled her close, trembling with desire, and kissed her.

Confused, vulnerable and unsure, she said, in a questioning tone, *"Uncle Festus?"*

"Ikesha, it's ok," he whispered, kissing her again, with more passion this time.

She didn't know why, but she trusted him. Was that Ikesha's problem? With all her head-screwed-on ideas, did she trust too much? And the wrong people too? Had she simply needed to get out more? Experimented with life like her peers did? Whatever it was, she was obviously lacking something crucial.

He turned her around and held her back against his chest. He kissed her neck, the side of her face and her sensitive earlobes. Trembling now with a rush of lustful desire, he manipulated her thin waistline and fumbled her firm breasts.

"Uncle Festus?" She needed no telling it was wrong, but somehow she didn't wanna be right. It was most certainly the wrong comfort, and from the wrong person, but she needed something.

"It's ok," he whispered in her ears, and still she trusted him. But what about Auntie Kizzy? Wasn't she thinking about her when she accepted his kiss?

A hard dick throbbed against her firm, young ass. Perhaps now, she would freak. No. She didn't. She simply, *'let it be'*. Nervous, shaky fingers reached for her once violated flower: its scattered petals quivering from his touch. Unlike the first time in Rock's car, she had strength to protest, but still, she allowed Festus' fingers to travel. Easing. Roaming. Fumbling. *Pitter-patter-pitter-patter-pitter-pitter*…

"Uncle… Festus… what if Auntie Kizzy…"

"She won't. She won't come, Ikesha" he whispered. "Come. Let's go upstairs."

He held her now, like precious jewels as they climbed the stairs to his bedroom. Before she had the chance to notice the absence of Auntie

Kizzy's toiletries etc, he laid her, silently on the king-sized bed and began undressing her with a tenderness he himself didn't know he possessed. He undressed and joined her on the sacrificial bed, kissing her hard nipples, touching her inner thighs, running his hands over her soft, tender body. And soon, he was inside her, moving his hardness in and out of her moist vagina. Something told her again that it was wrong, yet it felt so right. But would it have felt the same, had she known what he did to Auntie Kizzy? The physical abuse. The rape. The tarring her with the same brush as his father did, with his mother.

And now, she was floating. Her first orgasm. A thousand angels used her g-spot for a harp-string, rendering sensational touches to die for. She wasn't sure what was happening to her body. Sure she had read about orgasms, but if this was how it felt, Uncle Festus could touch her forever.

"Festus!" a voice boomed from downstairs, "Ikesha is here?"

Festus had never pulled his key from an ignition so fas before.

"...What's her car doin' outside yuh front door?" The familiar voice raced with footsteps, up the stairs and towards them. It was too late. Game over. No place to hide. "An' how come yuh leave yuh front door open?"

Then he remembered how the front door came to be left opened. In his shock to see Ikesha, he had invited her in and had forgotten to close it. And now, Lijah was in their faces, like a bare-faced cheek.

The only thing Festus had a chance to do was to whip on his boxers. Ikesha was only halfway on with his knickers when Lijah entered the bedroom, her legs weak from the orgasm she was having: disturbed midstream.

Lijah stopped in his tracks, his eyes wandering from Festus to his daughter simultaneously. *Was this real? Was this really his young daughter, nude, in the company of his idrin?* "Is weh de bombo claat me a si yah?" he said in a seething, murderous whisper. But the whispering was from pure shock. It wouldn't last. The eruption was bubbling uncontrollably in his throat. To him, she was a virgin. The *'sweet untouched'* like Festus had put it. He knew now that his intuitions were right. Festus had lecherous designs on his daughter, feh true. "Is weh yaah deal wid, Festus?! Not Ikesha! Tell me yuh not fuckin' me daughta! Yuh god-daughta! Kizzy's god-daughta! Yuh sick?!" He grabbed his idrin by the balls, intending to rip out the molesting organ. Forgetting his own strength, he twisted and squeezed the living daylights out of it, as he asked "Why! Why, Bredrin?!"

Both Festus' pupils met at the bridge of his nose and he squeaked like a mouse. *Literally.*

"Why, Festus?! Why Ikesha?!"

By this time, Ikesha was fully clothed and was hitting the stairs, crying.

"Why did you have to spoil her, Festus? She was different from other young girls. She was a virgin." Now, Festus freaked when Lijah produced a gun and held it to his dick.

"Ee... ee... ee... easy, Lijah. Is dat t'ing real?!"

"You should know if it's real or not. I do believe you have one, bredrin."

Festus looked at Lijah, and his eyes confirmed that the gun Kizzy had seen was real.

"Jus' watch it don't go off bredrin!"

"I said why did yuh spoil Ikesha?! Ansa me before me blow yuh fuckin' dick off!"

The threat felt real and Festus hastened, "I didn't spoil ar, bredrin! Rock did done spoil ar a'ready! He raped her!"

Ikesha was sat at the bottom of the stairs with her head in her hands. Festus' words wrapped themselves around her eardrums and she wished she were dead. *'Why did he have to tell him?'* she thought. *'Why?'*

"Weh yuh seh?" Lijah loosened the grip on Festus' dick. His hands fell lifeless to his side. He stared hatefully at his idrin as if his name was Rock. "Weh yuh seh 'bout Rock?" Shock seemed to have taken the strength from his voice.

"Rock raped her, Bredrin. She tell me."

Lijah heard his daughter's sobbing. He thought she was long gone.

Yes. It's true. Every man has it in him to kill. It just takes that special something to bring it out. Lijah saw red. " 'Keeshaaaaa!!" Reality had reached his brain. Sunk in and soaked up by its cells, drumming now, like racing heartbeats. His voice hurled like a herder's noose, pulling her daughter up from her ass and up the stairs. Its compelling force pulled her back towards the scene of her most recent crime of lust.

"Yes, Dad?" Tears reclaimed their place in her eyes.

"Is it true?"

Silence.

"I said, "Is... it... true?"

Silence.

"I said! Is! It! True?!"

"Yes! Yes! It's true, Dad. I... he... I... it was... er... I just..." She was confused. "I'm sure he put something in my drink. It was the last time I went out with Scorcha. I woke up and I was..." She was sobbing her heart out.

"Wha' yuh mean 'im put somet'ing in yuh drink?! What?! An' wha' yuh mean yuh woke up?! Where?! Tell me! Wha' 'im put inna yuh drink?!"

"I don't know. Maybe that GHB. That rape drug. I read about it. And I saw it on a documentary once. I'm sure I was drugged, Dad."

"Ikesha?" Lijah calmed now. He dropped his voice, lifted his daughter's chin with his right index finger and stared an abundance of condolences into her eyes. "Why didn't you tell me, Ikesha? Is dat why yuh was asking about Rock de las' time yuh was 'roun' de house? I t'ought yuh was actin' strange. I knew sop'n was wrong. Yuh wasn't ok at all."

"Dad, I just didn't want…"

"It's ok, Sweetheart. It's ok. Jus' leave Rock to me," he said gently. "Does your mother know?"

"No!… No, Dad… don't tell her. Don't tell her, please… don't tell her," she pleaded, knowing full well that if she told Gloria the first half, she would have to tell her the other. Although they had long gone strayed from the majestic life of true Rastas, the word abortion would still be a profane word to her parents.

"You don't want yuh madda to know yuh was raped?"

"No, Dad… No… I haven't kept anything else from her, but this…"

'Secrets,' Lijah thought. 'Secrets. The Benjamin family is built on secrets. From de ole man. To me madda. Meself. Kunta. Now Ikesha. Secrets bring only misery in the end.' Yet he knew there were newly accumulated ones on his part, he still couldn't divulge. Would it ever stop? In fact, he wondered, 'Is there another family like the Benjamin's?'

"Is a'right, Ikesha. If dat's yuh wish, I won't tell yuh madda. Like dem seh, 'what yuh don't know, won't hurt yuh'." And on that note, Lijah turned and landed an unexpected punch in Festus' gut, winding his last sexual pleasure out of him. It frightened the living daylights out of Ikesha.

"Dad!"

Déjà vu hit Festus as he hit the floor. The very same spot where Fiona had put him, previously.

"Yuh a'right, Ikesha?" Lijah asked.

"Yes, Dad," she said, looking down at Festus.

"Come. Let's go," Lijah told his daughter. He touched the deadly weapon (a legacy of Lucy) now concealed beneath his jacket, and, as clear as day, he saw Rock's face in his mind's eye. 'Vengeance is mine', he thought, 'vengeance is truly mine'. Was he now about to play God? That was the last thing he had challenged Papa Dread about.

CHAPTER * TWENTY-THREE

Kunta pressed his left index finger against his left nostril and leaned into the white powdery substance. One straight lick and he had sniffed his first fix for the day. Menilek's cry was just a distant murmur in his head. Shari's pleading, conveniently blocked out. He leaned back, ignoring his son's cry and his woman's pleading. His second child was due in three weeks, but he would be in no fit state to be around it.

"Kunta, why don't you get some help," his woman pleaded. "Why did you start taking that shit? How am I gonna cope with the new baby and Menilek when you're like this?"

He was spaced out. Shari may as well be talking to herself. She held her belly. Mopped her tears. Cuddled her son. And now, she watched him feed again, on another lick. "Kunta! Stop it!" But the horse she was flogging, was dead. Her man was hooked. Truly won over by the devil's food. He knew not its history. From whence it came. How many top dogs were getting rich on the substance that was destroying him. But he knew its destination. It surfed happily on the once, calm tides, of his bloodstream.

Menilek stared perplexed at his crying mother, then at his strange-looking father, not understanding what was going on.

Love *lived* there. It had not left. Young love that had only just begun. But without help, hope would *die* there. It was slipping. Fast.

Shari walked away from the confines of the small kitchen and the sorry sight of her man. She took her son with her to the bedroom and closed the door firmly shut. As if to shut out a pending disaster. She slipped in a cassette and turned up the stereo on a song that had been her favourite for the longest time. When she had first heard it, she had not dreamt that it would be a significant one in her own life. Now, she cried as she listened to the words, knowing it was too late. Too late to cry, that is. As she held her son close to her belly, she rocked, not just to the rhythm of the song, but the wild rhythm of confusion that surrounded her. TLC rode the airwaves of her heart:

Don't go chasing waterfalls
Listen to the rivers and the lakes that you're used to
I know that you're gonna have it your way or nothing at all
But I think you're moving too fast...

It was getting too much. After twenty minutes, Shari pulled on Menilek's coat, threw on a jacket and headed for the door. She needed to think. Clear her head. She dialled Lijah's mobile. The last time she saw him was at Fari's birthday party. Kunta had got worse. Now he needed daily fixes.

"Lijah? I need some help... whose baby is that?" Shari was interrupted by Shanique's loud screams. She didn't know Lijah's present situation. The child was clearly missing her mother or something.

"Just a minute." Lijah evaded Shari's question and pacified the baby. "What's wrong, Shari?" He knew she only called when something was wrong. Besides, he could have guessed what the problem was.

"It's Kunta. He's taking crack or coke. A lot more now. Lijah, I don't know how I'm gonna cope with the kids. The new baby is nearly here and..."

"Where's Kunta now, Shari?" Lijah asked.

"I left him at home," Shari sniffled.

"A'right. I'm coming over. Go back to the house."

But by the time Lijah got there, Kunta had disappeared. "Where could he be?" Lijah asked.

"I don't know. He's been hanging 'round with some guy in a black BM. I don't know what they're up to."

"Which guy in a black BM?"

"I don't know. He never gets out his car so I never see his face. He always just pulls up, toots and Kunta goes out. I don't know who he is, but Lijah, I don't trust him. I think he's gonna get Kunta into deep trouble. Once, I asked Kunta who he was, he told me to mind my own business."

Lijah had a think. A guy in a black BM? Could it be Rock? Perhaps the Mercedes he last saw him with wasn't his. Or perhaps he was sporting two rides. "Shari, describe dis Beema dis guy drives."

"It's just black. With gold caps. And I'm sure it had a private reg. When it drove off earlier, I tried to read it but it sped off too quick. I only got RO something."

"*ROCK*. I might have known. Kunta a lick head wid Rock?" Lijah had got caught up in some shit lately, but he would give anything to save his son from the hands of Rock, a man who was as deadly as sin, and to put the icing on the cake, he raped had raped his daughter.

"Who's Rock, Lijah?"

"Shari, you don' want to know who Rock is. Bad news. Nasty piece a work."

"And yesterday Kunta came home with a lot of money and I know he didn't work for it. He tried to hide it from me but I saw it. Lijah, I just want my old Kunta back. What's he mixed up in?" Shari started to cry.

"Listen. Nuh worry. Me wi' fin' 'im. Jus' cool." Lijah headed back to his Roadster, where the baby was fast asleep, and headed for the frontline. This was no life for a tiny baby. He seriously had nuff t'ings to sort out. Thoughts flooded his head. He knew that he himself hadn't been squeaky clean all his life, but he asked himself *'how can a parent protect his or her child from the perils of the streets, inna dis yah time. Any street. London. New York. Birmingham. Jamaica. The world over. You cannot be with them twenty-four-seven. And who did Kunta really need protection from? Rock? Jaro? The drug Lords at the beginning of the chain of destruction? Or Kunta, himself? Bwoy... I man don' know much, but me know one t'ing... it sipple out deh. Few real. Man an' man don' even know who to trus' to raas'.*

Lijah must have cruised the whole length and breadth of Handsworth, but there was no sign of Kunta or Rock. He cruised 'round to Papa Dread's shop where he found him in pain. His right leg was giving him a run for the good life he had lived.

"Yuh see Kunta todeh, Papa?"

"No, sah. Why?" Papa asked, trying to take leave of the pain that gripped him.

"He's been tripping on some shit again. I thought he bucked up, Papa. Me talk to him about de idea of getting private treatment. Kunta tell me seh him leggo dat shit. Seh 'im a'right. But a nuh so. Kunta is worse. Me one son, to raas. Is weh me do feh deserve dis, Papa? Shari is out of her mind. A don' know wha' duh Kunta. An' 'im linkin' head wid dat Rock. Dat man is bad news, Papa." Lijah hushed the baby, she was bellowing in his ears.

Papa Dread looked at the baby, but spoke through her. "Rock is not de only bad news out dere, Lijah. But yuh know dat, still. Bad news is all around us. It is a blessed child who can escape it. While we sleep, the machinery of evil turns. It needs evil hands to oil its cogs. There are always willing recruits. Wolves inna sheep's clothing."

Papa Dread was on a roll. His parabolic tongue was running. Lijah understood. Caught his drift.

"I neva had a son, Lijah. Died at birt'. Yuh know dat, still. *Kunta.* He would have been a big man now."

Lijah recognised the deep remorse in Papa Dread's voice.

"A t'ink dat is why I have dat passion feh de welfare of all a deh yout' dem. If I could snap me fingas an come up wid a solution, I would, but bredrin, a nuh so." He tensed his body in resistance to the pain that plagued him. He looked tired. Tired of life. Tired of bad news. Tired of the *'every day is a gun shot t'ing'...* But most of all, tired of the pendulum that swung daily in his head: *beat dem, join dem, beat dem, join...* Today, he sounded deeper than ever before. More sincere. Lijah noticed. Should he not have mellowed with age?

"How yuh feelin' anyway, Papa? Look like de leg still a badda yuh."

"Man cool, Lijah. Man cool."

Papa Dread and Reds sat waiting patiently in the ride they had borrowed from an unfamiliar source. Its windows were blacked out. Using their own cars would give the game away. Even with the streetlights, the surroundings had a bleak darkness about it. Like a couple of vigilantes, they were lying low, on the corner of a neighbouring street. Waiting. Watching. Anticipating. Eyes firmly fixed on the front door of the house: a house in which they themselves had sat, doing nuff reasoning. Bu'ning nuff calli-weed and chanting down Babylon.

But this was serious. Crack and cocaine, to them, were like germ warfare. They figured that might have been one root of this evil, but taking out one root would be better than leaving it to spread disaster.

They had been waiting for hours, but nothing.

Then something. Bunti and Sugar pulled up, looking around, casing the full length and breadth of the street, then walked up to the door and rang the bell. Jaro opened it. After the two men had walked in, he looked up and down the street suspiciously, then closed it again. Nothing unusual. Papa Dread and Reds didn't watch that. It wasn't the point they had come to prove.

Another fifteen minutes. Forty. Fifty. Then bingo! A brand new Mercedes pulled up. Rock was driving and Festus was in the passenger seat. The youth in the back was partly obscured, until he emerged and proceeded towards the infamous door.

Papa Dread almost fell off the edge of his seat, when Jaro opened and Kunta went in, only to come back out again with a suspicious packet.

Reds recalled the son he had lost. The youth was used as a drugs mule for the value of a few pounds, a quick fix and the promise of a fast motor.

On returning, Kunta had found Rock preparing quick fixes for the trio. Then after a little while, he sped off.

Papa Dread and Reds followed, but somewhere before the roundabout at the end of Soho Road, they lost them. It was unfortunate, but on the video camera they were equipped with, they had enough to make Jaro eat his famous last words: *"I man neva dish Kunta not'n, Rasta. Me nah tek de blame feh dat."*

"Yes, bredrin," Papa Dread addressed Reds. "Man to man is so unjust. I an' I don' know who to trus'."

"A dat me a show yuh, Papa," Reds agreed. "T'ings nuh pretty. Jah know."

Shari hated that '*It is impossible to connect your call*' response whenever she called Kunta's mobile. Lijah had called hours before to say he was still trying to find him. It was 1am. Worrying had brought on pre-mature labour, and excruciating pain had got a hold of her. The baby was not due for another three weeks, but she could not argue with nature. Her contractions were now seven minutes apart. Pain was licking her, but she was holding on, hoping she would hear the push of that key, followed by the footsteps of her man, climbing the stairs. But it was no good. Even Lijah's mobile was switched off the last time she called.

Shari dialled 999 and requested an ambulance.

Menilek, just a year old, was sleeping. Shari wished Gloria was around. She didn't call Ikesha. The last time she had bumped into her, she went weird when Shari talked about motherhood. She couldn't work out why Ikesha reacted like that, but put it down to something to do with babies. Shari knew it had to be a new phobia, since (although Ikesha wasn't ready for babies yet) she had never acted that weird.

She was lonely. She had fallen out with her best friend over something she could hardly remember now. She remembered how helpful and comforting Gloria was at Menilek's birth. The relationship between her and her own mother was still at the broken-down stage. It had broken down from the time Shari chose Kunta over university. Gloria could empathise. She had been the very same age when she fell pregnant, and from the outset, although they came 'round in the end, her parents had treated her the same.

Shari was lonely.

The doorbell rang and she didn't need telling it was the ambulance. Its blue flashing light flickered through her bedroom window, illuminating her fears. Not for the birth, but for the fate of her man. Where could he be? She didn't like the vibes she was getting.

"Menilek." She shook her sleepy son to consciousness. "Wake up, Darling. Mummy has got to go to the hospital. Your baby brother or sister is nearly here." She had already opened the door for two stout ladies. The driver helped Shari to the ambulance, and her assistant carried her bag and Menilek.

"Will Menilek be ok staying with me at the hospital?" Shari asked, "I can't get in touch with his father and..."

"Don't worry," one of them answered, "they'll sort something out. We've had situations like this before."

But Shari knew, that this woman couldn't possibly know her '*situation*'.

As they got to the ambulance, her waters broke and the nurse did the possible necessities.

It was almost like *déjà vu*. Shari found herself in the very same maternity room where she had been on the break of dawn, New Year 2002. The very same Barbadian nurse with her *singing-swinging-jolly* high-pitched voice was standing over her saying: *'now w'en we tell yuh to push, yuh have to push, young lady. Or we'll be here all night'*. Shari reckoned she must say that to every woman that comes in to give birth.

She looked across the room and saw the very same nurse that Gloria had clashed with and remembered her very words: *'Yuh tek de pleasure, now tek de pain!'* But at that moment, the memory of the pleasure had flown out the window with her dignity. Legs asunder and pain licking her, the only hand she had to hold was that of the Barbadian nurse and a young English one. There was no Gloria to tell her: *"Yes you can. I did it three times. Just look at dis big young stallion who put you in this position. I brought him here. He was eight pounds and I was much smaller than you... So you can do it, Shari."* Why wasn't Gloria there? She was like a mother to her.

And where was he now? That big, young stallion she loved so much? Shari had no time to dwell on whens, wheres and whys. Her second child was about to join a world that had failed its father. Or even a world where its father had failed to evade its dangling temptations. She hoped that he was not spaced out somewhere in a corner of it, high on some man-made substance.

The very same German-looking doctor that delivered Menilek, walked in. Shari wondered how many babies he had delivered, and would deliver in his lifetime. And how many of them had, or would grow up to be strong-minded. Strong enough to resist the temptations of the world.

The doctor meant business, but Shari had no great urge to push.

"Ok, Shari," the doctor said, looking not at her, but at her notes. He replaced the notes and pulled on a pair of rubber gloves. Pulling the sheets further up her legs, he fumbled, trying to find the baby's head. She wished he wouldn't do that. "Ok. I think you're ready now. Start pushing." He was so calm, he made it sound as if giving birth was easy.

Shari moaned. This time seemed much harder than the first.

She gripped the nurses' hands.

"Ok, Shari, push," the doctor commanded.

Shari panted.

Breathed deeply.

Pushed and pushed.

Then, for the second time, out slid a bouncing baby boy.

"It's a boy! Well done!" the Bajan nurse shouted.

Gloria and Lijah were grandparents for the second time.

"*Kunta*. I'll call him *Kunta Junior*," Shari said in a weary tone when the new baby was placed upon her tired chest.

Little Kunta had slept through the night. Shari was pleased, since it gave her a chance to sleep. She needed it. It was 8am. For her, the usual hustle and bustle of the maternity ward had just begun, although for the staff, what with the impartial timing of babies being born, it hadn't stopped. Shari wondered if Kunta had been in, seen her sleeping and decided not to wake her.

"Nurse," she caught the attention of a passing nurse. "Have I had a visitor this morning or last night?"

"No, love. I don't think so. Not that I know of anyway."

In the panic of the pre-mature labour, she had left her mobile at home. It had all her telephone numbers logged in it. She acquired some change, walked over to the payphone and dialled Kunta's mobile number. His and her home telephone numbers were the only ones in her head. But she got that '*the mobile phone you have called is switched off. Please call again later.*"

She rang home, but no reply.

It didn't feel right. The whole thing felt weird. She hadn't seen him since yesterday and now his phone was switched off. Butterflies danced in her stomach. She dialled Lijah's mobile. He had promised to find Kunta for her, but after that, she couldn't reach him.

"Lijah! Hello! Thank God I got you." Shari was relieved.

"Where are you, Shari? I was worried. I called your house phone... mobile... I was worried," Lijah told her.

"Lijah, I'm in the hospital. I had the baby. Have you heard from Kunta?"

"No, Shari. Haven't you?"

"No. I'm worried, Lijah."

"Listen, who's having Menilek?"

"He's here with me. I didn't have anyone to..."

"Why didn't you call Ikesha? She's his auntie, Shari. Wha' yuh mean yuh didn't have anyone? You know she would come."

"I just..."

"Listen, I'll contact her. We'll see you later. What ward are you in?"

"Ward 10... Lijah!"

"Yes."

"You're like a father to me. Thanks."

Shari replaced the receiver and wondered who he was. Her father. Her mother had always said, 'He spoilt me', and she had always imagined him as just that: someone who spoilt her mother. But had never told her who he was. It had never bothered her before. But now she was playing at being mother, and Lijah being so good to her, it had crossed her mind.

CHAPTER * TWENTY-FOUR

In a quiet corner of a derelict stretch of land, on the outskirts of Birmingham, a young ebony body lay dying, in the secluded arms of a marshy ditch. A deadly silence spread over him, like a wet blanket. Hours before, he had chased his last waterfall: the rivers and lakes he had been used to, had stopped flowing for what seemed like a lifetime.

His mother, oblivious to his plight, was swinging and singing in a hammock in Jamaica: a novel clutched with the fingers of pride, close to her chest and her eyes fixed on the face of P J Patterson on the front cover of *The Gleaner*.

His baby sister sang '*Shoo fly, don't bother me. Shoo fly, don't bother me*'. She had Hibiscus in her hair. The sun in her stride. And the hope of a bright future, in front of her. Her mother smiled periodically at her, as she played hide 'n seek, among Lignum Vitae.

His father tended to his latest offspring, brought to him on a whim, by a flighty, young babysitter.

His older sister nursed the mental wounds of a date rape and an abortion, while she examined the unnatural feelings she had developed for her godfather.

His woman fed his new junior – *Kunta Junior*, in a maternity ward in an infamous hospital, in Birmingham.

No one came by. '*Where are all the god-damn dog-walkers when you need them?*' was the young man's dying thought... '*So this is what it feels like to die?*'

A magpie perched on a nearby branch, its coincidental visit threatening to prove an old myth right.

The distant murmur of morning traffic rose from its rest. Life goes on, hustling and bustling, not minding him. '*What if I die here?... Oh my God... Gra'ma Fontaine...*' He recalled her caring cuddles when he was little. Almost felt it.

Now, his clouded, blood-filled eyes tried to focus on someone. Someone that lingered near. 'Who was he?'

Now, the smell of alcohol danced on his dying breath.

"Help... me...."

Now, the black drunken tramp overpowered him. Kunta, it seemed, was in his space.

"Help me... please."

Old, unkempt fingers opened a tired knapsack, trying to fish from its murky depth, a cloth. A tissue. Something. Something to wipe the blood away from Kunta's eyes. Kunta had no strength to protest against lack of hygiene. Not even to sniffle.

The tramp had no means to call 999.

Kunta hallucinated. His life flashed in front of his eyes. Now, he watched it. Piece by piece.

In his moment of reminiscence, a dirty, damp tissue wiped blood from his ebony eyes.

It shouldn't happen to him. No. It shouldn't. He had always been one of the stronger ones who managed to escape the pressures of his peers, and stayed out of the constant modern-day mischief that surrounded the youngsters of Birmingham. Yes. When guns and knives replaced the fists, and dangerous white substances and needle-filled fixes replaced the natural herbs.

No. It shouldn't happen to him. If rap, hip-hop, garage and drooping trousers were all his sins, he was an angel. But one moment. One careless moment. One deadly moment in time, he had *'tried'* and *'tested'* and *'failed'*.

The tramp's stench was high. Alcohol and months of unwashed body functions mixed in one. But he cared not for himself, but for the young man that lay dying. Lying there, helpless, Kunta reminded him of his own son, at around eleven years old, under the influence of a raging fever. And the memory brought with it, that of his wife. He saw her again: in that gleaming nurse's uniform. Always coming home smelling of another man. He remembered his uncontrollable rage. His only solace lying in the neck of a whisky bottle.

And now, in his drink-abused, devalued head, among other despised words, floated those of a black woman on the Lozells Road, saying: *'There's nothing so degrading as a black man drunk, laying in a gutter...'*

The young, near-lifeless, ebony youth hallucinated, his life flashing back at him, recalling recent happenings. Conversations. Family gatherings. Anything that mattered somewhat to him. Now, they swam like a whirlpool in his head:

'Nah man, Ikesha. Yuh cyaan do dat, man. Is only w'ite students do dem kinda t'ings deh. Dem t'ings is dangerous man. Yunnuh 'ear all

dem weird t'ings happening to back-packers... ?'

"It's a'right, Son. It's a'right," the tramp fussed.

'Kunta, don't be so narrow-minded. Bad t'ings happen everywhere. If they are meant to happen to you, backpacking or not, they will. Anyway, where's the dare in you? I wanna do t'ings before I settle down with any babies. Dem nappies, sleepless nights an all dat rubbish. That's not all to life you know...'

"Me wi' look afta yuh, Son," Montie told him.

'Don't talk like dat in front of her, Ikesha man. It won't be dat bad. I'll be there for her...'

Kunta's mind swayed. Shari. Menilek. His new baby. He didn't even know it was born. Who would care for them now? No chance to play dad. No. No chance at all.

He tried to cry.

"Don't cry, Son. Don't cry," the tramp petted, his alcohol-laced breath contaminating the little Kunta had left. All the tramp could see was his own son, Festus. Remembered how countless family feuds unintentionally chased him away from his Bristol home. How it must have been for him. Emotional torture.

Festus had just turned eighteen when he left Bristol for the big city of Birmingham. With a few things packed in a *'grip'*, he left saying he wanted to *'find himself'*. Montie had known, even then, that the far-from-pretty life he and his wife had lived had affected Festus. The young man had seen too many drunken storms. Too many beatings. Heard too many denials, outweighed by showers of accusations. Too many *'Women cannot be trusted'*. *'Pretty woman nuh good'*. *'Woman is de root of all evil'*. And he could not have known how much they had stuck in the crevices of his mind. Like black flies, caught on the surface of a freshly painted wall. Or leeches to the skin of an unsuspecting swimmer. In the process of *striking* at each other, they had emotionally *wounded* their son, forever.

And by then, the alcohol had got too tight a grip on Montie. Six months before Festus left, his wife had left, also for Birmingham. Later he pursued her. Sold his house in Bristol and bought himself a flat in Handsworth. They got back together. But he just couldn't hold life down. Alcohol Anonymous didn't help. He knew too, that only his willpower, could. But he had none. It had left long, long ago, with his pride. His dignity. His trust.

Then Festus found him one day on Soho Road. He had heard about the drunk everyone was talking about. Heard his name and decided to see if it *was* his father. The father he had told everyone had died, along with his mother, in a car crash. The father that was connected to the past he was trying to shut out.

But Festus kept it so. A secret. And like he would never have dreamt of Lijah's troubled mind, Lijah would never have dreamt that Montie, the Handsworth vagrant, was Festus' old man. Festus had covered the pain with pretentious joviality and constant clowning around. It was simply a show for the outside world. He would make sure that the payments on his old man's flat was kept up, even though he knew that the freedom of the cold, lonely, unfriendly streets suited him just fine.

"Yuh gonna be fine, Son."

But Kunta wasn't convinced. He tried desperately to tell Montie where to find his mobile phone. He could feel it under his jacket. He had turned it off while he waited in the get-away car. It was 10pm. Rock was driving. Kunta had reached the car before Festus and had panicked when the sounds of the sirens jabbed at his already confused brain. The rain of cocaine had left his head and he could see now, that he had gone too far out of his depth.

He wanted out. "Let me out!" he had pleaded. "Let me out! I have my family! Shari! Menilek! I have a new baby coming! Mum! Dad! Ikesha! Khamilla! Need to get my life together! Let me out man!" It was then that he found that he was still a baby, eating from big men's plate. *Stupid big men's plate.*

But now, his pleading had eaten too far into Rock's drugged-up head. The silencer of his gun took the sound away from anyone who would or might have heard.

The trigger he pulled was a slight extension to his ego.

The crowd of shoppers outside the off-licence was oblivious to Kunta's plight. The shot lodged nastily in his neck. Later, he was dumped and left to die. Thrown away like a piece of unwanted 'something'. Yes. The going got tough. And the tough simply dumped him.

Festus didn't make it to the car. He had no chance. Nerves overcame hi and he failed to pull the trigger. The Off-licensee had reached for his crowbar, delivering a blow that would immobilise him, at least until the police arrived. Now, for a while, the *nine-to-five-till-sixty-five* milestone would be the least of his worry. And his green-eyed monster would be well and truly, leashed.

Montie's senses must have returned again from their leave. *"Tom drunk, but Tom nuh fool!"* he shouted as he dialled 999 from Kunta's mobile. In his fiddling, he had found it. Although he didn't have one, he was familiar with it. Festus had tried equipping him with one before. But the chance of him keeping it would be like snow surviving in mid-July.

"Hol' on, Festus. Me won' let yuh dong again," he stressed, as if his brain was playing tricks on him again. For of course it wasn't *Festus*. It was *Kunta*. At that moment, Festus was looking at the four walls of a cell in a police station in Birmingham. It would be a while before he would pull Montie up about rummaging in bins.

Kunta hallucinated, still remembering past conversations as he went towards an infamous light.

'What d'you mean it won't be that bad? I don't see any tits on you, Kunta. Are you gonna help with the breast-feeding...?'

'Nah, man, we've got one a dem express t'ings to express the milk in advance. You don't need to frighten her sis.'

'Yeah, an' make sure you're not just there for the first few weeks. Always. Like Mum said Dad was with her.'

'Why yuh stressing me, Ikesha man?... Jus' because yuh at university yuh coming wid yuh righteous lecture. Yuh always 'ave yuh head in dem books. An' all yuh ever listen to is dat classical rubbish. Cha.'

'Classical rubbish, Kunta?... Why do you call it rubbish?'

"Hol' on Son. Dem comin," Montie shouted, looking around, his toothless mouth trembling. *"Tom drunk, but Tom nuh fool..."*

Kunta slid further away.

'... But Kunta, what's wrong with having my head in my books? You need to read more. Open your mind. Life is not all about rap, hip-hop, garage and trousers fighting for purchase 'round your ass, you know. Martin Luther, Malcolm X, Denzel Washington and Jessie Jackson read books.'

'Black woman an' chile'... Sizzler. He remembered Sizzler.

'Long Walk to Freedom.' He remembered Nelson Mandela too.

And now, the birth of his son Menilek. *'Now w'en we tell yuh to push, yuh have to push, young lady. Or we'll be here all night'... 'Kunta! Get Kunta, pleeease!'*

'She want yuh, Kunta. Come. Put dis gown on'.

'Kunta... It's horrible'.

'Yuh tek de pleasure, now tek de pain!'

'I can't do this'...

'Yes you can'... I did it three times. Just look at dis big young stallion who put you in this position. I brought him here. He was eight pounds and I was much smaller than you... So you can do it, Shari'.

'Ok Shari, push now, girl'...

'It's a boy! Well done!'

'Men,... One drop a blood and they're out'...

Papa Dread was in his head. The voice he should have heeded. "*So who you t'ink is filtering guns onto the street for our yout' dem feh get hold of?... Who yuh t'ink is filling the streets with crack, cocaine and all dis designer drugs shit? Tek me for instance. Look how long I've been using my herbs an' it don' mess up my head. Yet de first time a yout' man put one a dem E's in him mout' him due feh all dead to rahtid. From dem legalise de herbs, clean up de streets of guns, crack, cocaine an all dat shit, give us back our youth clubs and mek we deal wid we pickney dem ourselves, t'ings can work'...*

'Nuff a we yout' dem nuh need nothing but simple direction. The schools fail dem, so dem drop out. An' when dem drop out there's nothing on the street for them to do but get inna badness. Tek nuff a dem yout' out there on the street. Nuff a dem don't have an academic bone in dem body, but dem good at art, music an all dat. But once the system tell dem seh dem fail, them don't even bother feh show dem true creative potential. Dem jus' feel seh dem is a true failure. So it's up to us as elders to help dem'...

The sounds of sirens. Montie held Kunta's hand, his rough palms trying to comfort him. "Dem comin', Son. Ambulance comin." Then he hurried away from the scene, hoping to watch from a distance. Watch the rescue. Watch the saving of a young black youth. Watch with hope. Unlike the people of Handsworth watched him: with detest, and from a perverted voyeur's point of view.

But now, Kunta was floating. *'Bwoy, Ikesha, nuff sleepless nights, sis. Mum said Menilek is jus' like I was as a baby.'*

'How's Shari coping?'

'Ok. I think'...

'You think! Kunta, you should know. You talk, don't you? She don't seem happy to me. I hope you're doing your share with the baby.'

'Go talk to her, sis'. I think she must be having that post-natal depression t'ing. You're a woman'...

The voices of ambulance men were distant murmurs, but his thoughts vivid.

'Mum's seeing somebody else?'...

Then Papa Dread again. *'Look bredrin. Ovastan' me nuh. Me talking about the conditioning of our youth's minds. Yes, dis is a toy, but there are real ones on the streets looking jus like dis. Yuh don' want 'im get used to playing wid no toy gun! What next? Play-crack? Play-cocaine? Play heroin?'*

'One a de yout' weh get shoot up is me bredrin son. Even now it's grieving me, man. To de point where if I know who bring dat gun onto de

street weh kill him, I would deal wid him meself!'...

An ambulance man felt Kunta's pulse. "Any life?" another one said.

"Hardly," came the reply.

Kunta held on to hope. A glimmer of it. *'Shari? What's de matta, man? Menilek sick up...' 'I'm pregnant again, Kunta'... we can't even manage to look after Menilek. What we gonna do?'*...

'Pregnant again? How yuh mek dat happen, Shari? Why yuh neva tek de pill?

Papa Dread echoed, *'Kunta... yuh have a woman, a baby an' anadda chile on de way. Now is not de time to be getting spaced out on shit. What yuh t'ink will happen to yuh family when dem shit drugs mash up yuh head? Dem tings cause anxiety, Kunta. Paranoia. Tu'n yuh fool! Yuh see it on TV. Yuh know w'at it cyan duh. Why yuh waan touch dem cullu-cullu deh? Dem t'ings cause anxiety, Kunta. Paranoia. Tu'n yuh fool. Yuh eva see yuh dad touch dem t'ings deh? Yuh eva hear seh herbs mash up anybody's head?... 'Kunta, how yuh get mixed up in dem t'ings deh anyway? Lijah and Gloria a nuh bad parents. Dat is firs' t'ing people will be saying'*...

And now he had heard it. That song. Heard it with his last morsel of hearing life, as he slipped further away. Well above the frantic sound of the sirens. Sounds he had known would be hopeless. It was Shari's song. She had played it to him one night, when her own words could not do. One night when the lining of his nostrils pushed back some more, making way for a white substance that demanded entry to his body. A substance he had tried as an experiment. Given to him by someone who should have known better. And when it had clung to his soul like steel to magnet, his trainer Jaro had grinned. You see, Kunta needed Jaro's wares to calm his desire. Jaro needed Kunta to deliver. Kunta couldn't afford his new habit, so he simply worked for his fixes.

He could not refuse the deadly substance. From his first fix, it had claimed permanent *rights* to his body.

Yes, today he heard it again, but with a deep difference now. That song. That poignant, heart-wrenching song. Shari's song. He had not taken much notice of it before, but now, it had wrapped itself around him like a warm body bag:

Don't go chasing waterfalls
Listen to the rivers and the lakes that you're used to
I know that you're gonna have it your way or nothing at all
But I think you're moving too fast.

*

The morgue was no place for a family reunion. It was the most horrible thing any of them had ever gone through in their entire lives. Earlier they had hugged. Tears had flowed, not much words passing. Grief clammed them all up. Gloria had taken the first available flight from Jamaica. Ikesha was jolted from her own miseries. It was no place for a five-year-old, so Khamilla was staying with Kizzy - Gloria was staying with her, even though Lijah had offered her a pillow.

Shari was dazed. Her newborn baby and Menilek were at Shari's flat, being looked after by her mother Mitzi. She had heard it on the news, and had travelled up from London to be with her. They had even discussed the possibility of Shari returning to London with her. Said she was willing to forgive Shari for choosing Kunta over a decent future. But Shari wasn't sure how genuine she really was.

It was like being in a movie. Seconds after the undertaker pulled back the white sheet that covered her son's face, Gloria could heave nothing but bile. No food had passed her lips for days, since she heard the horrific news. She was weak beyond respite.

Ikesha couldn't cry. She was numb. Her only brother. Gone.

Lijah swallowed hard. Previously, he had cried enough for everyone.

Shari stared into space. So young, and this was the second boyfriend she had lost to the bullet. Her first boyfriend, Damian was Reds son. Caught in the same shit. A shoot up years ago. Pulled in with the wrong crowd and consequently, he was used as a drugs mule, for the value of a few pounds, a quick fix and the promise of a fast motor. Even now, Reds had not gotten over it.

"Wake him up, Lijah," she asked calmly, as if she truly believed it could simply be done.

They, all three, turned towards her.

"Wake him up."

"Shari," Ikesha coaxed, "Kunta is gone."

"I said, *wake* him up."

Lijah put his arms around her. He knew what was coming. Hysteria. It was slowly setting in.

"Wake him up, Lijah."

"Shari, come on. Let's go outside," Lijah said gently.

"Wake him up! Didn't you hear me! Wake him up! Why don't you wake him up?!"

"Shari," Lijah tried to comfort her. *"Shhhh... Shhhh... Hush... Hush..."*

"No... He's not dead... He's not dead, Lijah... Wake him up! Kunta! Stop it! Stop it! Stop messing! Wake up!"

Lijah held her. Tried to take her from the cold, morbid room.

She pulled back towards it, stretching her hands towards her lifeless man. Wake him uuuuup!" She fainted in his arms.

'Oh my God,' Ikesha thought. 'Is that really my brother lying there, lifeless? Kunta... Oh, Kunta. The brother I love beyond words. The brother who argued with me, not so long ago, over toys. Over stuff taken from each other's room. Whose named T-shirt I wore without asking. Where did the years go? When did we grow up? Or did we? My brother... My brother... oh, my brother. Are you really not coming back?'

"Come, Ikesha," Gloria's voice alerted her. "Come."

But Ikesha was lost. Recalling... 'Neva min' dat, sis. When was the las' time yuh tek een a session? ... Yeah... a real session. Dem play Sizzla inna dancehall, yunnuh... Yuh wanna get out more sis'. Get out an' dance... Ah tell me 'bout book.'

Gloria wrapped her arms around her daughter's shoulders, and pulled her away from her thoughts. She herself was suffering beyond words, a poignant song from her mother's funeral blowing through her mind. She wasn't sure of the words, but as tears rolled down her face, she sang in a sad, trance-like whisper:

Yes, we'll gather at the river, The beautiful, the beautiful river
Gather with the saints at the river, That flows by the throne of God...

A week later, Kunta was laid to rest next to Grandma Nettie. Gloria hoped that they would meet in that mansion in the sky. Yes. *In the sweet by and by.*

Dusk had fallen with a weird edge. Papa Dread and Reds slowed down and pulled into that same infamous spot, and watched the ride. The gathering of men outside Jaro's front door was familiar: Jaro, Sugar, Bunti and Rock. But the atmosphere was bordering on dangerous. A serious feud was about to take place.

Odd sentences could be heard from angry lips. "Yuh nuh waan fuck wid me yunnuh, Rock! Yuh nuh know who yaah deal wid yunnuh, bwoy! I feel is about time yuh leave dis town. Yuh don' fit een!" Jaro made his voice heard, his right index finger pointing profusely into Rock's face.

Rock lent against his car, arms folded across his chest, legs crossed at the ankles, staring him out. His body language asked, 'So?... what yuh gonna do about it?'

"Is jus' de adda day yuh come 'ere yunnuh, bwoy. So don' come gwaan like is you run t'ings!"

But Jaro was too much in his face now. Rock's patience boat was well and truly rocked. He didn't like it. He retaliated now, by pushing him away with more anger than a raging storm. But Sugar and Bunti were only too pleased to take up where Jaro left off. Perhaps it was a good thing for Rock, there and then, for as Papa Dread and Reds watched from the car they both sat in, they knew Jaro was simply holding his capabilities down.

Jaro spoke with his eyes.

A silent promise.

But promises have two roads. The *broken* and the *kept*. What would it be? Time would tell.

Bunti held Rock in a head-lock, while Sugar administered deadly punches to his stomach. Bunti let him loose and he fell to the ground like an over-used elastic band. Sugar sealed his landing, with the tough heels of his Timberlands.

As Rock lay there, winded and wrecked, Papa Dread and Reds knew that that wasn't the end. Jaro, Bunti and Sugar might have seen The Handsworth Riot and had a few run-ins with the law. But Rock had seen real carnage. Had more run-ins with the law than Eskimos had seen snow. Born to terrorise, his mother had band her belly on numerous occasions and cried. He cruised the coastlines of big cities looking for fresh waters to invade. Primed to terrorise, he had a host of weapon in his arsenal: a hard, persuasive nature to recruit, GHB (a deadly drug) in his pouch and a deadly piece of metal under his belt, he had no mercy. Rock had once claimed the title *'Jamaica's Number One Bad Bwoy'*. Later, he roamed the streets of the Bronx, where guns are like toys to gangsters. Teased the wanna-be gangsters of London, and was simply cruising for a while in the second city, Birmingham. So for sure, Rock would not be taking this lying down. *Feh real*.

"W'at was all dat about, Papa?" Reds asked.

"Bwoy, your guess is as good as mine. But yuh know seh two bulls cyaan reign inna one pen. Territory an' ting, yunnuh?"

"Feh real."

"Reds, I feel dere is goin' to be war inna Babylon, Rasta. Serious. *War* me a tell yuh. *War*. I feel seh evil is gonna tek care of itself, soona or lata. Yeah, man."

Reds stared into space, keeping his eyes on the area where the feud was.

"Come aan," Papa Dread urged. "Mek we ease out."

Reds hit the gas pedal, took the back street and left the scene, Justin Hinds speaking to them:

Sinners, where you gonna run? Where you gonna hide?

Sinners, where you gonna run? Where you gonna hide?

CHAPTER * TWENTY-FIVE
He had ran to the rock for rescue, but there was no rock

It was now nearly two weeks since Kunta was laid to rest, but the topsy-turvy air around Lijah was still whirling. He was missing his son like the sky would, stars. He remembered when the most he had wished for Kunta was that he would never pass through the evil gates of a Babylon's prison. And he remembered too that when he himself had had the misfortune of just that, and the most evil buggery had befallen him, he had wished himself dead. He couldn't tell how Kunta would feel had it been him, but just then Lijah knew that all he wanted was to hold his son. Touch his fist, father to son. Hug him, like his own father had never done to him. Reason. Whatever. He wished too, that he could open the heads of every youth, and pour enough sense into them. Enough sense to keep them from the fate that had befallen his only son.

He hadn't seen Bernadette for a while. He had been too preoccupied with the torrential happenings in and around his life. She had called him from London to give her condolences, and apologised for not liking funerals. Today, she had called him on a whim. She had returned from a long stay in London, and had invited him 'round for coffee and comfort. She knew a bit of what he had been going through, and had just the remedy. Lijah needed therapy and to him, she was no less than a love nurse.

He had no choice but to bring Shanique. She was cosy. Fast asleep in her carry-cot, breathing in the aroma of calming lavender that was wafting around Bernadette's sitting-room.

For Lijah, it was *déjà vu.*

"So you've inherited a baby, hey?" Her tone was carefree. Not surprised.

"Yeah."

"I heard."

"Who told you?"

"Never mind. That's the least of your troubles. But Kunta. He was such a nice kid."

Lijah was sad, angry, frustrated and confused. He remembered Bernadette's offerings and just then, she was the only remedy. He needed his release.

"You're tense, Lijah. So tense. Like the first time I touched you." She was moulding his shoulder blades with her firm fingers, her firm breasts against his back.

"I have nuff reasons to be tense. Don't know if my mind can take anymore. Lately I've been wondering what I've done to deserve all this."

"Wanna talk?" She kissed his neck and he leaned, clasping her face between his neck and shoulders.

"Not just talk. I want a lot, Bernadette. To talk, to know... Yes. To know. To know what I did wrong to upset Jah. Why is he dealing so harshly wid me? I want answers."

She touched his hard, eager bulge.

"D'you feel you're being punished, then?" she asked, moving like a doctor searching for the root of an ailment.

"Feh real. Must be for my sins.... Or the sins of my father... Whatever. But punished, yes. I am definitely being punished. Why did Kunta have to die? I brought him up well. We had a good relationship. We weren't such a dysfunctional family as he said."

She kissed his lips. He knew she was listening.

"My closest idrin lied to me for the longest time. Told me his parents were dead. His old man is the Handsworth tramp and his mother is married to my father, soaking up the sun in Jamaica. And her... Dora. How could she just... She gave birth to him. Regardless. Bwoy... dis world we're livin' in. I jus' don' know who to trust no more."

Bernadette unbuttoned his shirt and kissed his chest. The sink of his navel. She said nothing. As if she was an angel that already knew.

"What with Gloria leaving me," he continued. "Faithlyn turning up with the baby I'm not even sure is mine... taking my money... And Kizzy. Shit, Kizzy. At the time I saw it as nothing. Just two people giving and receiving pleasure. But it was wrong, Bernadette. Wrong."

"Why was it wrong?"

"It's true what Kizzy said, it was like incest. Yes, we're not blood-related but we were too close. She was right. We practically grew up together. She is Gloria's closest friend. Plus me an' Festus... Bwoy... to tell yuh de trut', we were like a little family."

"So, you feel you and Festus were like brothers, right?"

"Yeah. Like brothers. He was a bit secretive, but I feel we were closer than me and my own brother, Roy."

"I see what you mean. Like Faye and I. As close as sisters," Bernadette told him. She was now nude. So was Lijah. Yet he still talked. His heart was filled. So were his eyes. His desires burning. His manhood rigid.

She took his hand and led him upstairs.

Downstairs, the baby slept.

Now, the *déjà vu* was too much.

Bernadette dimmed the light. Lijah felt safe. Though it should, after remembering Lucy, the thought of bondage didn't frighten him. Not with Bernadette. Again, she pushed him firmly into her classily dressed bed. More than ever, he craved her.

She pulled out a drawer and pulled out two familiar strips of material.

"Trust me," she whispered, crossing his legs and tying them firmly at the ankles, again showering him with warm, moist kisses.

"Then Lucy,"... Lijah continued. He needed to empty his mind. It was what he was there for. Therapy. "She tortured me for what my father had done to her mother. Why should *I* pay?"

Her moist mouth on his genitals, she commanded, "Keep talking."

"I have a sister. She's mixed race. My father's daughter. I wonder if she's alive. She was put in a home. Left by her mother."

Bernadette teased him. Again she watched his sweet torment, stroking her breasts and vagina, slow and sensual. She teased the head of his dick with her warm mouth, this time pressing carefully with one finger on his scrotum, as she held his dick firmly, administering rapid hand movements. Her tongue, her fingertips and her woman worked over the most sensitive parts of his body, periodically allowing him quick licks of her firm breasts, deliberately denying him penetration.

And then came the mistake. The fatal mistake. The tragic unleashing of a disturbing subconscious... Her long nails, accidentally touching his forbidden zone.

Lijah freaked, remembering Conrad. The ordeal with Lucy. The nightmare. It had felt so real.

His brain fuzzed.

He kicked.

Screamed. "Untie me, Bernadette! Untie me!"

But she had mistaken his anguish for pleasure.

"Calm down, Lijah. You know you ain't seen nothing yet."

He settled for a moment, trying to show her his eyes. Let her know that he was serious. But it passed over her like a ghost to the untrained eye.

And so she committed that grave crime again, not knowing what she had done.

"Fuck you!" he protested, not knowing how to ask her to evade that area, fearing that the story might slip. Only Papa Dread knew.

"Like that, is it? I told you I was the best," she hummed. "Just enjoy."

With her strong yoga'd body she restrained him. She touched. Licked. Eased her tongue over his rigid, angry dick.

But now she knew. Suddenly he found strength and freed himself. It was like a scene from 'The Incredible Hulk'.

Her eyes filled with questions.

"What is it, Lijah? You are *really* freaking."

In his plunge, his feet hit the edge of her dressing table.

A framed photo that was lying face down, fell onto the floor, revealing a recent image of his brother Roy, in a compromising position with Bernadette.

Perplexed at his behaviour, Bernadette calmly picked it up and replaced it upwards, her placing delivering a subtle message.

"Why have you got a picture of you and Roy on your dressing table? A recent picture of Roy?" Lijah asked, perplexed. "Have you been fucking Roy? Is that what your trips to London had been about?"

"Lijah, don't ask me anything. You don't own me. Have you forgotten our last chat? *I am my own person*," she professed.

"So yuh fuckin' me and my brotha at the same time, and that's ok?!"

She lifted an eyebrow sarcastically.

"So that's why you kept escaping down to London? Does my dear brother know that you're fucking me?! He doesn't like sharing, don't you know?!" Veins reddened in his eyes.

"He doesn't own me either. What I do is my business." Bernadette's voice was calm.

"And anyway, is he not married to a blonde? Does she know?"

"Oh, Lijah. That's old news. That broke up a while back."

"So what's your game, Bernadette? Why me and my brother? Just tell me?" He shouldn't have, but he had developed a depth of feeling for her that could only turn to hate now.

"Oh for God's sake, get over it, Lijah. I was fucking you, not making a vow of marriage!"

He bit his bottom lip with anger as he tried to decide her fate. Held her neck. Flung her violently across the bed and jumped on her with more fury than hell's fire.

He used to be calm. Wouldn't dream of physically or sexually abusing a woman. Lucy triggered something in him, and now this.

Slap! "You women are seriously the root of all evil, yunnuh! Some of you anyway!" *Slap!*

"Lijah!"

"Me ole man said it!" *Slap*!

"Lijah, are you sick? Stop it!"

"Papa Dread said it!" *Slap!*

"Help!"

"Festus said it!" *Slap!* Now, he overpowered her, and it was almost as if Festus' spirit possessed him.

He thought he knew the answer to Bernadette's game. Thought she was simply playing *'scarlet woman'*. But she had a motive. The weirdest motive ever. Had no idea that the only two differences between her and Lucy were colour and wealth.

Now came the fierce hammering of jealousy.

The violating of her flesh.

The unleashing of pent-up anger.

Her un-heard cries.

Her questioned meaning of *'freedom'*.

"Bitch! Bitch! Bitch!" The fierce, painful hammering between her thighs...

The too-late realisation.

Now, Lijah sobbed like a baby as he climaxed, his locks soaking up his tears, Bernadette's insides resenting his warm, body fluids.

An *abuser* had *abused* an *abuser*.

An abuser that would not protest. She was hoisted by her own petard. She had played a callous game and had hoped to win. Everyone was getting even, playing their own made-up games. Clutching at the wrong straws. Lucy, Bernadette, Festus, everyone. But only two and two could ever make four.

Bernadette would never cry rape. Ring the *physical abused* bell. It was no use. And neither was it her intention to reveal to Lijah the reason for her weird double-dealing: that her best mate, Faye, Lijah and Roy's sister had taken her man, Jacques. And as far as she reckoned, he was loving her more than he ever did, her. The smile Bernadette wore and the carefree attitude she displayed were different shades of make-up she wore, since their devastating break-up.

She could not get to Faye and Jacques. Trying to break them up wasn't going to happen, so instead, she bided her time and took to wrecking the lives of her brothers with the deadliest weapon of all – sex. She had succeeded in wrecking Roy's marriage to the blonde, and watched her take him for every penny he had.

Commitment had never been, and never would be, what Bernadette craved. Just the satisfaction of watching something crumble: like she *thought* her marriage to Jacques had, when he discovered Faye. *Thought* being the operative word, since little had she known that Faye was the least of her problems. But that too was another story.

Like Lucy, Bernadette had a slight touch of madness. Something psychologists say we all have: some more than others. Like Lucy, she was like a poisoned arrow, aiming straight to the hearts of the Benjamin brothers. *'If yuh cyaan ketch Kwaku, ketch 'im shirt.'*

Apparently, Faye had no plans to return to England. Everyone was living with their own guilt, using everyone else's, as a shield to mask their own.

The baby cried.

In Lijah, *something* died.

That penultimate *something.*

Now, there was just one *'ultimate'* hope that could save him. Just a tiny glimmer of hope... Maybe.

Gloria. Yes, Gloria.

Now, he wanted her. *Like breath*

CHAPTER * TWENTY-SIX

Papa Dread walked out of the doctors' surgery dragging his right leg behind him. He had likened it to *'losing his dignity'.* His leg being pulled like an old tin can, that is. He hated it. Plus the pain was becoming unbearable. It had become cancerous and was now moving slowly, to his brain. No less than the same fate he was *led to believe,* befell Bob Marley, one of his heroes. He had already convinced himself that there was no hope. He had also decided that Chemotherapy or amputation was never gonna do for him, and hoped that when the time came, it would be a quick process. Death was one thing he didn't fear. He figured he had a good life and had made his will. He was ready *to bow* out like a man.

Now he remembered her again. His queen, Norma, dying in childbirth, and his stillborn child that was to be called *Kunta.* He rested, leaning against the wall outside the doctor's, reflecting on Lijah's son, Kunta. His funeral not long ago. His life had only just begun. Vengeance welled in the dread's belly, as that terrible pain gripped him again, to an almost paralytic state.

Now, he wondered about the *'heaven and hell'* thing. He had already decided that if there were another hell, this one here on earth would probably give it a run for its devilish activities. And if there were a heaven, would he be refused entry for what he was about to do?

He chewed on a painkiller and waited for a while. The pain eased and he took himself home.

Many were called, but just a few were chosen. Chosen to die. The flocking-together used to be more frequent. But then again, the birds used to be more *'of a feather'.* 'TRUE RASTAS'. The brothas all dealt in the teachings of His Majesty. Haile Selassie. They wanted no devil's philosophy. And they all found time to rock to Jah's music. But something alien had forced its way in. Evil. Greed. Material madness. Threatening now to turn the rastaman's plan into Babylon's meat, and the youth into useless, wild oats.

Now, Papa Dread had assigned himself the Robin Hood of Birmingham, with no intention of stealing from the rich to give to the poor, but to take the power from the *'dealers of shit'*, and liberate the youth. His Merry Men however, would be less than few. *One* to be exact. Reds had lost a son and had no problem *'assisting'* the *'assassin'*. They would only touch the surface. Nonetheless, a thick surface.

Déjà vu. Or so it felt. Papa Dread and Reds sat there again. Waiting. Watching. With vengeance in both their hearts and a metal piece under Reds' jacket. It was the first for them both. The only places they had seen pieces like the one Reds possessed, were on Crime Watch or on gangster movies.

From behind the blacked-out windows of the borrowed ride they watched. Debated. Waited for a time when Reds would make his move.

Midnight. Only this was no oasis. Just a plain old regular street, in an urban town, outside a house where greed and disregard for the welfare of the youth, lived.

"A'right Papa. Me goin' in."

"Walk good, Reds. Easy." Words were all Papa Dread had. His bad leg throbbed again. Only now, it was like a million stubborn toothaches all in one. He didn't feel too good. Worse than before. He just had to see this one out. But shouldn't he be praying to Jah for the deliverance of his soul? Thou shalt not kill.

Earlier, he had made his will, leaving all his earthly gains to Lijah, Gloria and Reds.

But something stopped Reds in his tracks. Before he could pull on the door leaver of the car, a gleaming Mercedes pulled up outside the infamous house. A *dude* 'if ever there was one' slid out. Trash an' ready or what? He oozed trouble. The aroma of bad air wafted across the road, in through their blacked-out window and up their nostrils.

"Hol' aan, Reds. Me smell trouble."

Reds had smelt it too. Stenching higher than an unattended pig-pen on a hazy day.

Rock got out. He looked up the road and down, patted his left breast pocket and eased towards the front door.

It was Bunti who answered the door and Rock floated in.

"What yuh t'ink, Papa? What's Rock doing there? 'im gaan een. I thought they fell out?"

"Bwoy, dat strange. Sop'n funny. But my guess is as good as yours, Reds. Mek we jus' hang feh a bit. Watch de ride."

But the *'bit'* they hung for was less than five minutes.

The random sound of dancing bullets.

A silhouetted frenzy of conflict.

A silent movie playing over the backdrop of drawn curtains.

A premier showing of disaster.

A calm.

A quiet escape.

The moving out of a dodgy Mercedes.

Rock was leaving. Leaving a house where greed once lived. Where wads of cash lay building like grains of sand. Wads of cash that Rock wanted. Cash he wanted as badly as the revenge he craved, ever since his last encounter with the three men.

But why was he just invited in?

Was there a truce?

That half might never be told.

Papa Dread and Reds didn't stay any longer than they needed to. As fate would have it, their work was done by someone else. A negative force had turned in on itself. *Evil had taken care of itself.*

Again, Reds took the back streets and eased out. Loud sirens greeted their eardrums as a convoy of police cars raced towards the scene.

Papa Dread got thinking, as sorrow drowned his soul... *'Don't you shoot your brother down, don't you shoot you bother down.'*

He was no warrior. Neither was Reds. Rock had saved them from a fate that could not be reversed, if it was carried through. Blood would have been on their hands for life, although Papa Dread did not have much left.

'It shouldn't be happening', Papa Dread thought. *'No. Not now. Not when the call for 'peace in the community' was at its highest. Not when events geared towards 'increasing the peace' had risen to an all time high. Not when community leaders were trying their hardest to hammer, ring and sing out love between brothers and sisters, all over Birmingham city. No. It shouldn't be happening'.*

But what driveth a man to want to take life, when he could never blow breath?

And now, Rock cruised the motorway to another town. Another city. Another life: with money in his pocket and blood on his hands. And as sure as the sun would rise in the east, more victims awaited his deadly touch.

That night, when the news had reached TV screens all over the West Midlands, Papa Dread was sat in his armchair with a peaceful look on his face. His soul was somewhere. Somewhere he himself wasn't sure of before he took the last breath. He was sat with a hot chalice, burning by his side, and a bible in his hand: his fingers purposefully resting on the tenth commandment: *'THOU SHALT NOT KILL'*.

A picture of Norma lay close to his chest.

The eyes of Haile Selassie looked down on him from a picture on the wall, its accompanying words: *'Behold, how good and how pleasant it is for brethren to dwell together in Inity... It is like the precious ointment upon the head, that ran down upon the beard, even Aaron's head: that went down to the skirts of his garments;... As the dew of Hermon, and as the dew that descended upon the mountains of Zion: for there **Jah** commanded the blessing, even life for Ivermore.'*

Earlier (not that it would have done him any good), he had read up on the one Melanoma, a classic type of cancer found in black people. He recalled too, the first time he had seen that infamous black and blue spot on his big toe. A spot he had simply ignored, thinking he had inadvertently stubbed his toe.

So he did not hear the news... *"Three men have been found dead in a house in the Handsworth area of Birmingham. The men, infamous for their street names, Jaro, Sugar and Bunti were found in the living-room of the house, which belonged to Jaro. Each man died as a result of a single gunshot wound to the head. Police are treating the shootings as suspicious.'*

"I hate you!" Shari shouted, "Gloria is more of a mother to me than you! I can't live with you anymore! I'm going back to Birmingham!"

"Well go then! Go! If you didn't get mixed in that messed up family, you wouldn't be here now with two kids you can't look after! So go back to Birmingham to your Gloria!" Shari's mother dragged on her cigarette. "And anyway, I want my life back! I can't cope with two screaming kids everyday! Nappies everywhere! Messing up the place!" *What manner of mother?* She stubbed the butt in a gold ashtray, skimming her long red nails like top models do.

"You never loved me!" Shari sobbed. "You're my mother but you're not maternal! Not like Gloria! Why did you even give birth to me?!"

It was too painful for words.

"Oh yes?! So maternal is she, this *Gloria*? Your nice... wonderful... *mother-in-law*!... All I ever hear is, Gloria this! Gloria that! God's cousin, is she, hey?!... So nice, and look how her family turned out! Losers! Losers!"

SLAP! Shari had forgotten herself. Rage had engulfed the young, hurting mother: still a baby herself. She stared at her palms that had just connected with her mother's left cheek. She stared at it. Stared as if to rebuke it for its profanity. *Shit.* She had slapped her mother's face and now, her nan's voice echoed in her head: '*Honour thy mother and father, so that thy days may be long upon the land which the Lord thy God giveth thee.*'

'*Honour?*' She questioned its meaning now. '*Honour? Don't it mean respect? How do I respect a mother that doesn't respect me?*'

Mitzi held her chiselled cheek, dumbfounded. It wasn't the blow, or the lingering sting from the slap that came with anger. It was the *shock* that got her.

"How... dare... you?! How dare you?! How dare you slap me, you bitch! I'm your mother!" She lunged at her young daughter and grabbed her braids.

Menilek cried.

Kunta Junior cried.

Shari fought back, holding onto her mother's Gucci top.

But the doorbell saved the day. They released each other. Mitzi tried to salvage a once-perfect look, and walked to the door.

She returned with a tall, handsome, black policeman, who looked as if he was paying her a '*chance*' visit. The handsome guy could sense the mood of the room: more so, as a handful of Shari's braids decorated the shiny wooden floor and streaks of tears flowed down hers and the boys' faces.

Mitzi found solace in another nicotine stick.

"Listen, Mitzi, I've obviously come at a bad time. I was just passing anyway. I'll come back when it's more convenient," the handsome guy said, feeling like a fish out of water.

Shari stared at the tall, handsome policeman and saw a shaven-headed version of Lijah. She remembered Kunta saying he had an uncle in London that was a beastman. An uncle that had kept himself away from the family, for reasons Kunta was unsure about. But of course it couldn't be. For one, this uncle was supposed to be married to a blonde, and by the look of things, this hunk-in-blue was more than just a friend to her mother.

Mitzi walked him to the door.

"Mother? You don't know the meaning of the word," Shari picked up where they had left off. "Gloria is my mother. You disowned me, but Gloria accepted me for who I am."

"Only because her son spoilt you, Shari! She had to accept you!"

"Is that what father did, Mum? Spoilt you? If my nan thought that, she didn't chuck you out, did she? She might have been upset, but she accepted you. Is that why you can't even tell me who my father is, because he was just a man who spoilt you! Then why did you sleep with him in the first place?!"

Mitzi did nothing but puffed on her cigarette.

"You haven't got a clue!" Shari shouted. "I wish my nan was alive!"

Shari picked up Kunta Junior and stormed off to the bedroom.

Menilek followed, crying.

Mitzi followed them.

Kunta entered her brain. Now she started to sob again. A deep, heart-felt agony. *'Kunta... Oh Kunta... Why did you have to die?'*

Mitzi looked on. She was confused. Shari was right. Not that she needed her daughter to tell her that, but she was most certainly not maternal. Not like Gloria. Right then, her top-modelling career (that was slipping away fast on the slippery slopes of age), high-flying friends and the freedom of a plush Kensington flat were her main concerns. She had got used to that, so a prodigal daughter and two screaming grand-kids could go amiss. She had become a creature of habit. A victim of her own selfishness.

'How can I go back to Birmingham?' Shari pondered. *'I gave up my flat. Gloria wants her own life. She won't want me hanging 'round her feet with two young children? Besides, she just came back from Jamaica. She needs to get her own life together again.'*

"Where you going, Shari?"

"What do you care?"

"I never said I did. I just asked where you're going."

"I don't know. Anywhere away from you. I'll come and get the rest of my stuff another time. There must be some refuge place around here, somewhere."

The young girl sobbed as she struggled to manoeuvre a child on one hip, a suitcase in the other, with the other child holding on, confused as to what's happening to his mother.

"Shari, you can't just venture off like that. Not with the kids. This is London. It's not like..."

"I'll survive."

Mitzi was familiar with the strong determination of her daughter.

"Have you got money, Shari?"

"A bit."

"Here. Take this." Mitzi stretched a wad of notes patronisingly towards Shari.

"I don't want your money, Mum. I want what you are not capable of giving. *Love.* You know that thing that mothers have for their children? Gloria gave that. Plenty of it. Love! Love! It might not have saved Kunta, but I bet he died knowing he was loved!" She sobbed again.

Mitzi went towards her. Unsure. She reached for her, but Shari shrugged. Pushed her away.

Now she trod the streets of Kensington, not sure if the people were unfriendly, or if it was her who had chosen to see them in the same light as her mother.

"Whaap'n, Baby Girl? Why yuh crying? Can I give you a ride?"

Shari ignored the voice of the man that crawled the kerb of the Kensington street, and trod on. To where? She didn't know.

"It really look like yuh need help, Baby Girl. Mek me gi' yuh a ride nuh?"

Shari couldn't believe her bad luck. Her suitcase came open just at the wrong time, spilling her belongings onto the pavement.

The stranger stopped his car, swooping down on her, like a vulture that had been waiting for something to die. He got out. "See. You need help, Baby Girl."

He bent down and helped her to gather her things.

Menilek stared in his face.

"Where yuh going, Baby Girl?"

"I don't know."

"Yuh don't know?"

"No." Shari started to cry.

Game over.

Vulnerability exposed.

Was she about to be hung out to dry?

As she sat in the back of a brand new Mercedes, Menilek hitched up to her side, and Kunta Junior gurgled on her lap, she remembered Ikesha's words at times. '*You would never be in this position would you, Ikesha?*' she asked hypothetically.

Shari didn't know where she was going.

But Rock did.

Yes. Rock.

He cruised like a film star towards his newly acquired abode. With money in his pocket, blood on his hands, and Kunta's woman in his grip.

He took a sharp left turn at an uncontrollable speed, and just about rammed his ride into a police car coming from the opposite direction. The officer glared at him as he slowed his Mercedes to a controllable speed.

Shari couldn't help but notice that it was the same officer that had not long left her mother's flat. Mitzi had obviously given him the all clear. By the look of it, he was on his way back.

CHAPTER * TWENTY-SEVEN

Kizzy had found her mother and had gained a substantial legacy. If she invested right, the notion of working again would be history – Festus had missed out, big time. A hefty proportion of what Beatrice had owned, was hers. Money could never compensate for love, but it sure would make life much easier. But although she had gained a material abundance, on top of the guilt she had carried for over eight years, she had gained another guilty stack on her conscience pile: she had slept with Lijah.

Festus' sentence was no joke. In fact, she had only taken up residence in her own house again, after he was sent down. The thought of any man behind bars wasn't one she relished, so that of her Festus was unbearable. But she wouldn't go back. She would run. Run as far away as she could.

Now she sat up in bed, looking back over her life. She was in a half-dream mode, as she remembered her last moment with Beatrice, her blood-mother. Earlier, she had heard Gloria tip-toeing downstairs and out the front-door, trying hard not to wake her. They had had a long talk earlier, although crucial bits had to be left unsaid. Although Gloria was sure about not returning to Jamaica just yet, she had seemed rather stubborn about getting back with Lijah. But Kizzy drummed in her '*devil I know*' theory and stuck to it. Regardless of the past, she felt Gloria and Lijah were good together. Now, as if in-tune with Gloria's thoughts, she figured she knew just where her sistren would be going.

Khamilla was sleeping like a log, and Fari's snoring helped Kizzy's thoughts, as she replaced her mind in the morbid hospital ward, where Beatrice had lain, dying:

"*Your father loved you, you know, Kizzy,*" the pale, frail woman had said, trying hard to make use of her last morsel of breath. Kizzy held her hand, feeling not so much sadness about losing a mother, but more like loosing a likeable, quick acquaintance. "*I know he did. I saw it in his eyes as I walked away from his door that dreadful night. Minutes before, he had your little fingers in his hands. His rough, black, hard-working fingers, contrasting with your soft, pale, delicate ones. Didn't want to let you go. S'pose, looking back now, it was hard for him. I remembered how he concentrated on your birthmark. That dark mark, just above your left collar-bone. Said it was the living map of Jamaica. Stroked it with his index finger, he did... As if he was reminiscing on the Island... Always said he wanted to go back. 'Home', he always said. 'Me want to go back home', he used to say."* Beatrice's aristocratic tongue didn't go well with the lingo, especially now she was dying, but she tried.

Kizzy hadn't known why finding her father wasn't an issue before. Perhaps because the way Mama Maya explained it, a father was not prominent in the story. That *'Father unknown'* seemed so vague. Careless. It had such nothingness about it, it was unreal.

"He loved me?" Kizzy had asked, *"But you never said that before. I thought he didn't want me. Didn't care about..."*

The piercing sound from the heart-monitor stopped Kizzy in her tracks. Beatrice was dying. A nurse rushed to her bedside, summoning a doctor.

But Kizzy knew it wasn't the end of the road. Something happened at that moment. A fresh bee had become trapped in her bonnet. A bee that demanded a fuller picture. Up until then, she had been prepared to let the paternal side of her life go, but from what Beatrice had just told her, it would be hard. *"My father loved me?"* she said in a low whisper. *"But where is he now? Who is he? Is he alive? Dead? Is he in Birmingham? What?"* Her brain raced.

"But what is his name?... My father?... Beatrice?... Can you hear me?" But Kizzy was speaking to a corpse. Now, she didn't care about her mother's *'dying'*, but was now clinging to a new hope of a father, *'living'*.

A nurse gently helped Beatrice's eyelids down and covered the pale, breathless corpse with a white sheet, then she pulled Kizzy away from the scene.

Lucy breezed in casually. *'Where was Conrad?'* Kizzy wondered as she walked away from the bed.

Now she stared into space. Though she loved Mama Maya, she felt cheated. Robbed of her true identity. Now it was a bigger deal than she had thought. The one thing that didn't matter at all was fast becoming the biggest issue of all: if she didn't know her father, how the hell could she truly know *who* she really was?

She eased her locks away from her neck, stroked her birthmark and was thinking deeply. *'Perhaps Festus was right. Perhaps I should have let sleeping dogs lie.'*

As the doctor pulled the curtains closed around Beatrice, a new train of thought opened in Kizzy's head.

'Everybody hurts, sometime,' Lijah told himself as he sat in his Roadster under a tree in Cannon Hill Park. Earlier, he experienced *déjà vu*. It didn't seem that long ago that he was there. He had sat in the very same spot after Gloria had rejected him that day after the last family dinner. Back then, a deep contempt for a red SAAB and its illusive driver was slowly devouring him. Now, he was being devoured by everything, but.

He leant back and cruised the highway of his mind, thinking of rivers he had crossed in the not-far-off past: the rivers of hurt, greed, loss, power, revenge, secrets, transformation, growth, courage, disgust, purpose, sacrifice, guilt. And love.

When you have troubles, don't cry, Just remember God is standing by...
When you have troubles, don't cry, Just remember God is standing by...
God is standing by... God is standing by
So... don't you worry, and don't you cry...

The chorus was a distant murmur in his head and it was the gurgling baby that brought him back to reality. He scolded himself for having her out so late and headed home.

It wasn't long before he was settled in bed with a kind of acceptance.

An hour later, he opened his eyelids reluctantly. The knock on the front door had a kind of strangeness about it. An *'unsure'* kind of rapture. He glanced over at the red digits on his clock. It was just past midnight. *'Who could that be?'* he wondered to himself, now heading downstairs in just his boxers. He didn't know why he should think so, but he felt sure it was Bernadette.

Lijah pulled back the blinds from the kitchen window and peered out. His heart skipped a beat when he found the spotlight shining on his queen, Gloria. Yes, his queen was standing on his doorstep, after midnight and he panicked. He had not long had a shower, yet, he sniffed his armpits and checked his breath and face. He consulted the long mirror in the passage and questioned his physique. *Dis was Gloria man, a wha' duh yuh?*

He had stretched the self-scrutiny a bit too long, and the doorbell rang again. A bit more piercing this time, waking the baby. A split-second pause, then he took a deep breath and walked to the front door.

"Lijah, whaap'n?" Gloria asked, clutching a book tightly to her chest. "Yuh took yuh time. I know you're a light sleeper, so when you didn't come, I was about to go... Thought you and the baby might be spending the night somewhere... Can I come in...?" She fixed her eyes on his head, the strangest sight she had ever seen. A prominent verse from the bible came home t roost in he head: Numbers 6:5: *'All the days of the vow of separation, no razor shall pass over his head. Until the day be fulfilled of his consecration to the Lord, he shall be holy, and shall let the hair of his head grow.'*

"Er... Yes...Yes... 'Course yuh can, G. How could you ask that?" He felt sorry for making her stand there so long, but shock has a way of shaking the brain.

"Sorry it's so late." Her eyes were still on his head. "Hope I'm not interrupting anything. Presumptuous, I know, but it was a spur-a-de-moment t'ing. Kizzy don't even know I'm gone. I couldn't sleep." She spoke as she walked to the lounge: as well as Lijah, that too needed her touch. It had been left to drop. Not dirty. Just untidy. A nuh not'n. Just a man t'ing. The naturalness of domesticity is way down on their line of priorities. It was no longer her house, so she had no say, though somehow, it felt as if she hadn't left.

"No... yuh not interrupting' anyt'ing... Sit down, nuh. Yuh want a drink?" Lijah fussed, not knowing how to treat her, trying too, to disguise the joy her presence had brought.

Arms folded across her chest, as if to close him off, Gloria rested her eyes questioningly again, on his head, but asked no question. Perhaps he would explain. It wasn't like that when they mourned together at Kunta's funeral over a week ago. Now she looked at his bare chest. Then his sturdy thighs, her eyes now coming to rest on the area of his inside leg. Now, she averted her eyes to a picture of Kunta, while he kept his on the book she clutched so protectively, to her chest.

"Ikesha will be fine, won't she? She didn't take the funeral too well," Gloria said.

"No, she didn't. They were close, G. Really close. But yes, I think she'll be fine. Ikesha is a survivor, G. Yuh done know."

"And what about Shari? Think she'll be fine with her mum? She was so hard on her before? So hard, she practically disowned her."

"Yeah. Like your mum was, with you, G," he smiled, "both her and your father were so hard."

"Yeah, but they didn't disown me. And they came round in the end. If this tragedy with Kunta didn't happen, Mitzi wouldn't show. Shari doesn't even know who her father is. I don't see the point in hiding that from your child, unless it's a rape case or sop'n like dat."

"Serious. Anyway, what book is dat?" Lijah asked, reaching out.

She passed it to him, almost absent-mindedly, her eyes still on her son's picture, and a lump in her throat. She hoped Kunta would be looking down on them, now anticipating the possibility of them '*getting back together*'. She reflected on his words: ones that never left her head: "*Is it true, Mum?... that you're seeing somebody else?... But Mum, you're my mum. Another man?... Did you bring him in the house like Dad seh?... Oh no, Mum. I can't see you an' Dad getting back now...*"

"Wha'? 'FALLEN RASTAS'?'...By Gloria Fontaine'?" Lijah's voice brought Gloria back. "G? Yuh get yuh novel published? To raas. Nice one, babes."

But before she could answer, the baby cried.

"Just a minute, G," Lijah said, hurrying upstairs with the book in his hand.

Gloria smiled at the thought of Lijah coping alone with a baby. She sighed and cast her eyes all over the room.

When Lijah entered the bedroom, he found Shanique frantically trying to find her dummy. He replaced it and she took it, almost as if her little life depended on it. He stopped for a moment and stared at the helpless infant, peacefully sleeping in her cot, not knowing what her mother had done. Shanique must have been having an angelic dream, for she smiled. And now, for the first time, through this angelic smile, Lijah saw it. The truth. The living, breathing truth. That he had been given a *jacket*. The baby was Rock's. Without the slightest shadow of a doubt. Only a blood test could convince him otherwise. But he wouldn't make it an issue. This new life had brought him *something*. Something he couldn't explain. Something he had become unbelievably attached and accustomed to. Kunta entered his head. And the fact that the baby wasn't a boy just didn't matter.

Now, soft warm fingers brushed his bare back. He jumped, and came to realise that he had left Gloria downstairs. She had stood watching him for a while: watching as he admired the sweet child, whilst still clutching her book.

"How are you coping?" she asked in the most understanding voice.

"Oh... Well... Could be better. I know one t'ing. Dis one-parent shit is no joke. But I'll survive," he said, now trembling at her presence in the bedroom. Nervous at the thought of them, being there together again.

"She's beautiful. I can't see you in her yet, though. Still. She's still young. Kunta didn't start taking on your features until..." She stopped, swallowed hard and summoned strength. *Kunta.* It was going to be hard.

"Yeah. I know..." Lijah's mind swayed. "G... I'm sorry. If only..."

"Shhhh." She stopped him in his tracks. "We've buried our son, Lijah. Now let's bury the past. The hatchet. Everything. Don' matter who was right or wrong. Too many people live to regret. We've only got one life to live, and we're gonna live it." She coupled his face in the palms of her hands and kissed his lips. Tears welled in both their eyes. "None of us are perfect, Lijah. So much has happened since we've been apart." They were now hugging each other tight. Lijah moved his hands all over her back, shoulders and ass. He stared into her eyes, and she read his look: *'I can't believe I'm holding you'*, it said. "We've lost our son," she continued, "I've lost my mother. Festus is inside. The shooting t'ing. And Papa Dread. Jesus... Papa Dread. I still can't believe he's gone... It's almost as if a dark shadow has passed over us."

Lijah listened in silence, his mind following her every word.

"And me," Gloria continued, "I thought I found someone better than you. But I was wrong. Glen is rotten to the core. The only sweet thing about him was his name. *'Baby Face Glen'.* She sniggered. "I soon saw his true colours. Never would I put my daughter's life in danger like that again. You are a warm frying pan compared to Glen, Lijah. He's a raging furnace."

Lijah wondered if he should pour out *his* troubles to Gloria. Tell her that he had taken another walk on the wild side of life while she was away. How could he keep such things from her? But how could he tell her? And now he felt he was betraying her again if he kept them from her. And should he decide to begin, he didn't even know where would be the easiest part to start, and in fact where it would end. And would she really forgive him? *The final showdown with Lucy and sleeping with Kizzy...* Would she really be comfortable with all that? *And for not telling her about Ikesha's encounter with Rock and Festus.*

Shanique smiled again, in her sleep.

"I want to start again, Lijah. Put the past behind us."

She had come after midnight. Unexpectedly. So he had half expected something. "Are you sure, G?" he asked.

"Yes. I'm sure."

"Yeah... but..." he looked perplexed at the sleeping child, "don't you mind the baby? I want to keep her."

"We have to keep the baby," Gloria stressed. "Unless you want to regret it all your life. I went to see your dad before I came. He told me that if she's still alive, you have a mixed race sister somewhere. Possibly in Birmingham. Said he told you. He has regrets, Lijah. Lots of regrets. Are you gonna try and find her?... Your sister?"

"No. I don't think so, G. I will just let sleeping dogs lie. It might open another can a worms. I called Dad a few days ago to ask a few more questions. I'm sure Kizzy must have told you already that Dora is Festus' mother. Montie, the Handsworth tramp, is his father. I still cannot believe it. So many people are living lies. It is as if Dora classed Festus as dead, just like he did, her. Me closest idrin's madda married my faada... Festus knew, G. And he didn't even say a thing."

"I know," Gloria said. "I've been talking to Kizzy. But you know, Lijah... worse things happen at sea." Gloria spoke as if she had been born again. As if nothing could ever shock her again. "We assume that our parents are saints. That they weren't young once. They have flaws. Imperfections. Emotions. Everybody makes mistakes. Some big ones, some little ones. Take my father for instance. I know how much you respected him, but there are things I haven't told you about him, Lijah. Now, if my father can show imperfect traits, it shows that we are all just regular human beings."

"Reverend Fontaine? What could he have done so bad?"

Gloria smiled. "It's a long story, Lijah. A long story."

"Yeah, well. Still... to go searching for my half-sister would mean asking my father more questions again. He's getting old, G. I have left a lot too late. Things I should have asked years ago, I'm only just asking now. I have been raking up a lot. I don't want to ask him any more on that matter. Plus, I t'ink he told me all he knew. He didn't even know what happened to the mother of this half-sister of mine. He didn't even want to say the woman's name. Kept calling her 'Her', 'De woman'. Anyt'ing but her name."

"Funny. Must be some psychological explanation to all this. Fear of utterance maybe?" Gloria leaned into her psychology again.

"Yeah. But I made the old man seh it de las' time I called him, G. 'She name Beatrice', 'im seh. Not that her name matters to me. I just wanted him to face his fears, like I did. Say her name. It didn't kill 'im. They had a child together, feh God's sake."

"It's up to you, Lijah, whether or not you want to trace your sister. She could be untraceable for all you know, but you neva know. Look at Kizzy, she traced her mother and it turned out fine. If she invests well, she doesn't need to work again for the rest of her life. I know money can't take the place of love, or make up for the years, but it's almost as if it was what she was owed. Your sister might even be a very nice person."

"True. Kizzy did well there though," Lijah, replied wanting to put that little episode with Kizzy out of his mind. He remembered the day when sex had helped to comfort both of them. When he had told her: "*But who's gonna tell them, Kizzy? Don't go beating up yuhself because a dis now. We were two human beings in need of a little TLC. We both gave and received. Gloria has left me. Yes I want her back, but she's not coming back. She's got a new man in Jamaica now. You and I aren't making promises. Just making love."* Kizzy was probably the deepest of all his secrets. That moment of uncontrollable lust with his woman's best friend. Now, all he wanted to do was to make love to his queen.

"G, yuh lookin' good. The Jamaican sun has kissed your face passionately." Lijah could be a real romantic when he wanted to be.

"Thank you."

Now he held her close and she felt a spark of magic moving through her body. *Déjà vu* gripped them both. The last time they touched, now seemed like forever, but the action replay took over.

"Have you still got John Holt?" Gloria whispered.

"Of course. I play our song most nights," he assured her, kissing her lips and reaching for the controls on his mini stereo in the bedroom.

"Let's dance," she commanded when John Holt's voice seduced her very soul.

Take the ribbon from your hair...

"Why not?" he responded, holding her close. And like the last time they touched: the last time she had cooked dinner for her family. Trembling, she allowed his warm, moist lips to caress hers, devouring her tongue, like the first time.

Then the pause.

The deep seductive staring of a non-verbal question into her eyes.

She held his stare.

Gently, he caressed her face, spread his arms around her shoulders, and down her back. Now he caressed her waist, her breasts, squeezed her firm pouty ass and kissed her neck. Her juices flowed. He knew her too well, and reached now for her inner thighs and remembered again, he was her first. And though not her only, he hoped he'd be her last - she was his queen.

She wanted him, badly, but something stopped her. Unlike before, it wasn't her pride, but a big crunch on her conscience. "No, Lijah. No."

He freaked. It was just at that point, that she rejected him last time.

"What is it, G? I thought...?"

All I'm taking is your time
So help me make it through the night...

"We've both taken different turns from each other, Lijah. Eaten from different plates. We both don't know where we've been. We're big people. We might have been stupid before, but let's be sensible now. We need to take that crucial step of getting AIDS tests."

"Oh... right... cool..." It hadn't crossed his mind." He mopped his brow. "You scared me, G. For a moment I thought..."

"You thought I was going to reject you again?"

"Jah know."

She kissed him. "And I'm not gonna stay the night either. I want Khamilla to see me when she opens her eyes tomorrow."

"Irie."

"And Lijah?"

"Yes, Empress?"

"Yuh know me love yuh, yes?"

"Likewise, G. Likewise." He penetrated her eyes, then asked, "Where did we really go wrong, G?"

Gloria smiled what could be referred to as a *'serious'* smile, but said nothing. Instead, she let him follow her eyes to where her answer lay. They rested on her novel FALLEN RASTAS. Started way back when, in the heart of Edgbaston, England, and completed under the sun and moonlit skies of Kingston, Jamaica.

"Serious," he said, "serious. Can't wait to see your reasoning."

"We took up a banner we couldn't carry, Lijah. Hats off to those who can. *The true Israelites.* Let them ring home the *'truth and rights'*.

"Serious t'ing," he agreed, pulling her close.

STOP!!! GO STRAIGHT TO PAGE 280 (CHAPTER * TWENTY-EIGHT)

There was no telling who Lijah would bump into today, since the aisles of Sainsbury's didn't discriminate. He had already bumped into Fiona and Grace doing their weekly shopping. And earlier he had had a trolley crash with Festus squeeze, Heidi, who had looked at him through guilty eyes.

But his next encounter was one he could have done without. *Bernadette.* His heart raced. A sprinkling of sweat gathered about his forehead. And the thought of Lucy coming the other way freaked him out. Being sandwiched between those two would have been a nightmare.

Now the hypothetical *'shall we dance'* would not have gone amiss, as he and Bernadette came unexpectedly in contact with each other. It was a very uncomfortable moment, to say the least.

"Where's your baby?" Bernadette asked after smiling at him.

Lijah looked around to make sure she was definitely addressing him. After all, their last encounter wasn't exactly a pretty one, so the most he had expected of her was a quick u-turn.

"She's... with a babysitter," he answered; unsure as to whether she was being polite or sarcastic.

"*Babysitter?*... Not another Faithlyn, I hope."

He paused after catching the definite sarcasm in her voice, and braced himself for a confrontation. "Excuse me?"

"Never mind. Heard from your sister yet?"

"What's with the questions? You and I know you don't really care."

"No. But I care to know if she's still fucking Jacques."

"Wha'?" Lijah's antennas were alerted. "Bernadette what the fuck are you on?"

"*Was* on, Lijah. *Was* on. I was on a mission to wreck Faye's brothers' lives."

"Listen. I know you're a fucking psycho. You're one of many, walking around the place looking normal, but you're fucking sick, Bernadette."

"I trusted your sister, Lijah, and she took my husband away from me."

"A weh de blood claat..." Lijah understood now. In fact he had understood from that first, *'But I care to know if she's still fucking Jacques'* comment. The details could stay. There was no need for Bernadette to go into any depth. "So what the fuck have me and my brother have to do with that?" He looked around the store as if to check who was listening. "Tell me sop'n," he said, leaning towards her, "yuh sure you an' Lucy aren't a double act? If not, you two should link up. Seriously."

"What d'you mean?" she quizzed, pretending she didn't know what he was talking about, and at the same time, casting her mind over Lijah's words on their last encounter: *"Then Lucy... She tortured me for what my father had done to her mother. Why should I pay?"* Bernadette had pledged never to literally explain *her* reason for her action. Just to watch the two brothers crumble under her plan of action. But it wouldn't end there. *No.* Bernadette had another plan. She was driven by *something*. Though not in the sense that she knew it. *Madness.* Feh real.

"Neva mind," Lijah said, kissing his teeth, discarding his half-filled trolley and leaving the scene. "If Birmingham isn't fucking big enough for me an' you, the aisles in Sainsbury's are hardly gonna be, to raas."

In his hurry to towards the exit, he bumped again into Fiona and Grace.

Lijah's action of sitting in his car with that solemn look on his face and a distant look on his eyes was almost becoming a trademark of late. He should have been hitting the road by now, considering the speedy exit from Sainsbury's, but instead, Bernadette, that infamous fly was in his soup again. It was her tapping on his window that brought him back to reality.

"And by the way," the cheeky bitch had said when he wound down his window, "don't think you've seen the last of me yet."

He stared vengefully at her, in disbelief, his eyes asking, *'Why the fuck can't you just ease off de planet, woman?'* "What's the problem now, Bernadette?" he asked.

"Problem? Who said anything about a problem?" She bent down towards him and was now in his face. *Literally.* "You're gonna have to be nice to me, Lijah. *Real nice,*" she stressed.

"Weh yuh seh?"

"You have become quite a nice lover. I taught you well. I think I'll cash in on my investment."

"What the fuck yuh talking about?"

"I want you in by bed from time to time."

"No fucking way! Are you sick, woman?! Gloria and I are getting back together. And even if we weren't…"

"You have no choice, Lijah. Have lips, will spill the beans. Unless, of course, you have ways of silencing me. And I wouldn't count on that. I have already taken care of that possibility. A kind of… verbal *safe-deposit-box*?"

"Too late, Bernadette. Gloria already knows all about you and me. She's forgiven me. Old news, yuh fucka."

She laughed a cutting laugh as she opened her car door. "Who cares about what Gloria knows?" she said, her voice administering a bitter-sweet cut into his soul. "You're so way off track, it's unbelievable."

"So… what?"…

"We all know what Gloria knows… but do the police know how one infamous *Rock* came to be lying dead in his London flat?"

Lijah's eyes widened. His face turned an ashy grey. "How d'you…"

"Like I said," Bernadette told him, "in my bed. From time to time. Gloria doesn't have to know you're fucking me. Like the police don't have to know where the bullet that eliminated Rock, came from." She started her engine.

"Are you fucking blackmailing me, Bernadette?"

"Lijah, you are such a clever boy," she said sarcastically. "No one would have guessed that. *Good boy.* Brownie points. *Kiss, kiss.*"

Lijah felt smaller than an illusive pimple, in his MRS. *'Gloria,'* he agonised to himself, laying his head on his steering-wheel. *'Gloria… Gloria… Gloria… what the fuck am I gonna do?'*

"*Secrets,* Lijah. *Secrets.* They're not really worth having, are they? You see, a secret is only a secret when only one person knows it."

Lijah could have killed her.

"And by the way, Lijah," Bernadette tormented relentlessly, "I've just picked up some more lavender oil. You know how much you love that."

She reversed out of her parking spot and left him in torment.

STOP!!! NOW READ FROM CHAPTER * THIRTY-TWO TO THE END

CHAPTER * TWENTY-EIGHT

When Kizzy had told Gloria of her plans to leave Birmingham, it didn't go down too well. It was Kizzy who had made her look long and hard at her relationship with Lijah. She had made her evaluate what they had, by the constant drumming-in of her *'devil I know'* theory.

Although she herself had left to live in Jamaica previously, it was only then that she had realised truly, how Kizzy must have felt. She was near and dear to her. She felt guilty too for keeping the *'Baby Face Glen'* thing from her, but back then, Gloria had doubted whether honesty was the best policy: if she had started, she would have had to finish, so she decided to keep it from Kizzy. In the heat of the moment, she had taken Glen to Lijah's bed.

Now, as Kizzy and Fari waited in the slow-moving queue at Kingston Airport, they could both murder tons of kisco-pops, or long cool glasses of Ting. Kizzy looked at Fari's hot and bothered face, and hoped that the heat, and missing Festus would be all his troubles. Fari had seen a lot. Heard a lot. She hoped that in time, his little mind would dispose of the negativities he had experienced. She could not forget his reaction to her battered face, at Fiona's house. *'Mammy! What's wrong with your face?! Has Daddy been hitting you again?!... You wait 'till a get my gun!... I'm gonna shoot Daddy! Shoot him! Shoot him! Shoot him!'*

But now, her mind swayed to how shocked she was, when a week after Gloria had told her that she was planning on getting back with Lijah, she had opened a letter Beatrice had written to her. A letter the old lady wanted her to have *after* she had passed. It revealed the name of her true father. *Lothan Zechariah Benjamin.* Lijah's father. And now she thought of how she had fought back the need to be violently sick over its pages, when reality had hit her. She thought of the brief moment she spent with Lijah, not knowing he was her half-brother. His words: *'But who's gonna tell them, Kizzy? Don't go beating up yuhself because a dis now. We were two human beings in need of a little TLC. We both gave and received. Gloria has left me. Yes I want her back, but she's not coming back. She's got a new man in Jamaica now. You and I aren't making promises. Just making love..."* And at the time, that had helped to minimise the guilt. But that was then: well before the letter. And this was now.

Everybody runs from his or her problems. She believed leaving England was the best she could do: thanks to Beatrice's legacy that helped her decision. She would not go to see Lothan either. In doing that, Lijah would know that the *'too-close'* thing she worried about when they had sex was more *real* than *she* had ever feared and *he* would ever care to imagine. So she had pledged to let her *paternal-sleeping-dog* lie. Forever.

At the airport's exit, a cute looking taxi-driver made his presence felt. He didn't seem to need the job. He dressed too well. Better than the average taxi-driver would. His neck and fingers were covered in gold, not to mention his mouth. A black Nike hat was slanted backwards on his head. He had a cute face with dimples to die for.

"Weh yuh goin', lady?" he asked, holding onto one of Kizzy's cases, allowing her no chance to refuse a ride with him.

"Right here in Kingston," Kizzy said. "Load my cases up. I'll give you the address."

"A'right, yout'?" he asked Fari, who smiled at him. "Me like yuh locks dem." He grabbed another case and headed for his car. "How long yuh been growin' dem?"

"From I was a baby."

"Wha'? Me respec' dat yout'." He turned and looked at Kizzy. "Yuh 'ere on holiday?"

"No. For good. I love Jamaica," she replied, climbing into his ride.

"Yeah, man. Jamaica nice. De only problem?... Dallaz nah run." He grinned as he stared at her through his rear-view mirror. "I thought foreign was where all de dallaz deh. How come you decide to leave?"

"Lots of reasons... but still. I'm here. That's the main thing."

"So w'at about yuh man? Yuh lef' 'im?"

"Aren't you getting a bit too personal? I don't even know your name, yet yuh asking me my business?"

"But kiss me neck! Yuh facety feh a English gyal, yunnuh."

"Yes, me facety. Yuh nuh see me wid me big face?" Kizzy was giving it as large as a native gyal.

"Bombo cl... yuh know wha'? Me like yuh, yunnuh. Yeah. Me like yuh. So tell me sop'n... yuh sell-up yuh house an' everyt'ing before yuh come?"

"Yuh too bright. Nosey. Is dat any a yuh business? An' yuh still haven't told me yuh name."

"Yuh neva tell me yours?"

It wasn't long before Kizzy was sitting inside that divine house Mama Maya had built to retire in. She had told Kizzy and Fiona, she had come there *'to die'*, but she seemed a bill of health and had more likely come there *'to live'*.

A pretty, gracefully aged, jet-black woman walked sure-footedly up the path towards the veranda. "Sweetie!" she called out. That strong, distinctive voice could be detected anywhere. Grey had now covered the whole of her head, but sprinkled itself randomly about it, giving her that distinctive *down-south-black-American-woman* look. It suited her. And she had lost the buxomness of her bosoms. She wore a pair of flat open-toed sandals, as opposed to the faithful heels Kizzy could remember back in England.

"Come, Pat! Kizzy is here!" Maya shouted back.

"Sweetie?" Kizzy quizzed. "Why is Aunt Patricia calling you Sweetie? Strong term of endearment, isn't it?" The word only stood out because of what Fiona had said back in England: *'Mama Maya is gay herself, Kizzy. Her and Aunt Patricia... Ok. Look deep into yourself and tell me that you don't think Mama Maya and Aunt Patricia were lovers.'*

"I'll explain later, Kizzy. It's a long story," Mama Maya said, looking towards Aunt Patricia.

"Kizzy? How yuh doin', young lady? Yuh lookin' well," Aunt Patricia boomed, as she neared the veranda where Mama Maya and Kizzy sat enjoying the cool air from the fan above their heads. "How is Englan'?"

"Just the way you left it, Aunt Patricia," Kizzy got up, walked towards her and gave her a hug, questions racing through her head. *'Was Fiona right? Were Aunt Patricia and Mama Maya really...? Could Fiona not have read more into it than what had met her eyes? Do older black women really...? Well, they were young once...'* No. This was Mama Maya and Aunt Patricia. Two black women who fried goatfish together in Mama Maya's kitchen. Swayed together in the narrow pews in their local Pentecostal church. Discussed the state of pieces of yams in Birmingham Bull Ring Market. Chose wads of brown nylon tights as if they were going out of fashion. Sported the best church hats. Chuckled, whispered and hummed in the dead of numerous mysterious nights. Two black women who, as far as Kizzy understood, *'Wouldn't do dem t'ings deh'*.

"How's Fiona?"

"Fiona's fine, Aunt Patricia. You know Fi'... the original survivor."

"I know she is, Kizzy. From the day she was born, I knew she was gonna be a suviva."

"From the day she was born?" Kizzy smiled. "You said that, Aunt Patricia, as if you knew Fiona from birth."

"Yes, Kizzy. I knew Fiona from birth," Aunt Patricia answered, placing her bottom on a bamboo-weaved chair, as if in readiness to lay a heavy burden down. Mama Maya gave her an *'are you sure you're ready?'* look.

"Yuh want a drink, Pat?" Mama Maya felt uncomfortable. Dere is carrot juice in de fridge. Cool-Aid as well. Dere's Lilt tuh. An' me did buy some Ting."

"Let me have some Cool-Aid nuh, Sweetie. Please."

Apart from everything else, Kizzy was wondering why she had never once heard Aunt Patricia called her Mama Maya, Sweetie, in England.

Mama Maya got up and walked into the house, barely managing to take her eyes off Kizzy's face, which was now a question mark.

Kizzy changed seats and sat down beside Aunt Patricia. "Wha' d'you mean, Aunt Patricia? Wha' d'you mean yuh know Fiona from birth? Were you there when her mother gave birth?"

Aunt Patricia sighed like an old, original African woman and said, "Kizzy... a me gi' birt' to Fiona. Fiona is me daughta. Like your mother, I gave her up. Later in life, I regretted it and went searching for her..."

Nutty Professor, eat your heart out. Kizzy needed to pick her bottom lip up off the floor. Aunt Patricia... could you... run that by me... again?"

"It's a long story... but when I found out she was with Maya, I was shocked. You see, Maya and I knew each other from right here in Jamaica. Went to school together. Sewing lessons. Everyt'ing."

"C'mon, Aunt Patricia!" Kizzy urged, "neva mind all dat. How... when... er... why did you give up your own...?"

"I had to, Kizzy."

"No! Don't tell me that. Not unless you're gonna tell me it was a matter of life an' death! There had to be another way!" She didn't want to wait for an explanation. The mystery of Aunt Patricia was slowly unfolding, and the respect Kizzy had for her was fast diminishing.

"Kizzy, I got pregnant by a pastor. Later, he wore the title *'Reverend'*."

"So? Does that justify giving away your child? Wouldn't it have been better if this... pastor... reverend... whatever had supported the child? Even if it was secretly?"

"Kizzy, he didn't want that. We talked about it. He had his family. He wanted it that way. I wasn't the only one either."

"He wanted it that way. What did *you* want?"

"Kizzy, we all make mistakes. Some we will regret for the rest of our lives. If me neva regret it, me wouldn't go searching for her. I made sure I spent as much time as I could with her when I found her. Every chance me get, me would travel down from Luton to see her."

"So... why didn't you tell Fiona this? D'you know what secrets like these can lead to? Fiona thought your visits were... she thought you were... you and Mama Maya... she thought you were..."

"We were what, Kizzy?" Mama Maya had returned with four glasses of Cool-Aid. "Fari! Come! Come have a drink!" He was playing in Mama Maya's beautiful garden. "What did Fiona think we were, Kizzy?"

"She thought you were... gay. Lovers."

"Oh Lord have mercy," Mama Maya said, both her and Aunt Patricia looking perplexed at each other, "she thought *that*?"

"Yes. Totally convinced."

"Oh Lord, Lord, Lord," Aunt Patricia lamented. "What is dis pon me? But w'at a somet'ing, eeh Sweetie? Gay? Heh, heh, heeeeye!" The laugh was more hysteria than hilarity. "Me affi tek bad somet'ing mek joke."

"Well, yuh cyan put Fiona straight on dat one," Mama Maya stressed. "Because yuh don't see a woman wid a man, it doesn't mean she is a gay."

Aunt Patricia kissed her teeth long and hard now, with disgust, dismissing what she saw as an absurd suggestion, coming from Fiona, and continued, "If yuh know how many times I tried to find de words, de right moment... Child, it's no easy tryin' to mek yuh undastan'."

"So... who is this... pastor? Or reverend person?"

"It don' matter anymore, Kizzy."

"Aunt Patricia, it's not for you to decide what matters to Fiona, from what don't."

"What good will it do now, Kizzy? I know Fiona has neva showed much interes' in fin'ing her blood parents. I didn't think she wanted to know. She seemed fine."

Kizzy and Aunt Patricia's eyes locked. Even though it wasn't *her* father, Kizzy wanted to know *who* he was. Her look was compelling, and Aunt Patricia said, "His name is Mr Fontaine. Reverend Fontaine."

"I know a Reverend Fontaine," Kizzy said casually, "Gloria's dad. So where does this other Reverend Fontaine live then?"

"If he's lucky, in heaven, if not, hell. He's dead. That's him. De same very one. Gloria's dad," Aunt Patricia assured her, taking a sip of Cool-Aid.

"But... Gloria's dad is from Leeds. You're from Luton."

"I was living in Leeds at de time. I left not long after I gave Fiona up. Left and went to Luton."

When the reality had settled in, the shock of it all caused Kizzy to splutter. She coughed, sprayed Aunt Patricia's face with a mouthful of Cool-Aid, and was now choking profusely.

"Kizzy! Yuh a'right! Hol' yuh breat'! It look like de Cool-Aid went down de." Mama Maya panicked, beating Kizzy's back.

When the coughing and spluttering had subsided, Kizzy asked, drying her eyes, "Gloria and Fiona are half-sisters? And all these years they had no idea? What if one of them was a male, Aunt Patricia? Think of the possibility of incest." Kizzy knew all too well what she was talking about. She thought of her and Lijah again. For them, it was too late. "Well, Aunt Patricia, I hope you're gonna tell Fiona now. She needs to know, and it would be better coming from you."

"Uh uh," was all Aunt Patricia said.

"I don't know," Kizzy despaired. "I really don't know. There's you with your too-late story, then there's the story of my father. I wonder what *his* side of the story would be?"

"The story of yuh father?" Mama Maya picked up quickly, remembering that her and Kizzy had not really sat down to any deep conversation, since she landed. "Yuh know the story of yuh father?"

"Why did you keep that from me, Mama Maya?" Kizzy attacked. "Is our whole existence one big, mysterious circle held together by threads of secrets?"

"Keep *what* from you, Kizzy? Me nuh know w'at yuh talkin' 'bout. I told you all I knew. Your father was unknown to me. I didn't even know your mother. I haven't lied about dat."

"You didn't know that *Lothan, Lijah's dad...* was my father?"

"Which Lot'an? Lot'an weh did married to Nettie...? Lot'an Benjamin?"

"That's him."

Mama Maya kissed her teeth long and hard, cutting her eyes at the same time. "Chile, stop talk foolishness inna me ears. W'at yuh mean Lot'an is yuh faada?"

"Beatrice, my blood-mother told me the whole story, Mama Maya. From start to finish, in a letter. I had it after she died. But I'm too worn out with Aunt Patricia's little surprise to even go into it, right now." Kizzy got up and walked out onto the lawn where Fari was playing with his football, but seconds later she rushed back onto the veranda when she heard Aunt Patricia shouting, "Lord have mercy! Sweetie?! Yuh a'right?! Kizzy!"

Mama Maya, it seemed, was suffering a mini-stroke. The realities of life, too hard to digest.

Gloria couldn't believe it when she bumped into Yvonne, her old work colleague. Yvonne looked great. She was rushing out of Rackhams with two fistfuls of bags. But the only thing Gloria could think of was that weird situation with her and that phoney American, Marlon: a guy who hid behind the church and his accent to play his *rat* game all over the

West Midlands.

"Hi, Yvonne. How are you?" Gloria asked, giving the bubbly girl a hug.

"Fine. Couldn't be better. So how about you? Didn't know you were back from Jamaica. Visiting?" Yvonne asked.

"No. Back in sunny Brum for good. Long story though. Anyway, you're looking well. Found a good man yet?" Gloria joked.

"Let's put it this way," Yvonne told her, "I've found a man. So far, he's brilliant, but I've got my eyes open very wide. Whether he's a good one or not, only time will tell. Well... you knew what happened with Marlon, that American drop-out."

"Yes. I was wondering... have you heard anything else from him?"

"No, girl. And believe me, I seriously don't want to." Yvonne looked sincere when she said that.

Gloria laughed, not realising how serious Yvonne was.

"You'd never believe this," Yvonne continued.

"What?"

"*Marlon* wasn't even his original name. He changed his name for a reason."

"What reason?"

"Wouldn't you like to know, girl? And he's not just here in England for the weather either. Gloria, there are dodgy characters everywhere. The thing is, more and more of them are using the church as a hiding place. It's as if nobody fears The Almighty anymore."

"I remembered you said before, that this Marlon went to church. But what's new, Yvonne?"

"Gloria, it's a small world. My cousin in the states called me a few months back. We were having a conversation and I just happened to tell her about this shifty character I thought was going to be my husband." Yvonne laughed mockingly at the thought.

"Don't tell me your cousin knew him."

"Yes. Knew him like the back of her hands. Small world."

"Looks like this guy did you a big favour by checking out, then?"

"The biggest favour of all, girl."

"Oh... did you ever find your passport?"

"No. But I believe that just as how God revealed Marlon's darker side to me, he will eventually reveal what happened to my passport. I still think it's funny how it had been in the same place for years, and as soon as he slid away like a snake, it disappeared."

"That's what I thought when you told me, but..."

"The guy I'm with now, took me to Barbados, but you should have seen the hassle I had to replace this one passport."

"Bwoy," Gloria said, "Jah know, you don't even know who yuh standing by in a shopping queue."

"Or even standing or sitting by on the bus!" Yvonne added, cynically.

"Could be a serial killer," Gloria said.

"Believe me," Yvonne said. "It's no joke. But this Marlon guy gets better – or worse, I should say."

"No. There couldn't possibly be more."

"Girl, from what I heard, Marlon had had more runnings in the states with the law than Asians ate curry."

"What?!"

"Big time woman-beater. And you know, once a beater, always a beater."

Gloria thought of Kizzy and Festus. "Oh no! You're well outa that girl."

"Damn right. Very violent person, I heard. Thank God he saved me that fate."

"I can't believe it," Gloria perplexed.

"Yeap. I got talking to a girl here in England too, who had first-hand info on Mr America. From what I gathered, he's still slithering from church to church like a serpent, having affairs all over the place. I heard he even got a church sista pregnant and checked clean out of the relationship. If he is doing things like that in church, Gloria, would he have any qualms about doing that outside? *No.* A man who doesn't respect *God,* wouldn't be giving *man* the slightest consideration, would he?"

"And to think, Marlon is still at large. It's frightening," Gloria said.

"Yes! Still at large. In Birmingham. West Midlands. All over," Yvonne stressed. "In fact, the joke about it is, he chatted up one of my friends in Wolverhampton without the slightest clue that we knew each other." Yvonne smiled with pleasure, knowing how lucky she was. "You know me, Gloria," she continued, "all I ever wanted was a peaceful life. If Marlon could do a thing like that to me without even flinching, or without the slightest regret, he needs serious help, wouldn't you say?"

"You're not joking," Gloria said, with shock-filled eyes. "Serious help, I'd say."

"So you see, Gloria, sometimes we think the next guy we meet is going to be better than the one we left. But no. You could end up with a snake like Marlon. Or even a gun man."

Gloria flinched. *'Did Yvonne know about Baby Face Glen? Or was that the most coincidental reference of all times? And why was she telling her so much about this American guy? Was she simply doing a 'the morale of the story is... ?'*

"But there are some more things I wanna tell you about *Mr Pretender,* Marlon," Yvonne continued.

"There are more?!... Oh my God."

"Yes. There are more. Girl, you haven't heard anything yet. Now I now know why he used to be so nervy, although, at the time, I didn't see it as anything. Jumpy. Once, he was sitting in my sitting-room. I walked in and spoke to him. Believe it or not, the man nearly jumped out of his skin! It's as if he was living in fear."

"Yvonne, I'm speechless. I just don't know what to say."

"Talk about living a lie, girl. Simple things like... for instance, he told me he didn't smoke. Not that I cared whether he did or not, most people do these days. But once I came home and was shocked to find a bong behind my bed."

"A bong?! What the hell's that?"

"You know, like a chalice. I think Americans use that more that the English."

"Is there an end to this man?" Gloria perplexed again.

"And conversation," Yvonne relented. "I used to think the guy was intellectually challenging, but later I found out that he was just a gibbering ass, faking intelligence and bluffing his way through life. He used to talk so fast, he stumbled over his words: *JibberJibberJjibber.* Chatted for England that man. Making so many damn promises in the process, it was untrue. He even chatted in his sleep."

"Yes, I remember you telling me that. Why do you suppose he had to pretend?"

"Apart from the fact that he's a rat?" Yvonne laughed out loud. "Beats me. And talking about pretending, I remember when I let him talk to my brother and my sister on the telephone. Marlon gave them both the same sell-sell spiel, in the sweetest American accent you ever did hear: *'Hi. I know you don't know me, but I have seven sisters of my own. I know you love your sister, so I'm gonna do my best to make her happy'.* Needles to say, neither my sister nor my brother fell for it. My brother simply said, *'If the guy had said any more, he would have fallen over-board and drowned himself. The guy isn't real, sis. He was trying too hard. Watch him. Too good to be true. Dodgy'.* And low and behold, he was. Dodgy. As dodgy as double-glazing salesman."

As Gloria listened, she cast her mind back to Baby Face Glen. She cast a shadow of concern over her two daughters who must face the relationship challenges of life

"And he sweated too," Yvonne continued. "That's another sign of a phoney. For no reason at all, he used to just break out in a sweat. You see Gloria, when a person lies, he or she might sweat. Marlon was simply living a lie – hence the constant sweating. To think that when I first met him, he came over so sweet. Perfect. And now, every time I think of him, I judder. Everything about the man is ugly. Nasty. So rat-like, it's unbelievable."

Gloria's face was a question mark. She couldn't speak.

"C'mon," Yvonne said, "let's grab a coffee. You're gonna die when you hear who Marlon *really* is."

As they headed back into Rackhams, Gloria couldn't help thinking, *'It really is better the devil you know. If a man could buy his woman a present, snuck into her house when he knew she wouldn't be there and stole it back, then left without an explanation, he had to be a slippery character'*. She knew now that giving Lijah a chance couldn't be that bad after all.

CHAPTER * TWENTY-NINE

Everything was happening so fast, Gloria didn't know whether she was coming or going. The unforeseen gap between the time she had paid Lijah that unexpected visit, to the time Kizzy had left for Jamaica, had stretched to just over a month. She had stayed on at Kizzy's house, just until the new tenant had moved in. Kizzy had left the house to Festus so he could at least have a base when he returned from jail, (a gesture Gloria had thought too humanly for words, considering what he had put her through). There was no mortgage on the house, so he was a lucky man. *'I owe him, Gloria'*, Kizzy had said when Gloria had asked how come she was being so generous. But *what* she owed him was a mystery. Besides, whatever it was, Gloria would have thought that all the years of beatings would have compensated.

The new tenant, unbeknown to her, was one Festus himself had recommended to the estate agents that were handling the property, as a *must*. So, although it was in the making, Gloria had moved back into Lijah's house, prematurely.

This was meant to be a spare-room thing until they had sorted out a few things, but Lijah was only too pleased to let her have the room they once shared.

Things weren't sorted. Lots had to be talked about. And amidst it all, Ikesha had announced she was moving to London, to a new job. Besides, what with so many other stuff going on, the AIDS test that they promised to take, had not yet materialised. Abstaining from the pleasures of the flesh wasn't easy, but they did it anyway. Besides, Lijah couldn't get used to that. Skin-to-skin with his queen was how things had always been.

Gloria woke in the dead of the night, to the ringing of the telephone that was placed adjacent to her head. She picked it up, still half asleep and was convinced the desperate sobbing at the end of the line was Shari's, but for the first few seconds, she couldn't be sure.

"Shari?!... Is that you?!... What's the matter?!"

But words failed to over-ride the young mother's sobs. "Y... *sniff*... ye... *sniff*... yes, it's me... *sniff*... Gloria...C... ca... can... can I come back to..."

"Calm down, Shari. Take a deep breath. I can't hear what you're trying to say."

Shari calmed herself down. "Can I come back to Birmingham and stay with you until I sort a flat out?" She had called that number, so news must have gotten to her that Gloria was back with Lijah.

"What's the matter? Have you fallen out with your mother?"

Gloria's anxious voice had awoken Lijah. He was now standing over her, perplexed.

"I'll explain later," Shari said. "I just don't want to stay in London."

"Where's your mother now?"

"She's right here."

"Hi," A toffee-nosed voice met Gloria's ears before she could think. Mitzi had obviously whipped the telephone from Shari, in an attempt to defend herself.

"Hello, Mitzi. What's going on?"

"Gloria, Shari left me for a while. I didn't know where she was until now."

"What?!... You didn't know where your daughter was, and you didn't even ring Birmingham to find out if she was here?"

"Well, she led me to believe she would be ok."

Gloria sat up. She couldn't get her breath. "So where was she?"

"The police brought her back. She was living..."

"What?! Police?!"

"Yes. She was living with some guy called Rock."

"Rock?!" Gloria was alarmed. That name rang an ominous bell in her head.

"Rock?! What about Rock?" Lijah jumped on the bandwagon.

Mitzi continued, "She said it was only in conversation she found out that this was the same Rock who Kunta was mixed up with, and..."

"Hello!" Lijah grabbed the phone from Gloria. "Shari?!"

"It's not Shari, it's Mitzi, her mum. Who's this?"

"It's Lijah, Kunta's dad. What's dis about Rock?"

"Hello, Lijah. This *Rock* guy beat Shari up. She said when she found out who he really was, she got hysterical and was leaving. He beat her up. Badly too."

"What?! Dis is a raas claat... excuse de language, yuh 'ear... Gi' de phone to Shari."

"Hello, Lijah. I just want to come back to Birmingham. I hate it here. I just hate my life. Nothing's going right. Everybody that loves me dies. My nan. Damian. Kunta. What's wrong with me, Lijah? Why did Kunta have to die?" She was sobbing her heart out.

"Shari, how are the kids?" Lijah evaded her last questions and turned his concerns to his grandchildren.

"They're ok. They're sleeping."

"Ok. We'll come to pick you up tomorrow. Gimme Rock's address." Lijah grabbed a pen and paper and quickly jotted down what Shari was saying. "A'right. Everyt'ing aggo cool, yuh 'ear? Here's Gloria. She'll arrange times an' t'ing wid yuh."

Lijah passed the phone and proceeded to punch the wall from sheer frustration. Why was Rock such a bane in his life? Why had he preyed so much on his family? It was as if he was sent by an old enemy to cause him pain. *'Have I upset Jah so much?'* he wondered.

"Shari, are there any bones broken?"

"No. It's just my face. It's bruised and swollen. Especially my lips."

"Did you call the police?"

"No... He said he'd kill me if I did."

"Oh my God... you poor thing." Gloria's mind raced back to Kizzy. Then the memory of her own situation in Jamaica with Baby Face Glen made her shudder.

"Listen. Try and rest tonight, Shari. I'll ring you tomorrow. It's true, Birmingham is where you should be."

"What's going on, Lijah?" Gloria asked as soon as the receiver was down. "Don't this family ever get any peace?"

Along with Rock's head, there was no doubt as to what Lijah wanted. He was angry. Gloria knew what anger and frustration did to him. *Sex.* He wanted it. Badly.

Gloria sensed it clearly, but she just wasn't in the mood. "Ok, Lijah. Good night. I'll see you tomorrow." The answer to her last question could wait. Besides, Lijah didn't have one anyway.

"G... can't we just cuddle-up together tonight? It's ok, I know we can't..."

"Lijah, I'll see you tomorrow," she dismissed. "Serious. I just want to be alone right now. Plus you know it's hard for you to refrain from sex when you're in this mood. Cuddling me won't help. It'll make you more frustrated."

He kissed her forehead, then left the room with mixed emotions. Angry, deflated and slightly perplexed. *'Why can't I stay the night with her?'* he wondered. *'Just cuddle her. Regardless of her explanation. Just one night until we sort things out. I know we can't go all the way until the AIDS test, but... The last we touched, she seemed so sincere. So passionate...'*

Seconds later he hit his single pillow, played solitaire and hoped she wasn't having a change of heart.

It was four days to be precise, after Shari had moved temporarily into Gloria and Lijah's, that Reds and Lijah hit the road to London. There was an unfinished business that needed fixing. It was only after visiting Festus in prison that the whole truth came to light, enforcing Lijah's desire to take him out. The fact that Rock had wasted Jaro, Bunti and Sugar didn't lie heavy on his mind. That was their shit. But after a long chat with Festus, Lijah found out that regardless of who had introduced his son to *The Devil's food*, it was Rock who had wasted him.

On the journey down to London, they had mixed feelings about what Papa Dread would have said. It wasn't so long ago that they had buried him - *Jah rest his soul.* They knew that at one time, he was passionate about weeding out the wolves from the sheep. There was a time when only peaceful solutions would have done. But there was a time too, when the *'by any means necessary'* solution was a strong option. But Lijah and Reds knew too, that in his final moment, the index finger of his right hand had found it's way to the tenth commandment: *'Thou shalt not kill.'*

But Lijah had his own axe to grind. Rock had taken Kunta away from them, raped his precious daughter, and later he had beaten Shari to a pulp, while her young children watched. So although he himself couldn't physically pull the trigger, and his intention was not to glorify and start a life of crime, Lijah was pleased when Reds had told him it was all over. Rock was *done. Non-existent. Finito. Kaput.* And while he and Reds would not be able to rid the world of gangsters, they could rest assured that Rock would no longer be terrorising the streets of Birmingham, London, Jamaica or the Bronx anymore.

Little things, like baby clothes shouldn't matter today, not after the *'wiping out'* of a life, anyway, but Shari had asked Lijah to pick up some of her children's clothes that she had left behind at her mother's flat. He had mentioned to her and Gloria that he was accompanying someone to Heathrow Airport, to pick up a relative. Telling them that he was about to *assassinate* an *assassin* just wouldn't do.

It was late evening when Lijah knocked on the door of the plush Kensington flat. It took a while before Mitzi answered, but when she did, Lijah gathered why. She was obviously in the middle of a passionate session.

"Come in, Lijah," she obliged, wrapping a silk dressing gown around her. "Sit down for a second. You should have rung before you came. I washed the clothes. They're just airing in the spare room. I just need to iron them quickly. Would you like a drink?"

' *'How are my daughter and grandchildren?'* would do for starters', Lijah thought, cynically. "No thanks, Mitzi. I have a friend waiting. I can't be long."

"Why don't you invite him up for a few minutes?"

'Is this genuine hospitality?' Lijah wondered, knowing how selfish the lady could be. "No, it's cool. Really. Anyway, it looks as if I'm already disturbing you."

And so he was. *Confirmed.* No sooner had Mitzi disappeared out of the exquisitely decorated living-room that was most definitely not child-friendly, a stocky brotha walked in, clad in an exclusive dressing gown. The piece of garment was extraordinary, and had most definitely cost a packet. In fact, it looked foreign.

"A'right?" the brother asked Lijah casually, reaching for a packet of cigarettes. He had obviously come to see the male who owned the voice that had seeped from the living-room and into his ears.

"Man cool," Lijah replied, but he had only to look closer. "Raas claat! Roy! Bombo cl…"

The stocky man looked at Lijah, "Oh!… Lijah!" He dropped the packet of nicotine sticks. "What you doin' here?"

"I should ask you that question, bro'. What *you* doin' 'ere inna yuh dressin' gown? Didn't you marry a blonde, from what I heard? Couple a kids? House an' cyar to go wid it?… Big beastman job an' all dat?"

A hug between brothers, after so many years, wouldn't have gone amiss.

"Yeah. But that's history…" He needed to get over the shock of seeing his brother after so many years. That was one thing. But seeing him in his main squeeze's living-room was the ultimate other. Never mind trying to answer personal questions. "She divorced me. Cleaned me out. Still, I don't blame her. I dogged her… So what are you doing…?"

"Divorced you? Cleaned you out? Wouldn't be anything to do with Super-bitch, Bernadette, would it?"

"Pardon?" He looked towards the bedroom as if to check Mitzi's proximity. "How d'you know about me an' Bernadette?" He lowered his voice.

"Didn't you smell me all over her every time you fucked her? Or did the aroma of lavender oil take care of that?"

"You were dealing with Bernadette?" Roy lowered his tone.

"More than dealing, mate. She was the best seductress I've ever met. Still, it wasn't all in vain. I learnt a thing or two."

Roy sat down. "You've always wanted her, haven't you? Always. I knew it. From we were young. She was my first girl, but you have always wanted her. Got her in the end though, didn't you?" He filled his lungs with nicotine.

"Why don't you have a spliff, bro'?" Lijah asked sarcastically. "Cigarettes are cancer sticks. Herbs is natural. Heal all ailments. Even *fuckriesitis*... Oh... I was almost forgetting. Beastmen don't indulge, do they?... Yeah right... Like pigs don't fly, right?"

Roy ignored him. The Bernadette thing was cutting him.

"Sorry, bro'. I know you don't like sharing your things. Especially with me. But how was I to know?... Listen, if you hadn't kept away from the family, this wouldn't have happened. We all know that one secret only leads to another." Lijah felt on top. Here he was, talking down to big brother who had served Queen and Country. A brother who he thought had hidden from himself for years. A brother who shared the same pum-pum with him, without even knowing it.

"How's your family, Lijah? I don't even know them."

"How's *yours*, Roy? *I don't even know them,*" Lijah mimicked. He kissed his teeth. "Cut the bullshit, bro'. You didn't want to know my family before, so how's knowing how they are now, gonna matta? At least you've met two of your grand-nephews."

"I have?"

Lijah laughed mockingly. "Now this is how I know you didn't care a damn about me or my family. If you had talked about me to Mitzi, she would have told you *who* the father of her daughter's children was."

Roy sought solace through the tip of his cigarette. He pulled so hard he almost consumed the damn thing in one go.

"What made you decide to play *Master*, Roy?" Lijah relented. "I can see you wanting to cut de ole man off for what you think he did to Mum, but what did I do? Why did you and Faye act like that?"

"I have no answers, Lijah. None, other than the fact that I wanted to forget my past. Mum must have gone through hell. The pain was too much. But that wasn't all, Lijah. I don't know how much you know, but you must be the strongest of all of us. You stayed. Endured. I might have defended Queen and Country, but you are more of a man than I'll ever be."

"You might have suffered mentally, Roy, but don't you think that if all three of us had suffered together, shared things, communicated... don't you think it would have been a problem shared? Don't you think I suffered too, Roy?"

Mitzi entered the room with two bags of baby clothes. "Oh, sorry. How rude of me. Roy, I didn't know you came out, or I would have come in and introduced you guys."

"Don't worry, Mitzi," Lijah assured her, "we've met. We go back a long way, Roy an' me. A long, long way. Came from the same place, to be exact. Our mother's womb." He fixed a daggered stare on Roy.

"Excuse me?" Mitzi perplexed.

"Roy and I are brothers, Mitzi."

"You're what?!"

"Listen, thanks for sorting these for Shari. Roy will explain – if he wants to, that is. I must make tracks. Me idrin's waiting downstairs."

Roy lit another cigarette. Mitzi walked Lijah to the door, still perplexing over his latest revelation.

"I wonder if you fuck better than Bernadette?" Lijah turned and rudely asked Mitzi. "You have to be seriously wicked in bed to stop him craving that ass. Still. Whatever. I think you all deserve each other. All three of you - selfish bastards. I won't give Shari your love. She's got ours. Mine an' Gloria's." He pulled the door closed behind him and Mitzi stood motionless for second or two. *Shocked.* Now, she walked back to her living-room with vengeful eyes.

"You ok?" Roy asked calmly, stubbing out his cigarette.

But she didn't answer. Instead, she lunged at him, throwing wild, girlish punches at his face, neck and shoulders, and random kicks to his shin and ankles. "Who the fuck is Bernadette?! What is Lijah on about, *'I have to be seriously wicked in bed to stop you craving her'*? What did he mean?! *Whack!* What?! *Whack!* You bastard!"

Roy had no problem restraining her. It was part of his job. "I have no time for this, Mitzi," he said, as cool as ice. "I'm gonna take a shower. I have to go to work. The streets of London are heaving with criminals. Not so long ago, there was another shooting." He kissed her as if nothing had happened.

Mitzi calmed down as if his kiss was laced with hypnotic juices. She slumped onto the settee, cuddled her knees and cried silently.

*

Stir it up... Little Darling, Stir it up...

When it came to music, Papa Ashley had the touch. *No messing.* He had been entertaining ravers from way back when: when most of Birmingham's younger DJs were still in nappies. Ask *him* about vintage, he had it all. Knew the musical score inside out. *Feh real.* With some guys, their first love is their cars, but with Papa Ashley, it's his music.

The session he was asked to play at was swinging, and so was Stanley Benjamin. Good old Uncle Stan. The brunette that held onto him looked half his age. She was under his spell, and he was under his waters.

"A'right, Stanley?!" Papa Ashley shouted over the music as he walked away from his deck, and past Stanley. He needed a drink and had left things in the capable hands of his nephew, Derek.

"Yeah, man. Man cool," Uncle Stan replied.

"Yuh unda yuh watas? Mek sure you not drivin' yunnuh," Papa Ashley told him.

"No, man. Me nah drive. Tracy 'ave de key feh de cyar."

"I'm driving," his woman answered.

"Yeah. Mek sure yuh don' mek 'im tek de key dem," Papa Ashley stressed, throwing his head back and laughing haughtily, then he walked over to the other side of the room.

"Yuh ready?" Uncle Stan asked his woman not long after that.

"It's not like you, Stan'," she moaned. "I've only just started to enjoy meself."

"Me jus' tired, Tracy. Plus me nuh feel too well," he told her.

"Ok, we'll go then. If you're not feeling well," she obliged.

But it was as plain as day that Uncle Stan needed to take it easy on his ticker. Of late, this young brunette was working him too hard. He was no match for her. Besides, he had never married, and over the years he had never slowed down when it came to women. He changed them like Buckingham palace changed its guards.

"Yuh gaan, Stanley?" Papa Ashley asked him when he returned to find Uncle Stan leaving his spot.

"Yes yaah, sah. Me a go home go lie dong. Me nuh feel too good."

"Too much liqua?" Papa Ashley threw his head back and laughed again.

"It look so," Uncle Stan replied.

"A'right, sah," Papa Ashley told him, taking up position again, over his deck. "A'right, Derek. Mek we gi de people dem some Beres."

"True. True," Derek replied, digging deep into Papa Ashley's selection.

CHAPTER * THIRTY

Kizzy tucked Fari in bed, kissing his forehead like she always did. Now, she pulled the mosquito net securely around and watched his sweet eyelids droop to the call of sleep. Last night, when she had tucked him in, she had cuddled him for the longest time, putting her mind back to his conception, eight years and some months ago. She was raped. It was no joke. Abortion was the farthest from her mind. She had lived a lie with Festus for the longest time. Just couldn't tell him. So she took the option she thought was best for her. The 'quiet life' option. Only, on the inside it was turmoil.

She loved Fari so much, it was frightening. Much more, she believed, than other mothers do their children. But she hated, resented and detested the man who had impregnated her through rape. He had come to the house to see Festus. Festus wasn't there, so he said he'd wait. Through trust, she had invited him in. And he had taken her, by force, on the living-room floor.

Although he had always thought the problem of not conceiving lay with her, Kizzy had always felt that Festus could never father a child. Prior to the rape she hadn't been using any form of protection, but only after the horrific ordeal had she fallen pregnant, and never again.

So, for the longest time, Festus had played father to Jaro's child. Yes, Jaro. One of the nastiest pieces of work ever to cruise the streets of Birmingham. So, she had always felt that she 'owed Festus'. She could afford to, so she left him a house. Whether or not that would compensate for him bringing up another man's child, was not the issue. The issue was, she didn't feel so guilty now.

Now she ran her fingers through her short-cropped hair and admired herself in the mirror. Her new look would take some getting used to. She didn't think she would ever see the day when she would allow a hairdresser's scissors to touch those faithful locks. Not even after she had seen Gloria do it. At the time, the act felt gratingly sacrilege. Now, as she stood staring in the mirror, giving Halle Berry a run for her cheek, sexy look, she realised that her locks were simply an old habit dying hard, as opposed to symbolising the mane of a lioness.

Like Gloria and Lijah, no one needed to tell her that the majestic life of a true Rasta needed to be lived with much more sanctity. Fallen? Failed? Or simply *'bowing out'*? Whatever the name of the game was, they could not play it to the fullest.

An' if we should live up in dah hills...

She had been playing the legendary tape down low, all evening. Mama Maya loved it too. The night had fallen with a strangeness that could be felt all around. Mama Maya was sat on the veranda rocking in her rocking chair, a worrying distance set deeply in her eyes, and her thoughts almost touchable: '*Lothan. The only man I eva loved. It was him who named me, Sweetie. Left me for Nettie, my best friend, whose best friend in-turn, took him off her. And to think... I brought up Lothan's daughter, without even knowin' it. It was like it was meant to be. I was meant to have a piece of him nearby. But if I didn't know, what good was dat? Only God knows de reasons feh dese t'ings'.*

Kizzy found her adopted mother on the veranda, in body, but not in mind. Her body was there, but her mind moved questioningly over the other side of the ocean. Over the streets of Birmingham.

A car horn tooted and alerted her, reminding her that Kizzy was going out on the town. Her first date in Jamaica, with an infamous taxi driver who once told her, *"Bombo cl... Yuh know wha'? Me like yuh, yunnuh. Yeah. Me like you. So tell me sop'n, yuh sell-up yuh house an' everyt'ing before yuh come?"*

The open-air dance he was taking her to, promised to kick, and she was looking forward. But firstly, she had insisted on a crucial port of call. *Feh real.* A couple of sistas had invited her to a '*Poetry Singles Release Party'* at La Maison De Sajoya. She had seen them performed before and had recognised real talent. Expressing female sexuality on stage took guts. And these ladies had that, alright. Sajoya, aka *Empress Erotica.* Chandis, aka *Poetic Princess.* Poppy Seed aka *The Warm Revolutionary.* And Italee '*Rude'* & Neto. With Mutabaruka as guest speaker, the sistas would make no excuses for tearing up the place with their '*tell-it-like-it-is'* act of poetic verses, music and drama. With two talented musicians, Mark Stephenson on violin and Ishion Hutchinson on drums, Kizzy was 100% down with that.

Both Kizzy and Mama Maya knew that they had lots to talk about. Kizzy was just pleased that that mini-stroke was not fatal.

"Kizzy, be careful a dese sweet-mout' men. Dem is ginnal."

"I'm not silly, Mama. Not this time. I'm gonna try to be real careful. No way do I intend to pick up anadda violent man. I'll see you in the morning." She kissed Mama Maya's forehead.

"Safe journey, an' rememba, be careful," Mama Maya stressed.

"Yuh lookin' nice, Kizzy. Real sexy," the sweet-mouthed brotha told her. "But I still t'ink it's sinful to cut off yuh locks. Numbers 6 verses 5 seh...'

"Yes," Kizzy cut in. "I know... *'All the days of the vow of separation, no razor shall pass over his head. Until the day be fulfilled of his consecration to the Lord, he shall be holy, and shall let the hair of his head grow.'*

"Awoah... Yuh know?" he patronised.

"Listen," Kizzy defended, "I've done much more sinful things than cuttin' my locks."

"Feh true?" I can't imagine anything you could do more sinful dan dat. Not a sweet girl like you." Flattery would get him everywhere.

She laughed. "Anyway, yuh not lookin' too bad yuhself. Yuh have such a cute face. Is dat why dem call yuh *Baby Face Glen*?"

The trickster answered only with a laugh and a prolonged squeezing of her right knee. He hit the road, handling his red SAAB with pure mastery as he headed for Barbican Heights, Kingston, 6.

*

I met a girl de adda day, Shi 'ave barb-wire in ar baggy wais'
Eye yie yie yie yie yie yie yie, Oye yoy yoy yoy yoy yoy yoy yoy
Woye yoy yoy yoy yoy yoy yoy yoy...

Festus picked at the walls of his cell as he sang the old song, changing its intended gender. His happy-go-lucky front was on display, yet again. His name was chosen as a derivative from the word festival. It meant happy. Joyous. His mother had chosen it as he was conceived in Barbados. She had gone there with Montie when they were young to experience Cropover.

Yes. Festus' singing, as always, was a front, for only less than fifteen minutes earlier, he got thinking hard about what a silly shit Rock had talked him into. And Kunta. He couldn't bring him back and that hurt like hell. And the sad thing about it was, he didn't even have a healthy stash to come out to. Still, he did the crime, so all he could do was serve the time. *Period.* One good thing that crossed his mind was the fact that Kizzy had found it in her heart to leave him the house, which was left on rent until his return. Although she had left him, he thought highly of her generosity. He knew too, that she had taken a lot. Given him chances upon chances, to try to change. Seek help. Counselling. But the final beating was the last straw, and she had bowed out while the going was good.

The jangle of keys outside his prison cell told him he had a visitor. At least he had something to look forward to. The guard led him to the room in which his visitor was waiting. He wished it could have been Kizzy and Fari, but that was only high hopes. They were under the sunny skies of Jamaica.

"Bejesus, Festus. How on earth does anyone manage in a place like this?" Heidi asked him, her Irish accent more prominent than ever before.

It was strange seeing her away from her post behind the glass partition in the bookie shop, and a few times in the dimness of his bedroom, after Kizzy had left him. They were more like friends who had slept together, rather than an item.

"I don't know, Heidi. Sleep, rise, eat, exercise, count de days and hope for some a dat *good behaviour* shit."

"Right shit-hole, prison, isn't it?"

But she had something to tell him. She looked distant. He had detected it. "What's wrong, Heidi? Is the house ok?"

"Yes. It's fine."

"So what's de matter? You look troubled."

"Festus, you know we've become good friends and all that, and I'm glad you let me have the house on rent for such a reasonable rate, but soon I won't even be able to keep it up."

"Why? Have you lost your job? Yuh nuh work a de bookie no more?"

"Festus... it's not that. I'm pregnant."

"Oh shit!"

"Don't look so surprised."

"Heidi... yuh sure it's mine?"

"Oh, Bejesus! What sort a person d'you take me for? Oi'm a good Catholic girl, me." She crossed herself.

Festus felt guilty, but he couldn't help but think: *'Good Catholic girl'? Dem moves deh weh yuh t'row pon me inna bed was more like de moves of a 'bad devil girl'. But who am I to judge?'*

"Soon I won't be able to manage the rent," Heidi continued. What with the baby and all..."

He held his face in his hands. "Weren't you on the pill, Heidi?"

"Yes. But I missed a few. And I don't believe in abortion, either," she hastened.

"Ok. Right. So... maternity benefit an' t'ing... you'll get dat, won't you?"

"Well, I haven't been at the Bookie's long enough to qualify for maternity benefit."

"Well... won't social help? Surely. If you're pregnant and unemployed..."

"Maybe. Something should work out. But I was just thinking… how you gonna contribute towards the child. You're in here. You don't even know how long you'll serve."

"Listen, Heidi. Dis is prison. Yuh cyaan be givin' me dem stress een 'ere. De house is paid off for. I don't deserve it, but Kizzy gave it to me. If you're having my child, the best I can do is to let you live there rent-free. What good is it to me, anyway? Like yuh seh, how long will I serve? Listen, I'll sort sop'n out."

It wasn't long before Festus was back in his cell. Such an evil place. He had a new cell-mate, but he just wasn't interested. Some burly, blonde geezer, in for some bank robbery shit.

"How you doin', mate?" the sturdy man said, in the broadest Brummie accent ever. He stretched his right hand towards Festus. "The name's Conrad. But you can call me, Con'. Appropriate name, I know." He tried to be flippant, but the air about him spelt danger.

"What yuh in for, Con'?" Festus asked.

"Bank job. But some geezer's got me loot. Fifty grand's worth of used notes, mate. Nicked it off me sister. The bitch told me when it was too late. Cops had already nicked me, ain'it. But he'd better not get too comfy. I have friends on the outside."

Festus lay across his bed, belly down, half listening.

Conrad stared hungrily at his ass.

CHAPTER * THIRTY-ONE

High-grade is going through my head
And that's the reason why my eyes are turning red
It's going through my head...

Reds lay across his bed, meditating. Along with the song that graced the airwaves, high-grade was going through his head. *Literally.* He needed a good lick to calm him. Too much had been going on lately. Besides, he had just taken a life.

When Lijah had put the idea of eliminating Rock to him, he had pondered, but something told him the cause was a just one. His punishment would lie with Jah.

But Reds' meditation didn't just stop there. It went back to twenty odd years ago, to the birth of his son Damian. And to not so long ago, when a bullet claimed his life.

But now, Reds' mind came to rest on a young woman he had met, while he was still seeing Damian's mother. He wasn't then, and would never now, be this woman's type. *Miss Criss Miss*. She had always felt she was too good for him. But, one day, under the influence of youth and firewater, she had lost control of herself, giving him permission to go further than she would have let him, had she been sober.

He had touched her.

Entered her.

Made love to her.

But what he did not know was that he had impregnated her with his youthful sperm. She went off to London with the foetus inside her. After a while of *to*ing and *fro*ing between her mother and her grandmother, the child expressed her wish to stay with her grandmother in Birmingham.

The child's name was Shari.

Her mother's was Mitzi.

Oh ye mothers and fathers, let your offspring know who they are.

Without Mitzi's knowledge, Shari had tangled romantically, with Damian. Her half-brother. It shouldn't have happened, but it did. How were the young, hot-blooded teenagers supposed to know?

And still, even now, Reds had no clue.

No clue, to the fact that Shari was his daughter. And Shari, no clue to the fact that the man she had simply known as Damian's dad and Lijah's friend, was her father.

So to the end, Reds would never know that he had had more reason to eliminate Rock than he had ever imagined.

Fiona pinched herself and read the beginning of the airmail letter again. The colour had drained noticeably from her face and Grace asked, "What's the matter? Who's that letter from?"

"It's from my mother," she said in a carefree tone, as if the subject of *'her mother'* was an every day one. Or as if she wasn't surprised at all. Only she was. Shock had simply plunged her into a half-sedated state.

"Your what?"

"My mother. Aunt Patricia."

"The Aunt Patricia you told me about?"

"Yes. Shhh. Let me read. Get the gist a dis."

Grace leaned over her shoulders and read too.

Fiona could not believe the newest revelation in her life.

"Pour me a brandy, will you, Grace? This can't be true. I have a mother who gave me up, acted for years as my surrogate aunt, left and went to Jamaica, and now she tells me in a letter she's leaving me all her worldly goods in her Will. What's with all these mothers? Do they think ignoring their children for years, then handing over a big cheque, or a big plot of land and a house is gonna make it ok?"

"Oh my God," Grace whispered, in shock. "So... who's your father then?" She was over-curious.

"Wait. I haven't got there yet. If it's there, that is. She might not tell me."

It reminded Grace of when she had asked her mother the same question. After a verbal battle, she had decided to tell her. But it was too late. Grace's father was dead and she felt cheated out of the chance to see him, touch him, or even have a conversation with him, even though he had expressed his wish not to get acquainted. Grace had never discussed with Fiona, the paternal part of her life. It wasn't a subject she enjoyed. In fact, she didn't discuss the maternal side much.

"Oh my God! Oh!... My!... God!" Fiona knocked back her brandy.

"What is it?! C'mon Fi', tell me!"

"I have a half-sister. And you'd never guess who she is?"

"How can I guess? Tell me!"

"Gloria. You know... Kizzy's best friend. The one you met while she was staying at Kizzy's for a while. The one I always said you have a slight resemblance to. You and her have the same bone structure."

"Oh my God! She's your half-sister? But you've known Gloria for years, Fi'."

"Damn right."

"D'you think she knows?"

"I doubt it, Grace. I think she'd say something to Kizzy if she did."

"Shit... This is like something you see in a movie. Ok. So... who is your father then? Did she say?"

"I doubt if you'd know him, although she said he lived in Leeds. He's dead now anyway. He was a reverend. Reverend Fontaine, it says here."

Grace's face turned an ashy grey. "What's did you say his name was?"

"Reverend Fontaine. Why?"

"Oh fuck... Oooooh fuck," Grace alarmed, though in a low tone.

"What, Grace?"

"Is... Gloria's... mum... called... Hortence?" She spaced her words deliberately, emphasising the crucial need for an answer.

"*Was*," Fiona assured her. "She's dead now too. Why, Grace?"

"Fi'..."

"Wha'?"

"You're never gonna believe this. Not in a million years. Well this one takes the biscuit. I would have said the odds of this happening would be more like one in a million, but..."

"Cut the fucking chit-chat Grace. The suspense is killing me, man. Wha'?!"

"You and I?"

"Yes?"

"We're half-sisters. We shouldn't have... Reverend Fontaine is my dad too. You, Gloria and I are half-sisters... That man... Jesus Chris'. He has surely done his rounds, man... Oh, my life."

"What?! How?! When?!..." Fiona was confused.

"Calm down, Fi', Let's start at the beginning."

The brandy glass fell, shattering against the wooden floor, echoing their fears.

Little blonde Heidi opened the front door of Festus' house to a big black man. It was her new squeeze. She had met him just after she had had her first rendezvous with Festus. Festus was her first black man, but now she had tasted black, she was never going back.

But this man was simply laying his hat for a while. This would simply be 'one of' his homes. Just another watering hole. She knew that alright, but what was she to do? She was carrying his baby and he knew it, but letting another man hold his jacket was no big deal. Festus' cartridges had never been full. Fired blanks all his life. But how was he to know? He had always thought that the fault was Kizzy's. That her eggs were difficult. And that Fari was made from one lucky egg.

"Cuppa tea, Bongo?" Heidi asked.

"Tea?" He kissed his teeth. "How unnuh English people luv drink tea so. Next week when yuh shop, get some Nutrament inna de place. Some Supamalt. Carrot juice. Guinness an' all dem t'ings deh... 'Bout tea." He kissed his teeth again. "Anyway, come upstairs. Me feelin' horny."

Bongo Dee was on form. Beat around nobody's bush. He was a deadly character that floated around Birmingham like smog on a winter's night. He had once severed the right index finger of a character who had dared to mess with a Don called Conteh Egyptian. But that was another story. Bongo had no time for women. No respect for them either. He simply took quick sexual fixes from them whenever the urge would take him.

Heidi followed him upstairs, where she would lay her body down to make rough love.

Meanwhile, somewhere in a wing of Her Majesty's prison, a burly blonde followed Festus into a cluster-phobic cell, where, by force, he made him lay his body down... for *rough, forbidden love*.

STOP!!! RETURN NOW TO PAGE 277.
START AT ... There was no telling...
READ TO THE END OF PAGE 279.

CHAPTER * THIRTY-TWO

Another funeral. They almost always bring families together. And who would have thought it? Who would have thought that Uncle Stan would have kicked the bucket before Lothan? A week ago when one of Uncle Stan's sons had brought the news to Lijah's door, he couldn't believe it. No matter how many times he had heard the phrase, *'In the midst of life, we are in death'*, he had always expected his sick, feeble father to go before Uncle Stan. Nasty pieces of work, heart attacks. They have no prejudices. Take anyone, at anytime: the young, the old, the good and the bad.

Lijah had turned up a little late and snuck into the church as quietly as he could. Gloria and Ikesha didn't come. They didn't go to Papa Dread's either. Too soon after Kunta. They simply couldn't bear the atmosphere.

Lijah was surprised to see Roy. He was looking at the back of his head. Sat right up there in the *'close family'* row, Roy was. No tears. Just a straight, solemn face. *'If he could make it to Uncle Stan's funeral'*, Lijah thought, *'he would surely make it to his own father's, when the time comes, regardless of all the bad feelings the lurked in the past'*.

Roy turned and glanced around the church. Lijah caught his eyes and remembered their last encounter. He remembered his last harsh words to him, in Mitzi's flat in London, not so long ago. And the rude comment he had made to Mitzi: *'I wonder if you fuck better than Bernadette? You have to be seriously wicked in bed to stop him craving that ass. Still. Whatever. I think you all deserve each other. All three of you - selfish bastards... '* He knew Mitzi would have told him, but he couldn't have cared much, since he didn't hurry his sorry ass down to Birmingham for a confrontation.

But Lijah's interest wasn't on Roy. *No.* It was on his sister Faye. France, it seemed, had released her from its grip, for this occasion. Who had told her? It must have been Bernadette. She knew. But why couldn't she have told her about Kunta's death? Or perhaps she did. Who knows?

Lijah had forgotten how many years it had been since he had last seen his young sister. And now, with age, she was looking more and more like the old man.

Faye sat sobbing. Sobbing her heart out. Strange. She was sobbing so deep for her Uncle Stan, it made Lijah well up even more. But it was understandable. She was his favourite, and she obviously hadn't forgotten. She held her wreath in her hand like a child would a cherished toy. *'Why?'* Lijah wondered. *'Why don't she just lay it down like everyone else has? Is that how they did things in France?'*

Time passed. Mourners poured out the church with faces like wet weekends. Blondes, brunettes and redheads: old flames of Uncle Stan's sprinkled themselves about the place like odd forgotten peaches under brown autumn leaves. A host of his mixed-race offspring of differing ages and from several different mothers, mingled freely among their brothers and sisters, as they found their way to their designated procession cars.

"Faye," Lijah said nervously. They were sitting in the same procession car, on the way to the cemetery. "How are you? I can't believe it took Uncle Stan's death to bring you back to England. Why didn't you...?"

"Lijah, there are so many things we should talk about. I hate saying sorry. It doesn't do anything. It doesn't change the past. Roy and I were talking earlier about a few things. Blood, they say, is thicker than water, but I don't know sometimes."

"What made you say that, Faye?" Lijah asked, although not doubting her surmising.

"Well, for one, Lijah, I wouldn't say our blood is thicker than water, would you? Look at the way we lived our lives. Our family problems are much deeper than you think."

'Does Faye know something I know?' Lijah wondered. "So deep, Faye, that you and Roy left me stranded in England, as if I did something to you?" he asked.

"We didn't leave you, Lijah. We left a whole heap a shit. I know, personally, there are things I'd like to wash away. Erase. Turn back the clock on."

"Are you gonna come round to the house after the funeral?" Lijah asked. It was his young sister. He wanted to make sure he didn't lose her again. Besides, it looked as if Faye was ready to talk. As for Roy, it would be up to him if he wanted to cross his doorstep.

"Yes, bro'. I need my family around. I have my children, but I need my brothers. We all need to talk. We need to take a trip to Jamaica and see our dad, also. We're all we have."

"Faye, that is the best thing I've heard for a long time. Feh real." It was as if Lijah had found a new lease of life. "But Faye," he perplexed, "why are you still holding the wreath? Why didn't you...?"

"I want to lay it myself. Finally. On his grave," she replied, with more sincerity than Lijah had expected. "D'you remember that dress he bought me one Christmas? The one covered in beautiful red roses?"

"Yes. I do."

"And d'you remember how he used to love to see me in it?"

"Yes. But you were always his favourite, weren't you?" Lijah said.

"Yes, Lijah, I suppose I was... I still have that dress."

"Always treated you just that bit more special. Rocked you on his knees for the longest time. I was wondering when Uncle Stan was gonna realise that you were getting too big to sit on his knees. At one time, I felt sure Dad didn't like it. The way he used to sit there in a mood. As if he despised his brother."

"I know," Faye said, "and Uncle Stan used to sit out Dad's moods. As if he was proving a point. Or protesting against something."

"Yes. I used to think he was just thick-skinned."

"Lijah," Faye continued, closing the subject on Uncle Stan's affection for her, "Mum told me a few things before I went to France."

"What things?"

"Well, did you know that Uncle Stan was Mum's boyfriend back in Jamaica?"

Lijah laughed through his nose. "Are you serious?"

"Yes. I'm serious. Lijah, there are always two sides to every story. Sometimes we hear just one side and not the other. And we make our judgements and assumptions from the half we hear."

"So how did Dad end up with Mum?" he asked.

"Well, apparently, when Mum came to England, she betrayed Uncle Stan with Dad."

"Dad didn't tell me that," Lijah said. "I wonder why he chose to leave that bit out?"

"Dad himself had left his girlfriend in Jamaica," Faye continued. "Someone called Sweetie. Sweetie was Mum's..."

Lijah cut in, "...best friend... yeah, yeah... yeah... and the rest. Yes, Dad told me that much when I went to Jamaica, but not that Mum was Uncle Stan's girlfriend. That's sick!"

Lijah recalled his dad's words from years ago: '*Stanley too dyam sneakin'. Him gwaan like 'im quiet, but 'im can be sneakin' at times. Ginnal.*' Now he wondered who was the biggest ginnal. His old man or his uncle?

"Lijah, the world is filled with sick things. The thing is, it's all about what is moral and what is immoral."

Lijah was fast sinking into a state of shock, then he asked, "So what else did Mum tell you, Faye?"

"Lot's more, Lijah. She also told me never to cry on another man's shoulder when you're lonely or when your man has hurt you. Mum needed a shoulder to cry on back in the sixties. Dad was there. That is how she came to end up marrying her best friend's man... and how Dad wound up with his brother's woman."

"What goes around, hey?" Lijah said, still in shock.

"I cried on Jacques' shoulder, Lijah. I didn't heed Mum's words. He was Bernadette's man. I'm not proud of myself, but I'm human. We are, none of us, perfect. The flesh is weak, yet powerful at the same time. And yes, what goes around sometimes comes around too."

Lijah said nothing. He had already caught more than the gist of the 'Jacques' story from Bernadette in an aisle and car park of Sainsbury's, and would never forget how he had paid and still is paying for his sister's sins in the form of blackmail. Like he had paid for his old man's. *'What am I gonna do with Bernadette?'* the question came to him for at least the hundredth time, now.

"So did Jacques come with you to England?" he asked Faye, pulling his mind away from the evil seductress.

"No. The kids are staying with friends. Jacques left me, Lijah."

"Oh no. Is there any end to this relationship game? I suppose the woman he left you for is out of this world."

"Out of this world, yes. But it wasn't a woman, Lijah. Jacques left me for a male model."

"What?! Jacques is gay?!"

"Bisexual. And believe me, Pierre is the sexiest specimen you ever did see. I was no contest for him."

"Oh shit. So how did you find out about them? Did he just tell you he's leaving you for Pierre?"

"No. I came back prematurely from a weekend away. Jacques was in the shower when I got in. He couldn't hear me, as the torrents from the shower were quite noisy. I decided to join him as I usually do, so I took my clothes off and walked into the bathroom."

"Don't tell me you caught them at it?"

"Pierre's dick was so far up Jacques' ass, there wasn't an inch to spare."

Lijah began to heave. Once again, he was taken to the disdain horror of an infamous prison cell. "Ok, Faye. That's enough. Shit. Let's talk about something else... *Jesus.* What else had Mum told you? Get this shit outa me head, please."

"Mum told me, Lijah, that Dad hadn't touched her since you were two years old, so there's no way I could be his daughter."

"What de fuck yuh talkin' 'bout? You're de spitting image of Dad. What was Mum...?"

"Yes, bro', and so is Uncle Stan. The spitting image of Dad. So how can you tell *who* I look like?"

"Wha' yuh mean, who yuh look...?" Lijah was getting the shocking picture now.

"When you look at me, all you see is a product of the Benjamin blood, right?"

"What the f..." Lijah was almost choking. How much more could he take? "What kind of family are we?"

"Don't be surprised, Lijah. We're probably no different from most families we see around us. Every family has it's own secret. If you give certain families the task to write their biographies, if they're honest, they might even shock themselves. Only God is perfect, Lijah."

"So... you're saying..."

"Lijah, I'm saying, Uncle Stan is my blood-father."

"Wha'?!"

"One day, when Dad wasn't there," Faye continued, "and Mum needed a shoulder to cry on, Uncle Stan was there."

"Faye, w'at yuh tellin' me?" This was hard to digest.

"I suppose Uncle Stan thought she was his girl in the first place, anyway. Now you know why I was his favourite."

"So... that's why Dad and Uncle Stan didn't see eye to eye," Lijah surmised.

"Yes. That's why. But even though Dad was hurting, deep down, he believed Uncle Stan's action was justified. Another black man would have killed him. Or even forbid him to come to his house. I suppose that was the way they battled things out. Weird, I know, but that was it."

"Oh fuck," Lijah muttered, not knowing what he was most shocked at. Shock grabbed him by the balls and he was pleased the procession car had stopped just outside the cemetery. He raced in and darted behind the nearest edge, heaving the entire contents of his stomach.

"You told him then?" Roy's voice connected with his eardrum.

"Yes," Faye answered, "I told him."

Lijah turned and realised exactly where he was standing. Kunta and Nettie's headstones greeted his eyes. He paused, looked at them, then allowed his tears to flow. The story of his life so far, began to run through his head like a sad, blockbuster movie. *'Is there really another family like the Benjamin's?'* he asked himself again. *'I doubt it'.*

Later he would come to realise that Uncle Stan had reserved his place of rest. *A special place, beside Nettie.*

Bernadette wanted jam on it. But little did she know how sticky her jam would be.

"Hi. Come in. Let me take your jacket."

"Nice place you have here, Bernadette," the cool Jamaican Indian told her.

"It's ok. *I* like it."

"I don't have to ask. *Red* is your favourite colour, right?"

"How observant, Nico."

"It signifies *passion*, yet at the same time, *danger*," he told her, placing his ass on her settee.

She looked at him with a joking question in eyes. "Are you implying something?"

"No. Well, I suppose I could say that about myself. Passionate yet dangerous."

"You don't look dangerous to me, Nico. Far from it. What would you like to drink?"

"Yuh have any brandy?"

"About to get Randy, Nico? You know what they say about brandy," she joked.

"Why not? If you'll let me. Live life to the fullest, I say. None of us knows when our time will be up."

"Don't be morbid, Nico."

"Well, it's true. You could be having the most fun one minute, then the next, you're given notice in the form of an illness or some shit like that."

"Well, I hope I have many years left, Nico. I've only just begun."

"So, tell me more about France."

She sat on the floor now, and patted the spot beside her. "Sit here, Nico." She couldn't wait to get her hands on him.

He had no intention of hesitating.

"We'll talk about France later," she said in an authoritarian tone. "Tell me about yourself."

"Me? There's not much to tell. I'm just a regular guy trying to live life to the fullest, till I die."

"Christ, you sound like a scratched record, with this *'living life to the fullest'* thing."

"That's because I mean it."

"Well, I'm sure a handsome guy like you must have a story or two to tell, but if you don't wanna talk right now, it's no problem. Besides, you're irresistible. Talking can wait." She leaned forward and kissed his lips.

"Have you had many lovers, Nico?"

"It depends on what you call *many*."

"I shouldn't ask. It's obvious. You're oozing sex. Women everywhere must find you irresistible. You're a right lady killer."

He smirked. "You could say that." Cocky or what? "Believe me, as we speak, I'm killing a few ladies."

"Hey?" she perplexed.

"Never mind," Bernadette.

She un-buttoned his shirt.

He eased his hand under her T-shirt and caressed her firm breasts.

She trembled.

"Hey. Let's not waste time downstairs." She got up and took his hand.

"Let's go upstairs. I'm gonna give you loving to *die* for."

'And I'm gonna give you loving to die from', he thought.

They headed upstairs where extra delights awaited them.

Nico would surely be going for the kill. *Literally.* For little did Bernadette know, but this handsome specimen of a man was exactly what she called him: a 'lady killer'. One of Birmingham's walking deads, who had picked up the AIDS virus from a once happy-go-lucky, mixed race stewardess called Pam. Pam was the best mate of sista called Simone, who was married to an infamous Conteh, aka *Egyptian* - Nico's best mate.

Yes, Nico was a walking dead who had pledged *'There's no way I'm going down, alone.'* But that too, was another story.

"What d'you think of bondage, Nico?"

"Do with me what you will, Bernadette. Do with me what you will."

He knew full well what she meant and was most certainly partial to a little *'slave-in-the-bedroom' romp.* In fact, he was partial to anything that would aid the passing-on of a deadly antidote that swam around in his bloodstream like a time-bomb.

She kissed him again. "You know, your kiss is so sweet, Nico."

He smiled as he bathed in the aura of an evil thought: *'Sweet?... If you say so... but me know one t'ing... it's de fuckin' kiss of death. And by the time they throw the 'biological grievous bodily harm' book at me, it won't matter anyway'.* He eased into her grip like putty.

CHAPTER * THIRTY-THREE

Lijah gripped Gloria's fingers as they walked into The Xaymaca Experience. The babysitter they found this time was trusting. She was older and more mature, so Gloria did not envisage any problems there.

Earlier that day, they had settled Shari in a flat the council had seen fit for her to have. A week ago too, they had settled Ikesha in a flat in London. She was sharing with a few others. Her feet in the BBC's door were looking as if they would be firmly placed.

And with all the settling they had been doing, Lijah had done a trading settlement. He had traded in his MRS Roadster sport for a 4X4 Jeep. Family man. Needed those wheels now. Feh real. But it went without saying: was that it? *Really.* Or would Lucy be back to reclaim the little gift she had given him?

And Faithlyn. Would she spill the beans as to where she got that infamous suitcase of cash?

And would he ever find out that Kizzy, his woman's best friend who he had given a little TLC, was his half-sister?

And what about the elimination of Rock? Would what was done in the dark come out in the light? How long would Bernadette hold him ransom over that one?

And Conrad: the convict that buggered him up good and proper. The one that had bestowed upon him, the bitterest taboo of all, way back when, in a cluster-phobic place called a prison cell. Had Lijah seen the last of him?

Nothing was sure, but for that present moment, Gloria and Lijah seemed relieved.

The ambience of The Xaymaca Experience was just what they needed to help them wind down. The Caribbean Restaurant with its warm, welcoming atmosphere and tantalizing delights were like a breath of fresh air.

They found a cosy corner and sunk slowly into the sweet serenity of the place. Before they ordered their meal, Lijah found himself merging into the calling comfort of the Mural that decorated the walls, hugged his being and rocked him tenderly. With the soul-searching music of King Melody in the background, who could care who was right or wrong?

"Are you ok, Lijah?" Gloria's voice fuzzed around him like summer haze.

"Yeah, babes. I'm cool."

And it was almost as if a voice had said, *'Come ye heavy laden. Lay thy burden down.'*

It was midnight, an hour after their return from The Xaymaca Experience. They had relieved the baby-sitter and were now lying, fully clothed on the bed in *'their'* bedroom: Gloria was lying between his legs, his arms wrapped around her. They had talked at the restaurant, but not as much as they could. Khamilla's snoring comforted them and the sound from Shanique, sucking on her dummy, made them feel new again. And it would be a denial of their existence, if they said they hadn't felt Kunta's approving presence.

"Isn't it great, Lijah, Ikesha starting with the BBC?" Gloria said.

"Yeah. She deserves it, G."

"She's always been so sensible. I'm kinda glad she didn't do that backpacking thing though," Gloria added.

"Me too."

"I think she's still a virgin yunnuh, Lijah. Yuh don't get much twenty-three-year-old virgins around these days. I'm so proud of her. I really hope and pray that when she finally gives it up, that will be worthy."

"Mmm... Yeah... true." With all the other things that he should feel guilty about, this one got Lijah real good. He swallowed hard and remembered his promise to his daughter, not to tell Gloria about the episodes with Rock and her godfather, Festus. Besides, it would kill Gloria. "Ikesha. My first baby-girl. She'll survive," Lijah finished off. He tried to empty his mind as he held his queen: their synchronized breathing displaying a seemingly perfect harmony.

"I remember the first time we met," he told her. "You were divine. I've always seen us as a kind of Rita an' Bob Marley," he said, chuckling.

She smiled.

He kissed the side of her face. "I love you, G. We shoulda neva strayed."

"It was your fault, Lijah."

"Hey. What's this laying blame? Are you forgetting our song? Are you forgetting the *'I don't care who's right or wrong'*, bit?'

She chuckled. They kissed. *Passionately.* It was gonna be ok to play. All the way. AIDS tests negative and all that. They would try, at least, to help each other through several nights. Hopefully, a lifetime of nights.

"I want you so much, Lijah," Gloria whispered, more sincerely than ever before.

"Not as much as I want you, G. Feh real... Just a second," he said, kissing her. He rose, then walked with purpose towards the bathroom.

Now, as he ran the bath, thoughts swam in his head. Almost in slow motion, he lit four lavender scented-candles, and placed them at the four corners of the bath. Lijah had never bought candles before, but it was as if he had known, the moment would come.

In the meantime, in the dim, silence of the bedroom: the baby' breathing, her backdrop, Gloria rested her eyes on the long plastic bag that hung over the bed. She walked over and reached out and touched its contents. It felt different. Lifeless. Unlike when they hung gracefully from the crown of his head and swung with ease down his back. *'What made him do it?'* she asked herself. *'Apart from his 'I'm not worthy' line of explanation, what made him decide to cut his locks? Really? What was*

*that one crucial, penultimate 'something' that made him take a pair of
scissors to the lion's mane?'*

Now, she let go and watched the bag swing freely, then settle into
position. She reflected on her novel, 'FALLEN RASTAS', and wondered
now, *'How would he take it when he finally completed it? How would he
interpret it?'*

Now, almost as if she had picked up on his telepathy, she followed
him into the bathroom. He was ready for her. Now, he unbuttoned her
blouse, eased it gently off her shoulders and watched it fall to the floor
like feathers in a dream. They spoke non-verbally, the sound of the
torrents and the lavender-scented air providing the backdrop they needed.

He engulfed her nipples.

Gently he traced the route to her navel and sunk his tongue into its
fold.

Eased his warm fingers between her thighs and hoped she would not
reject him again like she did last time.

Gloria touched his face, as heavenly sensations invaded her body.

Stroked his lockless head.

Kissed his tears and watched his manhood rise.

Seconds before, she had set a special tape featuring several of her
favourite songs, and now, John Holt helped them through the night, his
words seeping deep into their souls:

> *Take the ribbon from your hair, Shake it loose and let it fall*
> *Lay it soft against my skin...*

"G?.... Oh my God, I missed you," Lijah was helpless. "I love you so
much."

"Elijah... Zephaniah... Benjamin. I love you too," she responded,
shaking.

Lavender bubbles awaited them.

Now, she stepped into the foaming bath, following him. Never had
they known such a *bitter-sweet* moment, filled with love, hate, honesty,
deceit, truth, lies, misgivings, acceptance, and forgiveness. *Secrets*. And
the burying of ghosts. But the strongest of all: that crazy little thing
called *Love*.

His protruding organ stayed rigid, calling her moist woman. She eased
onto him and it felt like the first time. Gloria trembled and cried,
welcoming the sweet sensation of his warm tongue against her neck,
moving like volts to the tip of her toes.

> *Like the shadows on the wall*

The music moved them.

> *Come and lay down by my side*

Till the early morning light
"Will you marry me, G?" his breathy, trembling voice said.
All I'm taking is your time, Help me make it through the night...
His question was music to her ears. It was as if it was *he* who had invented the question. The concept. Love.

Beneath the still to*ing* and fro*ing* of the baby's breathing, the inner mysteries of a novel, lying unread, and the shadows of a sordid half that will never be told, she said, "Why not?... Why not, Lijah?"

Sinking him deeper into her, moving up and down his shaft like a fresh, new lover, and almost as if she had come with the vengeance of forgiveness, she moved him. Gripping him in a cow-milking fashion, she reminded him of somewhere he had been... But he knew where he'd rather be. Her vagina muscles tightened around his shaft giving him pleasure to die for.

She was like a new woman. In Jamaica, her gym regime had not lolled. Her pelvic exercises gave her a new approach to love-making. They were tight. As tight as a virgin's.

"G... All along... I had my phenomenal woman... *You.*"
She gripped him hard, understanding, but replying only with her climatic sensations.

"All the time... you were here. All the time, my queen," he panted.
Now, she gripped him harder, their aquatic tryst their heaven.

"In the palm of my hands," he relented, his utterance even more breathy as butterflies danced down below, calling his libido to play. "And I nearly lost you," he sighed, floating on ecstasy.

"Why shouldn't I marry you?" she said between sessions of devouring his   mouth, and while sweet sensations played with her G-spot. "After all, Lijah... *'You are... the devil... I know'.*"

And as their heavens came down, the tape moved on:
Cos you're loveable, huggable, touchable
It's you that I need right now
You're incredible, irresistible
It's you that I need right now...

*

'Relax, Lijah,' Bernadette told him. *'You're so tense.'* She kneaded the front of his shoulders and the side of his neck with her strong fingers. *'Oh, such knots. It's not good for you, you know. All this tension. Bad for your health. Besides... I want you healthy, if you're gonna be in my bed from time to time.'* She garnished her telling with a cutting laugh.

'But Gloria,' Lijah said. *'My queen. What about her? We're back*

315

together now, Bernadette. You and I shouldn't...' Lijah could not get the rest of his words out. His tongue went heavy. Dead.

'Who gives a shit about Gloria?' Bernadette asked, in a cruel voice. *'So, Lijah,'* she relented, *'tell me... who pulled the trigger? You or Reds? Who killed Rock?'*

Lijah's tongue got heavier and heavier. Words failed him.

'C'mon, Lijah... you know you can trust me,' she coaxed, massaging him at the same time. *'Who killed Rock?!... Killed Rock?!... Killed Rock?!'*... Now, her voice drummed vengefully into his head, taking him to a point of no return.

'No!!!... Stop it!!!' Rebooted. But that was all he could manage. Just three fear-loaded words, then he shut down again like a crashed computer.

'Hush now, Lijah. Would I ever hurt you?'

A cold shiver ran down his spine.

'Cho', unnuh English bwoy sof' een sah. All me want yuh feh duh is put yuh wood inna me fire. Gloria nah know not'n. Me piano waan tune'. That was Faithlyn's voice. Emitting with ease from Bernadette's lips. Whole heap a mix-up mix-up. What the hell was happening to Lijah?

'I was on a mission to wreck Faye's brothers' lives,' Bernadette's familiar tone rang back as she rubbed lavender oil all over Lijah's phobic, sensitive ass, as if readying it for a sacrifice.

Lijah smelt trouble. Horror. Fear.

'Noooooooo!!!' Rebooted.

'Touchy,' she patronised, reaching now for a sharp object.

How weird? Lucy's pendant was dangling from Bernadette's neck.

And Conrad. *Shit.* He appeared from nowhere. What was he doing there, standing over Lijah now, with intent?

'Noooooooo!!!'

Now, the burly blonde reached out and grasped the two cheeks of Lijah's forbidden. *'Different name, same entry,'* he said. *'And let's see who is the pussy bwoy now.'*

'Noooooooo!!! Noooooooo!!! Noooooooo!!!...'

"Lijah? Wake up,' Gloria's voice seeped into his head like a saving grace. "Wake up... some nightmare that must have been?"

"Empress?... Oh... Yeah.... Feh real... Some nightmare." Fear pumped a rush of adrenalin around his body. He held his woman tight and sought rescue in her warm and tender love. "Some nightmare."

END

316